ROYAL SEDUCTION

JENNIFER BLAKE

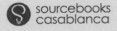

sourcebooks
casablanca

Published by Sourcebooks Casablanca, an imprint of Sourcebooks, Inc.
P.O. Box 4410, Naperville, Illinois 60567-4410
(630) 961-3900
FAX: (630) 961-2168
www.sourcebooks.com

Originally published in 1983 by E-Reads.

Printed and bound in Canada
WC 10 9 8 7 6 5 4 3 2 1

Part One

One

MADAME DELACROIX'S SOIRÉE WAS A SUCCESS. DESPITE the chill winter wind that whipped around the galleried mansion, the crème de la crème of St. Martinville had honored the invitations delivered by her groom. Dressed in their velvets and brocades, their satins and sarcenets, the guests had bundled into their carriages and driven to her house along the muddy tracks overhung with moss-draped trees.

It was not the *beaux yeux* of their hostess that brought them, Madame well knew, but the prospect of news. Though more than seventeen years had passed since the French men and women of Louisiana had become Americans, and though they had basked for as long as it lasted in the glory of republican France, there was among them a fascination with royalty. Was their fine town not known even now as La Petite Paris? And were not many of them aristocratic emigrés, or the children of such, who had fled the Terror thirty-odd years before? Quite a few could remember the rumble of the tumbrils and the flashing blade of Madame Guillotine.

To be sure, the prince lately come among them was from some Balkan kingdom one had scarcely heard of. Nonetheless, royalty was royalty. It was highly unlikely, of course, that he would put in an appearance this evening. *Mon Dieu*, but Madame Delacroix would have sent out criers to tell the world if such a thing were expected! Still, one could dance and eat and drink— Madame was famous for her suppers. And perhaps there would be someone present who had seen the royal personage passing through the town, or had a servant who knew the Negro slaves at Petite Versailles, the plantation of M'sieur de la Chaise where he was staying.

The music of violin, French horn, and pianoforte was gay, the dancing sprightly, and the conversation, consisting of gossip and matters of mutual interest to the area's closely interrelated families, mild through caution, since one must be careful not to offend. The long, silk-hung room, contrived by throwing wide the doors between the *grande salle* and the *petite salle*, was warmed by a brightly burning fire at each end. The air was scented with the faint tang of wood smoke, the medley of perfumes worn by the ladies, and the woodsy fragrance of the shining green streamers of smilax that had been used to decorate the mantels and doorways. The polished floor gleamed, reflecting the radiance of chandeliers overhead and the soft-colored gowns of the ladies. Dancers moved in and out, voices rose and fell, women smiled and men bowed.

There was one person who could not share in the pleasurable excitement. Angeline Fortin circled the floor, her finely molded lips curved in a mechanical smile. The candle glow caught the russet silk of her hair, dressed high in loose curls *à la Belle*, shimmered over her flawless skin, and touched the copper flecks in the depths of her gray-green eyes with mysterious, almost secretive gleams. The effect she made in her virginal white gown in the Grecian mode did not concern her. She wished fervently that she could have stayed away from this soirée.

Her attitude was stupid, her aunt, Madame de Buys, had declared. Nothing could have looked more odd or caused more comment than their absence. In addition, an appearance at Helene Delacroix's evening party was an opportunity to learn what they could of this prince before he sought them out. It was well to know your enemy.

Her aunt was right, of course, and there seemed nothing in the chatter and easy laughter around her to arouse concern. Still, Angeline could not be easy.

"You are quiet tonight, *ma chère*."

She glanced up with a smile in her eyes for her partner. A serious, dark-haired young man with the clipped line of a mustache above his full lips, he was the son of her hostess. "I know. You must forgive me, André. I—I have a touch of the headache."

"Why did you not say so? We could have forgone our dance. I would have been happy just to sit with you. I am not one who must be forever entertained." As he gazed down at her, the expression in his eyes was warm with concern and there was a flush tinting his olive features.

Angeline shook her head. "I know you better," she teased. "You are so wild and dissolute, I'm sure you would think sitting out a dance the greatest bore!"

"And I am sure if I were so dissipated, you would never dance with me at all. Such a character must disgust any female of sensitivity."

"How little you know us!" she returned.

"I know you well enough, I think, or should since I have watched you from your cradle." When she did not reply beyond a smile, he went on. "Does your aunt plan to travel to New Orleans for the *saison des visites* this year?"

"I'm not certain. No arrangements have been made."

"It will be dull without you, even though she keeps you close. If you do not come I would rather remain at the plantation myself."

"Yes," she declared, "and watch your precious sugarcane sprout!"

"Cane is the crop of the future, mark my words. Indigo is dead, killed off by blight and—"

"Listen!" She interrupted him without compunction.

"I don't hear anything."

"I thought there were horses on the drive."

"Who would come this late? It's nearly time for the supper dance." André glanced at the windows that lined the room. There was nothing to be seen except the reflection of the dancers in the candlelight.

"I must have been mistaken," Angeline said, relaxing.

She was not. Moments later came the sound of booted feet on the gallery. The flames of two hundred candles fluttered in the draft as the door swung open. The lustre of the chandeliers that held them tinkled with crystal coolness. Heads turned. Young women drew in their breath, faltering for an instant in the steps of the quadrille before recovering. Men glanced at each other, their faces stiff. The dowagers and spinsters ranged against the wall in lace caps stopped speaking and stared. A quiet descended in which the shuffle of feet and the thin trill of music was loud.

The candlelight gleamed across Angeline's shoulders as she turned to fling a look of alarm at her aunt. Madame de Buys did not notice. The stout, dark-haired older woman sat upright, her hands clenching the delicate ivory sticks of her fan. With her prominent nose and sharp upper lip, she seemed to be perpetually sneering. Now her black gaze was fixed on the man who stood in the doorway.

Madame Delacroix's liveried majordomo stood to one side, his chest swelling with the announcement he was about to make. "His Royal Highness, Prince Rolfe of Ruthenia, Grand Duke of Auchenstein, Count Faulken, the Marquis de Villiot, Baron—"

The prince lifted a hand gloved in white doeskin and the recitation of his titles was cut short. It was a natural gesture, made with an unconscious but supreme confidence in instant obedience. He moved forward, a commanding figure with the soft gold waves of his hair sculpted to his head, wearing a uniform of shimmering white with gold-fringed epaulettes, looped and tasseled cord over one shoulder, and gold buttons securing the gilt-lace-edged cerulean bars that slashed across the broad width of his chest. The enameled jeweled cross of some order winked above his heart, and precious stones sent prism fire from the hilt of the sword that swung gently against the gold stripe of his pantaloons. Of greater than average height, he surveyed the room with detachment, though the bright turquoise of his eyes, glinting from behind thick, gold-tipped lashes, missed nothing.

Behind him appeared another man, and another, until he was flanked by an entourage of uniformed guards, five in number. In the forefront was an older, craggy-faced man with cropped gray-blond hair, a patch over one sightless eye, and the bearing of a Prussian. Behind him came another man as broad and tall as the prince himself though a little heavier in build and with a peculiar half-moon scar at the corner of his mouth. Next, a slim, rakish-looking individual with aquiline features and black hair stepped forward, followed by a set of twins with brown curls falling over their foreheads, identical hazel eyes, and the selfsame stance, left hand on the hilt of the sword and legs spread.

Like a phalanx they advanced, glittering with braid and decorations, their movements as precise as if they were on parade. It was a magnificent cadre, as out of place in Madame Delacroix's small, country ballroom as a flock of peacocks in a dovecote.

The music came to an end. The dancers halted, standing in place. Madame, the lady of the house, in rose velvet underlined from the high, empire waist in pink taffeta, rustled forward. Dropping into a deep curtsey, she said in breathless tones, "Welcome to this house—and to Louisiana—your Highness. You do us… great honor! If we had expected, if we had imagined—"

"I have the pleasure to address my hostess, I presume," the prince said. He took her hand, bowing over it, his firmly cut lips curving in a smile of utter charm.

"Yes—indeed yes, Your Highness."

"M'sieur de la Chaise, who has most kindly provided a billet for my men and myself during our visit to your fine community, gave us to understand you would not be displeased if we descended upon you this evening. If he erred, if we intrude, you have only to say so and we will go away again."

"Oh no! We are delighted that you and your friends have condescended to—to come among us. One had heard of your arrival as the guest of M'sieur de la Chaise, but it was not dreamed that you—"

"Accept my infinite gratitude, Madame," he said, inclining his golden head in obvious dismissal. "Your fair name shall be mercy."

A frown creased the woman's forehead. "As you wish, Your Highness, but I have been called Helene from birth. And now, if it pleases you, permit me to present my husband."

Amusement, warm and vibrant, flashed across the features of Prince Rolfe of Ruthenia and then was gone as he turned to M'sieur Delacroix. With only half his attention engaged by the necessary civilities, he glanced over the room once more.

Angeline had contrived to be near her aunt as the music ended. As her partner bowed and left her, she stepped to the older woman's chair. "Tante Berthe," she said, her voice low, "what are we to do?"

"Nothing," came the hissing answer. "He can know nothing of Claire coming here. He is merely casting about for a scent."

"He must be amazingly lucky to have come so close then," Angeline answered with a touch of asperity.

"He has come because he knows St. Martinville to be my Claire's birthplace, for no other reason."

"And he has come halfway around the world on the off chance she may have gone to earth here?"

"Do not be pert! Nor, Angeline, do I enjoy hearing you speak of my dear daughter, your own cousin, as if she were a hunted she-fox. I will not have it, do you hear? And smile, for the love of *le bon Dieu*—he is looking this way!"

He was indeed. The amusement had vanished from the prince's face, leaving it tight and hard as he stared at Angeline. There was about him a sense of leashed power and implacable will overlaid by distinct menace. Angeline stood chilled to the core of her being, unable to look away. An instant later the prince turned aside, replying to his hostess, presenting the men that accompanied him.

Angeline took a deep breath and let it out slowly. She was not usually prey to nerves. It was the uproar of this day, and the sleepless night before, to say nothing of her aunt's snappish humor. Nothing was as it should be, nor had it been since Claire had descended upon them two nights ago, claiming to fear for her life and demanding to be hidden.

Claire of the fiery red hair and emerald eyes, her mother's greatest pride and most fierce joy. With what hopes had she been sent off to Paris three years before. She had lived with a distant cousin for a year of polishing, then at age seventeen had been launched into the *haut monde*. How Tante Berthe had missed her; with what transports had she read the letters telling of the balls, routs, and soirées, the *billet doux* and the poems written to Claire's eyebrows or the whiteness of her throat. What economies had been practiced so that dearest Claire could have a new gown or fresh ribbons to pin on her great fur muff. Nothing could have equaled the joy Madame de Buys had felt at hearing of the court being paid to her daughter by the heir to the throne of one of the small but wealthy Balkan kingdoms. An invitation to visit this country had called for even greater frugality so that a wardrobe could be ordered, one suited to the prospective bride of a prince. The journey was undertaken and Claire's safe arrival reported. More than once Madame was heard to whisper over her stitchery, "Princess Claire, Princess Claire..."

Then the ecstatic letters had become fewer, saying less and less. Finally, they had stopped. After weeks of silence Claire had come in secret, looking hollow-eyed and frantic, declaring that Maximilian of Ruthenia was dead, shot to death by the same hand that had tried to kill her in what was to have appeared a suicide-murder pact. She had lain unconscious after the pistol ball had struck her, then when she had come to and found Max dead beside her, she had fled for France in the most desperate haste. There, she had sold a few of Maximilian's gifts for the money to take her to Le Havre. From that port she had taken passage home to Louisiana, fearful all the while that she was being tracked by Maximilian's fiend of a brother, a man who had become heir apparent.

Now he was here, bowing in front of Angeline even as she drew back.

"My dear," Helene Delacroix was saying, "do not run away. The prince has expressed a wish to be made known to you."

He smiled with a trace of mockery in his manner as the introductions were completed. His gaze, smooth with insolence, moved over the auburn tendril curls that clustered around her face. It dropped to the tender curves of her breasts just revealed by her gown of white muslin banded with emerald ribbon, a castoff of Claire's with cap sleeves and a full skirt falling to a demi-train. The sweet symmetry of her form left him unmoved, though he seemed enthralled by the faint tremor of her hands in their white lace mitts that reached to her shoulders.

"Do you waltz, Mademoiselle?" he inquired in a tone that set her teeth on edge.

Angeline sent a quick glance to her aunt, who gave a warning shake of her head. "I regret, Your Highness—"

"Nonsense," her hostess exclaimed. "Have I not seen you twirling over the floor this evening with my son?"

Madame de Buys bristled. "Come, Helene, if my niece is reluctant she should not be badgered."

"La, *ma chère*. Of all the girls here, I was certain she would be the least likely to turn awkward with shyness. What a thing it would be to refuse a prince! His request must be perceived as a royal command."

"We are not his subjects," Berthe de Buys objected.

"But he is our guest!"

"It is of no moment," the prince struck in, a glittering challenge in his blue eyes as they rested upon Angeline. "If Mademoiselle is afraid, that will be the end of it."

A flush of irritation rose to Angeline's cheekbones. "Not at all."

"In that case…" He proffered his arm as the musicians struck up once more.

What choice had she with the interested gaze of the entire room upon them? Moreover, would it not arouse his suspicions more if she were antagonistic? With her face set in uneasy hauteur she moved onto the floor beside him.

There was muscle and whipcord sinew under the sleeve upon which her fingers rested. The sword that hung at his side on fine chains was something more than a jeweled toy, and she discovered as he swept her into the dance that he was adept at keeping the swinging weapon from becoming entangled between his partner and himself.

They circled the room quite alone, an excruciating experience as the man who held her kept his gaze fixed on her face. Never could she remember being so aware of a man's hand at her waist, of the brush of his thigh against her in a turn, or the sheer male presence of a partner.

"Angeline," he said, his voice deep as he tried the syllables on his tongue. "The name matches your pose of pale and offended innocence tonight, but in my country you were better known as Claire."

She stiffened, lifting her lashes to meet his gaze. "I beg your pardon?"

"I make you my compliments—that was well done. But I have no time and less inclination for the weaving of spells. I must speak to you."

"I think, Your Highness, that you have made a mistake," she said, a frown drawing her winged brows together. "I am not—"

"Did you think that I would not recognize you?" he cut across her words. "We have never been introduced, it's true. But I have seen you in my brother's company, riding along the avenue, sitting across the theater, a number of times."

"You appear to be speaking of my cousin Claire, Your Highness. I am said to resemble her from a distance, but I assure you I am Angeline Fortin."

Why had she not foreseen this possibility? As children, she and Claire, being much of an age, had been likened to twins. Angeline had come to live with her aunt, the wife of her mother's brother, when a fever had taken her own parents. As they grew older, Claire's coloring had become more vivid, her manner more bold. There were those who said Angeline had the look of a mirror image of Claire seen in a dim room, more muted in the autumn shading of her hair and shadowed green of her eyes with their thick fringing of dark lashes. During the years of her cousin's absence, the frequent comparisons had ceased, and Angeline had taken it for granted that the two of them would become even less alike as they grew older. And after seeing Claire, she thought that they had.

His grip on her hand tightened so that the seams of her mitts pinched her fingers. "Patience is no virtue of mine. What you choose to call yourself is nothing to me. My interest is in the knowledge you hold of my brother's death, and I swear on the moss-grown graves of my forefathers that I will not be denied it!"

At the low intensity of his voice, the odd choice and cadence of his words, a shiver ran through Angeline and she felt suddenly sorry for Claire. For herself, she knew the growing anger of frustration because he would not heed, much less believe, what she said. "If your brother is dead, I am sorry for it, but it has nothing to do with me."

It was a moment before he answered, a moment in which his face turned to iron and the light in his eyes grew more brilliant. His grip at her waist hardened so she was brought closer to him, much closer than was seemly. His lips actually brushed her temple with a fiery tingle as he spoke. "Have you any idea of the danger in which you stand? I am not Maximilian, all stiff decorum and unfailing politeness. I travel my own road, one some say will lead to damnation. Be assured that I will drag you along it with me, naked and without dignity, if needs must to achieve my purpose."

With a gasp, Angeline tried to jerk away from him, but she was held in a grip of steel. She flung him a quick upward glance and saw him smiling down at her. Memory shifted, and she recalled abruptly a letter Claire had written months before. Thinking she would one day become Maximilian's wife, she had taken an interest in his family and the country where she must live, troubling herself with his worries. At that time, they had been over the scandalous conduct of his brother, a nobleman who flaunted his common mistresses abroad, consorted with thieves and gypsies, had killed any number of men in duels, and was seldom entirely sober.

His wild careering across Europe was the despair of his brother and a cause of rage for their father, the king. With seemingly no idea beyond the pleasure and excitement of the moment, Rolfe was felt to be a disgrace to his family and his country. Regardless, by force of his personality, an incredible boldness that scorned safety, and a wild and sweet penchant for the lyric phrase that amounted to poetry, he commanded the loyalty of his chosen followers and the love of his countrymen. He was hailed wherever he went, called the Golden Wolf after some symbol in his arms, something to do with a Russian grandfather, or so Claire thought, though from what she had heard of the man, she saw little reason why anyone should feel emotion of any kind for him. The most provoking thing of all had been that Prince Rolfe's popularity had been far in excess of Maximilian's, or even the present king.

Around them, the floor filled. Several of the prince's guard had prevailed upon the mothers of young ladies to allow their daughters to dance. Angeline found herself hemmed in by white uniforms. They presented a bulwark between her and the other guests, a blind to prevent anyone from getting too close a look at the treatment she was receiving. She threw a harried look to where her aunt sat. Madame de Buys was frowning, her lips pressed in a tight line, her small black eyes hard with condemnation. The next instant, the straight shoulders of a laughing, dark-haired young man blocked her view.

Angeline drew a deep breath as copper fire flashed in the depths of her gray-green eyes. "I've told you I know nothing. The fact that you don't believe me doesn't give you the right to insult me with vulgar threats!"

"It was not a threat, it was a promise."

"One you can hardly keep here in public, in a private home."

"It would be fatal," he said softly, "to put your faith in that belief."

He was so sure of himself and his ability to control the situation that she longed to flout him. He watched her with ironic appreciation for the quick rise and fall of her breasts and the rose color that bloomed on her cheekbones. "Now that we have come to an understanding, perhaps you will tell me exactly how my brother died?"

"I can tell you nothing, because I know nothing! How can I convince you I was never there?"

"You were seen leaving the house just after two in the morning, some hours after my brother must have been shot in his bed. Several long red hairs were found among the bedclothes, along with a chemise of green embroidered silk his servants identified as yours. You were there."

Angeline missed a step. Caught off balance, she stumbled against him and his arm clamped around her, pressing her to the armored hardness of his chest with his cold buttons and decorations gouging into her. She wrenched away from him in haste, lowering her lashes to conceal her confusion. "There must be some terrible mistake."

"There has been, and Maximilian made it when he allowed you to return for even one night after he had paid you off. I will admit that on closer acquaintance I find his lack of resolution more understandable."

There could be no doubt of his meaning. Claire had been Maximilian's mistress. Angeline would have liked to doubt it, but it fell so neatly into place. It explained the reticence of Claire's letters toward the last and her loss of interest in the welfare of Ruthenia, as well as a certain cynicism that Angeline had noticed while she was with her these last two days, and the odd looks she had intercepted between her cousin and her aunt.

"Distressing, is it not, to be found out?"

"If I am distressed," she grated, "it is because you have revealed to me something of Claire I would as soon not have known."

Iciness settled over his features. Through set teeth he said, "Have done, Mademoiselle. You will cooperate, or—"

"By all means," she agreed, taking him up with angry bravado. "Shall we discuss who may have wanted your brother dead? Shall we think between us, Your Royal Highness, who might have benefited most from his removal? Who might have had something to gain—wealth, honors, high position?"

Her voice was carrying. From the corner of her eye, she saw one of his men—the broad, sandy-haired one with the half-moon scar that quirked his mouth at the corner—look from her to the prince in surprise. The change in the man who held her was imperceptible, and yet she was abruptly afraid as she had not been until that moment.

"I believe a private interview will be best for you, after all," he drawled.

"It would avail you nothing, even if I should consent to it, which I will not!"

"For those who dare, a woman's consent becomes unnecessary."

There was a muscle corded in his jaw, and a hard gleam in his turquoise eyes.

"You wouldn't... you couldn't..."

"No? There are no means so foul or without honor, Mademoiselle, that I will not use them to find my brother's killer, proving him no suicide, or to exonerate myself in the eyes of my father and my country of the charge that you hint at so delicately."

The music was slowing, the dance nearly over. Since she no longer struggled, his hold had loosened, allowing her to put a proper distance between them. She could sense, however, the tension, like a tempered blade bent in half, that he held in such restraint. It vibrated through her too, in a faint trembling of her fingers in his. What he would do when the music stopped she did not know, nor did she mean to find out. As the last note of the waltz faded, she wrenched herself from his grasp and whirled to flee.

He sprang after her, snatching at her wrist, his fingers closing with such force that her bones ground together. She came up short, white to the lips. She stared into the face of the man above her, impaled by the blue fire of his eyes beneath oddly slanting brows.

"You must not be in a rush to leave me," he said softly.

"I must return to my aunt. She... everyone will think it peculiar if I do not."

"Let them think what they will," he answered with a lift of his head.

There was a movement beside her, and André was there, bowing, his dark gaze traveling from her to the man at her side. "Is anything wrong?"

"I—I was explaining to the prince the etiquette that prevails in this provincial backwater," she answered. Rolfe of Ruthenia had lowered his arm so that the wrist he held was hidden from view by the fullness of her skirt.

"I am sure these matters are much the same everywhere." That André sensed something odd in the situation between them was plain from his tone. "On that subject I will remind you, Angeline, that the supper dance next on the program is promised to me."

"So it is." She forced a smile as she reached out to place her free hand on André's arm. "It was not necessary to remind me."

The prince could retain his hold, descending into an undignified tug-of-war that must give away his persecution of her, or he could let her go. His decision was instant. Releasing her wrist, he stepped back.

The weakness of relief swept over Angeline, the effect so intense that she did not dare try to take a step. She covered it by sending a glance of smiling coolness to the blond man. "Madame Delacroix has a daughter who sings beautifully. I understand she will be entertaining us during supper. Will you stay?"

"I think not. My men and I have intruded long enough. I trust, Mademoiselle, that we will meet again—soon." With a nod to André, he turned on his heel and walked away.

His uniformed guards sprang to attention. The dancers leaving the floor parted as if cleaved by a sword, while the majordomo leaped to open the door. The cadre of the prince passed through the opening and was lost to sight.

"Angeline, *ma chère*!" Madame Delacroix said, rustling to her side. "Whatever can you have said to make him leave us in such haste?"

Angeline turned her wood-fern-green glance to where her aunt sat in brooding silence. "In truth, Madame," she answered, "I said little at all."

The remaining hours of the evening were a severe trial. At supper she was surrounded by girls exclaiming at her good fortune in being singled out by the prince, demanding to know what he had said to her, and what she replied, and wondering how she was able to retain her wits through the ordeal. In their voices there was more than one echo of the questions asked by their hostess as to why the royal gentleman, ignoring town officials and other important men and women of ancient lineage, had asked to be presented to her alone, departing after their waltz without speaking to another soul.

Angeline answered as best she could while giving away nothing of the revelations the prince had made and therefore nothing that might indicate that Claire had returned. Between the glances of suspicion-tinged curiosity cast in her direction, the sighing comments of first one girl and then another over the dashing men of his entourage who had led them into the dance, plus André's solicitous inquiries after the headache she had admitted to earlier, she was more than ready when Tante Berthe signaled her desire to leave the gathering.

The catechism was not over. During the carriage ride home Madame de Buys required to know every word uttered by the prince and every syllable of her

answers. She castigated Angeline for not having been
more flirtatious in her manner; surely, had she tried,
she could have charmed him into believing her, the
better to have protected her cousin? In all prob-
ability, she had merely put his back up with her tart
responses, making him all the more certain she was
lying. She might have expected Angeline to bungle it.
She should have refused the dance as she was bidden;
that was a piece of disobedience that would not soon
be forgotten.

The threats of the prince Madame de Buys
brushed aside. What could the man do? Force himself
into the house? People of his station did not behave
in so barbaric a fashion. And even if he should try,
there was a manservant to prevent him. As to coming
upon her elsewhere, the solution to that was simple:
she would not go out unattended while he remained
in the neighborhood. That was well thought of
indeed, for if Claire were to remain a prisoner in
her mother's house, she must have someone to help
alleviate her boredom.

Angeline, trailing behind her aunt into the house,
smiled grimly to herself as she nodded a greeting to
the butler, the man her aunt expected to protect them
from intruders. A grizzled, white-haired retainer shuffling arthritically and stifling a yawn with one hand, he
might be able to deny them to callers, but little more.

Claire tossed a piece of needlework aside and
uncurled from a wing chair before the fire as Angeline
opened the door of her bedchamber. "Well," she said,
her voice brittle, "it's about time. I was beginning to
think you meant to dance the night away."

Angeline closed the door behind her and turned to face the other girl. "What are you doing here? I thought you were to remain in Tante Berthe's rooms where her maid could look after you."

"Maria has no conversation, and staring at the *toile de Jouy* on the walls, however delightful may be its representation of the festival of Bacchus, was beginning to pall. I was, in short, attacked by ennui."

"After only two days?"

"I have become accustomed to a trifle more excitement." Claire stretched, a lithe, voluptuous figure in emerald satin.

"So I gather. If what occurred tonight is an example of the type of excitement you had with your prince, then you are welcome to it."

Claire straightened abruptly. "What do you mean? Not... not Rolfe? But he can't have come already!"

"Can he not?" Angeline's tone was laced with irony. Turning from the other girl, she removed her hooded manteau-cloak of dark-gray cloth and flung it across the bed.

"*Mon Dieu*, to think he has been so close behind me all this time." Claire shivered, hugging herself. "I might have guessed what he would be like, once he set out. But who would have dreamed he would exert himself so? There seemed little love, much less liking, between him and Max, and naturally the responsibility of being next in line to the throne falls upon him now."

"Whatever his reasons, he has come. For which you have my sympathy."

"Your sympathy?" Claire repeated.

"He mistook me for you tonight."

For long seconds Claire was silent, and then she gave a peal of laughter.

"It was not amusing!" Angeline exclaimed.

"No, forgive me," Claire agreed. "Was he unpleasant? You do not answer—of course he was, and I expect he was even more so when he discovered his error."

Angeline sent her a look of annoyance. "He might have been if he could have been brought to acknowledge it. As it was, he was not too pleased when I tried to point out his mistake."

At that moment the door swung open and Madame de Buys swept into the room. Behind her came Maria, a thin Frenchwoman in black, of indeterminate age and regal bearing.

"So here you are, *chère*," Madame said, the chill expression on her face dissolving into a smile as she addressed her daughter. "It gave me quite a start to find you gone. I suppose Angeline has told you what took place this evening?"

"Ridiculous, is it not?" Claire answered.

"I find it so myself, but then I have never been able to see this fancied likeness between you."

"The question is, can it be turned to advantage?"

Madame de Buys did not pretend to misunderstand her daughter. "How? I see no way it can help you."

"Nor do I at the moment. I suppose he would soon discover the fraud if he had the opportunity to speak to her above a few minutes' time."

Angeline, listening to the exchange in growing dismay, broke in. "If you think I am going to pass myself off to the prince as Claire, you are mistaken!

There can be nothing whatever to be gained by such a masquerade."

"I need not face him, or his wrath," Claire pointed out.

"But I would! I thank you very much!"

"You could plead ignorance of the events in Ruthenia so much better than I, dear Angeline. You have always been good at maintaining your composure, no matter the provocation."

Angeline brushed aside the half-coaxing compliment. "Oh, yes, claiming ignorance should be no problem at all, since I have been told nothing."

"There was something you wished to know?"

"A great many things," Angeline said, meeting the other girl's cool emerald gaze without evasion. "To begin with, why was no mention made to me of why you were alone with the prince that night? Or who may have tried to shoot you?"

Claire glanced at her mother, her expression wary. "There seemed no need to go into sordid details. I—I'm not at all sure I remember. The shock of seeing Max die before my eyes... of being shot. At the time I thought I was fatally injured, and fainted away. Luckily, it was only a graze to my side, quite minor."

"I congratulate you. Did one of the sordid details you neglected to mention have anything to do with your chemise being found in Maximilian's bed?"

"Angeline!" Madame de Buys cried. "That will be quite enough!"

The maid, though her mouth thinned into a tight line, did not seem surprised by the accusation. If anything her disapproval seemed to be directed at Angeline for her lack of taste in raising the subject.

Angeline persisted. "But I should know my exact position, should I not, if I am to pretend to be Claire?"

Her face like a mask, the older woman said stiffly. "We are agreed, I think, that such a thing will not be feasible."

It was a victory of sorts. Angeline looked to Claire, but could see no sign of discomfiture in her beautiful features. If she had thought she had hurt the other girl, she might have felt some remorse; as it was, it was her aunt who seemed more affected by the hint of scandalous conduct.

Abruptly Claire spoke. "I am sorry Max is dead. I was… quite fond of him, despite the way he… the way I was treated. It is wrong to speak of a murder-suicide pact, however. It was murder, no more, no less. Prince Maximilian of Ruthenia had no intention of ending his life. Nor, I might add, mine."

"But what happened?" The question could not be suppressed.

"I don't know, I really don't. One moment I was in his arms, the next he was lying across me. I saw the flash of the pistol, felt the ball strike as I was shot, and then—darkness. When I came to myself again, Max was dead and I… my only thought was to get away."

"That will do," Madame said, her voice sharp. "What matters now is finding a safe place for you, *ma chère*, until this madman who has followed you is gone."

"Surely I have only to stay hidden here?"

Madame's thick, dark brows drew together in a frown. "I think not. I have given the matter careful

consideration this past half-hour. You must have a
place secure and free of malicious gossip, yet one at no
great distance so that I may keep myself informed of
your well-being. Maria, just now in my room, made
a suggestion."

"Yes?"

"The Convent School of Our Sisters."

Claire's brows went up. "You can't mean it!"

"I was never more serious. The sisters will take you
in and give you sanctuary. There are few who would
dare pursue you into such sacred precincts."

"You do not know Rolfe!"

"Nor do I wish to," Claire's mother replied. "I will
not spare my feelings, however. When you are well
hidden, we will throw open the doors here and invite
him to search, to question the servants. No one knows
of your presence save Angeline, Maria, and myself, so
it will be safe enough."

"There will be a great many who will know if I am
to leave this house to travel to the convent," Claire
said in scathing tones.

"Not if you take the path through the woods under
the cover of darkness."

"You mean... go into the woods... at night?" Her
daughter stared at her incredulously.

"Just so. This night, in fact. Angeline will guide you."

"How very brave of her!" The words were edged
with sarcasm.

"There is a path, well worn in these past few years
while she completed her education with the nuns and
helped with their younger girls. When the two of you
arrive, she may awaken the Mother Superior and speak

to her about taking you. Angeline is quite a favorite there, and may easily persuade Mother Theresa."

"I am much obliged to her, I'm sure, but I have no wish to be shut away in a nunnery!" Claire swung away with an angry swish of her skirts.

Her mother moved to touch her shoulder. "It is only a school, not a place of training for novices, as you well know. It is a refuge that you cannot afford to refuse. Come, Maria will help you dress and put up your hair. It will not be so bad, you will see."

"Endless prayers and sackcloth to wear," came the bitter answer. "No doubt you think the experience will be beneficial!"

"I did not say so. I am thinking only of your safety, my dearest daughter."

Angeline turned away, moving to strip off her mitts and to search for stouter slippers as the maid stepped to the other girl, murmuring encouragement and endearments. Her own safety was not important; that much was plain. She was in no real danger, of course, not like Claire. Should she meet this Balkan prince again she must, given time, make him understand who she was. Still, it would have been nice if there had been some concern, some sign that any one of the other women in the room realized the risk she ran, some indication that it mattered. It might have been enough if they had merely pretended.

Two

THE MOON LOOKED DOWN WITH THE COOL RADIANCE of January. It slanted through the leafless limbs of the trees, leaving a dark tracery of moving shadows on the path. Dry leaves rustled in the wake of footsteps. Angeline stopped, tilting her head to listen as she stared back in the direction they had come.

"What is it?" Claire whispered, coming to a halt beside her.

"I'm not sure. I thought I heard something."

"Probably a wolf, or a panther. I still think Mother should have sent one of the menservants with us. He could have been paid to keep his mouth shut."

"Yes, and paid to open it again." Angeline's tone was acid. "Listen!"

There was a moment of silence. "Well?"

Angeline shook her head. Drawing her manteau-cloak around her, she moved on once more with Claire close behind.

They had come perhaps a quarter of a mile. There had been no difficulty in getting away from the house unseen. They had crept down the back servants' stairs of the two-story West Indies–style house, passing beneath the lower gallery, then kept to the shadows of the shrubbery before striking out for the woods. Where the path began, they had looked back to see the white house gleaming in the moonlight with Madame de Buys pacing the upper gallery, striking the railing with her closed fist with each step.

"Wait," Claire panted when they had gone half a mile more. "Can't we rest a bit?"

"No. There is still nearly a mile to go."

"Why didn't you tell me it was so far?"

"It didn't seem to matter since we could not have the carriage brought out anyway."

"I don't understand how you came to be taking this path. Your studies should have been finished two years ago, as mine were."

"I have been doing a little extra reading in Latin and higher mathematics with the Mother Superior, as well as helping with the younger girls. That is, I was until this winter."

"It sounds stultifying, not to say useless, for a female. Even so, why should you walk rather than take the carriage?"

"It was not offered," Angeline said, her tone dry. "Your mother did not approve of my studies."

"Ah," Claire went on after a moment. "I see no objection as long as no other alternative offered itself."

"If you mean so long as no man offered himself, that was a part of the problem. Tante Berthe was certain that if I made the effort I could bring André Delacroix to the point of proposing. She feared that if my interests were otherwise engaged I would never try to capture him, and so I have been forbidden the convent school." Angeline held her manteau-cloak close as she skimmed past a matted twist of saw-brier that had fallen into the path from a broken tree branch.

"As I remember, André was suitable enough, his family not only well-connected, but wealthy." Claire panted a little as she hurried at Angeline's heels.

"Oh, yes, and I'm fond of him. But only that, no more."

"So you are a romantic?" Claire's tone was shaded with ironic, if breathless amusement.

"Is that so odd? I'm sure you were the same when you met Maximilian in Paris."

The other girl did not answer. Ahead of them was a patch of brightness where the path broke from the trees to cross a road. To the left the thoroughfare curved sharply away toward the outskirts of the sleepy town of St. Martinville, with its scattering of Acadian-built houses on the outskirts. The convent lay a short distance out of town. It was possible to reach it by this road, but because of the windings and turnings of that narrow way that followed the twisting Bayou Teche, the distance traveled would be more than twice as far. *Teche*, from a French corruption of an Attapas Indian word, meant snake, and the bayou was as curving as any snake. In some distant time the waterway had been the channel for the mighty Mississippi River before it changed its course.

To the right, the road meandered through the woods, still following the bayou, to reach the homes of the planters who lived along its banks. Some seven or eight miles up the bayou lay the lands of M'sieur de la Chaise, the man who had offered hospitality to the prince, and also the Delacroix plantation, where the soirée had been held earlier that evening.

Angeline glanced back the way they had come. Though she did not want to alarm Claire, she could not rid herself of the feeling that something, or someone, was behind them. She reached out to catch the other girl's arm. "Come on. Run!"

They scrambled down the low bank to the road, snatching at their skirts as berry briers caught them, stepping over tussocks of dried grass. With Angeline dragging at Claire, they swung left, racing along the wheel-rutted track. Their footfalls thudded in the soft earth, sounding loud in the moonlit stillness. Their breath rasped in their throats and fear drummed along their veins.

They rounded the sharply angling curve and saw another winding away from them.

"Angeline—why—?" Claire gasped.

Angeline slowed, whispering, "Not yet."

A few steps farther, and she glanced behind them. Seeing nothing beyond the curving roadway, she dove into the woods once more. She crept deeper into the trees, moving as noiselessly as possible, Claire close on her heels. She wormed her way into a thicket of evergreen wax myrtle of the kind used for making candles, then stood still.

The night grew quiet again. The aromatic fragrance of the myrtle, brought forth as they brushed against the leaves, rose in the cool fresh air around them. The wind soughed through the trees overhead. Somewhere two branches rubbed together with a complaining creak.

And then they saw him through the trees, the dark-haired young man who had been with the prince. He came along the road at an easy lope, the front of his uniform winking with the gleams of burnished gold buttons. There could be little doubt that he was a sentry sent by the prince to watch over Claire. They must have caught him unawares, or else his orders had not included restraining the quarry, something for which they must give thanks. He could have caught up with them at any time, otherwise.

Claire started, and would have broken from cover at a run if Angeline had not clamped a hand on her arm. The chill dampness crept in under their cloaks as they stood watching the prince's man trot to where the second curve wound out of sight. He stopped there and stood for long moments with his hands on his hips before swinging around and pounding back the way he had come. As he passed where they stood concealed, there was grim determination stamped on his thin features.

The minutes ticked past. Angeline brushed a wisp of spider web from her cheek. A hunting owl swept by with slow-beating wings. Finally she moved. Motioning to Claire, she turned back in the direction they had come, back to the path that crossed the road, leading on through the woods to the convent's back gate.

The building that housed the nuns' school was an old one. Built of bousillage, a plaster made of mud, deer hair, and the gray Spanish moss that hung from the trees along the bayou packed between upright posts, it was surrounded by a tall fence of palings. It had been founded by a lady of wealth in gratitude for the return to health some twelve years earlier of her only daughter in answer to prayer. There had been plans to build a grand and imposing academy of learning for females, but they were curtailed due to the death of the school's benefactress. There was some discussion of closing the school now, with the three nuns in residence going elsewhere, a prospect Angeline hated to contemplate.

The rooms of the Mother Superior were at the back of the house. The lady who held that post, being an avid gardener and an herbalist of note, had caused a door to be let into the rear wall, the better to reach the area of the convent grounds she had under cultivation. That portal had for years served the women of the community well, since it was possible to reach Mother Theresa herself without going through the front gate. The stern nun who held sway there had made it her purpose in life to protect the Mother Superior from the importunings of foolish teenagers, nervous mothers, and garrulous older women.

It was late indeed, nearing three in the morning, but still Angeline did not hesitate to approach Mother Theresa's special door. It was well known that the *religieuse* seldom slept more than four hours out of the night, spending the others in the business of the order, keeping up her vast correspondence with clerics both in the parishes of Louisiana and in France, or else on her knees at her *prie-Dieu*.

Mother Theresa's personal servant, a gnarled free woman of color wearing a white turban and apron over her dress, opened the door. Urging Claire ahead of her, Angeline stepped inside.

A woman of acute intelligence, Mother Theresa grasped the situation quickly. Turning to Claire, she said, "You must come to us at once, my child. You will be given a room where you may remain hidden, even from the students. It will be quiet, not at all what you are used to, but there will be time for repose of both body and soul, time for you to repent of the past and consider what is to be done with your future."

Claire glanced at Angeline, her expression wry, before she dropped into a curtsey. "I am humbly grateful, Mother Theresa."

"You realize, Mademoiselle de Buys, that you cannot bring reminders of worldliness with you into the convent? This rule is not to mortify you, but to preserve the order of the community by preventing jealousy or, as in your case, to avoid reminders of a luxurious and decadent past."

"I understand," Claire murmured, though she did not sound happy.

There was not a great deal more to be said. Directing the servant woman to find clothing and clean bedding for Claire, Mother Theresa took up her candle and led the two young women along the dim hallway to the cubicle where Angeline's cousin would be staying. There, she left them alone to say their good-byes.

When the door had closed after the Mother Superior, Claire glanced around her at the bare chamber, its rough-plastered walls adorned only by a crucifix. The crude bed, side table, and chair were all of the plainest construction in native wood. Her voice brittle, she said, "Charming."

"It will not be for long."

"Let us hope not. I am like to go mad with the dull sanctity of it."

"I can see it must be very different from what you have become accustomed to in the years you have been away."

"You cannot imagine how different. I fail entirely to see how you could have supported coming here every day, much less have chosen it."

Angeline shook her head, smiling a little. "People have different tastes."

"So they do. You can hardly be blamed for the fact that you have had no chance to develop any other. I, on the other hand, have had that chance, which will doubtless be my curse."

Claire unfastened her cloak, letting it fall from her shoulders to the floor in the manner of one used to servants hovering ready to catch doffed clothing. She stood, a straight figure dressed in a traveling costume of amber-shot silk with the candlelight gleaming on her hair and a brooding look on her fine features. She was selfish, imperious, calculating; these things Angeline knew, and yet there was also a listlessness about her and a haze of despair in the deep-green eyes that brought unwanted compassion.

Angeline glanced down at her hands. "I'm sorry— that your affair with Maximilian ended the way it did."

"No more than I," Claire said, her lips curving in a bitter smile. "Dear Angeline, may I give you some advice? You will never need it, I expect, and it is not original, but still, you should remember it. Put not your trust in princes."

"I don't understand."

"If Max had been trustworthy, I would not be here—and he might still be alive. But never mind. Had you not better go? Or will you stay the night?"

Angeline shook her head in answer to the last question. "Tante Berthe will be expecting me."

"I don't envy you the return journey. Rolfe will be searching."

"Hopefully in the wrong places. I will be fine."

"Before you go," Claire said, frowning in something akin to embarrassment, "I suppose I should express my gratitude."

"There is no need." Angeline moved toward the door.

"But there is. Human dignity requires it, both yours and my own. Max taught me that. I—I pray you will accept this token as part payment of what I owe you."

Angeline turned reluctantly to see Claire removing a fine gold chain from around her neck, drawing it and the small, gold-chased vial suspended from it out of her bodice. The sickly sweet scent of lilies of the valley permeated the air, coming from that small, skin-warmed bottle. The chain shimmered with red-gold fire as she held it out.

"I can't accept anything so valuable," Angeline protested.

"It's no great treasure, only a gift from Max. It means little now, and since I must give it up, you may as well have it."

"You wouldn't be losing it forever, you know, only until you leave the protection of the convent."

"Oh, I understand that well enough, only I choose to give it to you. Don't make such a to-do over nothing. Take it!"

"Very well. Thank you, Claire." Angeline took the odd necklace, slipping it on over her head while a smile lingered in her eyes for her cousin's quick descent from graciousness into irritability.

Claire gave a short laugh. "Go ahead. You may grin as you please. You can leave this place, come and go as you will. How I wish I could exchange places with you. What I would not give to be so free, so innocent and untouched again!"

It would have been uncivil for Angeline to say how little she herself wished to reverse their roles. Promising to visit when she could, Angeline bade Claire goodnight and left her.

It was still nearly a half-hour before she could get away. Mother Theresa insisted she have something warm to drink before setting out, and while she sat sipping her milk flavored with vanilla bean and sweetened with honey, the nun also extracted from her the remaining details of Claire's history. The moon had set by the time the elderly *religieuse* let her out the back door. Even then Mother Theresa tried to prevail upon her to rest awhile, to take a dormitory cot until dawn. Failing that, she tried to press a shuttered lantern upon her. Angeline refused. She was not afraid of the darkness; now it was her ally.

She had not gone far along the dark path before she wished she had been less adamant. The going was much slower without the moonlight to aid her. The woods seemed to close in upon her, becoming sinister, impenetrable. To make matters worse, the night wind brought the scream of a prowling cat, a panther or lynx, both of which were known to attack human beings if they crossed their trails. She tried to hurry, but tree limbs seen too late to be avoided slapped her in the face and vines thorny and pliant snaked out to catch her ankles. It was a relief when she came to the cane brake that lined the main road. Safely on the other side, she would be over two-thirds of the way home.

She brushed through the towering natural bamboo, so thick-growing it crowded out all other vegetation. She was about to step out into the open when she came to an abrupt halt.

Voices. Faint, mixed with the thud of hoof beats, they came from a distance, steadily drawing nearer. One expostulated, the other was quiet. There was a rumble of bass laughter. The horsemen came abreast of where she stood.

It was the prince and his men; it could be no others. One of the *on dits* of the night had been of the fine horses bought by the prince at great cost in New Orleans, and the gold and bronze mounted tack brought from Ruthenia so that the men might enjoy riding for exercise and pleasure, or hunting in their accustomed style. She could see the precious metal now winking in the starshine, while the straight, military seat of the riders was unmistakable. As they came even with her they drew rein. The dark-haired man who had been left behind earlier was speaking.

"It was just here the two women left the wood and took to the road. They rounded the curve ahead, then— disappeared. I went back for my mount and retraced the route nearly into the town, but saw no sign."

"We can depend on you, I suppose, to recognize females?" The words laced with irony came from the prince.

"They were both wearing skirts," came the stiff reply.

"Not always certain proof, but we will accept it. A maid trailing along, whimpering and whining to add cachet, or at least propriety, to a clandestine escape. It seems unnecessary."

"I don't know about that, but I know there were two," came the fading reply as they moved on.

She should have guessed they would come. What now? To use the path leading to the De Buys house would be foolhardy. She could backtrack, then force her way through the woods at another point, or else return to the convent and wait for daylight. Neither choice pleased her.

She stood staring at the dark gap in the trees on the other side of the road, where the path continued. There was one other possibility. The prince and his men were not expecting her to return. If she could cross the road to the other path without being seen, she might race homeward, getting well out of sight before they came back, as they surely would, to investigate at this point.

No, it was too risky. The men might well go no further than the second curve, where the sentry had lost sight of her and Claire earlier. There would not be enough time. The convent it must be.

Angeline swung around, then drew back with her breath caught in her throat. Not ten steps away on the trail she had just covered was a furry shape merging with the darkness. A soft rumble sounded in its throat and its eyes were luminous. Its short body and its pointed ears pitched forward marked it as a bobcat or short-tailed lynx, and dangerously unpredictable. It might gather itself to leap or, with its curiosity satisfied, just amble away.

Seconds slipped past. The cat, unblinking, stood its ground. Angeline allowed herself a shallow breath. She could not stay where she was forever. With the return to the convent blocked, she was forced to go home. She must move at once, or lose her chance.

With infinite care, she took a step backward. She essayed another, turning her body to ease through the tall cane. One more, and she was on the low bank at the road's edge. There was no one in sight. Picking up her skirts, she jumped to the roadway and hurled herself across to the other side.

A whoop split the night. It was as she was pulling herself up the far bank that it came, like the call on the hunting field when prey is sighted. She flung a swift glance toward the curve of the road where the horsemen had sprung into sight once more. The slim dark-haired sentry was pointing, urging his horse forward. Without waiting to see the others, she threw herself into the woods at a run.

With her head down and her face shielded by her arm, she followed the worn trail by instinct for a few yards, then swerved into the undergrowth to the left, plunging deep, putting as much distance as possible between herself and her pursuers. She ran on until she could hear their crashing progress behind her, then slowed. Knowing they must also be able to track her by sound, she tried to step lightly as the Indians did, the way her father had shown her in a childish game long ago.

"Halt!"

The command meant for the following men came from frighteningly near. Neither loud nor harsh, it was instantly obeyed. The night grew quiet; not even a bit jangled. With set teeth, Angeline herself froze on one foot.

After what seemed an endless time, a harsh voice, belonging to the heavy, one-eyed veteran, asked, "What did you hear?"

"Before, our quarry. Now, nothing. Which means she is close enough to hear and act on my orders for her own preservation."

"In that case, Your Highness, shall we fan out and search?"

"Not unless your aim is to provide a cover for her retreat."

The other man grunted. "We await orders then."

"Amazing," Rolfe of Ruthenia said, and proceeded to give them in succinct phrases in a foreign tongue.

Angeline set her teeth against the tremor of fear. To hear what was to be done to capture her and be unable to understand was worse than not hearing at all. Did he realize it, this prince?

There came the creak of saddle leather as the men dismounted. The sound was ominous. On horseback the men were at a disadvantage in the dark, thick swampland with low branches thrusting everywhere to knock a rider from the saddle and tough vines to trip a hard-pushed horse. On foot, they were equal to her, and she was far outnumbered. Angeline's muscles tightened and she breathed deeply, making ready to run.

"One thing more," came the quiet, incisive voice. "Let no harm come to our quarry this night, on pain of instant dismissal."

Was it a mistake, those last words in impeccable French? Did he mean to reassure her of her safety from physical injury? Or was it a ruse to make her less wary, less frantic in her determination to escape them? There was one other possibility. The prince intended to keep her unharmed against the time when he had the leisure to seek his own vengeance.

A horse snorted, stamping nervously, shaking his head so that the bridle jingled. A man cursed. Prince Rolfe began to speak, and then the night was torn by the frustrated scream of the hunting cat. The sound rose to a rasping crescendo, and the mounts of the men whinnied in terror.

Angeline wasted no time. Under the cover of the disturbance she glided away, twisting and turning as she fled through the dense, damp woods. Behind her, she heard a crisp, sharp order and the crash of pursuit. Still she ran, ducking under tree limbs, leaping over rotting logs, feeling her hair slipping from its pins. Then came a shout, followed immediately by the hollow echo of listening stillness.

Angeline checked, and tilting her head, turned slowly. From a few hundred yards away came a faint call and a low-voiced answer. It was repeated in different tones from farther to the right. The men were moving in pairs, keeping in touch with each other, quartering the woods with method and certainty. They meant to flush her out like a hunted animal.

But the night was dark, the forest wide, and their

numbers were small for the task. More, Angeline
knew the woods, knew how they lay in relation to
the road, the bayou, and the house of her aunt. As an
added advantage, she would know at all times where
the men were as they called back and forth to keep
from chasing each other. She drew air into her lungs
to steady her nerves and shook back her hair so the
silken skein tumbled down her back. Let them hunt.
She would not be easily taken.

With her heart pounding, she eased by degrees to
a position between the nearest pairs of men. If her
calculations were correct, there were only four men
in the woods near her, leaving two unaccounted for.
They were either searching on the other side of the
path, or else, supposing one to be the prince, waiting
with the horses like a general and his aide-de-camp
at the rear of the battle to control and order develop-
ments. Her bottom lip curled slightly at the thought.
She might have guessed a royal personage so conscious
of the worth of his name would not soil his hands
apprehending such as he thought her to be.

The men moving steadily toward her expected
her to fly in panic before them, with the inevitable
result that she would be run down and caught. If she
could get behind them, she might creep back to the
path well ahead of where she had left it, ahead of the
waiting prince, then make a headlong run for the
house where safety lay.

They were coming nearer. The tramp of their booted
feet crushing the dry leaves sent a chill across the back
of her neck. Almost without conscious thought, she
drew her dark cloak around her and swung toward the

low mound of an evergreen wax myrtle. Such cover had served her well once; it might again. She pushed into it, crouching, going to one knee. Immediately she regretted it. This was foolish, a horrible risk. She should have taken her chances, trusted to her fleetness of foot. How humiliating it would be to be found hiding here like a frightened child.

The underbrush crackled and a man stepped out, a dark shadow near enough to touch if she stretched out her hand. Scarcely breathing, she held herself immobile.

"Oscar!"

Angeline started as the man, young and slim in the starlight, gave the shout. It was one of the twins, she thought before her mind leaped to wonder if he had heard her, perhaps seen her, if he were calling for reinforcements before he launched himself upon the place where she was concealed.

An answering hail came from a few yards away on the other side of the myrtle. The first man grunted. "Don't get ahead of me, brother mine. I like to know whether I'm tackling a soft female, a wild cat, or your bony hide."

"Keep shouting like that, and you won't have to worry about tackling any of them. The idea was to maintain quiet contact, not create such a ruckus it would drown out the trampling of a herd of goats."

The man beside her snorted at this caustic rejoinder as he moved away. "Two to one, there never was any girl, just Leopold trying to make up for losing her trail in the first place. Not that I blame him. With Rolfe in one of his white rages, being around him will be damned unpleasant for all of us until she's found, but especially for the man who let her get away."

"As you will find out personally if we fail to turn up this phantom female."

Their footsteps faded. Angeline rose from her cramped position and stood listening. They were moving deeper into the woods, all of them. It seemed unlikely they would stop until they reached the bayou. She had done it. Fierce exultation gripped her for a moment, then subsided. She was not safe yet.

By the time the galleried De Buys mansion rose up before her, Angeline was gasping for breath and there was the ache of a stitch in her side. The windows were dark. Tante Berthe must have given her up, retiring to her bed without leaving so much as a night candle burning. She had not known there would be trouble, but still she might have waited to be certain all was well. So unwelcoming was the house in the predawn blackness that Angeline felt she might count herself lucky if she were not locked out.

Throwing a last glance behind her down the empty path, she flitted toward the back stairs. Keeping to the dimness near the wall, she climbed to the upper gallery and hurried along it to the long French windows that opened from her own bed-chamber. She stood staring for a moment back toward the woods from which she had come, but could see nothing, hear nothing. Grasping the knob of the long, glass-paned panel, she slipped inside. Then she pushed the French window shut and dropped the bolt into place.

Only then did she let out her breath. Still grasping the cold brass handle, she leaned her head against the cooling glass panes of the window and waited for the relief and triumph that was her due to flood over her. They did not come. Instead, she grew aware of the smell of smoke and warm wax in the room, as from a candle newly extinguished. There was a whisper of sound, the merest slither of cloth against cloth. It came from close behind her, so close that in the heightened awareness of her senses she thought she felt the wafting warmth of a body's heat before a soft voice spoke at her ear.

"The vixen," Rolfe of Ruthenia said, "comes always at last to her lair."

Angeline stiffened, wrenching at the knob under her hand, pushing at the bolt. Even as the door came open, hard fingers bit into her arm, whirling her around. Abruptly the smothering folds of a coverlet swirled around her, covering her head, confining her arms. As she drew in her breath to scream, the air was trapped in her lungs by a hard hand clapped bruisingly across her face, while her head was held in the curve of a muscled arm like a wheelwright's vise of tempered steel.

She could not breathe. Panic beat up into her mind as she writhed, struggling with all thought of escape banished by the need to dislodge that hand. In a suffocating red haze, she felt herself lifted, carried out along the gallery and swiftly down the stairs. She kicked and tried with aching neck muscles to turn her head, but could feel herself growing weaker. A deeper darkness than the night and the encircling coverlet crowded upon her vision, closing in. With the last vestiges of reason, she accepted the will of the man who held her, allowing herself to go limp.

Immediately, the hand was removed. Air—pure, cold, and life-giving—rushed to her brain. There could be little doubt that it would be taken away at once if she moved or made a sound. The threat was not spoken, and yet it was a palpable thing between herself and the man who held her. And so, docile, blind, and cold with fearful rage, she lay still and allowed herself to be swung through the brushing shrubbery and handed up to a man seated on a horse. The prince mounted to the squeak of saddle leather, and then she was transferred to his arms and held against him, lying against his chest. The horses were set in motion.

"No trouble?" came a muffled question from the man who rode with the prince.

"None, but then she was worn out with the dance she led the others."

"Take care. From all that has been said, she has teeth, and claws."

"Your concern for my well-being unmans me, Leopold."

"You need not laugh. If she carves your heart out for breakfast the others will find some way to blame me!" By his voice and the name given to him, Angeline took the other man to be none other than the sentry.

"You think she has reason."

There was a moment of silence before Leopold spoke. "Why do you ask such a thing?"

"You did not stop her earlier," the prince reminded him with a reprimand in the quiet timbre of his voice.

"I had no orders to abduct her, only to watch and report her movements."

"But that isn't all," the prince insisted.

"No. At the ball this evening she... she seemed a lady, and—"

"What?" the prince took him up. "Winsome and without guile?"

"Something like that."

Angeline stirred and might have spoken, but the man who held her laughed, a bright and brittle scourge of mockery that vibrated in his chest long after the sound of it had died away.

They joined the remaining members of the *garde du corps*, hailing them from the woods. As they waited Angeline realized that her face and head were free of the coverlet. Had the prince thrown it back, or had it been loosened by the movement of their ride? She did not know, though she preferred to think the latter. She had no wish at the moment to temper her hatred for this man with gratitude.

The face of the man who held her was a pale blur in the darkness. By slow degrees her first terror was receding. Despite the iron grip of the arm around her and the hardness of the chest against which she lay, there was no reality in what was happening to her. She held herself stiff, aware of the curving edge of the English pommel beneath her and the ridged thighs of the prince as she sat across his saddle. Where he was taking her, what he meant to do, she did not know, but she was glad all of a sudden, fiercely glad, that she was not Claire.

"Your Highness," she breathed in unconscious entreaty, "this is a mistake. You must believe me."

"Pleading for clemency, Mademoiselle de Buys? Your misfortune is that I feel none."

She did not speak again but used the remaining
time to clear her brain of the last traces of fearful
excitement, the better to marshal her arguments and
bring her facts and proofs into line. She would need all
the wits she could gather, she thought, when this man
turned his full attention upon her.

Riding fast with the cadre streaming around them,
they came at length to the plantation of M'sieur de la
Chaise. They did not approach the main house, but
took a drive leading deep into the several-thousand-
acre property, to where the plowed fields gave way
to virgin swampland. They drew up before a square-
built, porticoed house of stucco-covered brick scored
to look like stone, a hunting lodge constructed by de
la Chaise in imitation of the nobility of Europe. It was
well known that his wife had refused to allow him to
hold the all-male revels that he had envisioned there,
and so it had seldom been put to use. It had served for
a time as a *garçonnière* for the older sons of the family.
Since their marriages it had been used intermittently as
a guest house, though not a popular one, being so far
from the main residence.

The doors stood open now, and against the yellow
glow of candlelight loomed a squat, broad man with
bulging muscles that stretched the taut sleeves of his
livery of military cut. He had a great shock of coarse
brown hair, eyes that were set in his head at a slant, in the
manner of a Mongolian from the steppes of Russia, and
an expression like an amiable bear cub. If he was surprised
to see a woman in the arms of his royal master as the
prince approached, no flicker of it appeared on his face.
Bowing, he stood aside as they passed into the house.

They entered a great hall. At one end was a fireplace large enough to hold an entire tree trunk. It was flanked by a pair of settees in the style of Napoleon's Egyptian campaign with faded velvet upholstery and crocodile feet for legs, obviously rejects from the main house since the decline of the fashion. To one side sat a long table holding the remains of a meal that appeared to have been hastily abandoned. High overhead, the ceiling was vaulted and sectioned with arched beams between which were frescoes painted in smoked pastel colors from classical mythology, all with a hunting theme: Diana with her bow, Daphne pursued by Apollo and being turned into a laurel tree. The antlers of deer and tusks of wild boars made a frieze around the walls of the room, while beneath them hung banners in faded silks and medieval tapestries to soften the plastered walls.

Directly before the door a great staircase rose, with outward-curving arms carved of dark oak. It was toward this that the prince turned, mounting the oaken treads with sure steps, ignoring the badinage of his followers below as they entered behind him.

He pushed into the first room on the right, an enormous chamber with a flickering fire on the hearth. Angeline had a glimpse of a vast armoire, a secretary-desk, a small table, and more jeweled-toned tapestries depicting wooded scenes where foxes, rabbits, and deer played among the laurel and holly. She saw a set of steps leading up to a high tester bed hung with crimson brocade shot with gold thread, and then she was swung dizzyingly and dropped upon its soft, yielding surface.

Angeline flung herself from him, rolling free of the
clinging coverlet, plunging to the far side of the bed,
where she dropped to the floor and came to her feet.
Disheveled and breathless, she sent a quick glance
toward the door. The prince moved with negligent,
almost casual grace, and yet in an instant he was
between her and the opening, reaching to pull the
door shut.

He turned toward her then. A smile curved his
mouth, creeping brightly into his turquoise eyes.
"Now, Mademoiselle," he said, the timbre of his
voice deadly with satisfaction, "let us seek among
the masks and low disguises, beneath the feminine
draperies and coy protests of modesty, for the sweet
kernel of the truth."

Three

FIRELIGHT GLIMMERED ORANGE-RED ON THE WALLS, THE only light in the room as the candle gleam from the stairwell was shut off. Angeline moistened her dry lips with the tip of her tongue, her wide gaze fastened on the prince as he swung away from the door, and her mind vibrating like a struck chord with the musical challenge he had issued. Rolfe of Ruthenia stepped to a small table near the front windows and took up a tinderbox, making a spark. With his strong, well-shaped hands sculpted in flame, he lit the wax tapers of a silver candelabrum. The glow caught the sheen of old gold on his finger in a ring crafted in the form of a Romanesque wolf's head with bared teeth. It illuminated his face, casting the prominent cheekbones into high relief, flickering with dancing points of blue fire in his eyes.

Angeline drew a deep breath. "There's no need to search for the truth. I make you a gift of it. I am not Claire! My name is Angeline Fortin—as I told you not five hours ago at the soirée!"

"You will forgive me if I don't believe you any more now than I did then?"

"Forgive you for calling me a liar? For carrying your unbelief to such lengths that you abduct me from my home? I am not so magnanimous!"

"If my behavior disturbs you, there is a way to put an end to it. You have only to tell me what you know of my brother's death."

"That is easily done." As his head came up, she snapped, "I know nothing. I tell you I am not the woman you are looking for, but her cousin!" In as calm a manner as she could manage, she continued with a concise history of her life beginning with her birth date, the names of her parents and grandparents, her relationship to Claire through her mother, sister to Claire's father. Though his face grew tight with impatience, she told him too of the manner in which her mother and father had died and the arrangement by which she had come to live with her aunt, ending with her long-standing resemblance to Claire. When she had finished, she waited expectantly for some alteration in his expression.

There was none. "I felicitate you on the convenience of having a look-alike. Does she, like some child's make-believe playmate, take the blame for your misdeeds?"

"Blame? There is no question of that."

"But I'm afraid there is."

Angeline stared at him with Claire's tale of betrayal and attempted murder running through her mind. "For what?"

"The wrath of a woman scorned that led you to plot my brother's murder, the use of your undoubted attraction and past intimacy to gain entrance one last time to his rooms, and, finally, for the crime of leaving him to die in a welter of blood—both his and your own. That should be enough for a beginning."

The color drained slowly from Angeline's face as he spoke. Her voice was no more than a whisper as she said, "You can't be serious."

He moved toward her with lithe ease, a powerful, athletic man in white carrying an air of indefinable danger in every springing step. "I assure you I can. Permit me to take your cloak."

He did not wait for an answer, but raised his hands to the looped closure, slipping it free, drawing the edges of the manteau apart as he lifted the weight of it from her shoulders. Abruptly, Angeline brought up her hands to clasp his wrists.

"I will not be staying," she said.

"Will you not?"

There was no curiosity in his tone, only certainty as his eyes burned into hers. Beneath her fingers she could feel the steady beat of his pulse, the leashed strength of muscle and sinew that could break her hold with ease. That he did not use it was somehow more threatening than a violent reprisal. A tingling ran along the nerves of her arms, shivering through her, and she released him as if she had touched hot metal. An instant later she was swept by rage at the irrationality of her reaction, but she could only stare at him with glittering gray-green eyes as he drew her cloak aside and tossed it over a chair.

He studied her a long, speculative moment, then reached to take her arm. "Come to the fire," he said in dulcet tones.

She wrenched away from him, moving with stiff-backed dignity to the fireplace, where she turned to face him once more. He was so close behind her that she stepped back involuntarily. He caught her elbows, snatching her against him. Off balance, she was molded to him from shoulder to thigh, with the buttons and bars of his uniform pressing into her breasts and the hilt of his sword prodding her hip. For an instant she was still, then, with a gasp, she pushed at him with her hands braced against his chest.

"Self-immolation is neither necessary nor, at the moment, desirable, as much as I might have enjoyed the spectacle not so long ago."

She ceased struggling as he spoke, breathing in the faint whiff of scorched muslin from the back of her skirts where she felt increased heat. Through set teeth she said, "Have the goodness to let me go."

"Goodness? Why should you suppose I will have any such thing? Or mercy?"

"I'm sure I don't know," she flared in unsteady bitterness. "Forgive me! For a moment of madness I thought you might have the same humane responses as other men."

"My responses," he said slowly as his gaze drifted down over the lovely line of her throat and shoulders and the shining swath of hair that had spilled forward across her breast, "cannot be faulted."

Her eyes widened. She felt as if his turquoise gaze had stripped her naked, and realized in the recesses of her mind that he intended it to be so. "I—I meant that I expected you to act the gentleman."

"Appealing to my chivalrous instincts? A fatal error. I have none."

His grasp on her arm loosened, sliding over her shoulder, slipping under her hair where his spread fingers cupped the back of her head. He bent then to touch his lips to hers. She tried to turn her head, but he held her immobile, exploring the tender curves of her mouth, tasting their sweetness, testing the resistance of her set teeth.

When he drew back finally, his breathing had deepened and his eyes were a darker blue. "No, there is nothing wrong with my responses, but yours intrigue me. You shy away like a filly who has never known the bridle, or else like a mare too wary from hard experience to allow any man to come near."

"What... what did you expect?" she whispered.

"A promiscuous bitch, all tail and talons." His dark gilt brows drew together in concentration. Then, as he surveyed her pale face, he added, "You did ask."

Color flooded up to her hairline in a suffocating rush. "You arrogant, presumptuous—"

"We begin to know each other, do we not?" he took her up. "You I find deceitful and sly, among other things. I underestimated you, which I freely admit was foolish. I should have known the woman who entered Max's bed then destroyed him would be more complicated. The only question remaining is whether it behooves me to revenge him in kind, or if that prompting is the result of your siren song—"

She wrenched back from him then, but smiling grimly, he held her fast in a bruising grip. She swallowed against a creeping desperation, though it shaded her voice as she spoke. "I am Claire's cousin! Ask anyone—my aunt's servants, Madame Delacroix, the parish priest—they will tell you! I never knew your brother, have never been farther from St. Martinville than New Orleans in all my life. I was here while Claire—"

"You grow repetitious. I have followed you halfway around the world, over mountains and valleys and along beckoning miles of roads. The width of the ocean was not too great a barrier to be crossed to find you, nor the fetid reaches of wilderness muck. My men and I have breathed down your beautiful neck, riding horses into bellows-broken dust, fine beasts more gallant and loyal than you have ever dared to be. We have asked a thousand questions, describing, explaining, cajoling with threats and gold, always coming closer. Now with my hands on you at last, do you think I will be beguiled by a piteous look and a hoaxing tale of two women who look the same, two women of lovely, armored intelligence fit to make rattling husks of men?"

The flow of words was a silver-tongued torrent edged with pain. Angeline stared at him in impotent, discerning fury as he went on.

"My brother was the future king, nurtured on almonds, mare's milk, and fatherly affection, strengthened with bouts on the field and bloodsport, and with a disciplined mind bent carefully to matters of state. He was not meant to die in a tumbled bed with a harlot's musk in his nostrils. I, by contrast, educated and strengthened to no purpose and through less exalted methods, with a blessing of paternal scorn to consort where I pleased, have reached at last this point where I confront my brother's murderess. Never say that existence is without design."

His turquoise eyes blazed though his voice remained steady until, abruptly, it stopped. He bent then to thrust an arm beneath her knees, lifting her. And so shattering was the wave of understanding Angeline felt that she did not move or protest in those seconds it took to reach the bed.

He had cared for his brother, admired, respected him, and sought now to ease the ache of his senseless, shaming death by the pursuit and punishment of the woman he held responsible. Did he also hope, in proving his devotion, to show his fitness to be the future ruler of Ruthenia? Did he seek, in fact, the accolades of his father by his diligence?

The bed ropes creaked as he dropped her on the mattress and then flung himself down on one elbow beside her. He kicked off his boots and began to work the gold buttons of his uniform tunic free from their laced holes.

Her muscles twitching with her tenuous mastery of the impulse to flee, she put out her hand, not quite touching his arm. "Your Highness, wait. Could— could you at least try to confirm what I say?"

His gold-tipped lashes shielded his expression as he shrugged from his tunic. "To postpone the inevitable, giving you time to think? I must decline. There are two ways you may protect yourself now. The first, supposing you are indeed Claire's cousin, is to tell me where she is concealed."

"And if, despite my innocence, I—can't do that?"

"You must and can, if you are who you say. When last we had word of Claire de Buys she was heading straight for St. Martinville and her mother's house. If you are a relative in residence in her home, then you must have seen her. The servants there declare that as of last evening only one young woman was in the household; therefore, if you are not Claire she must be somewhere else nearby, perhaps in town. Angeline Fortin could indicate where, and be freed at once, if there was such a person."

"And the second way?" She had to force the words through the tension that blocked her throat. Her failure to betray her cousin must be taken as an admission of guilt. It could not be helped; she could not do as he suggested. Endangering Claire for the sake of her own safety would be more than she could reconcile with her conscience.

His glance, his words, came with silken suddenness. "You could resign yourself to my mercy and confess, telling me why and how you took Max's life, and who was your accomplice."

It came to Angeline that the entire charade had been leading to this question, that the threat hanging over her had been carefully contrived to force the answer he sought. It seemed to hint at more than a woman's act of rage, a suspicion bolstered in her mind by Claire's tale of a botched attempt to make the death a murder-suicide with her cousin a second victim. What chance had she to convince him of the truth while his mind was clogged with flashing, sharp-edged words and intricate devices to incriminate her?

She drew a deep breath before she spoke. "A great risk, surely, since you have yourself acknowledged your mercy to be—somewhat strained?"

"You did remember," he said, his voice soft with satisfaction. His movements slow, he shrugged from his tunic and began to unfasten his pantaloons.

Moss-green with distress, her gaze held to the brilliant blue of his eyes until her control broke. She thrust away from him, reaching, sliding toward the far side of the bed. He lunged in instant reflex, his fingers clamping on her shoulder, catching in the fragile white muslin sleeve of her gown as she wrenched free. The fabric parted with a ragged sound, exposing the pearly contour of her shoulder. For a suspended instant she hesitated as recognition of her desperate plight drove deep inside her, then she tore from his grasp, leaving the limp sleeve in his hand.

She had lost a slipper and the wood floor was cold under her bare foot as she plunged toward the door. She had a brief vision of the prince's men waiting below ready to stop her, converging on the stairs, but it did not matter; she had no choice except to try to get past them.

The exercise of imagination was wasted. In a noiseless rush, she was caught from behind. An arm like a steel band constricted her chest, her knee gave way to a forward thrust, and she was falling. She did not strike the floor, but was lowered, turned in a wrestler's grip to the hearth rug before the fireplace, her shoulder blades to the rich red and blue wool.

"First fall to me," the prince said in soft satisfaction.

Fury, heated and wild, surged inside her. She arched her body, striking like a clawing cat for his face, her nails raking in wet furrows down his cheek, just missing his eye. He caught her wrist in a merciless, numbing grip before he twisted it behind her back to bring her up hard against him. Her breasts were flattened against his chest, pressing warmly with the rise and fall of her panting breath, while her futile writhing only served to make her aware of the hard maleness of his body. With teeth gritted against the sickening grind in her shoulder, she braced on the arm trapped beneath him, kicking, straining for purchase. His knee came up, and he shifted to bring it across her own, stilling movement with his weight. She subsided, glaring with the frustrated malevolence of a caged animal.

The hissing crackle of the fire was loud in the stillness. The light flickered over the face of the man above her, gleaming red and raw on the long slashes she had inflicted, glittering in his eyes. With nerve-stretching slowness, holding her gaze, he lowered his head to take her mouth with his own.

The kiss was searing, thorough, with brutal pressure that forced her lips to part for a deeper, more degrading invasion. Never had she known physical violence. She was chaste, untouched, with only a vague idea of passion as a companion to love like some gentle refrain heard over a nunnery wall. Her uncle, years before his death, had saluted her dewy cheek, and André Delacroix, her gallant suitor, had carried the tips of her fingers to his warm lips, but no more. This violation was of the spirit then, a bleak thing that drained her vitality, leaving only the blight of useless distress.

He brushed aside the gold chain of the perfume vial so that it spilled in a refracted shimmer over her shoulder. It made a gleaming line across her throat while the small, chased bottle sank into the shining mass of her hair. He drew aside the wide white-on-white embroidered shoulder band of her underdress, baring the proud mound of her breast. His lips burned a teasing, circular path to its rose-pink crest. His fingers grasped the torn muslin of her bodice, rending it with agonizing slowness before he served the thin underdress the same. He pushed the material downward over her hips, jerking the wadded gown and underdress from her.

At the sensation of his open palm on the naked skin of her abdomen, she drew in her breath, turning her head from side to side in negation. Her blood poured tumultuously through her veins, suffusing her body with fiery humiliation allied to something more, a faint stir of anticipation, joyless, but undeniable though she shut her eyes tightly against it with the fine fan shadows of her lashes quivering on her cheeks.

Her struggles grew more feeble. She inhaled sharply as his caress grew bolder, slipping between her thighs in unbearable intimacy. Though she held herself taut, he would not be denied, but increased the pressure of his weight, taking her lips once more as his gentle trespass continued inexorably. She swallowed bitter tears as her response grew, burgeoning beyond restraint. The fullness of her loins was shaming. She longed for darkness in which to hide, but she was not sure, given the chance, she would have the strength to use impenetrable night to evade what swiftly approached.

The slow and tantalizing arousal continued. A shudder rippled over her, and then another. The muscles of her abdomen grew rigid. He went still, lifting his hand, his breathing fast and deep as the seconds ticked past.

This was refined cruelty, a ravishment of the senses. To bring her with practiced care to this vibrant, reluctant desire was diabolical, but to leave her there deliberately in agonized recognition was the act of a fiend, a punishment to strip the soul.

She lay bathed in fireglow, scarcely breathing, her breasts jarring slightly with the pounding of her heart. As she raised her lashes in a slow sweep, her eyes were luminous with her discovery, huge in the oval of her face.

He watched her with blue-flamed coals for eyes and stark warfare on his features. The muscles of his face, arms, and shoulders were ridged in restraint, etched in shadow and glistening with a fine sheen of perspiration. In spite of his undoubted experience, his certain expertise, he was not indifferent. Intent on breaking through her defenses, he had neglected to tend his own. The knowledge was balm. It gave her the strength to force her bruised mouth in the semblance of a smile as she made as if to turn from him.

His hand swooped, pinning her where she lay. The timbre of his voice was savage as he spoke. "Second fall to you, a forfeit."

A strange, trembling triumph sustained her as he stripped off his pantaloons and drew her beneath him, parting her thighs, her moist flesh, guiding his surging, searing entry. He sensed the resistance, checked with a soft-breathed curse and sudden tensing of tempered steel muscles, but it was too late. A strangled cry caught in her throat as pain washed over her. She could not breathe, could not move, had no awareness other than the stretched, aching fullness inside her.

Time hung suspended, and then he released her wrist, smoothing his hand over her shoulder, tightening his hold to mold her closer to him. Against her hair he said in low remorse, "Cry truce, and as I have wronged you and injured you, let me salve your wounds."

His hands moved upon her, soothing, stroking. He brushed his lips over her temple, her eyelids, trailing a path to the sensitive corner of her mouth, teasing the smooth contours of her lips until they parted infinitesimally. He cupped her breast, sliding his thumb over the taut peak that slowly lost the contraction of fear, becoming supple, yielding as the tension left her. He eased deeper then, sending a prickling of unexpected pleasure along her nerves. It spread through her, an astounding thing that caused her to fill her lungs with air, breathing out in slow and grateful release.

He set a rhythm then that grew stronger, quickening by degrees. She lifted her hands to his shoulders to hold him away, but instead spread her fingers over the corded muscles of his upper arms, lost in pure sensation.

There was no reality but this, no future, no past, only the growing tumult of the blood, the blind reaching toward white-hot oblivion. It burst upon her, a wondrous fearsome thing shared in panting ardor, fused, clinging bodies, wrenching effort, and sudden cessation of movement.

They lay for long moments with their bodies entwined. She could feel the thud of his heartbeat against her breasts and the slow ebb of fever from her body. He gathered himself then, withdrawing, raising to one elbow. She lifted her lashes to stare at him, her eyes gray-green and shadowed with vulnerability. He watched her with his bronze features contained, his fine gold hair tousled above the brilliant blue of his gaze. He gave nothing away, Prince Rolfe of Ruthenia, except for the brief offering of compassion he judged her due. As recompense for what he had taken, it was not enough.

She looked away, lifting a hand to the gooseflesh rising on the shoulder away from the fire, aware suddenly of the chill pervading the room. He heaved himself up, rising to one knee, then pushed his hands beneath her, rising to his feet with her cradled in his arms. He reached the bed in a few swift strides, placing her upon it, stretching out a hand for the coverlet, tugging it free to throw it over her.

He swung away, moving to the door in magnificent, impervious nakedness. His body was perfectly proportioned, with wide shoulders, a flat belly, and lean, tapering limbs without an ounce of surplus flesh. The muscles of his back stretched with smooth power as he pulled open the door and sent a shout ringing through the house. "Sarus!"

The servant was there before the echoes of his master's call had died away. He stood bowing just inside the door, silently awaiting orders. He did not glance in Angeline's direction, and yet she knew he missed no detail of the clothing strewn about the room or her pale and disheveled appearance. If such circumstances offered any occasion for surprise, it did not register on his saffron features.

"Brandy for two," the prince ordered, "and a supper tray, the same."

He closed the door upon the man and came slowly back into the room. He knelt to replenish the fire with quick, unthinking efficiency, as if he had no recognition that it was not a task for royal hands. His expression shuttered, he took up his pantaloons, stepping into them, then turned toward her, moving toward the bed as he fastened the waistband.

The testered four-poster was of cherry wood, intricately carved in a design of lilies surrounding a shell. At the foot was a smooth wooden bar, a part of the bed frame itself used to smooth the surface of the feather mattress when the bed was made. He braced his hands on the bar now, leaning on stiff arms as he surveyed her.

"You seem to have discovered a third way to prove yourself, Angeline Fortin."

She accepted the use of her name without surprise. "It was unintentional, I assure you."

"I regret the necessity. I don't make a practice of raping innocents."

She believed him, but that did not allay the bleakness that gripped her. "No," she said, "only your brother's mistresses."

They were interrupted then by a scratching on the door. Sarus entered with a tray on which stood a decanter of brandy and an assortment of meats and pastries, along with plates, cutlery, and glasses. He sat it on the table, which he then brought near the bed. Unstoppering the brandy, he poured measures into two glasses and stood back, waiting. The prince cast a glance over the tray, before nodding his dismissal. When the man had gone, he picked up a glass and handed it to Angeline.

"Thank you, no. I—I am not used to strong spirits."

"No lady is. I understand that well enough," he answered with tight-reined impatience. "But this is not an occasion when ratafia or watered wine will do."

"I don't need it, really."

He lifted a brow. "Can it possibly be that you suspect me of trying to make you drunk? I would remind you that there is now not the least need."

A flush of anger stained her cheekbones and she pushed herself up higher on the pillows, catching at the coverlet to cover herself. "Such a thought never crossed my mind!"

"What, then, did? Do you require that I force you to drink it? Is that your pleasure?"

Sending him a glance of revulsion, she reached out to snatch the glass from his fingers. As the full implication of what he had said struck her, she took a too hasty swallow of the fiery liqueur. It caught in her throat, taking her breath, but she would not let him see. She swallowed, though the effort brought tears to her eyes.

A gleam of amusement came and went across his face. He sipped from his own glass, moving to seat himself on the end of the bed. "Brandy and rage, a most effective combination to banish unreason—"

The chain she wore had slipped back into place as she was carried to bed. The perfume vial nestled between her breasts. As she drew back at his approach, it swung forward, catching the light on its intricate scrolled surface, drawing his abrupt attention. He leaned toward her, and the brush of his fingers was warm against her skin as he reached to pick up the vial, turning it this way and that. His gaze lifted to her wide green eyes.

"Drink your brandy," he said, "then tell me where she is."

"I—I don't know what you mean." It was not the burning strength of the brandy that made her hesitate, but the hint of danger she saw in his expression.

"Don't bother to lie. If I could think Max was fool enough to have a virgin mistress I would throw his death in your face yet again, but it defies the imagination. Therefore, because this thing you wear around your neck is marked with his cipher, the initials of his name entwined on the kind of bauble he liked to hand out for favors received, you cannot deny having seen Claire de Buys. And so I ask you once more, and once only: Where is she?"

"And if I won't tell you, what then?" She lifted her chin with a defiance she knew to be unwise, but could not help.

He released the perfume vial, letting it swing with a soft thud against her breastbone. "Rage as a restorative was a mistake, I perceive. It would be foolish, however, in this moment of bravery, to think you have nothing to fear."

She lowered her lashes, swirling the brandy in the glass she held so that it coated the sides with an iridescent film. "Even if I had seen Claire, if I knew where she was at this moment, how could I tell you? It would betray a member of the only family I have, the same as giving my sister into your... hands."

"Your scruples are endearing, but have you considered what they are likely to cost you?"

Her gaze was straight and clear as she met his. "How much higher could the cost be?"

"Consider," he replied, tilting his head to one side. "Your aunt's house was quiet when I entered earlier, and there was no alarm when we left it. It seems likely your absence has not been discovered, in which case, if I return you there by morning it will be as if this incident had never happened. Your character will remain unblemished; there will be no evil rumors to make miserable your future. If, on the other hand, I deliver you in full daylight, riding up with you across my saddle in unimpeded view of your neighbors and your aunt's servants, what will be the result?"

There was no need to guess. The story would be whispered from ear to ear. The older women of the community, the arbiters of conduct, would unite in drawing their skirts aside. Her friends would be instructed by their parents to avoid her, indeed would do so of their own volition for fear of being smeared with the same dirt. The young men would cease to call, unless in the midnight hours to hoot and shout beneath her window. She might as well resign herself to the life of a reclusive spinster, or else, when the loneliness became too much to bear, the part of a strumpet in the town.

"A daunting prospect," he murmured, his gaze on her still face.

"You—you could not be so callous."

"A fallacy. I can do and be far worse things in the cause of finding my brother's killer."

Angeline turned her gaze toward the fire. "If that is the way it must be, then I cannot prevent it. You will do as you must."

"I don't think you realize what you are accepting so stoically," he told her, his voice edged with acid. "Has it occurred to you to wonder if Claire is worth such sacrifice?"

"I don't think I am doing this for her, but for my own honor."

"So you do know where she is, and dare to sit there in all sanctimoniousness, denying the knowledge to me. Have you any idea, my dear Angeline, how close you are to being beaten?"

The words fell harsh from his lips. The marks of her nails down his face stood out, blood-crusted and livid. The blue light in his eyes was cold as he leaned toward her. She met his gaze with contempt. "I wondered how long it would be before it came to that."

"Wonder no more."

"Am I supposed to cower before you, pleading that I not be hurt? I have good reason to think it would be useless. Your tactics, you see, have been at fault. A threatened person fears what he does not know. Since you have already subjected me to the ultimate in abuse for a woman, I can no longer be brought to cringing terror for what you might do next."

Was it the brandy she had drunk that gave her the courage to say those words? She did not know, and yet they spilled from her in effortless challenge, an echo of his own untrammeled speech.

He drained his brandy glass and set it on the table before he swung to place a hand on either side of her, resting his weight upon them. "If you think what I have done to you is the worst you can suffer, let me assure you that you are mistaken. It was not one tenth of what can be inflicted if I so choose. You are my prisoner. No one will interfere, no matter how I may decide to use you. If you remain stubborn I will keep you here in prolonged torment for as long as it takes to get the answer I want."

"My aunt will miss me come morning. She will raise the alarm."

"That may be, but I wonder if she will mention to the search party the possibility that you are with me? It would give rise to so many inconvenient questions, would it not, such as why I should find it necessary to abduct you? No, I don't believe we will be disturbed just yet, you and I."

She stared at him, unable to refute it. Her eyes stormy, she said, "It won't work."

He shifted to one arm, reaching to pick up a lock of her hair, letting it drift over her shoulder where it lay in a shimmering ringlet upon her breast. "Oh, I think it will. You have helped already, since we now know Claire is somewhere near. Given time to think, I am convinced you will be of greater assistance. In the meantime, I will have the... stimulus of your company."

"You will be bored within twenty-four hours!"

"It's possible, but I'm willing to take the risk." His fingers trailed once more to the vial where it lay between her breasts. "Just now the scent from this bastard joining of the goldsmith's and the perfumer's arts offends me. It is well enough for Claire, but suits you not at all."

With deft movements he found the clasp and released it, drawing the necklet from her. He took her brandy glass then, transferring it to the table, spilling the gold chain beside it, letting the vial clatter to the polished top.

He turned back to her, sliding his hand behind her back, gathering her to him, drawing her across his lap. Her protest was smothered on her lips as he possessed them in the rise of slow and scathing desire. Angeline lay rigid. What use was it to fight him? What was there to defend? And yet he would have no pleasure of her, no outward sign of the inward turmoil he caused. Let his boredom start soon, for no matter the cost, no matter the outcome, she would escape him. And do what he would, from her he would learn nothing. Nothing.

Four

THE AROMA OF COFFEE DRIFTED ON THE COOL AIR. Tantalizing, inviting, it teased Angeline awake. There was the brightness of day behind her eyelids and a heaviness about her limbs, as if she had slept deeply and long. She was warm and immensely comfortable, and it seemed a pity to move, but she could not stay where she was forever. Breathing deeply, smiling, she stretched, pushing her hands above her head, reaching for the foot of the bed with her pointed toes.

With a gasp she drew back as she encountered the warm hardness of another body. Like a cataclysm, the events of the night before returned to her. She swung her head sharply, to stare into the bright blue eyes of the prince. He lay watching her with only slightly less stunned surprise in his face than she felt herself.

"I give you good day," he said, his features closing in like a mask descending, a mask marred by the raw marks left by her nails.

It was no dream, her abduction in the early-morning hours, but a nightmare made no more bearable by the light of day. "Good morning," she murmured.

"Oh, it's later than that, past noon I would guess, and I fear your ruin is now complete."

"How—how kind of you to remind me. I am sure that otherwise it would have escaped my notice."

"Feeling waspish, are you? Good. Any sign of a decline would call for drastic preventive measures."

"Threats before breakfast? Your conversation is somewhat limited, is it not?"

He smiled suddenly, the brown skin about his eyes crinkling into fine laugh lines. "A just complaint. It shall be remedied. May I direct your attention to the tray at your elbow? And request that you pour?"

Frowning a little, wary of this new affability, Angeline turned her head to see a breakfast table drawn up to the edge of the bed, placed there no doubt by the soft-footed Sarus. It bore a silver pot with an eddy of steam rising from the spout, a pitcher of hot milk, a set of silver and crystal preserve jars, and a basket of fragrantly yeasty croissants covered with a thick linen towel. She pushed herself up in the bed, then as the sheet slipped, revealing the naked globes of her breasts, snatched at it with a gasp. The intimacy of this situation to which she had awakened was like a slap in the face. She was unclothed in the bed of a strange man who sat calmly waiting for her to pour his *café au lait*.

There seemed nothing else to be done except comply, though she felt ridiculous pouring the coffee into a china cup, mixing in the milk, handing it to the man beside her with all the conscious grace of a lady presiding over a tea table.

What was even more disturbing was the fact that she was hungry, and had no difficulty in disposing of two of the flaky pastries.

As she picked up a third crescent-shaped roll, she thought that the prince flicked her a glance of approval, but since she had deliberately avoided looking in his direction during this informal breakfast, she could not be certain. The more the idea grew, the more positive she became that she held his attention, the harder it was to swallow. It was almost a relief when he passed his cup to her for a refill.

He took the cup from her, requesting another croissant, buttered and generously spread with fig preserves. "It occurs to me that I have underestimated you and, possibly, Claire."

"How so?"

"There were two women who left your aunt's house last evening, according to Leopold. Being used to European females who will not stir a step out their door without a maid or footman to lend them protection, females who require an escort even to the lazaret, I concluded naturally that one of the two women seen was Claire, the other her maid. Later, when you were sighted on the road alone, I took it that your servant had either gone ahead to clear the path for you, or else been frightened into flight. In either case, the other female was of no concern once I had you—or rather Claire, as I thought. You proved me wrong, but that raises an interesting question: What became of the other woman? Was she in truth a maid? Was she with you at all by the time my men and I had returned with Leopold? Or was, perhaps, this second woman Claire? Could it be that you took her from her mother's house, guiding her through the darkness to a place of refuge before returning homeward along the same route?"

Dismay washed over her. Covering it with a cold stare, she said, "Surely, Your Highness, you cannot expect me to confirm or deny it?"

"I think under the circumstances," he said frowning, "it would be as well if you were to call me Rolfe. And no, I don't expect it. Still, *fortune favet fortibus.*"

Latin had been among Angeline's studies. "Fortune may favor the bold, Your Highness, but it will take more than that to find a woman who is not there."

"That may be, though what a shame it would be to deprive my men of the chase."

When she made no answer, he leaned across her to place his cup on the table. Instinctively, she recoiled, drawing back as far as the headboard upon which she rested would permit. He checked, a frown flitting across his face, to be replaced by a grim smile. He rested his hand beside her hip, his weight on the covers drawing the sheet away from her breasts, exposing their creamy curves.

"I gave you permission to use my name, but I have yet to hear it on your lips."

"There—there has been no need to address you."

"I think you mean to set distance between us by formality. This I cannot allow. I command you to speak my given name."

He bent his head to brush his lips along her collarbone, drifting lower to the valley between the perfect, conical mounds he had uncovered.

"Really," she protested in breathless tones. "What can it matter how I call you?"

"I am used to having my will obeyed, and will countenance nothing less."

As she felt his warm breath upon her breast's most sensitive peak, she lifted her hand to his head, sinking her fingers into the soft waves, grasping. "Then you are spoiled beyond belief!"

"Do you seek to thwart me for the good of my soul, or merely out of pique?" He gave no sign that he felt her tugging. The warm flick of his tongue rasped at her nerves as with his other hand he pushed the sheet down farther. He then slid his hand over the slim indentation of her waist, smoothed it over the enticing contour of her hip.

At that moment there came a knock at the door. Angeline drew a breath of relief. "There—there is someone at the door."

"It's only Sarus," he said, unheeding, unpausing.

The knock came again. "Please—please, Rolfe."

He raised his head, replacing the sheet he had dislodged, withdrawing to his side of the bed with stiff reluctance in his muscles and wry disappointment on his features. "The man," he said with grim amusement, "is entirely too well trained."

Sarus had brought a copper tub and the water with which to fill it. That the bath was a daily ritual seemed obvious since she had not heard it ordered, and neither manservant nor master saw fit to comment. Though Angeline herself enjoyed bathing, such cleanliness of the person was sufficiently a novelty for her to concentrate upon it instead of

Rolfe as, ignoring the dressing gown of brown velvet with gold satin revers Sarus had laid out across the foot of the bed for him, he sprang from the mattress and went toward the tub.

He bathed as he did everything else, with quick competence and an economy of motion. The coolness lingering in the room despite the fire Sarus had kindled appeared to affect him not at all as he soaped and splashed with wisps of steam rising around him from the hot water. Stepping from the tub, he allowed the manservant to dress him in a clean uniform of sparkling white, though one not so formal or so grand as that of the night before. Sarus set out his freshly polished boots so he could draw them on, handed him fresh gloves, and flicked a brush over his hair. More than once during these attentions, Rolfe met Angeline's eyes, enjoying her discomfiture. He was playing the prince, she thought, with a bit more royal helplessness than was customary, judging from the way in which Sarus hesitated before stepping forward with his sword and buckling it about Rolfe's narrow waist.

His amusement vanished when he stood ready, however. To Sarus he gave orders to refill the bath for Mademoiselle, ending: "You will perform any service for her that is required, up to, but not including, finding the means for her to leave this house. Gustave will remain as guard."

Knowing the last had been added for her delectation, Angeline asked, "And who is Gustave?"

"The oldest and therefore the most trustworthy of my men for your case."

Enraging in his fulsome good humor, resplendent
in his white uniform, he stood waiting for her reply.
She managed a smile. "I will have to try his nerve."

"I would not advise it," he said, moving toward her
in his lithe stride. "He is not that old."

With one hand on his sword hilt, he leaned as if
to kiss her. She drew back, and his hand came up,
cupping her chin, forcing her to meet his lips, saying
against them: "That is a habit I am going to have to
cure you of, when I return."

"I may not be here," she said, lifting her chin with
more bravado than she felt.

He straightened, striding toward the door, turning
as Sarus opened it before him. "You will be."

Angeline waited until the manservant had closed the
door behind both himself and his master, until Rolfe's
booted footsteps on the stairs had died away. She looked
around for her clothing, but it was not to be seen. She
remembered then a bundle of white that had been
clasped in the manservant's hand. Why had he taken
them? Perhaps to keep her from leaving? But no, she
had heard no order to that effect and Sarus would not
have done so on his own. Maybe he had thought they
were rags, from their appearance a natural assumption.
She would have to ask when next the opportunity arose.

She glanced speculatively at the prince's dressing
gown at the foot of the bed, then turned away. She
would not encroach so far as to wear his clothing
herself. Draping the sheet around her like a toga,
she slid from the bed. She padded to the window
that faced the front of the house, and drew aside the
drapery, looking out.

Below her, horses tied to wrought-iron hitching posts stamped and sidled, their coats shining in the sun. Deep voices called. There was the sound of masculine laughter suddenly cut off. A door slammed somewhere. And then in a blaze of white, the prince and his men poured from the house. They mounted their horses, swinging into the saddles with practiced ease, controlling the nervous beasts with reins and muscular thighs. Rolfe raised his hand, the sunlight glinting gold on the ring on his hand and catching gilt highlights in his hair, and then they plunged away in a muffled thunder of hooves, disappearing down the wooded, overgrown drive.

Angeline stood for long moments with her forehead pressed against the glass, staring at nothing. She felt suspended in disbelief. Alone, finally, without the vibrating tension of Rolfe's presence, the unreality of what had taken place grew ever more pervasive. Such things did not happen, not to young women of innocence and community standing such as herself. It seemed almost as if she must be to blame in some way, and yet she could think of nothing she might have done differently.

She wondered if her absence had been discovered, and what her aunt thought of it. Would there be any sign that the prince had been in the house? It seemed unlikely; the back door had been left on the latch for her and there had been no need for him to force an entry. To all appearances, it must look as if she had not returned, had not slept in her bed. Would Madame, her aunt, consider then that she might have spent the night at the convent? Knowing Mother Theresa and her concern for Angeline's welfare, Tante Berthe must consider it a possibility. In that case, might she not delay sounding the alarm? She would not think of the spectre Rolfe had raised: that Madame de Buys would not sound the alarm at all.

At a soft knock, she jumped, startled, and whirled around. Moving quickly back to the bed, she stepped up onto its high surface, slipping under the coverlet before she called out, "*Entrez.*"

It was Sarus, bringing the fresh hot water for her bath. He stood bowing in the doorway before he stepped inside and set down the cans he carried. With apparent ease, he wrestled the copper tub, tipping it to pour the cooling, soap-scummed water it held into the refuse cans. Setting it down nearer the fire, now roaring on the hearth, he refilled it, then left the room, returning with a folding screen that he carefully placed to cut off any drafts. Laying out a length of toweling and a bar of scented soap, he inclined his squat body once more, picked up the cans of cold water, and left the room.

Such attention to her comfort was unexpected, with little taint of the prison. It was wonderful to step into the steaming tub, to ease into the soothing water. There was a bruise across her ribs where Rolfe had caught her to hoist her into the saddle, and a slight tenderness about her mouth. Blue and purple splotches marred the white, blue-veined skin of her wrists and there was a vague soreness between her thighs, but other than these reminders, there was little to mark the events of the night. She felt no different. Though it was doubtless a flaw in her character, she knew no urge toward vain gestures such as self-destruction this morning. Knowing she might be forced to repeat the performance was not pleasant, but neither was it cause for despair. She hated the man who had brought her here and imposed his will upon her; she would like to see him drawn and quartered, hanging in pieces from a scaffold. But there seemed such little likelihood of it coming to pass that she could not exercise her temper over it. Of what use was it to stamp her feet and scream? Raging, pacing, shouting defiance would only deplete her energy without effect.

What was left? There might be some means of exacting her own revenge, and yet he was so formidable, so imperturbable that she must proceed with care. In any case, her concern in the near future was defense. She must steel herself to resist the attacks upon her will, her self-respect. Her best weapon in that endeavor, it seemed, would be her wits.

How long would the patience of the prince last? How long would it be before he resorted to physical means to persuade her to tell him what he wished to know? He had not done so the night before, but she could not expect such constraint for long. And if she managed to sustain her denial through that ordeal, what then? Must she stay here indefinitely? Would she become Rolfe's mistress, complete with the nightly obligations of such a title?

The prospect was chilling, but the thought of returning home was not much better. The picture Rolfe had painted, though unattractive, was probably highly accurate. In the bright light of morning, her character lay in shreds. Nothing could restore it, even if she regained her aunt's house. How the tongues would clack! Both men and women would shake their heads and suddenly bare long-held doubts about her moral strength. She had always been headstrong and undutiful, they would say. Any girl of the properly retiring maidenly manner would have been wed and out of her aunt's way by now. Such a pity that Madame de Buys had to be saddled with her!

But she would not be allowed to return to her aunt's unless Claire were found. If that came to pass, what would Rolfe do? Would he bring her back here? Would she be treated to the same form of inducement he had used on her?

She frowned. That it would be any more successful with Claire seemed doubtful. What could her cousin know of Maximilian's death other than what she had said? It was unbelievable she could be involved beyond the role of bystander; someone in the wrong place at the wrong time. Rolfe seemed to think that Claire had in some way enticed Maximilian, distracting him so that he met his death. That could not be; Angeline was positive of it. Still, no more than twenty-four hours ago she would have said it was impossible for Claire to have been Maximilian's mistress.

One of the most disturbing factors in that line of thought was Claire's fear. If she had been present at the time of the murder through no more than chance, then why her headlong flight? Why had she not gone to the authorities and given evidence, made herself available to aid in finding the killer of the man she professed to love? The notoriety would have been unpleasant, and there might have been a shade of suspicion, but it could not have been so distressing as the harried, hunted existence she had led these last weeks.

Looked at from that angle, Rolfe's request to speak to Claire did not seem so much to ask. Why could her cousin not be reasonable? Perhaps when she learned of Angeline's failure to return home, Claire would remember the sentry on the road and guess at who held her and why. In that case, would she come forward and voluntarily give to the prince the information she had? Remembering Claire as she had last seen her, armed in fear and unconscious selfishness, Angeline could not find comfort in the hope.

There was one other possibility. Could it be that Claire's fear and Rolfe's determination both stemmed from the same source, information Claire might have that would implicate the prince in his brother's death? Angeline sat staring into the heart of the fire for a long time before she shook her head and turned to the matter at hand.

She soaped herself with care, rinsing, soaking in the warm, scented water, taking her time with the ritual because there was nothing else to occupy her. She gazed about the room, at the tapestry-hung walls, the rich though faded bed hangings, the cypress wood floors with their scattering of rugs. No doubt those quarters suited the prince and his men far better than the de la Chaise mansion, despite their lack of burnished grandeur. Still, if they had not been available, her own fate might have been less drastic.

When the water began to cool, she stepped out, drying herself on the length of linen toweling. Her face grim, she wrapped the linen sheet around herself once more, tucking the free end between her breasts. Moving to the washstand, she picked up a comb made of solid silver and drew it through her hair, bringing some order to the snarled auburn skein.

Had Sarus been listening to determine when she finished her bath, or was it coincidence that made him return then? She could not tell. He carried over his arm her gown and underdress, plus a white, freshly laundered linen tunic of the type he wore himself.

He inclined his head. "I fear, Mademoiselle, that the work done on your clothing was not enough to make it whole again. I have a thought to cover the damage, if Mademoiselle will permit?"

His manner impersonal, he held out first the gown and underdress, then the tunic. For all that, he watched her closely, his eyes dark under his slanted brows as he managed to stay between her and the door.

The tunic was a blouson garment that pulled on over the head with pockets on the breast, one marked by a coronet in satin stitch embroidery, and with a sash of cerulean-blue twisted silk. Sarus meant for her to pull it on over her gown, effectively concealing the ragged, roughly darned tears in the fragile muslin.

As he began to turn away, Angeline held it out again. "I couldn't."

"It is not of sufficient... beauty and fashion?" the man inquired, a worried look appearing in his eyes. "There is little else to offer here, among men only."

"I would not deprive you of it."

"That is no problem," he said, his face clearing as he moved once more toward the door. "Take it,

Mademoiselle, and perhaps when you have dressed you will descend the stairs that I may ready the room of the prince for his return." -

The tone was respectful, but firm. The man was as highhanded in his way as his master. The annoying thing was that her inclination exactly paralleled his suggestion.

The tunic was not so bad. It looked, in fact, a little like a pelerine called the Cossack that had been the *dernier cri* the year before. The sleeves hung well below her hands, but she rolled them to her elbows. With the sash knotted at her natural waistline instead of higher, underneath her bust, she had a dashing peasant look. This was emphasized by her hair, flowing free in a shimmering russet curtain over her shoulders, and her cheeks, flushed from the heat of her bath. Lacking the pins lost in her flight, her hair would have to stay unconfined; there was nothing else to be done with it. Searching out her slippers, finally finding one bundled in the bedclothes and the other nearby, she slipped them on, then moved to the table beside the bed.

The necklet Claire had given her lay there, glinting in the morning light. She picked it up, then let it fall back again. Rolfe was right; lilies of the valley did not suit her and, in truth, the vial was too heavy, too ornate for her taste. As she stared at it, a vague suspicion touched her. No, Claire could not have known she would be taken by Rolfe, could not have wished for her to be confirmed as Claire, it could not be. And if it were, if the idea had been there in Claire's mind, it had been a mistake. Without the perfumed necklace Rolfe might not have been so certain she knew her cousin's whereabouts, might not be so determined to hold her. In any case, she could not wear it, would never wear it again. Leaving it in a gleaming tangle, she crossed the room and let herself out the door.

Apart from the great hall below, the house was built in the Georgian style with the upper floor bisected by a wide hallway. Angeline could not resist a small reconnaissance down its length, which was carpeted by a Persian hall runner. Bedchambers similar to the one she had just left opened along it at intervals, six of them in all. At the far end was a flight of narrow wooden stairs for the use of servants as they emptied slops and carried trays back and forth. Half afraid she would meet Sarus returning, she swung back in the other direction.

The great main staircase beckoned with wide-flung arms. She paused at the top, then descended step by cautious step. At the foot, she glanced around the great hall, seeing no one though a fire burned smokily on the enormous hearth at the end, and there was a silver-chased pistol lying in pieces on the table as if someone had taken it apart for cleaning. The front door stood open, and beyond it was the drive that led past the de la Chaise mansion after winding its way through the woods. M'sieur de la Chaise would be shocked to discover that she was being held on his property against her will. Surely he would help her, if only she could reach him.

Before she could move, heavy footfalls were heard approaching from the rear of the house. A man appeared, coming from a doorway on the far side of the stairs. He carried a tankard in one hand and a piece of bread wrapped around a chunk of cheese in the other. It was the one-eyed, grizzled veteran, Gustave.

"So you are up, my pretty one," he said in tones that rumbled around the room. He waved his tankard at her. "You will have a swallow and a bite to tide you over until dinner, yes?"

"No, thank you."

"Come, sit down. Talk to me while I eat. It is a sad man who sups alone."

"I will not be very good company," Angeline said, her tone restrained.

"To look at your face across from me instead of the beard-stubbled louts who left me behind will be a change so welcome you need say naught if you prefer. Come. Sit."

There was nothing in his manner to indicate that she was under his guard, and yet Angeline had the feeling that he missed nothing of her stance there, hovering between the stairs and the open doorway. Since she could not return to the bedchamber for the moment, there seemed nothing to do except bow to his brusque invitation.

"There, that's better, yes?"

He introduced himself then, rolling off names and titles in harsh, guttural accents, adding varying terms of servitude and degrees of rank from half the armies of Europe. He took a great swig of whatever alcoholic-smelling brew his tankard contained, and went on. "I have been with Rolfe these ten years, since he reached his majority. I have seen him stop a spent musket ball with his bare hands, race his horse for a wager down the steep and winding cobbled streets of the capital of Ruthenia in rain and darkness, snatch a famous actress from the stage with a silver rope to haul her to his box after her final curtain call, and fight a gypsy king in a duel with stilettos for the favors of a wild wench, but never have I seen him so bent on anything as he was on taking you last night."

"You flatter me—or else Prince Rolfe," she said in cold tones.

"No," he said simply. "When Rolfe came down a while ago, he said you were the wrong one after all. A great jest that, one we of his guard will enjoy at his expense for long days to come. He does not often make a mistake."

Angeline clasped her hands together on the table in front of her. "There's nothing in the least comic about it to me."

"I doubt it not, *meine liebe*, knowing the temper that flayed him. We felt for you as it was, but if we had known you were... a maiden we would have—"

"He told you that, too?" Her voice was tight as she spoke.

"Ah, no. He says little, our prince. But it was plain from what he did not say, and from the careful instructions he left for me concerning my conduct."

"I see. It... is a pity that you have to stay in on such a fine day to guard me."

"It is a duty like any other. Are you sure you will not join me? A cup of chocolate, perhaps? A glass of wine?"

She shook her head, glancing along the length of the table made of oak dark and stained with age. It had seen rough use. It was scraped and scarred, and there were places along its edges that looked as if a diner idle between courses had used his knife to occupy himself, chipping at the wood. She reached out, and with a finger traced one of the innumerable rings from tankards or glasses that marred the surface. The silence creaked with lack of ease. Finally she said, "Have you any idea how long you will be here?"

"As long as it takes." He sent her a glance from under thick brows, his one good eye narrowed. "Do you worry about what will happen with you when we are gone? You need not. Rolfe will make handsome recompense."

A laugh was forced from her. "Such a paragon."

"Do you doubt me? I swear that since he has taken a hand in your fate, he will not abandon you."

"If you think I desire a place in his baggage train you are much mistaken." Her tracing finger trembled and she closed it tightly into her fist.

"You are afraid of him?"

"Of course not!"

He stared at her as if ruminating. "I have been, at times, when he had drunk deep. You are a female, light of weight and with puny defenses, and so have more reason."

"It is so kind of you to reassure me."

He smiled at her as he took an enormous bite of his bread and cheese before diving into his tankard. Swallowing, he wiped his face with a callused hand. "That's the spirit. With Rolfe, you must give him back word for knife-edged word. It will make him think, give him distraction, and that is what he needs these days."

"Now I am to provide entertainment for him? No doubt if I could dance that would be well received also?"

He stared at her in concentration, his head turned slightly, the better to see her. "You are joking, but if you could turn his mind for a short time from this affair that plagues him, you will earn the gratitude of the men of the guard."

"And that is my sole object, of course."

"You are as bad as Rolfe," he grunted, throwing down the last crust of his bread, then sitting back to rest his tankard on the arm of his chair. "Perhaps it will not be so difficult for you to understand him then, especially if you are given some idea of his history."

There followed a rambling discourse with many asides and no few pungent observations. Rolfe, second son of the sixth king of Ruthenia in his line, had killed his mother with his birth. A sickly child of high nervous irritability, he had been left to his nurses while his father supervised the upbringing of his robust older son and heir apparent. Maximilian's education from boyhood had been the responsibility of a phalanx of teachers, each of them an authority in his field.

Rolfe had been placed under the tutelage of a Venetian scholar of many eccentricities, which included aesthetic leanings, notably poetry, and a passion for science. Lessons were held out of doors. A regimen of exercise and simple, fresh foods was introduced, along with a rich diet of ideas. The weak child-prince grew strong and wily and accomplished. But though he came to be able to argue his elder brother to a standstill in all debates with a rhapsody of words, and to defeat him in five athletic contests out of six, his father the king could not be brought to appreciate the grace and ease with which he did so. It was as if, preferring that Maximilian be ever victorious, the king could not grant that Rolfe could defeat his older brother without trickery.

Maximilian bore him no ill will. The two brothers were close until they came to manhood and began to keep their own establishments. Rolfe was excluded from much of the social life of the court, and all its responsibilities, and so he consorted with gypsies and other such rabble, and developed a habit of enlisting in causes not his own as an outlet for pent-up energy. And so he had careered across Europe with his handpicked cadre, fighting, brawling, visiting the Russian grandfather whose arms bore the head of a wolf and who had an affection for the wildest of the Ruthenian princes. Max he saw now and then in Paris, Venice, or Rome, though he seldom returned to Ruthenia.

Some weeks before his brother's death, he had heard disquieting rumors. There were those who wished to change the order of succession in Ruthenia, those who wished both the king and his heir dead and were willing to pay well to achieve that situation.

Returning to his homeland, Rolfe could discover nothing. All seemed normal, except for the beautiful mistress from the young United States whom Maximilian had taken, a woman fit to be a princess by her breeding and beauty, in every particular except character, or such was Gustave's opinion. Maximilian himself had seemed no different. Making his usual appearances at the opera, at the beer gardens, and on the hunting field, dancing attendance on his father, and, after a time, putting aside the red-haired woman in his keeping as if tired of the novelty, he went on exactly as always.

Then it had happened. Maximilian lay dead. When the news was brought to the king, he suffered a stroke. It was not his first; there had been another the previous spring. But it was severe enough that for several hours there was fear for his life. Then Rolfe, leaving the palace after his bedridden father had blamed him for his brother's death due to some foul rumor, was attacked by footpads. If not for quick action with his sword, he would have fallen a victim, too.

Angeline studied the face, craggy with scars, of the man across from her. "Are you suggesting there was a connection?"

"There did not seem one at first. Later, when the second attempt came—a knife thrown from a dark side street as he called at the former lodging of Mademoiselle de Buys—it began to look a possibility. When a crate being loaded at Le Havre broke its chain, narrowly missing Rolfe as it fell, the thing had to be faced."

"With Maximilian dead and his father seriously ill, then Rolfe had, overnight, become the future king."

"True, *meine liebe*."

"Who, then, would be next in the line of succession if Rolfe were killed?"

"The question leaps to the mind, does it not? The answer is Leopold, his cousin, the son of his father's sister."

"The dark-haired man who is with him now?"

"The same." Gustave shrugged massive shoulders. "And yet it was Leopold who, hearing of the attempts on Rolfe's life, gathered the *garde du corps*. It was he who spoke for us, saying we would not be denied the right to go with him, to live up to our name."

The *garde du corps*, literally Rolfe's bodyguard. "Could it have been a ruse, a trick to evade suspicion while staying near enough to try again?"

"Anything is possible. The attempt at Le Havre as we waited to take ship makes it all the more likely." He paused judiciously. "Then there was the trouble in New Orleans."

"Another attempt?"

"It's hard to say. One of the stallions we bought came close to trampling Rolfe, an animal that seemed high strung but of good heart when he came from the dealer's ring. If Rolfe had not been agile beyond most, he would be dead now. Afterward, the horse died. It may be that he was fed some poisonous weed to make him seem more spirited for the sale, though the dealer swore it was not so. It was odd that the mount was the one chosen by Rolfe, and not one of those left to the rest of us."

Angeline could only agree as she sat frowning. The threat to the prince meant that she must readjust her ideas. Under the circumstances, it was unlikely he was responsible for his brother's death. She must admit the idea had become more and more remote for her since the moment she had suggested it on the dance floor last evening. All the efforts to kill him had been unsuccessful thus far, but it was hard to believe he had gone to the trouble of arranging them to shift suspicion from himself.

"I understand the need of the prince to question my cousin concerning Maximilian's death, but would it not have been just as well to have sent someone else after her?"

"You mean an official of the law? Such a man would have no power outside Ruthenia. More, he would not have traveled as hard and as fast as we did, would not, after finding Mademoiselle de Buys, be so anxious to get to the truth of how Maximilian was killed. To Rolfe, suicide in connection with his brother's name is as repugnant as murder, a stain on his honor. But there is another thing. I can only guess, but I think sometimes it is in Rolfe's mind that by leaving Ruthenia he is drawing the pursuit after himself and, therefore, away from his father."

"Draw it after—or take the pursuer with him?"

"Just so, Mademoiselle."

Her green eyes were dark with dismay. "But to match wits with a murderer, trusting to skill and fortune to avoid his strike, never knowing when it will come again; it is a terrible risk!"

"You begin to know our prince." Gustave, his face creasing in a fierce smile, slapped his empty tankard down on the table with a force that made it ring.

They spoke of other things, moving to a settee before the fire as the early winter dusk drew in. They were assailed by the faint scent of dinner being prepared, wafting from the outdoor kitchen where Sarus, coming and going, supervised a Negro cook provided by their host, M'sieur de la Chaise. There were carved figures of men enjoying the hunt over the fireplace mantel, a hearth of slate, and tiles painted with stags, boars, rabbits, and squirrels in natural colors surrounding the openings. The settee was of dark

carved oak and jade green horsehair fabric, stiff and
scratchy and with scant comfort.

Gustave was restless. Sometimes he glanced at her
as if in growing unease, as if he regretted the impulse
that had made him seek to enlighten her.

It was during that time when it was not quite dark
enough to have the candles lighted and not bright
enough to see well that Rolfe and the others returned.
The front door swung open. Rolfe, his uniform a
blur of white, paused just inside. He drew off his
gloves, throwing them onto a side table, his swift gaze
missing nothing.

"Do I detect an air of maudlin twilight confidences?
Poppy red is the color of guilt, Gustave, and of that
rabbit-holed hunting course you call your face. If I had
known that was the way she would affect you, I might
have left her with Oswald and Oscar."

"You gave no orders about speaking to her,"
Gustave answered with heavy meaning.

"An oversight," came the biting reply. "My fault
for relying upon your discretion."

The other men crowded in behind Rolfe, standing
with strained patience, their faces lined with tiredness
and interested amusement. There was one especially—
the broad, sandy-haired man with gray eyes and the
small scar at his mouth—who met Angeline's eyes for
an instant with an expression of wry sympathy.

Angeline came to her feet. "I am afraid, Your
Highness, that the fault was mine."

"I am aware." His glance barely touched her, and
yet it carried the sting of a reprimand for interfering
between himself and his follower.

"No," Gustave said in bull-like tones, his one eye glinting with pale-blue light. "She did no more than listen to prattle that I began."

"A defender of fair flowers, Gustave? If it was your purpose, as I suppose, to soothe her alarm by filing the teeth of the ogre, then you have just nullified your case." He moved toward the stairs, indicating with a flick of the wrist that he wished Angeline to precede him upward.

In the bedchamber, he stripped off his tunic and tossed it onto the bed, then, unsnapping the wrist bands of his shirt, moved to the washstand. He poured water from the china pitcher into the bowl and laved his hands, splashing his face to remove the grime of miles of hard riding. Taking the small linen towel from the washstand rack, he turned with narrowed turquoise eyes.

"Was it necessary to fascinate Gustave?"

"A peculiar question," she answered, moving away from him to the window where she stood watching the men below grooming their horses. "I cannot answer yes to the charge because it is not true, but if I say no, then I will be admitting that he has been fascinated."

"I am to take that for a denial?"

"As you please."

"My pleasure," he said, tossing the towel aside, moving to stand with one fist on his hip and the other braced on the windowsill, "is to find out why you were prying."

She flashed him a quick look, uncomfortably aware of his nearness and the warm male scent, combined with a distinct smell of horse, that emanated from him. "Surely even you can see that it would be to my advantage to find out the kind of man whose prisoner I am?"

"To that there is a simple solution—ask me."

She lifted a brow. "I feel sure you would give me an answer in your own odd fashion, but why would you expect me to believe it?"

"That is a matter for your own intelligence. Every human being must carry his own saltcellar his life long. To refuse the burden is the act of a laggard, or a fool."

"You have no use for trust, I perceive. And yet you object to the grain of salt of my choosing."

"That is my prerogative."

She sent him a long, searching glance before allowing a smile to curve her lips. "One would suppose from your unreasonableness, Your Highness, that your afternoon was unproductive."

Ignoring the sally, he said, "That is the second time you have thrown my title in my face. I can see that you will require a firm hand. Henceforth, I will consider any use of it as an invitation." His meaning became abundantly clear as he reached with deft fingers to unknot the sash at her waist, letting it fall.

She brought up her hands, bracing the palms against his chest, feeling the warmth of his skin through his shirt. "You—you can't do this—not now!"

"I should not, I know, but the sight of you so pristine and bravely *en garde* inclines me to ignore the moral view."

"To—to crush my meager defenses?"

"No, no. To salute them!"

He clasped her forearms, his blue gaze bright with mockery as it raked the delicate oval of her face, the parted softness of her lips. Holding her gray-green eyes, he lowered his mouth to hers.

Five

THE DINNER HOUR WAS LATE, ACCORDING TO THE standards of St. Martinville. The candle flames in the black iron chandelier hanging low above the table wavered in the drafts that eddied in the great hall, leaving its cavernous corners in darkness, sending dancing shadows across the ceiling. The fire on the open hearth was like a good-sized log cabin ablaze. The leaping flames enameled the faces of the men around the table in orange, red, and blue, highlighting the edginess that each held in restraint.

Rolfe, red-gold and uncertain of temper, sat at the head of the table with a decanter of brandy at his elbow. On his right was Angeline in blouson tunic, muslin skirts, and stiff dignity. She had been introduced, formally, to the men gathered at the board: to Leopold, dark-haired and defiant, sitting on Rolfe's left; to the large, quiet man called Meyer who sat beside him; and to Oswald, one of the twins with light-brown hair, hazel eyes, and the mouth of a sensualist. Gustave sat across the table from Oswald. Angeline had flashed him a smile as she sat down.

He had nodded, his manner subdued, but there was a twinkle in his uncovered eye. Next to Gustave, on Angeline's near right, was the other twin called Oscar, a quieter and more observant young man than his brother.

They had feasted on turtle soup and two kinds of fish, followed by a haunch of roast venison basted in wine sauce, and pigeon pie. Their glasses had been filled again and again with Malaga and Bordeaux, and now the brandy was making the rounds, along with candied fruits flavored with liqueur, cheese, nuts, and a bowl of small brown apples.

Though it was not the habit of the French ladies of Louisiana to withdraw at the appearance of the brandy, Angeline had heard that it was the custom in some European countries. She had tried, therefore, to make her excuses and escape, but Rolfe would not allow it. She sat on, toying with her wineglass, nibbling at raisins while the voices of the men grew louder, their gestures more boisterous, the result, she thought, of the high-strung tension of fatigue. In their restless irritability they reached often for their brandy snifters, and in time the often interrupted tale of a race involving a milch cow and a camel grew so garbled that it was hard to be certain that Leopold, who was telling it, knew himself how it ended.

Oswald leaned back, teetering on the rear legs of his chair with one knee propped on the table edge. "Speaking of cows, I saw a sight this afternoon to bring to mind a herd winding its way homeward behind the bell. 'Twas a nun leading a gaggle of adolescent girls, each in white with little aprons and their hair in braids down their backs. And as they went along, the *religieuse* rang a silver hand bell with every step."

"An edifying spectacle, I'm sure. Adolescent girls, you say? I can see at once why your attention was caught." It was his twin who spoke. Oscar, the quieter of the two, had brought a guitar painted with odd Romanish signs to the table and sat tuning it, paying only slight heed to the conversation.

Oswald gave an elaborate sigh. "It was most depressing. To watch such a string of nubile, untouched females, and so closely guarded."

Like a file on a saw, Gustave rasped his throat clear, nodding in Angeline's direction. Oswald, frowning in irritation, fell silent, though a shade of color came and went under his fair skin.

Rolfe looked up from the contemplation of his brandy glass. "There is a nunnery close by?"

"Not as such, no. It is a small convent school run by three Sisters of Charity."

"I trust you did not overlook the obvious?"

The words carried an acid ring. It was easy to see that Oswald was glad to be able to give the expected retort.

"No. I checked into it as best I could without drawing suspicion. It is a small place with not more than twenty or thirty young girls in attendance, most of them boarding for the winter season. It was established by a lady of the community due to a vow made while her youngest daughter was ill. The young lady to whom I spoke, a charming minx who stopped to tie her slipper just as I dismounted to check my saddle girth, said the only adults in residence were the three nuns who serve as teachers. There were no new boarders, and no women of the advanced age of twenty or so had come to visit of late."

"I cannot envision Mademoiselle de Buys removing to a convent school." It was Meyer who made the observation, the scar at the corner of his mouth disappearing as he smiled, though there was a doubtful light in his gray eyes.

Rolfe swung toward Angeline in sudden challenge. "What say you on this fascinating possibility?"

The question, or something like it, was not unexpected. "What can I say? If you believe Claire to be there, you will probe deeper. If not, you won't. It might help in your decision if you will remember that those of the holy orders are not given to subterfuge."

"That has not always been my experience, but we will let it pass," he said, his eyes shuttered. "You are familiar with the school?"

"I was a student there from my twelfth birthday until recently."

Brief irony shone in his turquoise eyes for her deliberate alignment of herself with the innocents of the school.

The catechism did not end there. One by one, the men made their reports, describing the countryside through which they had ridden and the people to whom they had talked, older men on street corners, a woman dragging Spanish moss out of the trees to stuff a mattress, a boy leading a stray cow homeward. They had been down along the bayou, speaking to the Acadians. They had engaged in conversation a slave or two jogging toward town on errands, and had even spoken to the parish priest at the small chapel dedicated to St. Martin of Tours.

Gustave, with nothing to contribute after his day of guard duty, picked an apple from the basket on the table. The carefully piled fruit slipped and another fell to the cloth, rolling. The one-eyed man picked up the second apple, tossing it in his hand while he bit into the first, crushing it with large white teeth. Tossing the core aside after a few minutes, he plucked another apple from the basket, throwing it, with the one he held, from hand to hand. The brownish-red apples shone like polished spheres in the flickering, shifting light.

Gustave eyed the basket once more. Making room for a third apple, he juggled the two he held higher and higher. Absorbed in his play, he forgot the iron chandelier overhead with its load of half a hundred burning candles. As he made his grab for another, the apple that had just left his hand struck an iron candle base, and a wax taper jolted loose to fall smoking toward the tablecloth.

With a curse, Gustave jerked his hand away from the basket and snatched the candle in midair, flinging himself forward in time to catch the apple that had been deflected off course, wrenching back to keep it in play, and, with a frantic twist, adding the candle to the rising, falling, spinning apples.

The men at the table burst into ragged applause and catcalls. Oswald, with a reckless laugh, jumped to his feet. Grabbing an apple, he flung it upward. It missed the chandelier, coming down squarely upon the apple basket, sending fruit rolling in every direction.

Suddenly the air was filled with flying apples, caught and thrown with superb, well-honed reflexes. The iron chandelier swung crazily as it was struck from all sides. Another candle tipped and fluttered downward, and then another, until guttering lights and doused tapers trailing evil wisps of black smoke were hurtling in the air with the apples, like dead and dying shooting stars flying around wayward planets.

It was mixing horseplay with fire, accompanied by base laughter and hooting taunts that rumbled against the smoked divinities on the painted and groined ceiling. Only Rolfe sat aloof, staring into the fire. Oscar protested mildly as he ducked an apple, though he seemed hardly to notice the furor whistling around him as he coaxed a tune from the guitar on his lap. Angeline watched with a smile in the depths of her eyes. Nonetheless, she could not help wondering how long the men could, or would, keep it up.

The chandelier swung to the bombardment, and then at the height of its outward arc, Leopold struck a square hit. Flaming tapers tumbled, somersaulting in midair. A half-dozen or more of them thudded on the cloth at the same time, skittering, knocking over half-filled brandy glasses. The aromatic spirits caught in a rush of leaping, dancing blue, spattering flames in flickering azure droplets. The reek of scorched cloth and brandy rose in a stifling cloud. Small, sky-blue blazes danced over the strings of Oscar's guitar, playing across his pressing fingers.

He rose to his feet with an oath, slapping at the instrument to produce a nerve-jangling discord, his detachment shattered.

Leopold laughed. It was an easy sound, and yet carried in it a grating note of satisfaction that banished bonhomie and raked strained tempers. It was Oswald, Oscar's twin, who with mottled fury on his fair skin, turned a stream of apples and guttering candles toward the dark-haired young cousin of the prince. Leopold, amusement fading from his narrowed eyes, deflected the missiles toward Gustave, who hurled them in Meyer's direction in a steady flow. To defend himself, the large man sent a portion toward both twins, the expression in his gray eyes one of angry calculation.

A vicious, honed edge of temper had entered the game. Faster and faster flew the objects through the acrid, throat-catching smoke and swaying shadows, each thrown with accuracy and frowning intent to inflict pain. Angeline leaned back in her chair as far out of range as she could get, not daring to take her eyes from the dangerous skill being displayed, though the burgeoning tension made the hair rise on the back of her neck.

There was a slight sound from the head of the table, a wafting of air as Rolfe came to his feet. Like silk unfolding, he slid behind her chair, moving toward the fire. From the corner of her eye, Angeline saw him kneel as if he would tend the fire, and then he rose with a clutch of burning brands in his bare hands. Suddenly the air was filled with woodsmoke and showering sparks. The flaring torches descended upon the men, hard thrown, dangerously glowing. They caught them by reflex action, flinging them away with agonized yelps an instant later. Candles and apples fell in a rain as the brands were hurled from hand to hand, returning one by one to Rolfe. He sent them crashing into the red-hot heart of the fire, and the last shattered, spraying red coals over the hearth. An ember skated over the floor and came to rest at the tip of Angeline's slipper. It winked red and died in a curl of smoke.

Rolfe placed his hands on the back of her chair. "The evening is done, my children," he said. "We ride hard and long on the morrow and you must have your rest. You may each take up a night candle to light your solitary ways to bed."

They stood as stiff as statues, glowering at each other and their leader. With a soft splatting sound, wax dripped on the floor from a taper lying near the table edge. The fire crackled. Then a rueful smile broke. Another man grinned. A rumble of laughter came from Gustave. Shaking their heads, slapping each other on the back, nursing blistered palms, picking up overturned brandy glasses and raising them hopefully to their lips, the men of the cadre followed the oblique order. Their instant obedience was the most surprising occurrence of the evening.

It had begun and ended so quickly that the last blue brandy flame only burned itself out as the footsteps of the men retreated on the stairs. Surveying the ruin of the dinner table, Angeline felt a rush of gratitude, quickly suppressed, toward the man who had put an end to the incident.

"What a mess," she said.

"Sarus will deal with it. I suggest we leave him to it."

Rolfe moved to the head of the table, picking up his brandy glass and the heavy decanter that sat beside it. He did not wince as the cut glass bit into his seared fingers, but he was still for a breathless instant.

"You are hurt, not that it's a cause for wonder." Angeline's tone was sharp with the release of taut-stretched nerves. "Whatever possessed you to do such a thing?"

"To separate fighting hounds, you throw water on them. There was none available."

His gold lashes shielded his expression and there was nothing to be learned from the even timbre of his voice. "These were not dogs, but men," she said.

"As you will. They are fighting men, trained and drilled for action and with nothing but a chimera against which to use their skill, men of deeds forced to inaction, men pressed to the edge of exhaustion by long weeks of unremitting travel on an endless quest that is not their own. They crave an outlet for their pent-up energy, and have no one to turn it upon but themselves."

"Something you cannot allow."

"Something I will not allow. There is no time for sulking and petty feuds."

"Why could you not have ordered them to stop?" she asked in what she thought were tones of great reasonableness.

"With what result?" he asked, his shrug impatient. "Obedience at the cost of resentment, corked ire and suspicions of favoritism because I did not choose to enter the fray until Oscar was involved? You must consider longer, Angeline, before you seek to give me lessons in managing my men."

The sting of his last words sent the blood surging upward to stain Angeline's cheekbones. She compressed her lips, rising to her feet, clasping her hands at her waist. "Have you any healing salve, anything to put on your hands?"

"There is no need."

"It would serve you right if you got blood poisoning. I assure you it is not impossible. This climate encourages such infectious disorders."

He sent her a hard turquoise stare. "I told you there was no need."

"It is my belief," she said, lifting her chin, "that you are too far gone in drink to feel the pain."

"Could you also be brought to believe that the condition is deliberate—and apt to be of long duration?"

"If that's the way you want it. It matters not at all to me. How you die, and when and where, is your affair."

"And if it were to be a painful demise, I expect you would enjoy the spectacle," he said, a twisted smile hovering about his mouth as he indicated with the brandy bottle that she was to precede him toward the stairs.

"How astute."

Stiff-backed, she moved ahead of him. Despite their quarrel, Angeline was completely conscious of the fact that they were ascending once more to the bedchamber she must share with him. His quiet tread behind her sent a shiver along her nerves as they climbed upward into the darkness. Speaking to him as she had below seemed foolhardy when she considered what he might require of her when they were closeted together for the night.

She flinched a little as he stepped past her to open the door for her entrance into the bedchamber, and was not surprised when he slammed it to behind them.

The bed had been turned down. The light from a newly tended fire flickered on the hearth, and a branch of candles glowed on the small table that centered the room. Lying in the pool of light it shed were several strips of linen, a bottle of spirits of camphor, and a tin of salve. Angeline flicked a glance over the assembled medicines before looking to Rolfe with a lifted brow.

"Sarus seems the perfect servant: quiet, efficient, a good cook, able to anticipate your needs, if not your wishes—"

"He takes a good deal upon himself at times."

"To do less would surely not meet with your approval. Is there no pleasing you?"

"In the past, no. Now I am beginning to wonder." Without pausing to allow time to guess at his meaning, he went on. "Will it give you pleasure to press and pry at my self-inflicted wounds, or will you play nurse-maid, clicking your tongue over the errant child most women are convinced lies in all men? Either way, I am at your disposal."

He set the brandy decanter on the table with the glass beside it. In a lithe motion, he seated himself then, leaning on his elbows, spreading his hands with palms upward. The candlelight slid over the planes of his face, gilding the bone structure, etching the scratches that ran down his cheek in red-gold while leaving his eyes in hollow shadow.

His volte-face was disconcerting. Angeline stared at him a long moment. What was his purpose? She had come to understand him well enough to guess that he did nothing without a reason.

"Courage," he said, his voice soft, "unless tending my hurts has lost its appeal?"

The words were plain enough. Why she should sense a threat in them she could not have said, and yet it was there. To cross the few feet that separated them required an effort of will beyond anything she had ever asked of herself. To pick up a piece of linen, soak it in camphor, then lay it across his hand and smooth it upon his skin with the sensitive tips of her fingers was more difficult still. He sat in perfect stillness, his blue gaze resting not on what she was doing, but upon her face. She soaked another strip, laying it upon his other palm so that the cooling effect of the camphor would relieve the pain. But if he noticed any such effect, he gave no sign.

With both hands covered, she took up the tin of salve, twisting it open. The contents were pale pink, smelling faintly of attar of roses and some other exotic ingredient she could not name. An experimental touch found it to be slightly oily in texture, yet powdery, as if the grease were no more than a base for some medicinal herb.

Avoiding his gaze, concentrating solely on what she was doing, Angeline dipped the tip of her middle finger into the salve. She glanced at his set features, then on impulse reached to touch it to his face, smoothing it down the first of the raw scratches she had made. He did not move, though beneath her finger she felt the muscles of his face tighten. She was aware of an odd constriction in her chest. A lock of her hair fell forward, the ends trailing along his arm.

She flung it back with a quick shake of her head. With the movement, her knee touched his thigh, increasing her confusion. Still, she did not hesitate. Touching the salve once more, she went on to the next place where her nails had torn his skin, tracing the downward path to his throat in an odd expiation.

She turned her attention to his burns once more, lifting the linen strips, spreading the salve in a thick layer. There were calluses on his palms and along his fingers, she discovered, the hard, ridged skin of a man accustomed to using his muscles, one who did not begrudge exertion. The calluses were at variance with her image of him as a wastrel and hard-drinking carouser, and had prevented his injuries from being as serious as she had expected. There were angry red blisters rising in the center of his palms, however, and between his thumb and forefinger. With the greatest care, she bound linen strips around them, tying a flat knot across the back of each hand.

Her face was impassive as she picked up the lid of the salve tin, pressing it on and putting the metal box down before she recorked the bottle of camphor. She turned away then, but he pushed back his chair, rising to his feet, blocking her way. He put out his hands to cup her shoulders. His grasp was firm, but not so tight that she could not have twisted free. The problem was that in doing so she must cause him agony. She stood quite still, the breath shuddering in her chest. Slowly she lifted her lashes, angry vulnerability shading the gray-green depths of her eyes.

"I was right," he said, his tone musing. "No matter the provocation, you would not willingly cause pain.

You resisted the temptation to probe my burns, even given wanton opportunity. The question is, having discovered such tender sensibility, do I have the strength of will to refrain from taking advantage of it? The answer, I regret to say, is no."

He drew her nearer, lowering his lips to hers, a sheen of mockery in his blue eyes for himself as well as her. His kiss tasted of brandy and desire, and something more, a blind seeking for surcease from the anguish of remembrance. His arms were warm and enveloping; the sensation, combined with the lean hardness of his body, seemed to sap her will. His mouth brushed her cheek, burned along the turn of her jaw, moved aside the auburn cascade of her hair to press the tender curve of her neck. Her lips parted in a sigh and she rested against him, quiescent, as her mind accepted this virtuous reason for permitting his embrace. His hands moved upon her in the gentlest of caresses, his touch feather-light and tantalizing. Her senses expanded, reeling under the delicate assault of unforeseen sensation. She scarcely knew when he turned with her toward the bed. In any case, she did not resist.

❧

The guard was changed on her second full day of captivity. It was Oscar who stayed behind while the others pounded the roads in search of her cousin. He kept his guitar beside him, fingering the strings, playing now and then a soft and melancholy air. For all that, he was more obviously on guard than Gustave had been. He waited for her outside her bedchamber when the others had gone, lounging on the top step of the stairs, and, whether from conscientiousness or orders, escorted her downstairs where he lingered at her side. If she paced the room, he followed her with his eyes. When she moved to the window, he rose and came to stand beside her. When bright sun burned away the morning fog and she suggested taking the air, he walked at her side, alert but uncomplaining.

During that walk Angeline had considered making a try for escape. If she broke and ran in broad daylight, Oscar was certain to catch her in short order; if she made some excuse to step into the undergrowth, she would have not put it past him to insist on accompanying her, despite his blushes.

Oscar, along with his twin, was one of the younger members of the cadre. Conversation did not rank high among his priorities and, for the most part, he answered her desultory attempts to talk to him in monosyllables. That was until, as they strolled, she chanced to mention a great mat of fox grape vines that overhung the road. His interest flared then and questions poured from him in a torrent. When did the vine bloom in this climate, when did it fruit, and what were the grapes like. From there they moved on to the live oaks that lined the drive while he exclaimed over their green leaves during the winter season, wanting to know how old the trees were, and how large they would grow.

As they walked, Angeline identified for him also pin oaks, red oaks, and white oaks, swamp maples, magnolias, and bay trees. She pointed out wild azaleas with fat buds ready for early-spring bloom, the green twigs of low bush huckleberries, and the arching canes of blackberry brambles. Mother Theresa had been fond of nature walks, and of expounding on the flora and fauna of the New World, so different from the dry and sere hills of Spain from whence she had come. Still, the store of knowledge she had imparted to Angeline was soon in danger of depletion. It was a relief when a chance remark about wild cherries and the fermented drinks that were made from them by the Acadians turned his thoughts in another direction.

The Acadians were French-speaking citizens of Nova Scotia who had been forced to leave their homes by the English in the middle of the previous century. After many years of hardship and deprivation, they had made their way to Louisiana, where they could be among people who spoke the same language, were of the same religion, and shared many of the same customs. Hard-working, but pleasure-loving, they had settled along the bayous where they made their livings as they had in Nova Scotia, by farming and the raising of cattle, and also hunting, trapping, and fishing. There was a large concentration of Acadians around St. Martinville. Being of peasant stock, they seldom moved in the same circles as the plantation society of La Petite Paris, though that was not always so. Madame Delacroix, their hostess just two nights earlier, was of Acadian stock, and proud of it. Still, it was a pleasure to see the Acadians in the town, going to Mass, standing on the street corners gesticulating and arguing, driving past in wagons filled to overflowing with large families; the scrubbed and polished children, the sturdy, affable, mustachioed fathers, the plump mothers, the *gran'mères* in their best black dresses with their heads covered by small white bonnets tied under their chins and their skirts protected by crisp white aprons on which reposed the latest black-eyed *bébé*.

Regardless of Angeline's success in drawing him out, she thought Oscar was happy when they turned back toward the house, where his vigilance need not be so constant.

Rolfe returned early and alone. It did not escape him that Oscar, deep in a conversation with Angeline over hunting for snipe, seemed almost disappointed at being relieved of duty. There was a curt note in Rolfe's voice as he outlined an assignment for the young man, and a frown lingered at the back of his eyes as he watched him take his leave with a graceful bow and shy smile.

To Angeline, Rolfe said nothing, and yet the manner in which he shepherded her upstairs, after calling for sherry for himself and afternoon tea for her, made her feel more truly the prisoner than at any time since the hours immediately after her capture.

The sunlight faded and the afternoon drew in quickly as clouds gathered. Rolfe, it appeared, had returned in advance of his men because of correspondence that needed his attention. With a sherry decanter at one elbow and a candelabrum before him, he sat at the secretary-desk sending the tapered goose quill clamped in his fist, unbound since breakfast, slashing over the parchment.

Seated in a chair before the fire, Angeline drank her tea and nibbled at a slice of spiced currant cake, glancing at him from time to time. It was not cold; the air seemed to be growing warmer, though there was dampness in it also.

Getting to her feet, she moved to the window, staring into the lavender-blue twilight. What was Claire doing now? she wondered. No doubt eating her simple evening meal of bread, cheese, and milk, since it was the practice of the convent to have its most important meal of the day at noon. Did she know what had happened to her cousin? Did she care? It seemed doubtful.

At a slight sound behind her, she turned. Rolfe sat leaning on his elbows, brushing the tip of the goose quill back and forth over the ends of his fingers. There was a considering look in his turquoise eyes as they rested upon her, one that filled her with disquiet.

Without stopping to consider and lose her courage, she spoke. "How long are you going to keep me here?"

He paused. "Until the oracle speaks."

"I cannot tell you what you want to hear."

"Then," he said, deliberately withdrawing his attention, "it is an impasse of your own making. The key to release is in your hand. Use it or not as you wish."

That smoothly confident dismissal brought her blood to the boil. She curled her fingers into fists, the nails biting into her palms in the effort to curb her temper. "Since I must stay, are there any books in the house, anything I might use to pass the time?"

"Having gained a fairly close acquaintance with M'sieur de la Chaise, I would say it is unlikely."

"You, of course, had no time to throw anything so mundane into your baggage."

"A Latin treatise on the campaigns of Alexander, a copy of a German work on the botanical specimens found in the Amazon basin of South America, and a volume of Sanskrit poetry, beautiful but a trifle risqué. If you read any of those three languages then you are welcome to raid my library."

"Thank you," she said in the driest of tones. "The campaigns of Alexander should while away a few hours."

The flicker of arrested interest in his eyes was gratifying, as was his wave toward the armoire. She did not avail herself of the privilege so carelessly extended, however.

"There is a more mundane subject that I must bring to your attention. I cannot go on wearing the same clothing day after day."

With scant attention he said, "Sarus will launder your gown for you."

"I know, and he is very good, but it is in tatters already and will soon fall to pieces."

"The solution is obvious."

She glared at his bent golden head. "Not to me!"

"I have given you free use of my library. Now I extend the privilege to my wardrobe, which you have already raided. What more do you want?"

"Your…" she began, glancing down at the tunic that covered her, fingering the sleeve. "Sarus brought this to me. I thought it was… his."

"No, no. With a pole and guy wires, you could set up housekeeping in one of his coats."

With shaking fingers, she began to work at the knot in the sash at her waist. "I would rather not accept it."

"No?" He tilted his head, amusement bright in his eyes. "The alternative should be interesting." As her movement slowed he went on, "I had considered nakedness as a means of holding you here in my absence."

"You what?" she exclaimed wrathfully.

"Oh, I dismissed the idea for lack of practicality. The first factor was the weather; a healthy captive is much less trouble than one ill from exposure—to the cold. Another consideration is the strain the knowledge of your state must place on my men. The mere fact that you are here, moving among them with sweet smiles and yielding grace, just beyond their touch, though not mine, has strained their tempers. To test them further would be to invite anarchy, or so I thought. That was before I realized you would be so cooperative."

The images he conjured up were far from pleasant. "You know very well—" she began, then stopped, swinging away from him. Of course he knew. His purpose was to bring home to her the ambiguity of her situation and its dangers. He had succeeded, but she would never let him know it.

She moistened her lips. "I hardly think that one of your tunics can be considered sufficient covering. From what I have discovered of late, the base appetites of men can be stimulated by much less provocation than that."

"Quite right," he said, coming to his feet in a single fluid movement, moving toward her. "Sometimes the mere hint of a woman undressed—the idea in the mind—is enough."

What he might have done then she could not know, for as he neared the window his attention was caught by the jogging shapes of two horsemen emerging from the shadows of the trees below. That he recognized the men instantly was plain. He caught Angeline's arm, whirling her from the window before she had time to react, almost before she could realize that she too knew the identities of the riders.

The first was Meyer, returning for the day. The second was André Delacroix.

Six

Rolfe's eyes blazed down at her, their bright amusement replaced by a hard, opaque stare as he said, "Make one sound, scream, try to attract his attention, and you will place him upon his bier with lilies in his crossed hands. Do you understand?"

The copper flecks in her eyes were vivid as she stared into his face. She saw no indication that he recognized any authority, any honor or morality other than his own unshakable purpose. Her voice was a thread of sound as she answered, "Yes."

He stared down at her a moment, then stepped back abruptly and strode from the room. She could hear him calling for Sarus. Was the manservant to be posted outside her door to insure her discretion, or was he to join in the defense against the intruder? If the last, then what chance did André have to win out over the prince and Meyer, plus Sarus?

She stood still in the center of the room with her hands clasped together. Why had André come? Had Tante Berthe, guessing where she was, sent him? Or had he come for his own reasons, because the presence of the prince in the district coincided too perfectly with her disappearance? What would they do to him? Would he be made a prisoner, kept as she was, until Rolfe either had what he wanted or gave up the search? Or, supposing he was a greater threat, would he be killed regardless of her conduct?

She moved to the door on tiptoe, listening. So thick was the panel and so sturdy the walls of the house that she could hear nothing. Slowly, stealthily, she turned the doorknob, pulling the panel open the merest crack.

The sounds that came to her were of voices raised in pleasant greetings, of laughter and the clink of glass on glass as drinks were poured. She need not have concerned herself. André had not come for her sake at all, or else he was hiding his purpose well. He was here merely to pay a call upon the royal visitor. Rolfe, all urbanity, was welcoming him to the bachelor household.

She straightened, the fine curves of her mouth set in a grim line and her green eyes dark. What a fool she was to expect rescue by one man, rescue in any form. By all rights there should be a cavalcade of men of the neighborhood before the house, beating down the door and demanding her release. If André, her suitor, her champion in all things, could come to call, accepting the hospitality of the prince, enjoying his wine, then it could mean only one thing. He did not know she had been taken, did not dream that she could be there in hiding.

That conclusion led to one other. If she was to be pried from the iron grip of Prince Rolfe of Ruthenia, then she would have to provide the lever herself.

She could not endanger André. She would not risk his death by trying to enlist his aid. But what if she could leave the house by herself, could make her way unseen to a point along the drive where she might intercept him? He could take her up before him on his mount and they could be far away before her absence was discovered. Now, while Rolfe was involved with his duties as host and Sarus was serving their guest, would be as good a time as any.

She swung to the wardrobe where Sarus had put away her manteau-cloak. She drew it out and draped it over her arm before she turned back to the door. Giving herself no time to hesitate, she eased the panel open inch by inch. The glow from the flickering candles behind her seeped into the dim hallway. There was no one there, no one on guard just outside. She drew the panel wider, her heart leaping in her chest. She started forward, then stopped, her muscles locking into place.

Across the hallway was the bedchamber where Meyer slept. The door stood open, the room dim. But silhouetted against the panes of the window was the figure of a man, tall and broad-shouldered, standing with his feet spread and his hands clasped behind him. He stared out, a still shape in the gloom of the evening. That he was supposed to be on guard seemed plain. For the moment he was inattentive, but that could change in the flicker of an eyelid. Most likely it was her acceptance of her situation thus far, her lack of complaints or threats to escape that made him less conscious of the duty to which he had been assigned. For that she should congratulate herself, and would, if she could manage to slip past him.

She took a slow step, then another. As she moved onto the Persian hall runner, a floorboard under it creaked with a deafening sound. She paused, her gaze fastened on the back of the man at the window. It seemed he stiffened with consciousness, but he neither moved nor turned his head. Holding her breath, keeping her skirts close so they would not rustle, she quickly made the long strides that would take her out of his sight. When there was no outcry, she moved on, down the hall toward the rear of the house and the landing above the servants' stairs.

There was a light shining at the bottom of that steep and narrow stairway. It came, she discovered, from a single fat candle left burning in the butler's pantry, a small, dim room where food brought course by course from the outside kitchen was kept warm until ready for serving, and where soiled dishes were collected before being washed and put away. She could hear voices. Faint and deep, they seemed to be coming from near the entrance door, as if André, reluctant to impose on the prince, had drunk down his sherry and was already on the point of leaving. It was a natural thing, perhaps, but inconvenient.

Where was Sarus? If he was in the detached kitchen, busy overseeing preparations for dinner—a fair guess from the rich food fragrances that permeated the still, damp air—he might well see her as she left the house by the back entrance. It was a chance she would have to take.

She crept downward, rounding the bottom newel post, skirting a worktable topped by a marble slab. The cloak on her arm brushed against a silver tray holding glasses. One goblet wobbled and she snatched at it as the others clattered together with a musical sound. They steadied, and after a frozen instant she breathed again.

At the back door she paused, but could hear nothing. Turning the knob, she drew it open, stepped through, and closed it softly behind her. She crossed the rear gallery with light steps, swinging her cloak around her as she went. There was a light in the outdoor kitchen, and through the open door she could see Sarus moving about inside, a shadow against the glow of the fireplace where black pots hung suspended from double cranes. A few steps more and she was around the corner of the house, out of sight.

A light mist was falling, feathery wetness that felt good against her flushed skin. It coated the trees, making them drip with great fat spatters that wet the hood of her cloak as she hurried beneath them and clung in jeweled drops, dampening her gown.

The barn and carriage house lay half hidden among the trees to her right. If she swung in that direction, she might lead out a horse, one of the extra mounts. She could ride; both she and Claire had been given lessons as children when her cousin had developed a passion for horses that lasted an entire summer. She doubted her ability to stay on without a saddle, however, and there was no time for such refinements. She could hear the sound of hooves on the drive, a signal that André was leaving. At any moment Rolfe might discover she was gone and be after her with hue and cry. Before then, she must cut through the woods to reach the curve where André would pass. She must.

"Hey!"

The exclamation came from somewhere nearby. Whipping around, Angeline saw the flash of a white and blue uniform outlined in the darkened doorway of the barn. It was Leopold, she thought, from the sound of his voice. He must have arrived while she was on the stairs, and was rubbing down his mount in what was left of the evening light. He dropped the brush he held now and started after her. She whirled and, catching her skirts higher, plunged into a run.

It was instinct that made her turn toward the front of the house and the horseman trotting along the drive, disappearing among the trees with his back straight and a rain cape of gutta-percha spread over himself and his horse like the mantle of a knight. Forgetting the threat to his life, forgetting everything in her need to win freedom, she drew in her breath to call.

Her cloak was caught at one shoulder. Thrown off balance, she tripped in tangled briers and tussocks of dried grass, falling headlong. The grass prickled under her forearms where she caught herself, the smell of it surrounding her as Leopold went to one knee beside her. Twisting, she scrambled to sit up, staring at him in indignant despair.

Then came the sound of another step, soft, decisive. Above them a voice spoke. "Rough wooing seems ever to be your fate, Angeline, my sweet."

"No such thing!" Leopold defended himself, scowling up at Rolfe. "I leave such pleasures to you."

"I am overjoyed to hear it. And how does it happen that I find you cavorting in the grass with my... prisoner?"

"Your prisoner was escaping while you were engaged with your visitor. I only stopped her."

"How obliging of Mademoiselle Fortin to allow you to exonerate yourself for losing sight of her two nights ago. Instead of waiting for my gratitude, you should make yours known to her—or at least inquire after her injuries."

The anger that had made Leopold clench his teeth was wiped away as by a chamois. He looked quickly down at Angeline, his black eyes shadowed with concern. "Are you hurt, Mademoiselle?"

"Not at all," she snapped.

"Fortunate," Rolfe drawled, his gaze on Leopold even as he held out his hand to assist Angeline to her feet.

The other man colored, coming erect. "If you mean that as a threat—"

"How can you think it?" Rolfe spared not a glance for Leopold now as with consummate attention he reached to brush droplets of rain and wisps of clinging grass from Angeline's face.

"Easily."

"There is no need to exercise your imagination. If it had been a threat, you would have been in no doubt."

With his hands knotted into fists, Leopold took a hasty step forward. "Damn you, Rolfe, you accept aid with less grace than any other man living."

"Is that why you came along uninvited?"

"I was speaking of what happened just now!"

"Were you? But I was not."

"All right," Leopold ground out in bitter tones. "You did not want me to come and I knew it, but I am beginning to tire of taking the slicing edge of your tongue for something that is as much my right as yours."

"You attach yourself to my baggage train like an itinerant whore following her sergeant major on campaign, and you expect me to applaud?"

"It is as much in my interest as it is in yours to discover who killed Max! With him gone and your father ill, they are saying that I am the one with the most to gain should—should you meet with a convenient accident. Or didn't you know that?"

"I know, my bantling boy, and in the deep consideration you have given this subject, has it occurred to you what a precious scapegoat you will make while here in my company? Whereas, were you in Ruthenia when woe befell me, they could rise up and call you King Leopold, last of our line, without a qualm?"

"I have no wish to be king in your place. It won't happen if I can prevent it!"

Rolfe laughed, a rich sound that hung in the clammy air with the timbre of ridicule. "My guardian angel, I am touched."

"Jeer as you please, treat me like a fool, my princely cousin and future king, but I will not leave you. I will not go back to Ruthenia alone."

Leopold turned on his heel then and walked away, striding through the damp grass with parade-like precision. Rolfe watched him, a frown drawing his golden brows together. He was still, his turquoise eyes intent until, abruptly, he shook his head. Reaching for Angeline's hand, he placed it upon his sleeve with formality before, turning, he led her back to the house.

She went with him partly because there was nothing else to do and partly because she felt a compulsion that had nothing to do with his warm fingers covering hers. It was something in the man, a strength, a magnetism that imposed his will without effort, carelessly, inescapably. And in the confusion of the moment of her recapture and the agitation of what followed, André was forgotten.

Dinner was a silent meal. That the men as they straggled in wet and chilled from the increasing rain had been informed of her escape attempt could not be doubted. They glanced from her to Rolfe with covert sympathy that was as unnerving as it was gratifying, because it seemed to suggest that some retribution would be forthcoming. There had been nothing in Rolfe's manner to indicate such a thing when he returned her to her bedchamber earlier. He had settled to his letter writing once more, scratching away with the goose quill pen, the continuous dry scrape of it a strong test of her composure. To see Sarus announcing dinner at the door had seemed a deliverance, and yet as she thought of it now there was something ominous in Rolfe's deliberate avoidance of the issue.

When the meal was done, Rolfe got to his feet, moving to stand at the fireplace. He turned with legs spread and hands clasped behind his back. Faces grew tense as the men glanced at one another. They shifted in their seats as the gaze of their leader rested upon them one by one. Even Angeline felt the sudden strain.

The candlelight glinted on his fair hair as Rolfe lifted his head. "I call a tribunal."

The word had meaning for the men; it was evident from their stiffened attention. Gustave, his scarred face solemn, came slowly to his feet.

"Who are we to judge?"

It was Meyer, rising also, who answered. "It is I, I think."

"And the charge?" Gustave asked.

"Dereliction of duty." Rolfe's voice was neither loud nor vindictive. The words fell into a thickening pool of silence.

"Who will give evidence?"

"Angeline."

She slanted her steady gaze to Rolfe's face at the sound of her name. He watched her, his blue eyes unwavering. She moistened dry lips. "I—I can tell you nothing."

"You underestimate yourself," he answered, his voice quiet, determined. "All that is required is that you tell us how you left the house this afternoon."

Angeline looked then to Meyer. He stood watching her, his bearing straight and military, and in his gray eyes a kind of pensive irritation as if he might now regret the impulse that had made him let her go.

The interrogation that followed was exhaustive. Each man, including the accused, had the right to query any point. There was nothing frivolous or half-hearted about the proceedings; it was a straightforward effort to get at the truth, to learn to just what extent Meyer had been at fault in permitting her escape. Through it all, Angeline answered as truthfully as she could, though her hands were clasped in her lap to keep them from trembling. But whether from real doubt, from sheer contrariness, or from a vagrant gratitude to Meyer for the impulse that had made it possible for her to evade his watch, she kept stubbornly to the claim that he had been unaware of when she left. When there seemed nothing else to be asked, Rolfe looked to Meyer.

"Would you prefer judgment and penalty announced by your peers, or trial by combat?"

Meyer tugged at his lip, a considering look on his broad face, then, smiling, he spread his hands. "I freely admit my negligence, though I protest that I was lulled into it. More, I cannot think it was so very wrong. There can be little useful purpose in keeping this woman here. On the other hand, knowing the balance and reason of my friends, I don't fear their judgment, even admitting that a reprimand is due. But because there is more honor in it than in public punishment, and because it gives me the chance to give as good as I get, I choose the trial."

The sudden light in Rolfe's eyes was the only indication of his satisfaction. "It is my privilege to name the weapon. To show that chivalry does not reside with you alone, I choose staffs."

"Staffs?" Gustave protested. "We have no such thing with us."

"The woods are full of saplings."

No other suggestion was necessary. With the exception of Meyer, they plunged into the rain-wet night, calling for axes, arguing in high glee over the thickness of pole required. As their voices faded, Angeline got to her feet. Her tone subdued, she said, "I think I will go upstairs."

"Stay."

It was a one-word command.

"I would prefer not to be a spectator."

"Then," Rolfe said, his dark gaze swinging to hold her own, "there would be little point in this exercise."

He knew what Meyer had done and he meant for the responsibility of his punishment to rest squarely upon the person who had trespassed, herself. Meyer, too, would pay, though not for mere neglect of duty so much as for contravening Rolfe's will, for interfering in his affairs, and for putting compassion ahead of their purpose in being there. The choice of staffs, far from being a concession to Meyer, had been made so that no man would suffer permanent injury. And yet the lesson administered would be painful.

That Meyer himself understood this was clear as he tilted his head. "Do I meet you, Rolfe, or will you choose a champion for the court?"

"You know my policy. I will fight no man among the guard. As for a champion, none will be needed. Your opponent will be Gustave first, then Leopold— and Oswald—and Oscar."

"All?"

"All. In sequence, of course."

"Of course," Meyer echoed, though the look on his face was grim and the scar beside his mouth livid.

The appearance of punishment with honor was false. A signal drubbing awaited Meyer. Though the strongest of the guard by virtue of his size, he could not hope to prevail against them all. As his strength failed, so must his opponents grow weaker and less able, so that when defeat came it would be at the end,

and might well be at the hands of the least violent,
least strong of them all. First of all, however, to tax
his will and stamina would be the wily and scarred
veteran Gustave.

The contest was just as harrowing as Angeline had
known it must be. Chairs were pushed back, leaving
an open space in the center of the room. The men
stripped to the waist. The smell of fresh-peeled green
wood was strong in the air, an incongruous note
against the smells of woodsmoke, rich food, and the
acrid sweat of the struggling men. Blows thudded with
a sodden sound against flesh, booted feet scuffled as
men circled and the staffs clacked like the rattle of a
stick on the spokes of a spinning wheel. There were
grunts and curses. In a short time both Gustave and
Meyer had purplish bruises on their arms and shoulders, and were bleeding from a dozen cuts on wrists,
arms, and foreheads.

Gustave was cunning and more experienced; he
gave Meyer a strong fight. But after a few minutes
he began to breathe in shallow gasps. Meyer went for
his ribs and diaphragm then, choosing his targets with
care. Several times he was caught extended, and once
received a blow above the ear that made him shake
his head and stagger. He recovered, and a short time
later Gustave, raising his staff with both hands above
his head, cried quits.

Leopold was fresh and athletic and, since he
had caught the backlash of Rolfe's rage because of
Meyer, was not loath to close with him. That Meyer
dispatched him quickly was more luck than skill or
endurance. Catching Rolfe's cousin off balance as he

slipped in a drop of blood, Meyer swung a glancing blow that stretched him on the floor, and with the fall the meeting of the two men was ended.

Oswald, next, was wary but grinning and eager. Much time was spent in feinting, dodging, and ducking with sudden catlike springs beneath Meyer's guard. The technique was designed to deplete the reserves of Meyer's energy just as surely as earlier Meyer had tired Gustave.

Watching the battle as it went relentlessly on, Angeline thought that the competition she was watching was extraordinary. There was not one man of her acquaintance who could, or would, have seized a slippery green wood staff and with it attempted to defend himself, much less attacked to win victory. The quickness and agility displayed by each of the men was the result of strength brought forth only by training. They were fighting machines, these men, and therefore the method they had chosen to settle the difference between them, though barbaric, was also correct.

Meyer had a purple-red splotch on his cheek now, and a cut on his brow was bleeding in a steady stream, running into his eyes. Oswald had not gone untouched. One ear was swollen and there was a long scrape across his ribs. As in a flurry of blows a patch of broken skin appeared at his hairline, pain and rage twisted his features and he charged in with a whoop. The staffs flailed. Meyer hooked his pole inside Oswald's arms, gave a heave, and the long green wand of the slighter man went flying.

His twin picked it up, and shrugging from his tunic came forward with dogged solemnity. Oscar's approach, unlike that of his brother, was calculated. Each movement, though lacking his twin's verve, was precise, driven with an exact amount of strength behind it to a carefully chosen point. He seemed never to be at a loss, never to find it necessary to adjust his behavior to that of his opponent, never to need to move out of step to avoid a blow, never to let one fall. And his own blows were telling. Meyer staggered under the first that struck him squarely, and the second. If he had been fresh he might have over-borne Oscar by sheer weight and height; as it was, the outcome was inevitable.

"Enough."

As if released from a spell by that sharp command, Oscar stepped back. Meyer, gathering himself to strike, seemed to hear through a haze. He could not stop the blow he had begun. Oscar tried to bring his staff up once more, but the green wand of the other man came swishing down. There was a cracking sound, and Oscar dropped his staff, clutching at his left wrist, which dangled at an odd angle, the fingers limp.

Angeline sprang to her feet, starting forward. Rolfe was at her side in a long stride. "A ministering angel might be a comfort to Oscar, but there is no need. Meyer has some skill as a bone-setter and dispenser of palliatives. Come, it is time to retire."

His hand on her elbow swung her firmly toward the stairs. She fought it. Her voice sharp, she asked, "Who will tend to Meyer?"

"For what he needs, anyone will do."

To struggle, to insist on helping, would have been futile. Even if Rolfe had permitted it, she was not certain the men would have accepted her ministrations. She was, after all, the cause of their bruises. The guilt she felt was blighting, and only slightly alleviated by the suspicion that Rolfe had intended just such an effect.

Did he also intend that she should be in a state of tightly strung apprehension at being alone with him now? Whether he did or not, she was just that. The snap with which he closed the door behind them made her nerves jump. It was all she could do not to swing around like an animal at bay. She moved to the fire in elaborate casualness, holding out her chilled fingers to the flames.

"Take off your clothes."

She jerked around. "What... what do you mean?"

"I think you understood me very well." He came forward in the light of the candles left burning on the secretary-desk. It glittered on the sculpted cap of his hair and shone on the polished buttons of his tunic as he leaned over the desk top to pick up the goose quill pen lying there, running it through his strong, supple fingers. Holding it in one hand, he moved to her side, inserting his fingers at the deep opening of the tunic she wore. "If I am forced to take them off for you again, there may not be enough left to repair."

"Why?" she demanded, forcing the word through the dried leather of her throat.

His blue eyes burned bright and steady into hers, though a muscle flexed in his cheek. "Can it be that you doubt your attraction, or is it that you fear for the perfection of your pearl-white skin?"

"Why not both?" She lifted her chin to stare at him, her gray-green eyes dark.

"Such honesty deserves compensation."

"Your Highness… Rolfe…" she began, but could find no way to put her appeal into words that did not have the sound of cowardice. As his fingers began to move deeper into her bodice, brushing the skin of her breast, she brought her hand up to catch his wrist.

He glanced down at her white-tipped fingers, his lashes shading his expression. "If my touch distresses you, there is an easy way to avoid it. You have only to tell me what I want to know, and you will be returned at once to your aunt's house."

"I can't tell you what I don't know!"

"I think you lie, Angeline. I think fear and loyalty hold you silent, that they will continue to do so even though I hold your ruin in my hands."

"I am not afraid of you," she flashed.

"No, I don't think you are. Shall I introduce you to fear?"

"It will make no difference!"

"Possibly, to you. Perhaps it will suffice for me to tell you that your removal from the de Buys household has not yet been noted in the community. To those who ask after you, such as André Delacroix, it is said that you are laid down upon your bed in a darkened room with a fever so intense that none may approach, that you were taken suddenly sick in the night after the Delacroix ball." He paused. "You don't seem surprised."

"No. André would not have been so cordial otherwise. You, as a stranger, must have immediately have been suspect in my… disappearance, especially after the way you singled me out at the ball."

"Very true." He gave a short nod. "But the length of time so flimsy a tale can be kept plausible is limited. Another day, two at the most, and people will expect to see either you or your funeral cortège. Save yourself, Angeline. Don't force me to keep to this course that must make you an outcast."

"I force nothing on you," she told him, her voice not quite steady.

"Ah well," he said, dropping his free hand to the sash at her waist, slipping the bow with dexterous ease. "To say the same would brand me a fool as well as a despot. Since you will not have reason as a safeguard, protect yourself as best you may."

Seven

To be undressed forcibly yet again, to be unable to prevent that invasion of her self, her privacy, was insupportable. Angeline fought him, twisting and turning with the blood pounding in her brain and the edge of fear giving her increased strength. He broke her grasp again and again as she caught at his hands, and seemed not to feel the bite of her nails, the blows she landed with flailing fists. Her hair whipped around them in a shining curtain, swirling like a heavy silken mantle between them, impeding them both.

With an exclamation of impatience, he stripped the tunic she wore upward, pinioning her arms in its heavy, suffocating folds. Pulling her hard against him, he unhooked her gown, then bent to lift her over his shoulder. He swung to the bed, and with one foot on the step, boosted her to the high mattress. He threw himself down beside her, then casually, ruthlessly pulled the tunic over her head, casting it from him while retaining the sash that had been caught in its side loops. As she gasped for air, he tugged her gown and underdress downward, freeing her arms of the tight cap sleeves. Before she could strike out at him, he clamped his fingers about her wrists and, holding them in one hand, twisted the woven silk sash about them. Knotting it, he forced her arms above her head.

Cold with shock, Angeline quieted. Her eyes were wide and shaded with copper as she stared up at him. Her breasts rose and fell with the agitation that gripped her, their soft peaks straining against the laced bars of his uniform as he lay over her, constricting her movement. His face was shuttered, closed in, the chiseled lines of his mouth firm as he thoughtfully turned the goose quill he still held in his fingers. She glanced from it to his face and her stomach muscles tightened.

"Anticipation, they do say, is the most difficult stage of torture to bear. Have you any idea, my sweet, innocent Angeline, what I intend?"

A faint intimation lurked in a corner of her mind, but she denied it. Nor did she give him the satisfaction of an answer. Mute, using her strength to conceal her apprehension, she lay in total stillness.

"Pleasure is a sensation of the nerves. Stretch it too far and it becomes pain. The nerves affected lie close to the skin, clustering at the openings of our bodies, here, here, here—and here."

Gently he flicked the tip of the feather across the smooth curves of her lips, the shell-like opening of one ear, the crest of a breast, and downward over the taut muscles of her abdomen to the most secret recess of her body. His voice was detached, without malice. It was as if he had steeled himself to the task, willing himself to feel neither enjoyment nor repugnance.

Angeline gathered her wits with a conscious effort. Fighting him would avail her nothing; words might. "This afternoon you were incensed with Leopold for less than this. Are—are threats and—and torment privileges you reserve for yourself?"

"So it seems."

"I have done nothing to you. I can tell you nothing."

"If I believed you, I would bid the trumpets sound and set you free. As it is, you force me to the vulgar choice of tyrants to discover the truth. Every shining hair upon your head shall be a precious and protected jewel and your modesty shall be cloaked in untouched sanctity if you will only speak."

The melodious sound of his voice with its odd phrases was like a drug dulling the senses, allowing the meaning of his words to trickle through, distilled and pungent. "Even if I could help you, you have no right!"

"None, except what I take for myself."

"And if you are wrong, how will you justify your— what you are doing? To commit this crime while clearing your name of another, though it may be more vile, cannot be right."

"What you say may be true, but the soul blot will be mine to bear while you in all righteousness condemn me. That is, of course, if I am wrong."

What answer was there to that? In agonizing helplessness, she watched as his eyes narrowed, as he twirled the quill between his fingers and then deliberately shifted higher, resting on one elbow above her. He drew the feather tip across her parted lips.

The sensation was exquisite, tantalizing. She clenched her fists, straining at the bonds that held them, turning her head away. The feather drifted over her cheek, stroked a quivering eyelid, moved lightly down her hairline to the lobe of her ear. It hovered there as she strained away from him, then floated gently down the curve of her neck and across her collarbone to the mound of her breast.

With delicate care, he plied his refined instrument of torture until she felt her nipples contract, knew the onslaught of perilous languor. She drew in her breath with a soft sound, setting her teeth in her bottom lip. Her skin felt flushed with the heat of rage and embarrassment and kindling desire. The pliant quill traced lower over the fluttering muscles of her abdomen. She shrank away from him, trying to close her legs, but remorselessly he held them open with the force of his knee across hers. Taking full advantage, he trailed the tip of the quill along the tender insides of her upper thighs, circling, drawing nearer to the apex of the triangle they made. He paused, hovering while her taut nerves shrieked and her heartbeat thudded in her ears. And then lightly, almost as if by accident, he touched her.

The sensation vibrated through her, rising to her skin with the prickling of gooseflesh. Reality receded. A mass of raw sensitivity, she waited with tensed muscles and unwilling, debasing fascination for the next touch, and the next.

It was a sweet and piercing pleasure, a captivating affliction that grew boundlessly so that she ceased to avoid it. Her throat closed until she could hardly breathe and hot tears of despair welled into her eyes, running from under her lashes, making salt tracks into her hair. With consummate artistry, he brought her nearer and nearer the point of anguish so she could sense the form it must take and the brand upon the spirit it would leave behind. In the sweep of emotion she also felt, in a way unimaginable only minutes before, a closeness to the man who held her, a bond of violent intimacy greater than anything she had known. The realization brought stillness, though with no lessening of the painful pleasure that held her in thrall.

She opened her eyes, lifting her drowned gaze to the man above her, whispering, "How could you?"

There was a grayness about his features that had not been there before and a faint dew of perspiration across his upper lip. His movement stopped. He released his pent-up breath in a laugh of sardonic self-knowledge before, with a wrenching twist, he sailed the quill into the corner.

"I can't," he grated.

With quick fingers he unbuttoned his tunic and threw it aside, ridding himself of boots and pantaloons. He gathered her close then, cradling her against him as he spread her stiff limbs, entering her tender flesh with throbbing insistence. She wanted to protest, to resist, but the intense rapture of the moment took her breath. He pressed deep inside her, filling her with such acute and perfect pleasure that her mind reeled, drunk with the sudden gratification of over-stimulated senses. With a low cry, she rose against him, moved in unison with him. She lifted her bound hands, passing them over his head, clasping them behind his neck. Their breaths mingled, their mouths met and clung.

Frenzied ecstasy swept them, spiraling higher and higher, carrying them in its vortex.

It was ravaging and wild, a pairing in defiance of terrible, unendurable enjoyment. It surged through them, obliterating their differences with the relentless force of a river in flood, and ebbed in waves, leaving them spent and aghast, stranded together in their implacable antagonism.

He eased from her, bending his head to release himself from her tied hands. Taking them in his warm fingers, he slipped the knotted sash free, then lay gently chafing her wrists for long minutes. His grasp tightened briefly, then he sighed and, crossing her hands over her chest, rolled, sliding off the bed. He searched for his pantaloons and jerked them on. He watched her, his turquoise eyes dark as he buttoned the waist. He bent to take up his tunic and boots in one hand, then, running his fingers through his hair, swung away to the door and wrenched it open.

He stopped then to look back, a hint of baffled fury on his features. With an oath he stepped from the room, slamming the door behind him.

Angeline turned onto her stomach, moving with the slow care of one who, having been beaten, fears the return of pain. She pillowed her head on her arms and, without questioning for whom or what she wept, let the difficult and cleansing tears come.

Rolfe did not return to his bed that night, nor was Angeline disturbed when morning came. Deep in exhaustion, she slept on until the sound of a banging door, distant but sharp, brought her awake.

The rain had stopped. The warm, moist gulf air that had brought it lingered, warming the day that beyond the window showed the somnolent brightness and short shadows of noon. So pleasant was it that she had no need of a fire as she dressed. She longed for a bath, but none had been provided and she hesitated to put her head out the door and yell for Sarus, as did the others. There was no breakfast tray in evidence either, as there would most definitely have been if Rolfe were there. It was only after she had pulled on her clothes and ventured forth that she discovered the tray of cafe au lait, the coffee cold, the milk scummed, outside her door.

The men had gone. Only Meyer sat in the great hall, propped in the corner of the settee near the fire that burned regardless of the weather. Before him on a low table was a fresh pot of coffee and a plate piled high with smoking croissants.

He got to his feet, moving stiffly, favoring his left side. Bruises mottled his face with purple and blue, one eye was half closed, and there was a piece of sticking plaster on one temple. Inclining his head in a bow, he said, "Mademoiselle Fortin, good morning. At last my duty begins. I was beginning to think the day would end without the sight of you."

"Have you been up so long then?" she inquired, striving for normalcy, allowing her gaze to rest a moment on what was, apparently, his breakfast.

"Knowing you had not eaten, I waited as long as I could," he assured her with a slight smile as, following her glance, he took her meaning. "Will you join me now?"

It would be churlish to refuse. Moreover, she was ravenous, a state heightened by the fragrance of the

coffee and fresh-baked rolls. In addition, his excuse
rang true, for there were two cups on the tray before
him. With a murmured word of gratitude, she took
the place he indicated on the settee beside him.

He leaned to take up the plate of croissants,
wincing a little as he turned to proffer them. Angeline
chose one quickly so that he need not stay in that
position for long. As he turned away, she slanted him
a quick glance.

"I—I'm sorry that my attempt to escape caused
trouble for you."

"My greatest regret," he said with a slight shrug,
"is that it was necessary for you to try to leave us in
such a way."

He eased forward to pour the coffee, but Angeline
forestalled him with a touch on his arm. "May I?"

"I would be grateful." He settled back, watching her.

She filled a cup, passing it to him, then tended to
her own. Taking up the saucer on which it sat, she
sipped at the steaming liquid before she ventured, "I
may be mistaken, but I think, sir, that you let me go."

He threw her a startled look. "Last evening when
you were questioned you never breathed a hint."

Her heart leaped, then she quickly lowered her
lashes. He could not know of what had passed between
Rolfe and herself in the night. He was referring to the
interrogation during the tribunal. "Your punishment
would have been more severe, I think, if I had spoken.
As it was, it was bad enough."

"Then I have to thank you for your forbearance.
And I must also readjust my thinking as it touches you.
You stood Rolfe's questioning superbly. I have seen

men reduced to stammering wrecks before him, ready to confess to anything to escape his flaying tongue. You must be made of stronger fabric than I imagined, or he of weaker, and I cannot believe it is the latter."

"You—all of you—treat him as if he were a demigod. Why should he not have weaknesses like other men?"

"Why not, indeed. But there has never been a crack in his armor that I have seen, unless perhaps it is in a certain carelessness with his life, or a tendency to seek refuge from perfection in drink. He is the future king, you know, and that is what he must be, perfect in all things, with the strength, the prowess, and the omnipotence of a god indeed."

"Surely that is too much to expect?"

"How can you say so, when Maximilian embodied those virtues and more, and Rolfe walks in his shadow?"

"You sound—"

"Bitter?" he questioned. "A temporary thing because I still hold a grudge this morning for my public punishment. Besides, why should I not recognize the faults of Maximilian and Rolfe? I am of the same blood."

Angeline's head came up. "You are related?"

"Has no one told you? It's a thing of little moment, scarcely worth mentioning. I am Rolfe's half-brother with the bar sinister on my shield, the son of a common tavern wench brought to court and married to a nobleman of one of Ruthenia's oldest houses for the convenience of the present king, Rolfe's father—and mine."

"No, no one told me." As an illegitimate son he would not be in line for the throne and, though older by a year or two than Rolfe, she thought, he must take orders and accept the reprimands of his half-brother.

"You can see, I hope, that I have as much right as anyone to judge him? As we grew up at court, Maximilian and Rolfe, Leopold and I, I was always closer to Max, possibly because we were nearer in age and temperament. All I object to at the moment is Rolfe's way of going about the gathering of information. I will admit that under the circumstances I find his… excesses at least partially understandable."

"You will not think me unreasonable if I cannot?"

He shook his head. "If it gives you any satisfaction, I think Rolfe is beginning to regret what he has done. He seldom makes mistakes, but when he does he pays in dear coin, inflicting his own discipline. He was quite as drunk this morning as I have ever seen him."

"Why can he not just let me go?" The words were wrung from her.

"Perhaps he will."

There was no point in discussing it. They spoke of other things, of the directions the men had taken in their searches that morning as separately they quartered the countryside, even Oswald and Oscar taking different directions. Angeline, for something to say, commented on the youth of the twins.

"They may be young, but they have been with Rolfe for ten years or more. He owns them body and spirit, though you would think he was their property, so great is their care for his welfare."

"He owns them? What can you mean?"

"They were given to him by their father after Rolfe saved the old man's life and his farm from raiding bandits. It's a Ruthenian custom, the bestowing of younger sons of the yeoman class upon royal princes in return for favors. They were meant as body servants, but Rolfe would not have it that way. The benefit to Oscar and Oswald has been great, since otherwise they would be spending their days hunting and overseeing peasants in the fields."

"Oscar scarcely seems the type to enjoy warlike pursuits," she said.

"He considers it a fair exchange for the privilege of delving into Rolfe's library. Still, don't underestimate him, or Oswald for that matter. There is ferocity under the surface, as in all Slavic people, that and an ingrained fatalism. It is my opinion—gained the hard way—that either of them would die for Rolfe, or kill for his sake, if they thought it necessary. It was Oscar who gave me this." He touched the corner of his mouth where the half-moon scar formed an indentation.

She followed his gesture, frowning. "Oscar?"

"Oh, he had reason, or so he thought. He came upon Maximilian and myself wrestling with Rolfe—Max had decided it was time his younger brother tasted humility and had enlisted my aid. We never meant to hurt him, of course. Oscar didn't see it that way. He chose to even the odds with the king's walking cane with a sharpened ferrule, of the kind used for fending off beggars and dogs. I was lucky to escape so lightly. It was all a long time ago, of course, shortly after the twins came to Rolfe."

"I… doubt somehow that Rolfe was grateful for the defense," she said.

"Quite right. It was he who called Oscar off, much to the chagrin of Max and myself. Still, that is the kind of thing that makes him a leader, one for whom we are all willing to accept the most stultifying assignments, such as beating the forest for your cousin."

"Or keeping watch over me?"

He refused the gambit with a smile and a shake of his head.

"What of Oscar's arm? I trust the damage last night was not great, since he has gone out this morning."

Meyer sobered. "A regrettable accident. I wouldn't have had it happen for a fortune. I blame myself, bitterly. However, it is only a small break, soon healed, and as befits a member of the guard, he has not let it deter him from his duty."

"Perhaps he will not stay out as long as the others."

"As to that, I'm sure he will complete his given task. Still, you may be sure every man of the cadre will return before dark."

She sent him a quick glance. "Why do you say so?"

"We had an early visit this morning from M'sieur de la Chaise. That fine gentleman has arranged entertainment for us this evening, or perhaps it would be more accurate to say he has arranged it for himself."

"You mean a soirée?"

"No, no, nothing so respectable. I mean he has arranged to have a fine meal prepared in his own kitchen and served here by his own servants, has contracted for the delivery of fine wines and liquors, and has hired the services of a group of itinerant musicians and dancers who, he assures us, play the liveliest music ever heard on the Teche."

"I can see why he feels entitled to be present. It will add luster to his boast of having entertained royalty. No doubt his dinner-table conversation will be enlivened with a description of this party for years to come."

"Not, I think, in the company of the ladies."

"What?"

"To add the necessary *soupçon* of enjoyment to the festivities, there is to be a consignment of females from New Orleans."

Angeline met the man's gray eyes for a long moment before she looked away, reaching to place her coffee cup on the table. "I see. How obliging of M'sieur de la Chaise, to be sure."

"It has the ring of procurement, does it not? But then, as I said, the gentleman will be the one who most enjoys his own hospitality. That is, if Madame his wife does not get wind of it. We were cautioned most strictly to say nothing if we should chance to meet her."

Angeline could not keep the stiffness from her smile. "He may be disappointed. Such elaborate arrangements cannot be kept secret, especially if a meal is to be prepared under his wife's nose. Madame will know the full details by now, if she has not been aware since the day he placed his order with the merchants."

"Poor little man."

"Yes," she agreed, though her thoughts were elsewhere. She allowed a small silence to fall, then took a deep breath. "You—you are the only one left on guard today?"

"Other than the indispensable Sarus, yes."

She sent him a doubtful glance, biting the inside of her lip before she plunged. "If we agreed that you allowed me to leave the house yesterday, could you not—perhaps—"

"Do the same again?" He shook his head. "I wish that I could."

"I... understand."

"If you think it is because of the trouncing I took last night, then you are wrong. It is a question of principle now. Yesterday, I could look the other way out of pity and it could be taken as no more than a moment's inattention, something not to be tolerated in the *garde du corps* of Rolfe of Ruthenia, but not traitorous. Today you are my sole responsibility, and the complexion of the thing has changed—which is exactly what Rolfe intended when he left me behind today. He is damnably acute."

"It is a test for you, then?"

"Just so."

"Does he always treat his men this way?"

A wry smile tugged at Meyer's bruised mouth, making a deeper indentation of the odd scar that cut into his cheek. "We are his friends. We are also members of a fighting unit, a small but deadly army that can at any time become the core of a greater force of immense value to any country who needs such a thing. There have been times, and will be again, when we have had to depend upon each other for our lives. A man found lacking among us is a danger to all."

"An uncomfortable way to live," she observed.

"Agreed. Which is why men unable to stand the pace Rolfe sets, the degree of concentration and loyalty he demands, come and go. No man is bound, except possibly by the excitement, the feeling of being intensely alive and capable of anything that may be asked of him."

"You admire him," she said in tones of discovery, "despite what he did to you last night."

"It is difficult not to," Meyer answered. Draining his cup, he held it out for a refill. The closed-in look of his face did not invite further comment.

Meyer provided her entertainment for the remainder of the day. He pointed out a cupboard holding a stack of yellowed and maltreated periodicals, most concerned with farming and hunting though the few featuring literary pursuits were considerably less dog-eared. There was also, however, a small, hand-sized volume of *The Compleat Angler* by Izaak Walton that beguiled the hours with its sage comments and philosophy sandwiched between angling tips.

Later in the day when she admitted her reluctance to order the Mongolian manservant, Meyer commanded a bath for her. Sarus, on this occasion, brought the water, then moved to the side of the room away from the fireplace, lifted the tapestry that hung there, and disappeared behind it. He emerged a few moments later carrying the copper tub, which he then filled. When he had gone, Angeline moved the tapestry aside herself and discovered a door that led into a small dressing room that she had not dreamed was there. It contained a slipper chair with one leg broken and its horsehair padding spewing from the torn seat, several pairs of much-worn boots lying in a corner, molding in the damp climate, and a day bed with a cornshuck mattress on its rope springs, possibly the sleeping place, once, of a valet required to be on call against the return of the young masters of the de la Chaise family. A small dust-covered window high in one wall shed a faint light over the gray and uninviting interior.

Dropping the tapestry, she turned away, untying her sash and fastening it around her hair as she moved toward the tub.

She luxuriated in the hot water, slipping down until it came up to her chin, letting the tension and the strange aches in her muscles left from the previous night's ordeal ease away.

She allowed her mind to drift to her aunt. What would she be thinking now? Would she be concerned about her niece's prolonged absence? She had been so certain there would be no danger once Rolfe discovered who Angeline was; she had been wrong, as she must have realized if she had thought the matter through. Rolfe certainly had had no problem in seizing upon the salient point, that Angeline must know where Claire was in hiding. He could not be blamed for trying to use that deduction to his advantage.

What of Claire? Did her cousin know by now that Angeline had been taken? What would Claire do? Anything? It was unlikely. Where then would it all end, and when? If the episode did, finally, draw to a close, would she ever be the same, or would memories of it haunt her beyond forgetting?

There was no point in dwelling upon it. For now she could do nothing.

A small fire burned on the hearth against the gathering coolness of the evening. Its warmth was pleasant, soothing. She lay back, resting her head against the high copper tub back. She smoothed the scented lather over her limbs, untroubled for the moment by the thought of Rolfe. No duties, no decisions awaited her. She was oddly at peace.

So relaxed was she that she failed to hear the horses on the drive. Her first inkling of Rolfe's return came when he thrust open the door and stepped into the room. She sat up. Then, as her breasts, wet and glistening, rose from the water level, she subsided once more.

He paused before swinging the door shut with a hard push and moving into the room. In sharp contrast to his usual faultless appearance, he appeared unkempt. A gold stubble of beard glinted on his face and his uniform was wrinkled, the tunic worn without a shirt underneath. His hair was windblown in ruffled blond waves, and his eyes were red-rimmed and shadowed. There was no difference in his carriage, however. It was as controlled and vital as ever.

"Just what I need," he said, bright amusement in his eyes. "A bath."

"You will have to order your own." She searched with her eyes for the towel left for her on a chair within arm's reach.

"But I prefer to share yours." He began to remove his tunic.

"There isn't room," she said, following his movements with no small apprehension.

He surveyed the copper tub with a measuring eye, taking careful note also of her form only half concealed by the soap-clouded water. "A pity. It appears I will have to speed your progress. Shall I scrub your back for you?"

"I can manage it myself," she snapped, but he paid no heed, going to one knee beside the tub. He plunged his arm into the water, making a great show of groping for the cloth, though his hands glided over the slippery-smooth curves and hollows of her form.

"Is this what you are looking for?" she asked, her tones icy as she held up the cloth.

"Where did you have it hidden?" He twitched it from her grasp and dipped his hand into the water once more, sliding it downward over her abdomen. She closed her hand on the soap and, grabbing his wrist, slapped the wet cake into his palm.

"Oh, yes," he said, shrugging in mock disappointment. "Sit up, if you please, and lean forward."

"Aren't you back early?" she asked through set teeth, holding her place.

"Somewhat, though I pray you will restrain your joy. It happens we have exhausted the coverts of the area. It was either travel farther afield, or else return for consultation with the one who has been of such… invaluable assistance."

He shifted, moving behind her. Before she could guess his intention, he had encircled her with one strong arm and lifted her higher, bending her over his hand. She gasped and he soothed her shoulder as one might gentle a fractious mare.

"What do you think you're doing?"

"Scrubbing your back. Be still!" He soaped the cloth he held, then began to glide it over the white, tapering expanse of her upper body, massaging in tight circles, the pressure firm, a little too firm.

"Wait—don't."

"Stop wiggling," he instructed, slipping his free hand around her waist, seeking purchase on her water-slick skin, finding it by closing his hand over one breast. As she reached to pluck it away, his grip tightened.

She inhaled sharply. "If this is some new form of torture to make me tell where Claire is—"

He released her so suddenly that she rocked forward and water sloshed from the tub onto the floor. Coming to his feet, he stood over her with his hands on his hips.

"It was not," he said, the words clipped, "though I suppose you cannot be blamed for thinking so."

She had spoken from anger and irritation, not from any real belief that the accusation might be true. She would not give him the satisfaction of knowing it, however, the simple reason being that judging from the past it might well have been. Without looking at him, she splashed to rinse the soap from herself, then stretched out her hand for the toweling. Shaking out the folds, she draped it around her, coming upright with grace and self-conscious poise. Still, she was less troubled by her nakedness than she had been moments before. His hands upon her, the way in which he had come to her, as if he had the right, convinced her of the uselessness of reserve.

He watched her, his blue gaze moving over the tender symmetry of her body glistening with wet and glowing warmly with the orange-red fireglow behind her. Thrusting his hands into his waistband, he swung away.

He did not go far. Leaning on the footboard of the bed, he observed with disconcerting intentness her movements as she blotted the water from her skin. His glance followed the look, reluctant but resigned, that she sent toward her much-worn gown hanging over the back of the chair with her slippers placed neatly beneath it.

"The sparseness of your wardrobe still distresses you? I did tell you how to remedy it." Lithe and swift, he moved to the armoire. From a shelf within its depths he took a garment of white linen as fine and smooth as silk. He shook it out, revealing it to be a long nightshirt with voluminous sleeves, a wide flat collar, and a coronet embroidered in gold thread on the left shoulder.

As he held it out, she kept her hands clamped to the towel draped around her. "I couldn't take it."

"I assure you," he drawled, "that I have no use for it. Sarus packs them because he was taught such things are indispensable for a gentleman's wardrobe. They have little purpose in mine."

He did not wait for her to accept the offering but draped it over her shoulder. Then, moving behind her, he scooped up her clothing, rolling it into a bundle that he deposited outside the door for Sarus to deal with.

When he turned back into the room, she still stood where he had left her, her eyes dark with fury. "Such high-handed tactics may appeal to some, but not to me. Bring my clothes back!"

He made no move to comply. Instead he began to remove his boots, levering them off with the brass jack on the hearth before stripping off his pantaloons. Magnificently naked, he stepped into the tub and settled down with a sigh. As she turned sharply away he said, "Why? You know you don't want them. You know too, if you will admit it, that you are just as happy to have your hand forced."

"That's ridiculous!" The soft linen draped over her smelled delightfully fresh in its crisp, new folds, but she would not be beguiled by it, any more than she would listen to his soft, insidious words. She could hear him splashing water over himself, lathering the bath cloth.

"Is it? Perhaps the substitute I have provided lacks appeal. What would you have then? A Parisian gown fit to outshine the odalisques of Araby or a douche of demimondaines?"

She stiffened. "Are you suggesting that I want to compete with—"

"The demimondaines? Who else, though I may have been too kind in giving the women expected this evening that title. Your cousin Claire, now, may belong to that tasteful breed, but I fear those imported for our delectation tonight are likely to be less discriminating."

"Neither their relative merits nor the question of my wardrobe are matters of concern this evening. I will not be going downstairs."

"No?" The sound of his vigorous soaping ceased.

"Surely you can't desire it? It would present a certain risk, I think." Despite her best efforts, her tone held something akin to defense of her position.

"If you expect to be recognized," he said in dry humor, "then you are something more—or less—than I have uncovered so far."

The warm red stain of blood under the skin crept to her hairline. He referred to her lack of ardor in his arms until compelled by his caresses to abandon her defenses. In the agitation of the moment as he invaded her bath, she had been able to skirt in her mind what had passed between them the night before. Now with a few light words he had brought it forth, deliberately, to taunt her.

"Angeline——" he began, the water sloshing as he made as if to rise.

But she had recovered, lifting her chin. "Certainly I don't expect to be recognized, but these women cannot fail to notice and to comment, when they return to New Orleans, concerning the woman you have in your company. The town is some distance away, and yet not all that far when you consider that the people of St. Martinville have many relatives there, elderly women and curious men with nothing more to do than sit down and write each other about the curious tales they hear."

The noise of his bathing diminished. "I thought we were agreed that you cared nothing for your loss of character. Why this sudden concern?"

Had he been going to deny the taunt? The idea was astounding. If he did not want his every word weighed for hidden meaning, however, he should not load them so often with pricks and probes.

Ignoring his question, she went on, "I understand M'sieur de la Chaise will be present also. Easygoing he may be, with a love of good food and drink and—and other pleasures, but he will not accept my presence at your side without an explanation, no matter what you may think."

"We are not to have the honor of his company, it seems. We overtook a messenger on a mule on the drive as we arrived just now. M'sieur sends his regrets, but he must sup with his wife." He splashed a few more times, then she heard him step from the tub. "May I borrow your towel?"

The urge to refuse his polite request was strong. She resisted it, but swung to send him a fulminating glance as she shook out the folds of the nightshirt to hold against her while she whipped the towel away and threw it to him.

He met her gaze and held it as he caught the length of toweling and began slowly to wipe the droplets of water from his bronze torso. "It is the women you object to, isn't it? You would prefer not to join the vulgar array, preening for the benefit of my men—and for me."

He had it, despite the fact that she had not been certain herself of why she so disliked the idea of going downstairs this evening. "What is wrong with that? I have never—that is, I don't—"

"You have no experience of such bachelor gatherings and would prefer to acquire none."

"Yes." She stared at him defiantly, half expecting some explosion of wrath or amusement.

"I doubt," he said slowly, "that such forthright and unbowed innocence as you can claim, despite a small matter of what goes by the name of seduction among noblemen and other gentry, would be sullied."

"On the other hand, how could I be less than a dampening influence?"

He stared at her, his vivid blue gaze raking the proud tilt of her chin and the steady regard of her gray-green eyes despite the flush of color across her cheekbones for his oblique reference to his violent possession of her. Her forthright disdain he accepted, though it made no impression upon his chiseled features. As he reached for his discarded pantaloons he gave a nod of agreement. "There is that. Stay here then, well above the swilling and rutting. A portion of the feast will be sent to you—the debauchery I will leave to your imagination!"

Damnably acute, Meyer had called him. It was an accurate description. Because she could not let Sarus in with her evening meal while dressed in a length of toweling, she had to don the nightshirt he had presented to her. Because she was human, and female, and curious, she could not prevent herself, later, from wondering what was taking place downstairs. And because Rolfe had left her alone to go below, she could not help asking herself if the reason was the other women.

It didn't matter, any of it. Still, it was irritating to be predictable while she could not even begin to guess what Rolfe would do, or say, or think.

The sound of breaking glass came as the evening advanced, rising above the rumble of male voices and the vigorous scrape of fiddles in cacophony with an off-key squeeze box. A woman's laughter trilled, ending in a smothered yelp. The smell of liquor and cheap scent seeped upward, a nauseating combination.

Angeline paced, the slit sides of the nightshirt flapping about her ankles, exposing her slender legs to the knees. The long, tasseled ends of the blue silk sash she had used to gather the folds about her waist flew out from her feet with every step. She had rolled the sleeves to her elbows where the fullness hung in deep cuffs, threatening to descend over her hands again at any moment. The neckline, of width ample to pull over a man's head, plunged deep on her smaller frame, exposing the curves of her breasts, while the coronet embroidered on the shoulder struck her just right to emphasize their rose-shadowed peaks, which could be seen through the fine linen weave.

Angeline paid no heed, had not in fact taken note of her appearance in the nightshirt, any more than she had noticed the shimmering russet cloak of her hair as it shifted over her shoulders, falling well below her waist, the soft flush on her cheekbones, or the vivid gray-green of her eyes. It was the looks of the other women that concerned her.

Were they beautiful, those cackling harlots? Did Rolfe find their blatant allure and excessive availability more to his taste? He was welcome to them. She did not care if he consorted with every one of them, of course she didn't.

Were they fair or dark, these women, young or old? She hoped they were the last. That would serve him right, and also put a damper on his debauchery.

She stopped, listening. The inane giggling coming from below, mixing with the rumble of bass laughter, did not sound like older women. It had a silly ring, in fact, empty-headed and vain and stupidly excited. How any man could be attracted by a woman making such a sound she could not imagine. It was to be hoped that the foolish tittering would stop when they were bedded.

What was so funny? Angeline stood listening with compressed lips to the gales of laughter rising to her bedchamber. Abruptly she swung toward the door.

On the landing outside she paused. There was no one in sight down the long corridor of the upstairs hall. Beyond the stair railing, the great room was a well of light, a beckoning glow that drew her toward the stairs. She placed her hand on the banister, leaning to peer downward, but she could see very little. The men appeared to be gathered at the table, though all she could catch sight of was their feet. The fact that the feet of the women gathered nearby were bare was enough to make her drop to one knee. Still unable to see the entire tableau, she crouched lower, pressing her head to the carved balusters of the railing.

They were gaming, the men lounging in their chairs holding cards in their fists, each with a wineglass at his elbow. They had drunk deep, for their voices were loud and their faces flushed, and they had removed their tunics, sitting in their shirt sleeves. Meyer sat with his eyes half-closed, flicking his cards with a thumbnail. Oswald leaned back in his chair talking to Oscar, who had about him an owlish look as he hunched over the table. Leopold was flushed, his dark hair falling over his forehead to give him an appearance of dissipation not wholly undeserved. Gustave, the black patch askew over his eye, laboriously counted the marks on his cards, touching them one by one with a callused finger.

The women were gathered to one side, behind a single player. As Angeline watched, it seemed plain that they were being used as stakes in the game, a proceeding that suited them very well. They twined their arms around the man who had won them, touching his hands, drawing their hands slowly across his shoulders.

His blue eyes bright with wine and amusement, Rolfe accepted their caresses, and also the sacrifices they seemed anxious to make to stay with him as his luck began to turn. The women, young and attractive, most of them brunette though there was a brassy blonde or two among them, were in a state of undress, taking off items of their clothing and tossing them onto the table as stakes in their stead. The sight of a lace-edged garter, rolled still in its stocking tube of shining silk, was greeted by shouts of encouragement and anticipation, especially since the woman who had contributed it had nothing left to her except a low-cut chemise. It joined two gowns of gaudy color and design and several pairs of slippers. Before long, if matters continued along the same course, the women must be passed naked one by one to the men whose luck held the longest.

Angeline registered the situation, then ignored it. It was Rolfe, at ease, enjoying the discomfiture of his men and the ludicrous necessity of keeping the women behind him clothed that caught her attention. She had never seen him in this mood, without tension or his rigidly imposed self-control, without guile or the shadow of subterfuge. The relaxed charm of the smile that curved the planes of his face and set laugh lines crinkling around his eyes was devastating. This was the way he must have been before his brother was killed, she thought, before he had been accused of trying to take his father's throne. This was the man who had fought and played his way across Europe, the man who had flaunted his gypsy mistresses while winning and keeping the affection of his countrymen, as well as his own personal cadre. For the moment, with her out of the way, he had thrown off the weight of unwanted responsibility, seeking forgetfulness in the pastimes of other days, not the least of which was drink.

He was not sober. It took long moments to realize it, and even then there was no evidence except a feeling in the pit of her stomach. His hands were steady, his gaze was clear, his speech precise as he placed his bets, and yet there was a recklessness about him, a sense of heedless enjoyment that could only be the effect of the wine. The gold stubble on his face was brighter and his eyes more bloodshot than earlier. And if she needed further proof there was the fact that, despite her stealthy movements above him, he did not once look up. She was grateful for the omission, but for such a thing to go unnoticed he must be drunk indeed.

There was one person in the room below who was not enjoying either the play or being a part of the stakes. It was one of the women, a girl of no more than seventeen from the way she looked. She stood some distance from the others, staring at the floor with downcast eyes. As Leopold addressed a quick remark to her, she sent him an anxious smile as if trying to please, then glanced quickly away again.

The girl had the look, Angeline thought, of a young Acadian woman with her soft brown hair and eyes, her sturdy shape yet delicate face and hands, her sweet, nervous manner, though without shyness. Where were her people, her family, or was the girl alone, as she herself was?

His attention drawn by Leopold's banter, Rolfe glanced at the Acadienne. He sent her a slight smile and, ignoring the other women who fawned over him, reached to catch the girl's wrist, pulling her toward him to perch on his knee. As the girl settled herself, she sent him a strained, frightened look through her lashes. He picked up his wineglass and took a sip, then handed it to her. She drank without hesitation from where his lips had touched.

Angeline came to her feet with great care. Her limbs stiff with cramp and an odd, disconcerted awkwardness, she eased backward until she was out of sight. Turning, she went back into the bedchamber and, being careful not to slam it, closed the door.

Eight

THE SOUND OF A SHOT CRASHED THROUGH THE HOUSE, exploding against the walls. It was followed by a high-pitched scream reverberating with terror. Angeline sprang up, coming to a sitting position on the bed. She had not meant to sleep, only to close her eyes for a moment. She had turned down the covers, slipping between them only because her feet were cold. Coming awake so suddenly, she felt disoriented and unbelieving, as if she hovered on the edge of some nightmare that would soon fade.

Another shot blasted the night, followed by the echoing whine of a ricochet: this was no dream. The scream came again, and on the tail of it rang a sharp, feminine jeer. A babble of voices ensued, faint but deep, coming from the great hall below. It was cut short by a sudden order for quiet.

What was going on? Angeline pushed back her hair and slid from the bed, pulling the nightshirt straight around her as she jumped down from the bed step. The thought of rescuers, arriving at last, crossed her mind before she dismissed it. There was no urgency in the sounds from below, no surprise; the only panic was that etching the tones of the woman who had cried out.

She had reached the door and pulled it open when the third shot came. Its counterpoint was a sobbing moan: "I can't—I can't—"

"Hold it still, for the love of God."

The pleading admonishment came from Oscar. The answer was a hiccoughing sob as another shot exploded, then another and another in quick succession.

By the time the echoes had died away, Angeline was halfway down the stairs. She paused as quiet descended, surveying the scene.

The acrid smell of gunpowder was thick in the open room. Gunsmoke lay like gray muslin upon the air, swirling around the flickering candles of the chandelier, muting the light in the dim, tapestry-hung room. The table had been pushed aside, leaving a straight path to the one plastered wall where the covering had been removed near the front windows. Against that ivory surface the Acadian girl stood alone, clad only in her chemise and flanked by floor candelabra holding burning tapers. Her face was streaked with tears and she was trembling in convulsive shudders. In one shaking hand she held a playing card while behind it the plaster was pocked with holes.

Down the room at the long table stood Oscar with Rolfe beside him. On the oak top was an array of pistols, five in number. All similar in size and style, they had carved handles rounded to fit the hand and long barrels intricately chased and scrolled in silver. A sixth pistol Oscar handed to Rolfe, who began to reload it in swift, economical movements.

The other men, and the half-dressed, clinging women imported for their pleasure, stood near the fireplace, well out of the firing line. The drunken cadre were wagering back and forth among themselves in slurred undertones, or shouting encouragement to the girl holding the card.

"Change the card," Rolfe said, laying the pistol he held back on the table, aligning it with the others.

Oscar, with his left arm held close to his body in a sling, walked down the room, a six of diamonds in his hand. He pulled the six of hearts from the girl's viselike grasp, substituting the other card. He drew the girl's arm out more level and farther from her face, and, having positioned her for her greater safety, turned back toward the table.

"Four out of six," he called in gratification, "but all shots in the card. Not bad shooting, by all that's holy!"

Rolfe picked up the first pistol. The Acadian girl cringed, turning her face away. Her free hand flew to her mouth and a tinge of green appeared under her skin in the candlelight as sick horror surfaced in her eyes.

Rolfe aimed, fired. A ragged tear appeared in the new card, obliterating a red diamond. The girl shrieked, doubling over. Oscar averted his eyes from her, his thin face determined despite the lack of color under the skin.

Angeline could stand no more. She abruptly descended the last treads of the stairs with swift steps. "What's the matter with all of you? Can't you see that girl is terrified?"

Without waiting for an answer, she crossed with impulsive strides to where the girl stood, imposing

her own body between the men and their target. She
snatched the card from the girl's nerveless fingers, holding
it for the moment in her own hand as she reached out
tentatively to touch the Acadian girl's shoulder. She
dissolved into tears, weeping like a punished child.

"Here," a man called, "the wager isn't settled.
Nothing is settled."

Angeline did not answer as she led the girl to a chair
off to one side.

"She has the card," one of the women called, her
voice feline with suspicion. "Maybe she would like to
hold it?"

The suggestion was taken up, repeated, applauded.
Angeline flung a quick glance at Rolfe. He stood with
the second pistol in his hand, shuttered blankness on
his bronze features.

The drink they had consumed that evening had
made them all inhuman; ready, even eager, to make
game of someone. They were past caring for the life
that must be endangered for the sake of their stupid
wager. Anger such as she had never known swept
over Angeline. As she hesitated to comply with their
suggestion, the taunts turned to abuse. She wanted to
shout back at them, but there was a streak of perilous
pride inside her that forbade it. She would not sink to
their level. The only thing to be done then was to defy
them with raw courage.

With her head high, she straightened from the
Acadian girl and swung toward the candelabra. She
marched to the pockmarked wall and turned with her
lovely mouth curved in a smile of contempt, raising
high the six of hearts with its one shattered mark.

The quiet of surprise descended. Into it came Meyer's voice, quietly speculative. "Since the person who holds the target has been changed, does that also change the prize?"

Rolfe's dark-gilt brows drew together, creasing the space between them. Oscar, a brown curl dangling forward on his forehead, glanced quickly from Angeline to the Acadian girl and then, with sudden doubt clouding his hazel eyes, to his leader.

It was in that instant that Angeline realized to the full what she had interrupted. The wager had been to settle the final question of who would have the Acadian girl for the night. Through some oversight or mischance only five women had been provided, one short of the number required for the six men of the cadre, Gustave, Leopold, Meyer, Oswald, Oscar, and, of course, Rolfe.

How democratic it was of Rolfe to choose this way of deciding the issue instead of asserting his authority. How had it come about that it was necessary? Had Rolfe's luck turned so that he had lost his female stakes one by one? Had it come perhaps to a point where the young girl now trembling on her chair would have lost her chemise to Oscar and, rather than allowing her to be exposed naked in her tender inexperience, he had proposed this contest? Was the man who proved the better shot under these circumstances of uncertain light and unsteady reflexes to receive the chemise and the one who wore it, while the other got nothing? And having taken the Acadian girl's place, was she herself now, as Meyer had asked so delicately, to become the prize? Was this the point where she ceased to be the bedmate of the prince alone and began to be passed among his men?

The acid interest of the men and women around the fireplace, the importance of the wager, was explained. The distress of the Acadian girl was also made understandable since she was to be the forfeit of the game as well as the half-naked target of the less-than-sober players. Very well. The situation, as bizarre and without reality as it was, could not be changed. The best thing that could be done was to get it over with quickly.

Angeline stood straight and still with the candle gleam caught like molten copper in her hair, slanting over her pure features and shining in her eyes with gray-green defiance. It shafted through the fine line of the nightshirt draped around her, outlining the graceful symmetry of her form in a pale-gold nimbus that made her seem ethereal and yet divinely wanton.

Rolfe stared at her, his turquoise eyes grim. The line of his jaw tightened. Ignoring Meyer's question and the tension that flowed suddenly in the room, he swung his glance to the card she held, narrowing his concentration to that oblong of painted cardboard. The light slid along the chased length of the pistol he held as he turned to his side in a dueler's stance, drawing the weapon down level and steady, sighting down the barrel.

The sound of the first shot was deafening in that close room. There was a noise at her ear like a buzzing insect, and a tug at the card in her hand, and then bits of flying plaster stung her cheek as the ball struck the wall behind her. She narrowed her eyes, but had no time to flinch before Rolfe fired again and yet again in a near volley, moving down the line of pistols laid ready, each shot aimed separately and from a slightly different angle. As the explosion of the sixth and last died away, he stood wreathed in blue-gray powder smoke.

Slowly he lowered his arm, but did not move from the leashed tightness of his stance until Oscar, going quickly toward Angeline, let out a yell. "All six!"

They shouted and yelled for wine to celebrate. When it was poured they drank a toast to the bravery of Angeline, then, turning as a man, flung their glasses crashing into the dying embers of the fire. The women laughed and squealed as the men squeezed them in an excess of exuberance with hands groping playfully over compliant bodies. Rolfe hurled his goblet at the blackened back of the fireplace, then swung around. He skirted the table edge, making his way through those crowding around him, striding toward Angeline.

It was then that Oscar, flipping the card he had taken from her, spoke with a challenge behind the humor of his tone. "Do you claim both women, Rolfe, or since my cardholder was less steady than yours, will you permit me to shoot against you with the same holder in a second match, winner to take his choice?"

Quiet fell for his answer, the babble dying away as abruptly as it had begun. Rolfe stepped to Angeline's side, taking her hand. "There will be no second match," he said, his voice vibrant. "I carried through with the first for the sake of fairness, no other reason. You may say that I choose Angeline above the other, or else that, the odds being uneven, I waive my rights to the girl. Either way, there is no question of jeopardy for this woman. She is mine."

The words were a dismissal, an indication that the evening's entertainment was over. Without waiting for answer or argument, he moved toward the stairs, drawing Angeline with him. She suffered herself to be led a few yards, then with anger boiling slowly inside her for the callousness of the incident, the calm with which he had pronounced her his woman, and the assurance with which he escorted her toward his bedchamber, she jerked her hand free.

He turned his head sharply, his gaze resting on her scarlet cheeks an instant before he met her eyes. "You mean to enter an objection? By all means, but not now."

"I can think of no better time," she returned with a lift of her chin.

"Even if it means an uneven distribution of women? The numbers you will note are even now, an arrangement made without bloodshed or the clash of tempers, something I cannot guarantee will last if you mean to upset the balance again."

"Again?" she exclaimed, keeping her voice low in response to his own quiet tone. "What balance was there with you scaring the wits out of that poor girl, fighting over her with Oscar?"

"Half of that poor girl's terror was fear that I would win. Being the most tender parcel among them, I thought her best settled with Oscar, a state of affairs that would only be accepted if it could be shown he had won her in all fairness. If you had not appeared I could have, in another moment, disavowed the wager and left her to him in disdain for the prospect of a sniveling, screeching wench in my bed."

She felt a sudden easing in the region of her chest. "You—you wanted Oscar to have her."

"You might endeavor to hide your amazement at that small show of compassion. Are you coming, or have you decided to sample the delights of community closeness? If you intend to join the orgy I will have to reserve a place."

She turned her head with reluctance, following his hard nod. Oscar knelt before the Acadian girl, speaking to her in soft tones, drying her tears with his fingertips at one end of the room, while at the other there were couples entwined upon the settees or leaning together across the table. She looked hastily away again and, without acknowledging his sardonic bow, moved ahead of him up the stairs as if controlled with wires.

Inside the bedchamber Angeline moved to the washstand, where she picked up one of his silver-backed brushes. Leaning from the waist, she began to stroke the plaster dust from the silken mass of her hair. In the mirror, she watched through her lashes as he came to stand just behind her. For the flicker of an instant she thought he swayed, and her movements stilled. Then he was turning, drawing off his unbuttoned tunic and tossing it on a chair.

He spoke over his shoulder. "Bottled ire is the enemy of sleep—or anything else that requires a mind at ease. What is it you want to say?"

His indulgence was an added irritant. "You know well enough!"

"But I offer you the joy of flinging the words at my head. Have you lost the proper rage, or only grown wary?"

"All right," she said in goaded tones. "I am not yours."

"It is the public avowal that disturbs you, or fear that if it isn't so now it soon will be?"

"Neither!" With her hand clenched so tightly on the brush that her knuckles were white, she turned slowly to face him. "I am not a pawn or a plaything. I am Angeline Fortin, here through no fault of my own, and I belong to myself. Being forced to remain with you doesn't change that."

"Doesn't it? Suppose I said I had changed my mind, that no matter what you told me, no matter the outcome of our scouring and scratching on the trail of Claire, that I would not let you go. What is there, who is there, to take you from me?"

"You—you can't mean it."

Whether from necessity or the nonchalance of supreme confidence, he stepped to lean against the post of the bed. "Can I not? But even if the question is academic, what answer have you?"

She stared at him. "Eternal imprisonment, is that the threat?"

"The description is unflattering, but accurate."

"You would never get away with it—not that I am worried! Your interest in me would wane soon enough if you found Claire."

"A test, my dear? Unwise. You should know how hard I find it to resist the cast-down gauntlet."

The mockery in his tone was like a lash. "You are only trying to frighten me."

"Why is it then that, being so successful, I yet need consoling?"

"Wounded pride, I don't doubt!" she threw at him. "Did you expect me to melt into your arms in a dream of bliss and gratitude?"

"It would have been a novelty." His tone was pensive.

"If that is what you want, I suggest you try one of the women downstairs. Their counterfeit pleasure, bought and paid for, is as close as you will come!"

"Not," he said, his eyes narrowed to a blue glitter, "another challenge?"

The intelligent answer would have been to deny it. She was past that. "What of it? You can't treat me any way you want. Why you should try is more than I can understand—just as I don't see why you want to keep me here at all."

"Why? For the same reason that a priest wears his shirt made of horsehair next to the skin, a reminder of uncomfortable vows made for the most exalted of reasons."

"You enjoy being incomprehensible, don't you!"

"The meaning is there, if you look for it."

She turned back to the nightstand, flinging down the brush, aware of him watching her with all the assurance of a wolf with a rabbit in view. He had the upper hand and he knew it. What was more, she knew it, too. There was nothing to keep him from treating her in any way he pleased.

What was astonishing, she supposed, was his forbearance heretofore. If she could think him capable of the reactions of a gentleman, a man of honor, she would be forced to conclude it was guilt combined with confidence in his own ability to find Claire that had so far prevented him from using physical means to extract information from her. Granted, he had tried one method of persuasion that was less than parlor conduct, but it had not in all truth been hurtful. Was it possible that, his beating of the countryside having turned up nothing, he was ready now to use yet another tactic to discover what he wanted to know? What other explanation could there be for the apparent meaning of his words?

A slight creak of the bed frame as he pushed away from it warned her of his approach. His hand closed with gentle strength on her shoulder, while his arm circled the slim indentation of her waist, his spread fingers slipping around to draw her against him. He breathed the clean rose fragrance of her hair and his chin with its stubble of beard grazed her temple as he bent his head to brush with his lips the sensitive skin of her neck just below her ear.

"Don't!" she said on a sharp, indrawn breath. She tried to twist from his grasp, but he held her firm.

"Why? Are you afraid you might succumb to the lure of bliss after all?" His voice was low, his breath warm against her cheek.

As she flung her head back to stare up at him, her hair spilled over his arm in a cascade of shining auburn. "You flatter yourself. Nothing is less likely, especially when I have but to consider the purpose that drives you."

"And that is?" he inquired, his gaze on the enticing curves of her lips.

"I am not so gullible as to think that my appeal for you is personal. What else could you want except to—to use my emotions to bend me to your will?"

A smile gathered slowly in his eyes. "An enticement of kisses? An interesting idea. I wonder if it will work?"

"Not," she said through set teeth, "if I can help it."

"But can you? That is the question."

Holding her clear gray-green gaze, he lowered his head to take her lips. His mouth was firm and warm and achingly tender, flavored with wine. Against her will she felt the expanding of her senses and, though she tried to marshal a defense against that gentle, insidious invasion, she could not prevent the languor that seemed to melt her bones so that she yielded by infinite degrees, leaning against him. As he lifted his head, staring down at her, her eyes were luminous and her lips softly parted.

For a strained instant she was still, then she lowered her lashes. Her voice was husky as she forced it through the constriction in her throat. "Take care, or it may be that in appealing to my emotions you will leave your own unguarded. I will have no hesitation, I promise, in turning your own sword against you and, should that happen, in bidding you renounce your quest and return from whence you came."

"It is good of you to warn me, but you might bear in mind the risk you run even in that eventuality."

"Risk?" The strength of his arms around her was a secure and entrancing support that she could, with frightening ease, come to depend upon.

"Should I place my soul in fetters and become the willing captive of your sweet warfare, it is possible that my need of you will be so boundless that I must force you to go with me."

The prospect should have been cause for alarm. That it was not was more disturbing than anything he had said. She had no time to dwell upon it, however.

With an odd, pensive light in his turquoise eyes, he took her lips once more, exploring, tasting, his purpose as concentrated, his determination as steely as when, so short a time before, he had lifted the first pistol in the room below. His desire, directed by fierce intelligence and unbending will, created an onslaught that she could not hope to equal. She felt her senses giving way before it, absorbing the bruising strength, responding with honeyed sweetness. And in that one last flash of clarity she knew with instinctive, ancient wisdom that the ploy could not be bettered. Woman's answer to man's hard force had always been a soft encompassing. To fight him, knowing her strength to be less than his, was to invite defeat. But if she met him instead with yielding grace, he might be disarmed and left vulnerable, open to other, less obvious weapons.

His hand slid upward to cup the firm mound of her breast. His thumb brushed over the soft linen that covered the straining peak and she felt its tightening and the tingling of the nerves at that sensitive point. His hold strengthened so that she was pressed against him, made aware of the urgency of his heated need of her. She could not think how she had come from such violent determination to resist him to this boneless, formless acquiescence, but it did not seem to matter. She rested her head on his shoulder, her body pliant, her lifted hand just touching his arm.

Gently he turned her to face him and, sighing, kissed her eyelids before with easy strength he lifted her into his arms. His movements deliberate, he stepped to the side of the bed and placed her upon the high mattress. Discarding his clothing in a few swift moves, he joined her there, lean and nakedly golden in the light of the candles left burning on the side table. There was blue fire in his eyes as he stretched out beside her. He drew the hem of her nightshirt upward, smoothing his hand along the finely turned length of her leg to her hip. As he reached the sash constricting her waist he murmured a soft curse, though it was the work of no more than a moment before it fell free. He drew the voluminous linen garment off over her head, pausing to snatch a taste of one rose-crested breast as it was uncovered.

Casting the nightshirt aside, he stretched out beside her, then, gathering her to him, rolled so that she came to rest above him, every curve and soft hollow of her body molded to his long length. Her gray-green gaze was startled as she stared down at him. The chiseled firmness of his mouth curved in fleeting amusement, and then he pushed his fingers through her hair, drawing it forward so that it fell around them in a shining curtain. Cupping her face in his hard, swords-man's hand, he drew her mouth down to his.

She could feel the steady rise and fall of his chest, the jolting of his heartbeat, and the faint abrasiveness of the hair on his chest against her breasts. His belly was flat and firm, his thighs ridged with muscles. Engulfed in purely tactile sensation, she could yet perceive an easing within herself. Lying as she was, she could not be dominated so easily by his weight and strength, was not spread-eagled at his mercy. The sheer freedom of it was heady.

His hands smoothing down her back to the slender curve of her waist, gripping, kneading her hips, far from being repellent, brought a seething excitement, a sense of fluid fullness to her loins. He moved against her slowly, holding her tightly to him. Her breasts swelled, pressing into him. Despite the chill of the room, she felt flushed, glowing with warmth. Resting on one elbow, she lifted the fingers of one hand to his face, touching the bristled corner of his mouth where their lips were joined. The sensation was one of indescribable intimacy, of closeness beyond thought, and then it was swamped by abandoned vulnerability as he parted her thighs and with a slow twist of his hips, penetrated her with rigid, pulsing fire.

Her breath caught in her throat, then as he began to move with ever deeper thrusts, it quickened. All conscious thought retreated before the burgeoning pleasure. She levered herself upward, moving with him. She wanted to take him deeper and deeper within her, despite the effort, defying the consequences. Her body was a living flame, consuming, contracting upon itself until she knew nothing, wanted nothing but this fevered excitement, this white-hot joining. Her being seemed to dissolve, flowing outward, and still she strove, finding infinite delight.

Her muscles tensed, cramping. A dark shadow of frantic need touched her and she drew breath with a small sound of distress.

His movements ceased. His voice a deep rustle of sound, he said, "Sweet love, let me take you to the spring that ever fills."

He spread his hands behind her back and heaved himself up and over, taking her fused and trembling with him. As he hovered above her, she stared up at him, her eyes copper flecked with suspended wonder. He sank into her, plunging deep, and her lashes fluttered down as she accommodated herself to his smooth, gliding motion. She floated, drifting in a wondrous release of ageless enjoyment, and still he moved against her. With a shock, she felt the suffusion of excitement once more. It rippled through her, banishing all consciousness of who and what she was. She rose against him in panting joy and wild wantonness. She heard his ragged breathing, the strong thud of his heart, felt the shudder that ran over his frame. And then once more came the crimson explosion of surcease. Clasped together, they let it wash over them in pulsating liquid fire. Uplifted, they soared, bathed in its radiance, bound in rapture, indestructible and immortal.

Long minutes passed. Angeline lay unmoving, scarcely conscious. Rolfe shifted his weight so that he lay beside her though his arm trailed across her, the fingers enclosing her breast, and his face was buried in her hair. Their breathing slowed, quieted. The darkness left Angeline's mind, and though it seemed a long time later but was surely less than half an hour, at last she began to feel chilled. Rolfe's lean thigh was warm against her. If she moved she would draw his attention without fail, but if she did not she would have to endure the gathering cold.

She stirred a little, expecting him to release her, or perhaps to reach to cover her himself as he had once or twice before. He did not move. His chest rose and fell with a steady rhythm and his gold-tipped lashes lay still, shuttering his gaze. He was heavily, soundly asleep.

If she had doubted that he was drunk until this moment, she could do so no longer. Under no other circumstances could she imagine him falling so deep into slumber. Always before, her slightest shift of position was enough to rouse him. But if he was inebriated, then nothing he had said could be taken at its face value, nor could she read any meaning into her reactions. His tenderness, his attempts to please her, his hint of caring had been no more than drunken fancies. The realization was disconcerting, but more frightening still was her angry disappointment.

What a fool she was. There was nothing to be done but admit it. No matter her surface thoughts and resolve, somewhere deep inside she had been flattered that Rolfe had chosen her above the other women. The shortage of their numbers had not been an insurmountable problem, she knew; arrangements might have been made where all could have shared their favors. Instead, he had taken her upstairs, and she had allowed that fact to color her judgment. All her defiance and petty resistance were useless, useless. Her vanity had been pleased that a man who had abducted her, taken her in passionate punishment, and chosen to torture her with diabolical and degrading skill, had then, in a sudden about-face, chosen to make the most tender love to her. She should have known there was a reason, should have trusted her own instincts that told her he was not sober.

Now she was left with a terrible fury for the betrayal of her own body. The fervor of her reactions to him was both amazing and dismaying. But that was not all. There had been a moment as he held her when she had felt a shaft of something uncomfortably close to warmth for him. Not that she was in love with him, of course, or anything near it. Still it was impossible to be so intimate with a man without feeling something.

A shiver caught her unaware. In sudden revulsion for everything that had happened in that high-tester bed, she knew a desperate need to get away from Rolfe, to be by herself, beyond his reach or even accidental touch. She eased away from him, slipping from beneath his flaccid hand. She looked around for her nightshirt. It lay wedged between the two bed pillows, a sleeve under the one on which Rolfe lay. To retrieve it without disturbing him, she drew her own pillow down beside her in the bed and, catching the nightshirt, tugged it gently toward her. Rolfe stirred, and she went still, but he only turned closer to her, flinging his arm across the down-stuffed pillow.

She waited, scarcely breathing, until he was still once more, then slipped from the bed, carrying the nightshirt with her, skimming into it as her feet touched the cold wood floor.

The chairs in the room were not designed for comfort; she would have a hard night of it if she tried to sleep sitting up in one of them. She could curl on the hearth rug in front of the fireplace with her back to the dying embers, but the rug was thin and the floor hard. As she stood frowning, hugging her arms around her, she remembered the daybed in the connecting dressing room. It would be cold in there where no fire's warmth had penetrated for days, months, perhaps years. She would have to have a covering.

She eyed the rumpled coverlets at the foot of the bed doubtfully, weighing the possibility of waking Rolfe. Distance from him and discomfort, or proximity and prodigal warmth; that was the choice. Damn the man who could make things difficult even in his sleep! She would not choose, but would take her chance on snatching a quilt from those available. If ever the odds were to be with her where Rolfe of Ruthenia was concerned it should be now.

They were. With the quilt in her arms she turned away, then as her glance slid over his naked form she stopped. In his state it might be hours before he was alert enough to feel the cold, to cover himself. He would catch pneumonia in the damp, pervasive winter chill of this subtropical climate.

With her lips set in grim lines, she set down the quilt she held and, turning back to the bed, drew the sheet and the other woven coverlet up over him, pulling it with the lightest possible touch to his shoulder, spreading it to cover his arm that lay across the pillow. When it was done, a wry smile flitted across her mouth. Odd, but it looked a little as if his sleeping companion was still with him. For the space of a heartbeat, she stared down at the bronze planes of his face, then, swinging sharply away, stooped to pick up her quilt. She snuffed the candles in the holder beside the bed and moved toward the tapestry-covered door that led to the dressing room.

That small chamber was as dank and chill as she had imagined it would be. Without a candle, and with the moonless night crowding against the one window, it was also dark. Ancient dust, disturbed by her entrance, pervaded the air, along with the smell of moldy leather. Lying still on the daybed, wrapped in her cocoonlike quilt, Angeline became aware of the night sounds, both inside the house and out. Wind whined around the eaves and threshed the leafless limbs of the trees that grew close to the window. It made the walls and supporting timbers creak now and then, a natural accompaniment to the low moans and panting cries and squeaking bed ropes that echoed through the rooms beyond her. There was nothing ghostly about the sounds, however. The men of the cadre had brought their women upstairs. They writhed together now in their separate rooms, straining with entwined limbs. It crossed her mind to wonder if any such noises had issued from the room she shared with Rolfe, and if they had, if anyone had noticed. It didn't matter, but the idea brought a flush to her cheeks there in the darkness. Drawing the quilt tighter around her, she closed her eyes, willing herself to care not at all, and to become mercifully deaf.

A crackling noise intruded into her fitful sleep, becoming a part of the dream that unfolded around her. There was a column of flame towering into the sky and she was being forced step by step to walk toward it. She was both curious and afraid, filled with longing and despair. She could hear the fire's roar, smell the smoke. Her eyes smarted and began to run with tears. Fragments of burning ash caught in her throat and she choked.

She came awake coughing with the acrid sting of smoke in her lungs. Her eyes were burning and, indeed, from nearby came the ominous and greedy snapping of a fire. She sat up, swinging toward the sound from the next room. Through the crack under the door could be seen a streak of wavering red-orange light.

She scrambled from the bed, diving for the door. Jerking it open, she swept aside the tapestry. The bed where she had lain so short a time before was an island of fire. Scarlet and gold flames ate at the bed hangings, leaping and twisting, blackening the ceiling with their smoke. They ran across the top of the carved head-board and dripped upon the sheets, casting their bright light into the shadowed corners of the room, haloing the head of the man who lay beneath the covers as she had left him.

"Dear God," she breathed, then flung herself forward, fastening her hands on Rolfe's arm, dragging him away from the leaping, pouring runnels of fire. He was heavy, a dead weight, impossible to lift. A glowing cinder fell from the tester canopy overhead drifting to land on his shoulder. He did not flinch.

With her teeth set in her bottom lip, Angeline swung to the washstand and lifted the pitcher half-filled with water that sat upon its surface. She threw the contents over Rolfe and the bedding. A small portion of the fire died hissing, but the voracious flames that enwrapped the bed hangings roared on. She needed help. Now. At once.

Slinging the pitcher aside, she ran to the hall door and wrenched it open. She crossed the hall in a few swift strides to hammer upon Meyer's door.

"Fire!" she screamed. "Fire!"

A door opened down the hall and Gustave, slipping the braces to his pantaloons over his shoulders, appeared in the opening. "*Gott in Himmel!*" he said as he saw the reflected light leaping in the dark hall. "I was thinking I smelled smoke."

Angeline turned toward him. "It's Rolfe—I can't wake him!"

In less than a moment the hall was full of cursing men and screaming, cursing women. The cadre broke for the room where their leader lay. Heedless of injury or danger, they pulled down the bed hangings and stomped them, swatting, smothering the flames with snatched-up quilts and pillows, filling the air with flying ash and the smell of scorched cloth. Leopold and Oscar lifted Rolfe and carried him to the far side of the room, where they lowered him to the floor. As they stepped back, he roused, lifting his lashes with enormous effort. With the pupils narrowed to pinpoints, his blue gaze focused on Gustave and Meyer standing on the mattress, wreathed in smoke and bits of flaring ash as they slapped at a stubborn patch on the canopy. How much he understood of what was happening was difficult to say, but he greeted it in his own manner.

"What a pretty confusion," he drawled. "Hell, it seems, is no better organized than our exasperatingly precious earth."

The relief in the room was palpable. Sarus moved forward to kneel beside his master, his face pale beneath the yellow cast of his skin. Oscar flung a tight grin at Leopold and his brother Oswald, engaged in raking bits of burning cloth from the wall. "Thank God," Meyer said, while Gustave grunted and jumped down from the bed, moving to stand over the man on the floor.

"Just what is the idea?" the grizzled veteran demanded. "Were you trying to burn the house down around our heads, or only warming yourself a bit?"

Rolfe closed his eyes. "There is no need to shout. I am saving up apologies for M'sieur de la Chaise for the damage to his property so far, but to the best of my remembrance, this escapade is no doing of mine."

"I've seen you swallow as much and more than you did tonight with no effect, not even a yawn. How does it happen that you came so near to roasting yourself?"

"Do I disappoint you? It cannot be helped, nor can I solve this mystery for you."

Gustave frowned, then dropped abruptly to one knee. He reached to lift Rolfe's eyelid, staring at the contracted pupil in that expanse of brilliant blue.

"They work independently, but also together," the patient observed, and managed to prove it by keeping both eyes open while his brow quirked in inquiry.

"Drugged," Gustave said. "The fruit of the Turkoman poppy at a guess."

A silent laugh shook the man on the floor. "Decadent and debilitating. I don't think that I will throw up if I have something to drink, but I would like to test the theory. Nonalcoholic, of course."

"You didn't, yourself—" Gustave began, then stopped.

"If you need to ask," Rolfe said, closing his eyes, "then I have done something wrong. Perhaps been too liberal with the fruit of the vine?"

Sarus rose and slipped from the room. Angeline stared at the doorway where he had disappeared, now slowly filling with the white-faced women, their eyes avid with curiosity now that their fear had been banished. The question was, who had drugged Rolfe's food or drink, and why had he or she chosen that path instead of administering poison? Had someone felt that the drug combined with wine was enough to kill him, and finding it not so, used another means? Or had the point been to make the fire look like an accident, with the drug remaining a secret he would carry with him in death?

Oswald, who had moved to stand against the wall with one foot braced behind him, cleared his throat. "Are you suggesting that someone entered this house, sprinkled a dash of opium into Rolfe's food, then hid out until he was asleep, raced up here, and set fire to his bed? Impossible, not with all of us in the house. I will grant that there have been suspicious incidents in the past, but I cannot believe that whoever is behind them would venture into our own quarters. Besides, you will note the candlestick on the table beside the bed is close to the edge. Perhaps it was no more than an accident?"

"What of the drugs?" Gustave demanded.

"We have only your word for that. Could it not just as easily be that after the last few days he was overtired, and therefore more susceptible to his wine?"

"Only my word?" Gustave bellowed, coming to his feet.

Rolfe lifted a hand without opening his eyes. "The questions need to be asked."

It was Meyer who spoke next. "In any case, there is nothing to say that the person who acted came from the outside. There were five strange people in the house tonight, six if Angeline is counted. More than that, the servants of de la Chaise, bedded down even now in the outdoor kitchen, must be included. Then there are those who drove the wagons to deliver the supplies to the kitchens—"

"And ourselves," Oscar said, almost to himself.

As if by common consent, all turned their gazes upon Leopold. He came erect, his hands clenched into fists. "Now see here—"

"You can't count Angeline," Gustave said quickly, as if to avert the clash. "She gave the alarm, otherwise we might not have been in time. Besides, being here with Rolfe she was in just as great a danger."

"That's right," Meyer said, turning toward her. "Maybe she saw something, someone?"

"I—no, no one, nothing. When—when I awoke the fire was already burning." For some reason she could not bring herself to go into the details of why she had not been in the same room, much less the same bed.

In the doorway one of the women gave a smothered laugh. "She must have been sleeping sound. I wonder why?"

Meyer sent a glance in that direction, then with a significant nod said to the others, "This is getting us nowhere. I suggest we adjourn the postmortem until morning."

As he spoke Sarus returned carrying a goblet on a silver tray. Going down beside Rolfe, he supported his shoulders while he drank. On one elbow, the prince looked up. "Premature, Meyer."

The tall sandy-haired man turned, a smile in his gray eyes. "So it is, thankfully. Now what are we going to do with you?"

They remade the bed in Meyer's room for him. Meyer, whose suggestion it had been, took himself downstairs to spend the remainder of the night on one of the settees, the woman he had had with him taking the other, protesting bitterly until a gold coin was pressed into her hand. Rolfe walked to the bed unaided and lay watching with amusement in his eyes as Angeline, fidgeting and in high color, avoided joining him there until after the others had filed out once more, leaving them alone.

"I understand I owe you my life," he said as she climbed gingerly up to sit beside him.

"It was nothing."

"Perhaps to you, but I value the service more highly."

"I didn't mean—" she began, frowning.

"I know what you meant," he cut across her words. "I suppose now I will have to think of a reward."

"Don't put yourself to any trouble. My freedom will do." Her voice was tart.

Staring at her, his eyes brilliant and liquid with the effects of the drug, he said, "Anything but that."

Nine

ANGELINE EXPECTED ROLFE TO SLEEP FAR INTO THE day. He did not. Less than four hours after he had returned to bed he was up again, shaven, dressed, and in complete command. The only thing that seemed to have suffered was his temper. He was short with Sarus, whom he found sleeping across the threshold of his bedchamber door, surly with Angeline when she was not quick enough in answering what she required for breakfast, and cutting to Gustave when he offered something for the headache he was certain was bursting behind the prince's eyes. Descending to the great hall, Rolfe sent word for all the members of the cadre to join him there in uniform in half an hour.

Once the men, smothering yawns and surreptitiously straightening tunics, had gathered like a court-martial, Rolfe sent in the women one by one for questioning. So devastating was that interrogation that the flippant and hardened females emerged either white-lipped and silent or in tears. The young Acadian girl was so demoralized that Oscar had to support her from the room while she stifled her sobs with both hands. When it came time to go she could not be persuaded to stay behind at the hunting lodge, though Angeline heard Oscar's urging. She left with the others shortly before noon, climbing into the calèche provided by M'sieur de la Chaise for their return journey. She did not look back as the vehicle drove away.

The afternoon was devoted to a council from which Angeline was excluded. Before it began she was escorted politely to the bedchamber she had been sharing with Rolfe, where she spent the time helping Sarus bring it to some kind of order. They wiped down the walls, dusted the surfaces of the furniture, polished the wooden frame of the bed, and replaced the mattresses and bed coverings. The smell of woodsmoke lingered still, joined, when they were done, by the scent of soap and lemon-oil polish. Having made the chamber usable, Sarus left her alone while he went to see to dinner.

Several times during the afternoon Angeline heard hoofbeats on the drive, saw first one and then another of the cadre come and go on errands whose nature she could only surmise. It seemed that Rolfe had tired of his waiting game and was once more attempting actively to discover Claire's whereabouts. The cause was not hard to find; the incident of the night before had obviously jolted him by its similarity to his brother's death. A second heir to the throne of Ruthenia dying of unnatural causes in his bed would have been too much.

Though she tried not to dwell upon it, the fire was not far from her thoughts the entire day. Despite the suggestion put forward by Oswald, it had not been an accident; that much she knew. She herself had snuffed the candle that had been sitting on the table beside the bed before she had retired to the dressing room. What then did that leave? The idea of an outside culprit was plausible given the circumstances, but in order to take advantage of those same circumstances, that person would have needed either inside information or to have been keeping close watch. Even so, it was extremely risky. The more logical explanation, as Gustave had hinted a few days before, was that the person who wished Rolfe dead was one of his *garde du corps*.

Why was she worrying about it? She should be concerned for herself and for the untenable position in which Rolfe had placed her. She should be thinking of what lay ahead and of what she was going to do if his threat to keep her with him turned out to be more than just words. She would have to get away from him. How she would do it, she had no idea, but she could not simply do nothing, allowing him to treat her as he would. That way lay a life like that of the women who had been provided the night before, a life led from pillar to post without honor or respect, calling every man master and belonging to no one, not even to herself.

Darkness drew in early as clouds gathered and fog wreathed the trees, threatening to turn to rain. She bathed before dinner and washed her hair, ridding it of the smell of smoke. Combing the tangles from the long, damp, silken skein, she put back on her muslin dress and the tunic that Sarus had brought to her that morning, freshly washed and pressed once more. She was sitting before the fire, drying her long tresses, rubbing them gently between her hands, when Rolfe stepped into the room.

He paused, surveying her closely, then shut the door behind him, coming toward her with deliberate steps. He spoke almost at random, as if his mind was busy with other things. "Perhaps as a reward for last night you would like another gown?"

"Thank you, no."

"Not so long ago you were complaining about the lack of variety in your wardrobe."

Angeline allowed her gaze to slide over his shoulder, suggesting, "I have a more than adequate wardrobe at my aunt's house."

"One to which you have no access. If that rag you have on is any example you can hardly be heartbroken at the loss."

"What is wrong with this gown?"

"Leaving aside the fact that it is made out of the cheapest muslin, likely to tear like tissue paper," he answered, his bright stare daring her to comment on his role in causing its ragged state, "it is at least five years out of fashion. Moreover, it suits you not at all, though it was probably well enough for Claire as a *jeune fille*."

His words were biting, edged with a mockery more incisive than anything he had used against her since that first night when he had thought she was her cousin. Her gray-green eyes level, shadowed by anger and something more she would not admit, she said, "It's all I have."

"I was proposing to remedy that."

"That is neither your duty nor your right!"

"You are mistaken," he said, his voice soft. "If I desire to deck you with diamonds and petal you with pearls, I will. If it is my pleasure to see you garlanded in flowers with your feet nestled in fur and a ruby set in your navel, I will see it satisfied. Be warned. All I require from you is—"

"I know! My compliance. You must forgive me if my state of dress does not suit your consequence. I came away ill-prepared for a long stay and—and with little idea of the position I would be required to fill. You will have to make do with me as I am!"

He stood towering over her, his eyes holding the dark glitter of sapphires. "I am of a mind to return to the idea of restraining you with nudity. Not only would it be more convenient, it might prevent too close association with my guard, keeping you from making champions of them, from playing on their sympathies so that to a man they are ready to set you on the path to wherever you wish to go."

"You—you exaggerate."

"About holding you naked, or the reactions of my men? I assure you that in both cases I speak the absolute truth." He went to one knee beside the chair on which she sat and, reaching out his hand, trailed his fingers along her cheek and down the turn of her jaw to the hollow of her throat, then lower to where the valley between her breasts began. "It is a pity that we had to meet as we did, but I am not one to spurn a gift from the gods because of its wrappings. I am prepared to enjoy you for as long as the pleasure lasts, and to see that you do not lose by it."

His words, with their promise of payment, dropped like acid into her mind. He had done no more than confirm what she had suspected, but still, a fury such as she had never known rose up inside her. She flung off his hand, coming to her feet.

"So kind of you," she began, her voice brittle.

A soft knock sounded on the door. Rolfe had moved back, straightening to his full height as she rose. He took a step toward the door now, then hesitated. His gaze held hers, and in its vivid depths she thought she saw a flicker of something that might have been regret. Abruptly he swung, striding to the door, pulling it open.

Sarus stood outside. They held a low-voiced consultation, then the manservant stepped away. With his hand on the door, Rolfe looked to where Angeline stood.

"Dinner is served, Sarus tells me. There is a matter that requires my attention first. I will join you downstairs shortly." He started to turn away, then glanced back as if on an afterthought. "By the way, Claire's hiding place has been discovered. She will be in our hands before morning."

Angeline stood staring at the door long moments after it had closed upon his departure. She drew a deep, calming breath, pressing both hands to her chest. There was nothing she could do now. She would have liked to be alone, to forgo the meal that waited. If she did not appear, however, Rolfe might well return and carry out his threat; she would not put it past him. For the moment she had to do as he ordered, but it would not always be so.

Her hair was nearly dry. She brushed through it once more and, pushing it behind her back, let herself out of the room and moved toward the staircase.

She was frowning a little as she descended, her thoughts on what Rolfe had said, her lowered gaze on the oaken treads of the stairs and the baseboards along the wall of *faux bois*—literally false wood—painted artistically to look like marble. With her hand on the newel post at the bottom, she looked up. The front door stood ajar, as if someone had just entered in haste. Cool dampness seeped into the house through the opening and, almost without thought, she moved toward it, meaning to draw it shut. She put her hand on the handle, then paused, glancing out at the mist-shrouded night.

There was a saddled horse tied to the wrought-iron hitching post before the front steps. The mount moved restively, stamping. She stared at it with burning eyes, the urge to fling herself across the portal and down the steps, to throw herself into the saddle and race away like an ache inside her. Turning her head cautiously, she looked toward the great hall where the table was laid for dinner, shining with china and crystal and cutlery. No one was gathered there, nor did anyone recline upon the Egyptian settees before the low-burning fire. The others must be with Rolfe at the consultation he had spoken of, while Sarus was doubtless in the butler's pantry preparing the first course. Listening intently, she could just hear the rumble of voices coming from above her and the faint clink of dishes from beyond the great open room where they would dine. As incredible as it seemed, she was alone.

She slipped through the door, closing it with delicate quietness behind her, then moved on tiptoe across
the porch and down the stairs. Her fingers trembled so
that it was a moment before she could slip the knot
that held the reins to the hitching post. The horse was
a gelding with a silken white coat and wide, intelligent
eyes. She patted his neck with soothing whispers as
she backed him to the mounting block. Praying that
he had at some time in the past had experience with
women's skirts, she mounted to the block, stepped
into the stirrup, and eased upon his back. He snuffled,
turning his head to look back as if in polite inquiry,
but made no move to unseat her. Clucking softly, she
dug her heels into his side and turned him down the
drive at a slow walk.

The urge to kick the gelding into a gallop was near
overpowering, but she resisted it. The longer it was
before the alarm was raised, the better chance she
would have of escape. She was out of the house, with
a mount under her, but she had no illusions; she could
still be caught. She looked back over her shoulder at
the hunting lodge. Its windows glowed with candlelight, giving it an air of alert watchfulness, though
nothing moved at any of the softly shining rectangles.
Setting her teeth, Angeline faced forward, keeping to
the steady and quiet pace.

The relief when she was able to take up a canter
was enormous. Her chances were lengthening with
every yard she put between herself and the others.
They would have to saddle mounts to overtake her
and that would take precious moments. Even if they
were better horsemen with more reckless daring, their

chances of catching her were growing slimmer. The canter was a gait that the gelding could keep up for miles, and there were miles to go.

As she neared the de la Chaise plantation she was strongly tempted to turn in that direction. The sooner she reached people, someone to whom she could tell her story, someone who could help her, the better it would be. She thought of Claire at the convent school, perhaps making ready for bed, thinking herself safe. She must be warned. Angeline continued on past the de la Chaise mansion to the main road.

Once on this thoroughfare, headed in the right direction, she allowed the horse to have its head. In the darkness of the night clouded with mist from the river it was difficult to see the road, to keep to the ruts made by carriage wheels. The gallant white horse did so by instinct. The shadows of the trees flashed past faster and faster, whether because the horse sensed her disturbance or from the tightening of her grip upon the reins, she did not know. She allowed her thoughts to fly backward to the hunting lodge, wondering if she had been missed, wondering if Rolfe himself would ride after her, or if he would only send his men to overtake her.

Moments later, she thought she heard the sound of horses' hooves behind her, but with the pounding of her own flight, the rush of the wind against her and the thudding of her heartbeats in her ears, it was impossible to be sure. When it did not come again, she dismissed it as no more than an echo bouncing back from the thick, inward-pressing woods.

She was free, free of Rolfe, free to return to her aunt and resume the even tenor of her life. She had escaped, made fools of the precious cadre and the man who commanded it, slipping from under their noses with laughable ease. Triumph ran through her veins, merging with fierce joy. They had been misled by her lack of hysterics, her docility, her polite conversation. Perhaps they even thought that she had been happy to be Rolfe's kept woman. They must have thought that after her efforts to save him the previous night, there was no need to be so much on their guard. They had grown lax, and this was the result.

But then as the road wound away beneath her horse's hooves, a sense of unease crept in upon her. Rolfe had not thought her resigned; the taunts he had made, his attitude, the way he had studied her when he thought her unaware pointed up the exact opposite. His men might grow careless, but it was not in his character to do so. A leader could not afford that kind of mistake. And yet he had sent her downstairs alone when he must have known none of his men would be present, must have guessed Sarus would be busy with preparations for the evening meal.

She had been right. Her escape had been ridiculously easy. The empty hall, the open door, the horse standing saddled and ready; it was too easy, much too easy. She had escaped, she knew in a sudden flash of bitter recognition, because Rolfe had wanted her to do so, had in fact, with his cutting phrases and soft-voiced threats seen to it that she had every reason for trying to do it. To give her a more desperate motive, he had presented her with the news about Claire, knowing that she must, given the chance, try to warn her cousin that her place of refuge was safe no longer.

In the excitement of the lunge for freedom and the exercise of riding, Angeline had scarcely noticed the chill through the thin muslin she wore. Now she shivered in the fog-ridden night, feeling the mist clinging to her hair, molding her clothing against her, striking deep inside to pierce her heart with ice crystals.

Why? Why had she been allowed to leave the house? The answer to that was not hard. Rolfe and his men did not know where Claire was. The whole purpose, carefully crafted in the afternoon council, had been to arrange it so that she, Angeline, would lead them to her!

So absorbed was she in her thoughts, and so well concealed was the path to the convent, that she nearly passed it. Drawing rein, she sat for an instant, thinking furiously. If she was right, then Rolfe and the others would be close behind her, might have even sent out a scout from the main body to follow more closely, one who was watching her now. The last thing she wanted to do was to lead them to Claire then. The only other choice was the de Buys house and her aunt.

In the instant the decision was made, she kicked her horse into a run, heading for the opening to the path through the woods, barely seen between the trees. Her gallant mount took the ditch at a bound, scrambling up the bank, flashing onto the beaten trail with tree limbs whipping against his heaving sides.

It was madness, she knew. This way there were vines and reaching tree roots to trip the gelding, and limbs to knock her sprawling from the saddle. She would be lucky if she didn't break her mount's leg, her own neck, or both. Still, she was driven by the knowledge that she had stepped blissfully into Rolfe's trap. That she was doing exactly as he had planned, that he had outmaneuvered her once more while all the time she had thought she was making her escape, was so galling that it was unbearable. The possibility she might be wrong in her reading of events was scarcely considered. The design she could discern was so exactly like Rolfe that she did not question its truth. And if she needed confirmation, she had it, for behind her now could be heard the sound of horses ridden fast, a muffled pounding in the soft roadbed she had just left. Coming plainly, gaining fast, it was no echo.

Leaning low over her horse's neck, twisting one hand into his mane, Angeline urged the white gelding into a gallop. She spoke to him, scarcely knowing herself what she said, her straining gaze upon the dark shapes of the trees rushing toward her. She knew the way well, could have followed it blindfolded; she had that much advantage over the men behind her. They must follow more cautiously; moreover, they could not spread out to overtake her but would have to ride single file. If she could reach the house ahead of them, could raise her aunt or even the servants, then it was possible the prince might give up the chase. She would have liked to return quietly, without the servants' awareness, if it had been at all possible. Since it was not, she must do what she could to foil the man who had dared hold her prisoner.

Limbs lashed her sides as she plunged past them. Her hair caught on a tree branch and she was nearly jerked from the saddle, a fine, slender tress almost torn from its roots before it took the tip of the branch with it. The gelding's sides were heaving and clots of foam were blown back, spattering wetly onto her skirts. She spoke in low tones and he strained onward with flaring nostrils and flying hooves.

Then through the trees she caught a glimpse of light. It was the de Buys house standing foursquare in its gardens. There was a lightweight phaeton carriage standing before it, the blue paint gleaming in the light from the salon windows, but Angeline hardly noticed. She drew rein in a spray of the crushed oyster shells that covered the drive before the front door. Swinging her leg up over the horse's neck, she slid from the saddle, landing lightly on the ground. From the direction of the woods came a stream of riders, grimly silent, unchecking.

With her lips pressed together, Angeline flung them only a single glance before she picked up her skirts and ran headlong for the stairs to the gallery and the great fanlighted front door.

It was not the custom to lock the house until the family retired for bed. The bronze handle turned under her hand and the tall panel swung wide. There were voices coming from the salon to her left and she turned in that direction even as she heard hooves on the drive and an order rapped out in Rolfe's voice. From the back of the house shuffled the tall, white-haired Negro butler. His face lit with puzzlement as he saw her, then was engraved with scandalized horror as he noted the bedraggled gown she wore covered by a man's oversized tunic and the wild disarray of her unbound hair.

"Mam'zelle Angeline!"

"My aunt, where is she?"

"In the salon, Mam'zelle, but you cannot go in there, not like that. She has with her—"

Angeline did not stay to hear. She turned swiftly to the door leading to the salon and, pushing it open, stepped inside.

The room, designed expressly for receiving visitors, was softly luxurious with its cabriole-legged French furniture, velvet upholstery, and brocade hangings. There were gilt-framed mirrors topped by stylized flowers in gilded plaster, Watteau screens, and pastoral paintings in the Fragonard style around the walls, with bisque china bibelots, polished silver, and the wink of crystal ornaments upon the shining surfaces of the many small tables.

Her aunt was seated on a settee, dressed for dinner in a gown of ecru lutestring with a draped turban of ecru and black stripes on her head. She was deep in conversation with André Delacroix, who, darkly handsome in evening clothes, his mustache tilting upward with his polite smile, stood at the fireplace with one forearm propped on the marble mantel and an aperitif of ruby-red Burgundy in his hand.

Well-bred irritation for the unmannerly intrusion was etched on the features of Madame de Buys as she looked up. At the sight of her niece a ghastly pallor seeped over her features. "Angeline—" she said faintly.

"Angeline!" André came erect so quickly the wine sloshed from his glass, staining the marble hearth the color of blood.

There was no time for more. The prince and his men were at the front door, sending it crashing back on its hinges. The elderly butler could be heard remonstrating, and then Rolfe, at the head of the cadre, pushed through into the room behind Angeline. There was a cocked pistol in the hand of each man, purposeful weapons, the barrels steady and gaping as they were pointed at the people gathered in the room. Rolfe took in the scene with a single glance, then stepped to her, encircling her waist in a casually proprietary gesture. His hold may have appeared easy, but it had the bite of a steel band.

"Search the house." He rapped out the order, and saw Leopold and Oswald stride away to carry it out. Turning his attention to his hostess, then, he executed a bow totally lacking in both depth and respect. "Madame de Buys, I believe? I bid you good evening."

"What—what is the meaning of this?" the older woman demanded, rising slowly to her feet.

"A minor disturbance, soon over. Do not distress yourself."

"Do not—" Claire's mother caught herself, retreating into haughtiness. "I must know to what I owe the honor of this visit?"

"Surely you can guess, especially after the time your niece has spent in my company these last days."

André had not taken his dark gaze from Angeline. Now he turned to her aunt, his expression incredulous. "I thought you said Angeline was ill? Every time I came to ask after her you said—"

"A subterfuge entered into for her own sake, to protect her good name, a useless one it appears now."

"You mean," André said, color rising under his olive skin as he turned back to Rolfe, "that she has been with this man all the time?"

Rolfe smiled, his scathingly ironic words for André though his turquoise gaze rested upon the older woman: "Oh, against her will, I do assure you."

André snapped his head around to inquire of Madame de Buys, "And you did nothing?"

"You don't understand," she protested.

"Enlighten him," Rolfe suggested. "Tell him how you abandoned a tender young girl, leaving her to convince me of her innocence or make good her own escape—which she did this evening, wherefore this unexpected descent upon you." As Angeline made a small, abortive motion with the free hand not clamped against him, he reached to close his fingers upon her wrist, holding it tightly against her at the waist.

Madame de Buys, her bosom heaving and hatred in her dark eyes, remained silent. Overhead could be heard the tramp of booted feet as the upstairs rooms were searched. André stepped forward toward the prince.

"I must ask you to release Angeline."

"Even if I wanted to, which I don't, I would be forced to refuse," came Rolfe's answer.

"I insist!"

Rolfe sent him a straight glance. "You are an intelligent man, Delacroix, and a likable one. I understand your need to save the fair maiden, but you do not know what you are meddling in. I earnestly advise you to try the virtue of self-discipline."

There was in those soft words the lash-tipped flick of deadly reason. André's gaze moved to the pistol the prince held. His features tightened as if with resolve, and then came the sound of quick booted feet on the stairs and Leopold thrust back into the room.

"Nothing," he reported. "There is no one in the house except these two, the butler, and a ladies' maid we found upstairs."

"You have the servants?" Rolfe asked over his shoulder.

"In the hall. Oswald has them under guard."

Rolfe gave a nod. "Tie them up."

"How dare you?" Madame screeched. "This is my house, my servants! You can't—"

"I can." The Prince of Ruthenia swung toward André. "Forgive me, M'sieur Delacroix, but I must ask you to submit to bonds also. I regret the necessity, but your immobility for the next few hours is essential."

Before the words had left his mouth, Gustave had stepped to the window draperies and, to the accompaniment of Madame's screams, jerked free the tasseled cords that held them. Together with Meyer, he advanced upon the young Creole gentleman. A short and furious struggle ensued, but the issue was never in doubt. Within moments, André stood with his arms trussed behind him.

"This is monstrous, barbaric!" Madame de Buys shrieked in rising tones, flailing her fists and stamping her feet. "You are an animal, you picayune prince, a rapacious pig!"

"Madame," Rolfe said, "to quiet the squealing sow you slit her throat. The guinea hen who cackles the loudest is most likely to feel the axe at her neck. Do I make myself clear?"

The older woman was abruptly silent. She did not make a sound even when, at a nod from Rolfe, Gustave took her elbow and dragged her into the hall.

The first floor of the de Buys mansion, like so many others in the area, served as a raised basement, with all the main rooms of the house on the second floor for protection from flooding. The portion of the lower area that was closed in with *briquerte-entre-poteau,* bricks between posts, was used for the storage of foodstuffs and other supplies and, in one section, as a place of confinement for slaves recently arrived from Africa or the Caribbean, or for servants who awaited punishment for minor offenses. It was the butler who, with some encouragement at gunpoint, produced the keys to this place of incarceration and led them to it. He seemed to consider it preferable to be inside the dark damp room instead of outside with the prince's men. That Maria, Madame de Buys' maid, and André could not be expected to see it that way did not matter. Bound and gagged, they were pushed inside and the door locked and barred behind them.

There was some discussion then of making use of André's phaeton, but the idea was discarded. In the light of the lantern hanging in the entranceway, Rolfe gestured for Madame to allow herself to be put on the horse Angeline had ridden.

"What? You can't mean to take me?" the older woman cried, her small black eyes bulging from her head.

"Does the idea cause such terror? Surely not?"

"But I can be of no use to you!"

"That is as yet unproven. You will mount, now, or be tied over the saddle like a sack of potatoes brought to market."

In the end she was allowed to sit upright, but she was tied nonetheless, the rope that bound her wrists being passed under the belly of the horse and

the reins given as a lead to Gustave. Angeline was
handed up to Rolfe, sitting across his saddle bow.
He put his arms around her, enclosing her in the
warmth of his body. Feeling her shiver of reaction,
he cursed softly and stripped off his uniform coat,
wrapping it around her, ignoring her protests as
easily as her struggles.

Riding as if the invasion of homes and the kidnap-
ping of women was no more than an everyday
exercise, they swung the heads of their mounts back
toward the path that led through the woods, back
toward the hunting lodge.

The turban Madame de Buys wore was askew,
drooping over her eyes, when she was led into the
great hall. She pushed it back with a stiff gesture as
her arms were released. She was left to stand with
Angeline in the center of the floor before the dining
table. Rolfe and the others took seats behind the long
board, a piece of studied discourtesy that indicated the
suspension of ordinary rules of conduct.

Chairs scraped and male voices made a low
murmur. Sarus appeared to lean over the high back of
Rolfe's chair for a brief colloquy.

Madame de Buys sent Angeline a bitter glance.
"You are to blame for this, you ungrateful little
wretch. You led them straight to my home."

"I had gotten away from them finally. Where
else was I to go—unless to the convent school?"
Angeline's voice was soft but her gray-green eyes level
as she faced her aunt.

The older woman threw a quick look at Rolfe,
hissing, "Silence, *grisette*! Dare to speak of that place,

even to hint of it, and you will never pass through the doors of my house again!"

"I have kept the secret these last long days."

"*Oui*, when I think of you here with these men I am shocked. It is a good thing you were never betrothed to André Delacroix, for you are obviously not worthy of his attention!"

"May I offer you ladies a glass of wine to soothe your nerves?" Rolfe's sharp-edged words sliced across their private quarrel with the effectiveness of a well-honed knife. "No? Then you will not object if we indulge, along with our soup. Riding at night always affects the appetite, I find." Without pausing, he went on, indicating the chair at his right hand. "Angeline, my sweet, your place is here."

He rose to hold her chair, seating her as she moved with tightly held composure to the place he required her to be. It was only as she dropped onto the chair that she realized that her legs were trembling; the effect, she told herself stoutly, of the long ride to the de Buys house and back again.

As he resumed his place at the head of the board, Rolfe reached to close his warm fingers around her hand where it lay on the cloth. A slight frown flitted across his features as he felt the tremors that shook her. Sarus, entering with the soup plates then, was directed with a brusque gesture to serve her first, and Rolfe did not move or speak until he had seen her take a spoonful of the hot, reviving broth.

It was as well to be fortified, Angeline told herself, though it was difficult to force the soup past the tightness in her throat. If Rolfe had been made aware of

her frailty in that brief touch, then she had also sensed
the tension that vibrated through him. What he meant
to do, she did not know, but she could not prevent
stomach-churning apprehension. He was capable of
anything, anything at all, and now that her abduction,
and that of her aunt, was known, the time he had in
which to act was limited.

Her temper exacerbated by the treatment being
meted out to her, Madame de Buys drew herself up.
"I demand to know the meaning of this outrage. I
demand to know why I have been cruelly taken from
my home and brought here?"

Rolfe spooned his soup and drank a swallow of wine
before he answered. "I think, Madame, that you know
well enough why you are here. Nonetheless, I will
indulge you. We—my men and I—require to know
the whereabouts of your daughter, Claire de Buys."

"That is easily answered, Your Highness," came
the reply, a sneer in the woman's use of the respectful
term of address. "She is presently enjoying a visit with
relatives in France."

"No. Try again."

"I assure you—"

"Don't! Your desire to protect the child of your
body is natural, but unnecessary. I desire nothing of
her except a few minutes' conversation. Why that
should be a matter for such terror I am at a loss to
understand, but so it seems. I have followed her from
Europe to your doorstep for that purpose, Madame,
and I will not be balked."

In an attempt to match the biting force of his tone,
the older woman said, "You have my sympathy, Your

Highness, but I cannot whisk her here from France for you."

Rolfe leaned forward. "You may take me for a villain with my compliments, but do not make the mistake of thinking me a fool. You know, as do I, that she is not in France. You know where she is at this moment. If you value your dignity and a painless existence, you will speak. Now."

Madame de Buys studied him uneasily. "You would not harm me. André Delacroix knows it was you who took me from my home, knows that you have held my niece a prisoner for some days now. He will arouse the countryside to bring rescue!"

"Are you sure? Since you did not do as much in his place? Even so, he must first rescue himself, which will take time, more than enough time."

Angeline, no longer the center of Rolfe's attention, put down her spoon. He was right, she knew. It might be hours before the cook and the serving maid in the outdoor kitchen began to wonder why the butler did not come to tell them to commence serving dinner. More time still might pass before André, Maria, and the butler were found and released. It must happen eventually, and the results would undoubtedly be as Tante Berthe said, but the older woman could not depend upon it to keep her safe.

Angeline tried to catch her aunt's eyes, to signal caution, but the other woman would pay no heed. Her black gaze flashing with the strength of her conviction she said, "André will come, and you will be extremely sorry when he arrives. This is not Ruthenia, nor is it Europe where a nobleman may do as he pleases. You will find that here in Louisiana one may not lay hands upon a woman with impunity. Even if she is without a husband or close male relative, her friends and neighbors will avenge the insult, and your rank will be no protection!"

"Possibly. But long before then you will be stripped naked, Madame, and paraded before us hung with bells, bugles, and billows of flesh. Pricking with a sword should insure a dance for our amusement, macabre but of a certain obscene titillation. Will you be disappointed if it arouses no passion, only mirth?"

"You—you could not carry out such a threat. Angeline has been with you for days and has not the look of one so used."

"Do not be deceived," Rolfe said, his voice quiet, his eyes narrow and darkly blue. "She has suffered irreparable injury, the worst that may befall a young woman—and endured it in a spirit of grace and without hope of succor for endless hours while you, Madame, made no attempt to provide rescue, did not even make the effort to see her, though you must have guessed soon enough where she was. Certainly you did not come to plead that she be returned to your loving arms inviolate. You abandoned her to my tender mercy and sat at home rigged out in silk and perfumed lace receiving callers and pretending she was safe in her bed while she was imperiled in mine."

The rice powder on the older woman's face stood out yellow against the gray of her skin, but still she lifted a plump shoulder in a shrug. "For one who has been so ill used, she hides it well."

There was a growl from the men at the table at the snideness of that remark, but Rolfe's voice overrode it without effort. "Because she has a heart stalwart beyond your comprehension, and stubborn beyond mine."

"Still, she has no look of having been savaged," Madame de Buys insisted, studying her niece.

"Does that salve your conscience? The bruises are on the soul, a site, in my ignorance, I thought more suitable. A regrettable error. Shall I correct it now and disfigure her for you? Is that what you require?"

Angeline felt suffused with heat. Along the table there was stillness as the men glanced uneasily from Rolfe to Madame de Buys. Sarus was removing the soup plates, setting the entrée of roasted beef before the men. Gustave picked up his fork but only sat with pursed lips, watching Rolfe. Oscar frowned, his splinted wrist resting on the table edge.

"You are mad! I—I don't wish to see her hurt, but I cannot prevent it now any more than I could have prevented what has happened if I had come here earlier."

"Or than anyone can prevent what will be done to you in the next few minutes? Think carefully. Angeline, being young and beautiful and in possession of irresistible, innocent allure, required different handling from you, Madame, who can claim not one of those virtues."

Angeline's aunt shook her head, clasping her hands before her. "You cannot expect me, Claire's own mother, to betray her to you. You must do what you will. I can tell you nothing."

"By your own words you admit you know where she is," Rolfe charged.

"I admit nothing. I will tell you nothing!"

Watching her aunt, Angeline was touched by her bravado.

The older woman was afraid now, but was striving to hide it. And for all Tante Berthe's neglect of her niece, her love for Claire and her need to protect her could not have been more obvious. Angeline slanted a glance to Rolfe and found him watching her, his expression shielded by his lashes though there was a double line between his brows and tightness about his mouth.

Deliberately he picked up his glass of wine and drank before he turned back to the older woman. "You are quite right, Madame. It was wrong to expect you to reveal your daughter's hiding place. I gave you undue importance, I fear. Henceforth, you are no more than a pawn, a piece to be moved here and there, one of little worth, easily expendable. From this moment you will not be able to stop what will be done to you, no matter what you say, no matter how you plead. I will pay no heed to you, not even if you beg me to hear you, if you swear in the name of the Virgin and your husband's departed soul that you will speak the truth."

"You—you mean I can go?" Angeline's aunt took a stumbling step toward the table.

"Did I say so? Then do not assume it. No, the information I seek will come from another, one who will sit and watch your humiliation and pain knowing only she can stop it."

Angeline, watching Rolfe, had seen it coming from the moment he began to speak. She sprang to her feet in such a rush that she brushed the table edge, making the dishes rattle.

"No!"

"Yes." His hand flashed out to catch her wrist, forcing her back into her chair.

"You must not do this, not this way."

He only stared at her, his turquoise eyes opaque with the strength of his will.

"Angeline will not tell you what you wish to know. She won't!" Tante Berthe declared, her black gaze anxious as it clung to her niece's face. "What is done to me doesn't matter."

"Shall we see?"

The question was pleasant, and yet it carried an undertone of such limitless menace that Angeline was chilled to the core. She licked dry lips, her mind trying to come to grips with the terrible choice being forced upon her. She could save her aunt or her cousin, not both. Her voice a thread of sound, she said, "Rolfe, please. Don't do this."

"Give me an alternative, and I will salute your feet with kisses while the *garde du corps* sings hosannas." He waited while the seconds ticked slowly past.

She had no answer to give him. Her mind was in chaos, torn with conflicting duties, swept by a peculiar grief. As she stared at the man beside her there was accusation and pain in her gray-green eyes, overlaid by dread.

He released her arm abruptly, as if withdrawing from her, retreating into the fastness of his place as leader. Pushing back his untouched plate, he said, "Oswald, Leopold, Meyer, you are the chosen ones."

The men named glanced at each other, then came smoothly to their feet. Walking around the table, they stood on either side of the woman in the center of the room. Madame de Buys looked at them as they approached, searching their impassive faces, but she could find no relenting there. Licking her lips, she glanced at Angeline, shrinking a little as the uniformed men stopped on either side of her. Between them she seemed much less formidable, less authoritative, and altogether less assured than Angeline had ever seen her.

Rolfe made a flicking movement of his fingers and Oswald, a tight grin on his face that seemed to cover a basic revulsion, stepped before Angeline's aunt, lifting his hand to the turban on her graying black hair. She struck out at him almost in a reflex action. Her arms were immediately gripped and held by the men at her sides. The long pin that held the folds of black-and-ecru-striped material was pulled free and the turban dropped carelessly to the floor. Bracelets were removed from her plump wrists and rings twisted with difficulty from her fingers. Going to one knee, Leopold next lifted her feet one after the other, removing her slippers with their inward curved heels, rolling the gartered stockings from her strutted calves. Rising, he looked to Rolfe and, receiving a nod, stepped around behind the woman, reaching for the long row of small buttons that held her gown at the back.

Madame de Buys gave a low gasp, as if until that moment she had been holding her breath, as if only then could she bring herself to believe what was happening. The fire in the hearth crackled, sending out a shower of orange sparks. Gustave put down his knife and fork as if in sudden loss of appetite. Oscar crumpled a chunk of bread, his hazel gaze on his plate.

Angeline thought of Claire as she had last seen her, beautiful in her bitter pride, disdainful of the accommodations provided for her, yet accepting them out of fear, a consuming, scarcely contained terror of Rolfe of Ruthenia. She had been right to be afraid. Hadn't the treatment Angeline had received at his hands proven that, wasn't it being proved yet again at this moment?

She swung toward Rolfe. "How—how can you expect me to lead you to Claire when everything you have done, everything you are doing, only shows the treatment that will be meted out to her?"

Madame twisted against the hold of the men who held her, her breath rasping. "No, chère, you must not weaken."

Rolfe sent her the briefest of glances. "Shall I swear? But upon what? What will it take to satisfy you?"

The bodice of Madame's gown was loosening, falling forward as Oswald worked at the buttons. A moment more and the full pouffed sleeves were pushed down along her arms and over her wrists and, as the men transferred their hold from one hand to the other, the garment was allowed to fall in a heap around her feet. She stood revealed in a knee-length chemise with whalebone stays fastened over her ribs, compressing her shape like a sausage casing, pushing the full, overblown flesh of her breasts upward, allowing her hips to swell beneath. The pumping of her heart could be plainly seen in the trembling blancmange of her bosom above the low-cut chemise.

"You—you could swear upon the Bible," Angeline said hurriedly, "but I think there is something you revere as much, if not more. Swear then upon the honor of your *garde du corps* that you will not harm my cousin, that you will do no more than question her about your brother, as you have said."

"No!" Madame shouted, wrenching forward. "You little fool, you cannot bargain with Claire's safety. You cannot do this to her, you cannot!"

Angeline hesitated. Rolfe was still for the space of a heartbeat, then, reaching across the table, he picked up the carving knife that lay on the platter of beef and tossed it, spinning in the air, toward Madame de Buys. It was not a well-balanced instrument with its heavy ivory handle. It spun crazily, the blade flashing in an arc toward the woman's throat. Angeline gave a sharp cry as it looked as if it must bury itself in her aunt's soft flesh.

Oswald leaned forward, reaching in front of the older woman to snatch the knife from the air. He held it for an instant before her wide, staring eyes, then, stepping behind her once more, deliberately applied the blade to the tightly tied crisscross lacing of her stays. They parted with an explosive, snapping sound, like popping corn over the fire. Madame de Buys screamed, falling to her knees as the whalebone stays dropped away from her, sagging with all the boneless overabundance of her released flesh to the floor. As she was dragged to her feet once more, her features were ashen and her lips trembled.

Angeline gripped the edge of the table with both hands, her hold so tight that the ends of her fingers were without sensation. In horrified fascination, she watched as Oswald, his movements jerky, moved around in front of her aunt and, reaching for the neckline of her chemise, sliced at the embroidered white on white, semi-transparent batiste. The sound of ripping cloth was loud as blowsy skin was exposed.

"Wait," Angeline whispered, then forced strength into the word. "Wait."

Rolfe turned to her then, his blue gaze frank and without evasion. "I do hereby declare that Claire de Buys will receive no injury from my hands, that regardless of provocation and the promptings of vengeance, she will remain clothed in her damaged chastity and enwrapped in all her snobbish pretense. She shall be safe, providing only that she does not attempt a defense of deceit. This I swear on my honor, which is also that of the guard."

"And will you hold to it," Angeline asked, daring because the price of overlooking such a point might be high, "even if what you are told is not to your liking?"

"Even so."

What choice did she have except to believe him, to trust to a vagrant instinct and the hypnotic and steady brilliance of his gaze? Angeline drew a deep breath. "She is at the Convent School of Our Sisters."

Ten

"No! My daughter isn't at the school, she isn't! You can't disturb the good sisters at this hour. It would be sacrilege, and for nothing, nothing, I tell you!"

Madame de Buys might as well have kept her tirade to herself for all the attention Rolfe paid. As he had promised, he gave no credence to her protests. He did not appear to hear even as the woman screamed that Angeline was sending them on a wild goose chase. Within minutes after Angeline had spoken, the cadre was mounted and ready to ride.

It must have occurred to their leader that they might have need of a hostage for at the last moment he directed that Angeline and the older woman were to come with them. While Sarus searched out cloaks for them both, a mount was saddled for Angeline and led around to the front. Rolfe did not trust Angeline to keep with them by choice, however. Tossing the lead rein of Madame de Buys' horse to Gustave again, he took that of Angeline's mount in his own gloved hand.

The blue-gray of early dawn was spreading over the treetops as they rode up to the front gate of the tall, solid split-pole fence that fronted the convent school. The small building was engulfed in the deepest sleep of the night. In a quiet voice, Rolfe gave the order that sent Oswald and Gustave to the rear of the house to watch the back door. Dismounting, Leopold hammered on the gate with the hilt of his sword. After what seemed hours, they saw the faint, moving glow of a pierced lantern approaching. A querulous voice called from the other side of the gate, demanding to know who was without and the nature of their business.

"His Royal Highness, the Prince of Ruthenia to see the Mother Superior!"

"Mother Theresa is at her prayers and may not be disturbed," came the answer.

"It is a matter of greatest urgency."

"She will see no one. Come back in the morning at a decent hour, after sunrise."

"It cannot wait so long," Leopold declared, his face tightening. "I warn you, old woman, if you do not want to be put to the expense of another gate for this dilapidated fence—"

"Sister Marthe, if you please, it is I, Angeline Fortin," Angeline called, lifting her voice in an attempt to drown out Leopold's threat. "Will you let me in? I assure you it is important that we speak to Mother Theresa."

There was a long hesitation during which Angeline had ample time to wonder what had prompted her to help the cadre gain entrance to the convent. It was not that she wanted to smooth their way; had she wanted to do that she would have taken them to the rear entrance where they might have had direct, unofficial access to the Mother Superior. No, it was only that she did not wish violence to be used against these scared precincts and the women living inside who had befriended her as a young girl.

"Angeline, is that you indeed?" At her affirmation, the nun who kept the portal grumbled under her breath as she slid aside the great wooden bar that held the gate shut. "What are you doing with these persons? Can you stand surety for them?"

Rolfe swung down from his horse and lifted his hands to Angeline's waist, helping her down. Meyer did the same for Madame de Buys, now grimly silent, and Oscar, after dismounting, saw the horses were secured to the long hitching post. They moved toward the gate then. Rolfe, with one hand flattened against the rustic planks, pushed it wider for their entrance, forcing the elderly nun to retreat a step.

"Your pardon, Sister Marthe," he said, inclining his golden head in a bow. He gave her a smile whose warmth seemed to stun the elderly *religieuse*.

Sister Marthe gave way without a murmur. They mounted the steps to the front door that stood open and, stepping through, spread out.

From that point on, it was a military operation. Sister Marthe's lantern was commandeered, another was brought from somewhere. Gustave and Oswald were called in from the back, and while Angeline and Madame de Buys stood with Rolfe and Sister Marthe, in the central entrance hall, the guard divided into two groups and instigated a room-by-room search. No trunk lid was left unraised, no armoire unopened, no curtain unshaken. They reconnoitered the small, severe salon where pupils were allowed to visit with parents and friends, the dining room with its long table of bare wood and its hard, backless benches, the schoolrooms smelling of foolscap, charcoal, and old leather-bound books, the storerooms with their herbs hanging to dry, eggs packed in rendered lard, and bolts of cloth for the making of uniforms and habits. They even searched the small room used as a chapel, with its makeshift altar and crucifix of marvelously carved Bavarian oak.

By the time they came to the dormitory room, the long chamber lined with narrow virginal beds, the young girls living in as pupils were stirring. A few lay still in petrified fright, while others scrambled to stand on their beds or leaped this way and that with the lantern light shining through their nightgowns, shattering the night with their excited squeals and screams. It was impossible to tell from the noise whether the invasion of their chaste quarters by handsome men in uniform was the most devastating experience of their lives or the most thrilling.

"What is the meaning of this?"

The question, resonant with authority, came from Mother Theresa as she emerged from her chamber at the back of the house. Her habit without a crease, her wimple starched so stiff that it cut into her forehead, she came forward with a marching step, singling Rolfe out for her gimlet stare.

"Forgive the intrusion," he said, bowing. "It is regrettable, but necessary."

"That I cannot believe," Mother Theresa answered, her armor undented by his smile.

At that moment the two groups of men converged on the entrance hall, having completed their searches. Their lack of a prisoner, their impassive stares, told plainly of their failure. The Mother Superior glanced at them in immense and smoldering disapproval, at the same time dismissing the scantily clad girls who had ventured to leave their beds to trail behind the men. When the sound of their scampering feet had died away, she turned back to Rolfe, waiting in impressive silence for an explanation.

"My men and I are looking for a woman, Claire de Buys, who has information concerning the death of my brother. We have reason to believe that she is with you."

"And it was necessary," the Mother Superior said, lacing the last word with irony, "to descend upon us in the middle of the night to discover if your informant was correct?"

It was seldom that Angeline had felt the weight of Mother Theresa's displeasure, and though the elderly *religieuse* did not so much as glance her way, she was aware of it now. She would have liked to explain how she had come to lead these men here, to exonerate herself, but this was not the time.

"There was the danger that this woman would take fright and attempt to flee." The patience that threaded Rolfe's voice was unusual.

"I can, perhaps, understand your eagerness, but not your method of coming up with her. A simple request would have sufficed."

Rolfe lifted a brow, quickly seizing on the most important word. "Would have?"

"Indeed." The Mother Superior inclined her head. "She is no longer with us."

"I told you she wasn't here," Madame de Buys said in vindictive triumph. She started to laugh, gratingly, but stopped as Oswald stepped to her shoulder.

"She was here?" Rolfe insisted when there was quiet once more.

"She spent three days with us, until there arrived yesterday morning a message brought, I believe, by her mother's maid, Maria. I have no way of knowing what it contained, but as soon as it was dark yesterday evening a traveling carriage came for Mademoiselle de Buys. She entered it without a word of good-bye or, I might add, of gratitude for her stay with us before she was driven away."

"In which direction?" A frown drew the dark-gold brows of the prince together as he waited for the answer.

"I did not stay to watch. Sister Marthe?"

"North, Mother Theresa," the other nun answered.

It was obvious why Madame de Buys had tried to delay their arrival at the convent school, even knowing her daughter had gone. Traveling north by carriage, unaware that her whereabouts had been discovered or her flight made known, she would not be able to cover ground nearly as quickly as the cadre could on horseback. By her stubbornness, her risk of humiliation, Claire's mother had forced Rolfe to lose several hours and perhaps made it impossible for him to catch up with Claire.

"It appears," Rolfe said slowly, "that we must again turn centaur. I wonder what may be the female equivalent?"

Stepping toward the door as he spoke, he turned to catch Angeline's arm.

"One moment," the Mother Superior said. Her narrowed gaze was on the opening of Angeline's cloak where it fell away to reveal the crumpled and stained muslin of her gown, the same gown she had been wearing when she was at the convent school the night she brought Claire. She looked at her hair, falling around her in a wild tangle of auburn-brown silk. As Mother Theresa lifted her gaze to Angeline's gray-green eyes, her own mirrored shocked suspicion. Looking then to Rolfe she said, "I must ask you to leave this young woman here with me."

The men of the cadre, already beginning to move, halted, staring from Rolfe to the Mother Superior. Sister Marthe held her breath while Madame de Buys brought her head up as if the show of concern was an insult. Rolfe allowed his gaze to flicker over Angeline, remaining a moment on the gentle curves of her parted lips.

"It pains me to disappoint you, but such is the fabric of your life, is it not? If you must snatch a brand from the burning, however, I give you freely the other lady with me, Madame de Buys, along with the hope that you do not find cause to regret the impulse."

They turned then, sweeping from the convent school. Behind them Madame de Buys could be heard screeching, "Let her go! It's what she wants! Let her go with her picayune prince. I wish her joy of him, the little slut!"

Those last words followed Angeline, ringing in her mind as she rode with the guard. They seemed to strike deep into some close-held part of herself, taking with them an inevitable truth. She had made no demur, no protest, not the slightest twitch of resistance as she was escorted from the convent school to her horse. It was possible then that the description was accurate; she was immoral. She might not prefer to be with Rolfe himself, but there was no place else where she was so accepted as among the cadre.

She seemed in some way, perhaps because of the wrong Tante Berthe had done her, to have earned her relative's hate. It had not been soothed by her part in setting Rolfe on Claire's trail. The shocked disapproval of the nuns, their condemnation for her apparent behavior would have been unbearable, even if she had been able to stay. Mother Theresa might have been sympathetic, but she could not be expected to understand. As for the others, it was doubtful they would try, unlikely they would be resigned to having one who had survived so depraved an experience living in close contact with the innocent convent pupils. Their attitudes would be reflected in the community, of course; it could be no other way as soon as the tale was spread. Surrounded on all sides by scorn and tittering pity, why should she not feel an odd relief, even wry gratitude that Rolfe intended to keep her with him?

And yet there could be no future in it. The chase would end, Claire would be caught, and the needed information would be extracted from her. There would be nothing else to keep the cadre in Louisiana, nothing to prevent their return to the splendor and decadence of Europe. She could not hope that Rolfe would wish her to travel there with him, nor in all truth should she. She was going to have to learn to make her own way. There must be some way she could do that without sacrificing her honor and soul. There must.

They traveled rapidly along the bayou road, their hoofbeats pounding the soft, alluvial soil, the wind in their faces. Angeline rode in the center of the group of men, a part of their close-knit cavalcade. Her hair flew around her and her cloak fluttered, the collar slapping against her face. The increasing light, gray now with the moon only a ghostly shadow in the west, showed Rolfe at her right side, his attention on the road ahead. Gustave rode on her left, with Meyer and Leopold directly behind and the twins bringing up the rear. No one spoke, no one questioned where they were going or what they were going to do to push their exhausted mounts onward along Claire's slowly cooling trail. If they were tired after their active night or hungry because of their sketchy meal, no one spoke of it. It was enough that they were riding; the man who led them would take care of the rest.

Angeline glanced at Rolfe, wondering at the weight of responsibility that rested upon him. He seemed to accept it as a matter of course, scarcely feeling its press. He frowned a little as he rode, as if considering alternatives. Sensing her gaze, he turned his head to stare at her and a smile flitted across his chiseled mouth. He surveyed the pale oval of her face with its expression of doubt and puzzlement overlaid by fatigue. Sobering, he looked away once more.

They did not hear the posse of men that came hurtling toward them around a curve. One moment the road was clear and dew-silvered, the next it was filled from edge to edge with hard-faced men. In that first flustered moment of surprise, Angeline recognized the friends and neighbors of her aunt, and also the hatless, dark-haired young man who rode at their head. It was André.

"There they are! It's them!"

There came the chilling slither and scrape of drawn swords. Pistols were dragged out. A shot crashed and a man yelled, as much in anger as in pain. The two groups of horsemen clashed, coming together with the thudding impact of fighting bulls. Steel clanged, grating with blue fire and a shower of orange sparks. Men grunted and cursed. Horses whinnied, curvetting in alarm as they were jostled this way and that. The numbers were evenly matched, though if André and the others had reached St. Martinville where they were bound the size of the group of men would have been greater.

"*Sacre bleu*," a balding neighbor grunted, "they fight like fiends, these strangers!"

Then André came thrusting toward Angeline with his sword uplifted and an expression of absorbed determination on his face. Rolfe, swinging, engaged him.

"Ah, Your Highness," André said, parrying in breathless haste. "You are surprised to see us so soon, I think."

"Some busybody came to call, I presume?"

"The cook's son, an inquisitive lad, sent to see why dinner was delayed, heard our knocking."

"I felicitate you on your good fortune." Rolfe's swordplay was leisurely, though intent.

"It appears better than yours, does it not? But what have you done with Madame de Buys?"

"Done? Do you see her bedraggled in a ditch? No, no, though it might have been a fine thing. She was left at the convent shouting maledictions, though whether damning us for her deliverance unscathed or the little she had suffered I cannot begin to guess."

It seemed to Angeline that as they stood in their stirrups, lunging and retreating, there were several times when with a little more effort, a bit more extension, Rolfe might have injured André, ending the fight. It was as if he waited for the opportunity, instead, to disarm him without hurt. The same might have been said for the other members of the cadre as, forming a phalanx with Angeline in the middle, they fought off their attackers.

The men shifted, and Rolfe was being pressed on three sides. With his attention diverted for an instant, André disengaged, pushing through toward Angeline. He snatched her rein from Rolfe's hand. At that sudden jerk, her horse reared, plunging, then reared again. With no reins to hold on to, no pommel on the English saddle, Angeline gripped with her knees, leaning forward with her hands twisted in the horse's silver mane.

And then she was jostled from the side. Her knee was wedged between her own mount and that of the man next to her. Pain shafted through her leg, doubling as she felt a blow to the kneecap. Her horse, close pressed, unable to move, staggered. She felt herself slip, then she was falling, sliding down among the churning hooves. A cry rose to her throat and was caught there in a strangled rasp. Pain exploded in a blue-black flare along the side of her head, and darkness reached out, cushioned and enfolding, to catch her.

Angeline grew slowly aware of a rocking motion. The ache in her head pulsed with the movement. Illness shifted inside her and she swallowed hard against it. Pain rippled along her temple as something smoothed over it. It was a hand, warm and firm, brushing her hair back from her face and the sore spot on the side of her head, though in her sensitive state it was as if the strands of her hair were being tugged out one by one. She frowned, turning her head aside with an irritable murmur.

"Your beauty remains unimpaired," came a well-remembered drawl from above her, "though I can't say as much for your temper."

She realized she was being held in strong arms whose comfort contrasted with the goading words with which Rolfe greeted her. Her fanlike lashes fluttered open and she met his bright turquoise gaze, saw she was lying across his lap, close against his chest and covered by a fur lap robe, while he was wedged into the corner of a carriage seat. Lined with maroon velvet and fitted with carved rosewood door panels, the vehicle was rumbling down the road at considerable speed, if the trees lashing past the window were any indication.

Angeline closed her eyes again. "What happened? How did I get here?"

"Fortunate girl to have slept through the entire tedious business. Do you really not remember?"

"No."

There was a trace of laughter in his voice as he answered. "I picked you up when you fell and gave you into the charge of Gustave and Oscar. They were sent on ahead while the rest of us stayed behind to fight a rearguard retreat against opponents the like of which I have never seen for sheer clumsy zeal and useless bravery. Jousting with gentlemen farmers and their sons, all spleen and no finesse, is not my idea of sport."

"I'm sorry you were not suitably matched. Did you leave them lying bloodied on the field?"

"There were a few skewered shoulders and wounds that will give one or two interesting limps at the next ball, but nothing serious. The elders in the group bethought themselves of the better part of valor and their future grandchildren and allowed us the space to make good our escape without greater carnage."

His lack of heat, or notice of the sneer she had uttered so recklessly, sent a flicker of remorse through her. "It… was good of you to take the time to see after me."

"Not good—imperative. Without you to shatter my pretension, where would I be?"

"Farther along the road after Claire, I don't doubt."

"No, no. You must not fret yourself that you are holding us up. Gustave chose your chariot with an excellent eye. It is lightweight and able to travel very nearly as fast as we can ride."

"I meant that if you had not troubled with me in the beginning—"

"Dear Angeline," he said, his voice silken with suppressed amusement, "it was no trouble, I assure you."

Her lips tightened, though her eyelids remained obstinately shut. "I see your clash with Madame de Buys' neighbors did nothing at all to teach you humility—or even common courtesy."

"No. Why should it? They came at the behest of your suitor, André Delacroix, and if you think he was concerned for the overblown charms of your aunt, then it is you who need a lesson not in humbleness, but in how to overcome it!"

"André—was he—"

"Enraged and wrestling with a half-dozen wiser heads who sought to restrain him from following after us, the last I saw. Quite unharmed."

Unconsciously she let her breath out in a small sigh. "I'm glad."

"I am aware, though had I known you would be so much affected I would have caught him up by the scruff of his neck also and brought him along for your entertainment. I have never been involved in a *ménage à trois*, but I have it on the best authority that the arrangement can be diverting."

He was at his most outrageous, she had discovered, when he was disturbed, though his voice was light, holding nothing of stiffness. "A diversion? And I thought your preferred restorative was anger—that and brandy. I'm surprised you haven't forced strong drink down my throat."

"Unconscious females are in no case to savor fine spirits, but I was about to send for burnt feathers to awake you from your swoon."

"Swoon?" she uttered in accents of loathing, opening her eyes. "It was more than that!"

"Was it?"

"You know very well it was!" Why he should make light of it, she had no idea, unless to discourage her from playing the invalid—something she had no intention of doing.

"Do you doubt my ability as a learned physician?"

"Only your knowledge, and your disinclination to allow me some small weakness, such as fainting when I am knocked on the head." Her gray-green eyes were dark as she glanced away from him. At the sight of the bouncing carriage windows and dipping, dancing trees outside, sickness rose inside her and she hurriedly closed her eyes again, raising a hand to her mouth.

"Shall I stop the carriage?" he asked, his voice abrupt.

She shook her head and immediately wished she had not as pain clanged through it.

"Perhaps it was a mistake to revive you just yet. You have a mild concussion. It should not be dangerous, but of course this method of travel is not the best treatment."

She forced her eyes open to tiny slits. The expression on his bronze features was pensive. It crossed her mind that he might be contemplating sending her back to her aunt. "I—I will be all right."

"Will you?" he asked, his mouth quirking in something not quite a smile.

"I... think so, yes."

"I had sleeping powders, efficacious and quick, in my baggage. Unfortunately, there was no time to alert Sarus to pack and come with us. Everything is still at the hunting lodge. It will have to remain there until we stop long enough to send a message and allow

Sarus to catch up with us, since I doubt we will be returning by the same route. It may be possible to procure something similar when next we draw up long enough to find fresh horses."

"That may be a problem," Angeline murmured.

"Yes, so we have discovered. There is scarce a decent posting house in this entire wilderness. What do people who travel the roads do?"

"They go in easy stages, not at this breakneck pace," Angeline said with a gasp as the carriage wheel dropped into a hole and she was flung forward before Rolfe could snatch her back. When he held her steady once more she went on. "Other travelers, for fresh animals, depend on the cooperation of their hosts, the people who own farms and plantations along the road and who provide hospitality for the night to all who come."

"I suppose," Rolfe mused, "that unless a man owns a plantation in this wilderness, he has little reason to venture into it. There is greater cause to go in the opposite direction, toward St. Martinville and New Orleans."

"The wilderness? That is the second time you have mentioned it."

"So it appears to me," he answered, his clothing rustling as he turned toward the window where the close-packed, leafless limbs unwound past the carriage without a break. "We are heading toward a community with a name I understand comes from some Indian tongue, Natchitoches—"

"An Indian tribe, actually. It's an old town, a French fort at one time and quite civilized."

"I am delighted to hear it."

"Why Natchitoches?"

"Your cousin's driver was heard to inquire the way there."

The town of Natchitoches had a certain refinement, with several sizable plantations in the vicinity, but the roads leading to it and the territory surrounding it were sparsely populated. During the more than one hundred years it had been in existence, the principal method of travel to and from the town had been the waterways, up the Mississippi River to its confluence with the Red River, and then to the town that sat on the banks of the latter. Only in the last decade or so had an overland route been established, the one they were taking. Madame de Buys had relatives there, though it was a sign of Claire's desperation that she would take refuge with them. If she considered St. Martinville a backwater, then Natchitoches would by comparison seem the end of the world, a dead-water slough stagnant and without amenities.

There was an element of danger in reaching this place toward which they were fast traveling. It had recently become the frontier of the country as settlers from the southeastern seaboard used it as a jumping-off place for the wide open lands of Spanish Texas. It teemed with the lawlessness and rough way of life usual to that forward-spreading edge of expansion. But it was also at the heart of a large section of neutral territory known as No Man's Land. Measuring some five hundred thousand square miles and lying along the Sabine River in the southwestern corner of the state, it had since 1806, some fourteen years earlier, been claimed by both the United States and Spain. To avoid clashes between the two countries that might lead to wholesale war, neither exercised legal jurisdiction over the narrow strip of land, nor was it patrolled by the soldiery of either country, as were the lands on each side. As a result, it had become the haven of thieves and murderers, the outlaws of both countries, preying upon the surrounding countryside and the westward-moving settlers. It was also used indiscriminately for any number of clandestine activities, among them the illegal importation of slaves and other contraband, some said by the now middle-aged pirate and hero of the Battle of New Orleans, Jean Lafitte. There were rumors too of gatherings of men bent on starting a filibuster campaign to take Texas from Spain, making it a part of the United States.

All in all, it was not a safe stretch of land to cross. Any man who dared enter there did so at his own risk; there were any number who had disappeared into the district never to be seen again. A woman who trespassed needed armed protection, no matter how old or ugly; for Claire to journey in that direction virtually alone was foolhardy in the extreme. It was to be hoped that long before she got that far Rolfe and his men would overtake her.

Angeline would have liked to convey something of the situation to Rolfe, but his grim silence suggested that with his usual thoroughness he was in possession of the facts already. There seemed nothing, then, to say. In any case, she could find no will to make the effort.

She lay still with her cheek resting against his chest, feeling its steady rise and fall, the regular thud of his heartbeats, and the movements he made to accommodate the swaying and jolting of the carriage. With every turn of the wheels, every tortuous mile, they were drawing farther and farther away from everything she had ever known: relatives, friends, community, church. She was alone with a mercurial prince bent on a quest of vengeance. She knew not how it would end, nor what would become of her when it was over. She was not content that it should be so, not at all. And yet neither was she entirely discontented.

Part Two

Eleven

TWO DAYS PASSED IN A NIGHTMARISH HAZE OF BOUNCING, rolling progress, pressing onward, ever onward. They stopped out of dire necessity only: to water and rest the horses, to arrange for fresh animals, to snatch a few mouthfuls to eat, to ask their way along the maze of unmarked roads. Angeline slept much of the time due to the merciful sleeping powders Rolfe procured; if he and his men rested at all they dozed in the saddle. Great care was taken in tracking their quarry with every man keeping a sharp watch to be certain they did not overlook her while she put up somewhere during the night.

They encountered little difficulty. Their way was paved by febrile charm and a glittering stream of gold, a combination that melted opposition, causing doors to swing wide whether of barns or kitchens or medicine cupboards, and set men to bowing as they watched them out of sight with puzzled expressions. That combination also opened an armoire door to Rolfe. Measuring a young matron with his eyes in a manner that made her stammer and blush despite her

heavy pregnancy, he struck a bargain with the lady for
a portion of her wardrobe that she was unlikely to be
able to wear for some time, if ever.

The items included a round morning gown of gray
faille sprigged with lilacs, a Norwich shawl with silk
fringe, a chemise and petticoat set, a riding habit of
a green velvet so dark as nearly to be black with a
high-crowned hat of dyed beaver that was swathed
in a narrow streamer of white voile. In her misery,
Angeline paid scant heed to the garments Rolfe
brought and heaped upon the seat opposite her.
Curled up with one arm beneath her head, she did not
even rouse enough to thank him. Still, each time she
woke, she felt a little less ill, less as if stepping down
from the carriage was an overwhelming task.

During the afternoon of the second day, she sat up
for a short time, gazing out the window. As evening
fell, she was able to take something more than broth
and rough cornbread for dinner. Rolfe shared her
repast of baked chicken, freshly baked yeast bread, and
dried apple pie as the carriage rolled along a moonlit
corridor covered by an arch of skeletal limbs. He paid
no heed to her suggestion that he take off his boots
and close his eyes for a moment. He only stared at her
in the light of the coach lanterns, allowing his brilliant
blue eyes to drift over her dewy and rumpled shape
with the pearly sheen of the curves of her breasts just
revealed by the deep neckline of the tunic she still
wore. A crooked smile flitted over his features before
he turned his attention to the chicken leg that hung
forgotten in his hand. A short time later, he found an
excuse to leave her.

Almost immediately the cadre burst into a rollicking, highly improper song about a maiden from Prague whose bizarre propensities in the matter of sleeping companions made Angeline's ears burn. Rolfe's voice rang out in an order, and their courtly and drolly lascivious French changed to Ruthenian that managed, in its guttural accents, to sound even more lewd. As a means of raising the dragging spirits of his men it was apparently successful, however. Alternately cajoled, cursed, cheered, and harried, keeping to the frenetic pace that Rolfe set, they drove themselves tirelessly forward into the night.

They learned after sunrise that Claire was just ahead of them. She had left her carriage behind, standing in plain sight with the shafts down before a farmer's cottage, and bought mounts for herself and her driver, pushing on by horseback. How she had managed to outdistance them for so long, what means she had used to persuade her escort to such efforts—for that was what they discovered her driver had become—they could not say. Still, they expected to come up with her by midafternoon at the latest.

The sun was bright. As the morning advanced, the air grew steadily warmer in the way that days sometimes did in Louisiana in January. Angeline was tired of being bounced and thrown from side to side in the carriage. She was tired of the musty odor of the velvet seats, the dust that seeped in through the cracks around the doors and windows, and the monotonous squeaking of the body in one corner just over the back wheel. To be outside in the fresh air, to feel the sunshine on her face seemed marvelously inviting. Reaching across to the other seat, she took up the velvet riding habit and shook out its folds. There was an extra mount, she knew, in fact more than one. These spare horses were tied to the back of the carriage so that the men could change as needed in a constant rotation, preventing any one mount from becoming winded.

The problem was how she was to change her clothing. She solved it by draping the wide skirts of the round gown and the petticoats over the windows, tucking them in place in the loose frame of the door. Behind that screen she quickly skimmed out of her despised muslin and once-white tunic, pulling on the riding habit. The fit was adequate, a bit loose in the waist and tight across the bust, but not enough to be of significance. Tugging the jacket, made like a man's short coat, into place, settling the lace jabot that went with the shirtwaist of lawn at the throat, smoothing the somewhat crushed velvet over her hips, she felt appropriately dressed for the first time in days. A bath would have been lovely, but she would not quibble.

She wished that she had the strength of mind to refuse to wear the habit or any of the other garments Rolfe had bought for her. It appeared, however, that she was deficient in willpower as well as moral character. With a frown, she leaned to take the other garments from the windows, folding them neatly before letting down the glass and calling up to Gustave, who was driving, to halt.

Mounting a horse in a long, flowing skirt, without tripping or showing an unseemly length of limb, was not the easiest thing she had ever done. Controlling both skirt and horse, keeping her hat, with its flowing veil mingling with her unbound hair, upon her head was also a problem. She managed all with as much grace as she could summon. Then with her soft auburn tresses streaming out behind her, she cantered to join the others. She was greeted with huge grins and shouts of approval. Rolfe gave her one of his rare, unshadowed smiles and reined to one side so that she could ride abreast with him.

His blue gaze flicked over her, missing no detail of her toilette. "Do you feel as well as you look?"

"Much better, I'm sure. I must commend your taste in habits—and thank you for your thoughtfulness in providing it."

"There is no obligation, no need to continue to thank me, especially for secondhand clothing scarcely fit for a governess or serving girl, much less the woman that I…"

"Yes?" she took him up as he paused. "The woman that you have made your mistress? Is that what you meant to say?"

"Does the idea distress you? Then let me say instead the woman who has been of aid to me in my search. I am grateful that you will now allow me to provide for you without suspicion."

"You know well enough that I have done nothing that I was not forced to do."

He stared at her, a grim sparkle in his eyes. "Oh, I know that, but then nothing was said of willing aid."

She did not want to quarrel with him. There was no point in it; she had nothing to gain and little left to lose. She spoke of other things then, exchanging banter with

Gustave and Oscar. The others joined in and the miles receded beneath their horses' hooves. At midmorning, they stopped to water their mounts at a small stream. Angeline went a short distance into the woods while Rolfe stood guard. When she returned, she joined him under a spreading, evergreen bay tree. He was scanning the little that could be seen of the sky, a frown between his brows. The sun had fled, put to rout by a great cloud bank of pewter gray rising in the southwest.

"It has felt like spring today," she said, "and now it looks as if it's going to act like it."

"To my men and myself, used to a more drastic winter climate, it has seemed like summer, but that doesn't mean we will welcome rain."

"Welcome or not, you are likely to get it. Do—do you think it will matter? Will bad weather prevent you from overtaking Claire?"

"She will be as impeded by it as we, if not more so. I hardly see how it can be a problem so long as it doesn't storm."

"It isn't very likely, not this time of year. The only problem might be flooding."

"I think we can safely expect to close in on Claire before that can occur."

"What—will you do—when you find her, I mean?"

He sent her a quizzical glance. "What are you afraid of? I gave you my word, did I not?"

"You said you would not harm her. That leaves considerable scope for someone of your… inventiveness."

"A scourge of mop strings or a flail of broomstraws? I would like to do more. I would like to pare her conceit to the bone and suspend her by her hair from the crenellated towers of my father's palace. I will not, because of the oath given to you. Can you not trust it, and me?"

"I do, yes, until I think of how self-willed Claire can be, and of the fact that she may know nothing that can help you. Have you ever considered how you will feel, what you will do, if after traveling all this far, the journey proves to have been useless?"

"Are you saying," he asked quietly, "that I cannot be depended upon to curb my impulses?"

"I didn't say that."

"And yet?" he inquired.

"You must admit you have given me little reason to think it."

"I admit nothing. Impulse plays little part in what I do."

"You cannot be serious!" she exclaimed. "Why else was I taken from my aunt's house, made to… stay with you, brought away with you from the convent school after Claire had flown? You cannot expect me to believe it was all calculated."

"Why not?"

"Such cold-bloodedness is frightening!"

"Oh, I never claimed it was done in cold blood. There were moments, in fact, when it was quite the opposite." His brief smile was laced with real amusement. "If you speak of what occurred between us… in private at the hunting lodge, then let me tell you that I wanted you and was determined to have you from the moment I held you in my arms at Madame Delacroix's soirée. Your innocence was unexpected, but I am not certain, I tell you in all honesty, that it would have made any difference had I known."

Whether his behavior toward her had been a thing dependent upon himself alone, something of the mind and emotions, or whether it had been brought forth by some element within herself—a word, a glance, a movement—she did not know. Either way, it was no cause for pride. She looked away, bereft of words and oddly vulnerable.

"You need not go into a decline, all lily-like and pale. You were not responsible."

Her head came up. "I never thought so!"

"No? The other possibility for your sudden lack of spirit is that you have overextended your strength and should return to the carriage."

"How complimentary you are, sir!" she exclaimed, bridling, despite the weakness in her limbs that told her he was not far from wrong. Her reluctance to admit it was caused in part by the light in his eyes that sent a frisson of unease over her.

"More so than you think," he answered. "I do not intend that you should go alone."

"You—you mean that you will ride inside with me?"

"The prospect appears to be reviving—or alarming."

She could feel the heat in her cheeks, but chose to ignore it. "I am not certain that I—that I am ready to be driven again."

"Must I insist? For the sake of your injuries, of course?"

"Insist? Why should you? I assure you my lack of staying power will not hold up your progress."

"Alas, that I might say the same thing of my own."

He was laughing at her determined efforts to pass over the hints he had so blatantly given. "You—you are so close behind Claire. Perhaps you and the others should press on, leaving the carriage, and me, to catch up later?"

"And permit you to travel through No Man's Land with only Gustave to protect you?"

"We are in No Man's Land already?"

"For these last ten miles and more."

"I didn't know."

"You were not meant to. Nonetheless, you see why I am determined to accord you my personal escort?"

"I don't believe it," she said stoutly.

"That we are in dangerous territory, or that I am anxious to... protect you."

"I think," she said distinctly, "that neither of those things has anything to do with why you mean to join me in the carriage."

"Intelligent as well as brave," he mocked with laughter rising in his eyes. He reached at the same time to remove the jaunty hat with its veiling that sat upon her head, tossing it away into the bushes before he drew an auburn lock of hair forward over her breast. "Now if only you were amenable as well."

She was given no chance to be anything else. He put his hand on her elbow, drawing her toward the carriage, where it stood waiting with Gustave on the box. Opening the door, he turned to hand her in. There was a moment when she might have refused, when she stood staring at him with her fingers clasped tightly together. He waited unmoving, and his voice as he spoke was so low only she could hear.

"Put it to the test," he recommended. "Can I be deterred? Will the guard intervene on your outcry, or will they applaud in envy? Will they support their prince or the adopted, unclaimed mistress of them all? And will you, when the choice is made, abide by the result?"

It had been only the flitting shadow of an idea. How he had divined it she knew not, but the venture, once put in plain words, was shown as too uncertain to risk. In that moment of hesitation, the first drops of the threatening rain began to fall, as if the elements themselves were on his side. Her movements stiff, she put her hand in his and allowed herself to be boosted into the carriage. But as she went she seethed with the indignant knowledge that intelligence could be a burden.

She did not realize how dark the day had become until she was inside the closed vehicle. The moment they were under way, the rain came down in earnest, spattering against the windows, hammering on the roof, pouring down the sides of the ancient coach as they rolled relentlessly onward. The ruts of the road softened, filling with water that was ground to mud under their wheels, and the holes in the track were like great pig wallows without bottoms, threatening to mire them to the axles every time a wheel dropped into one. With bent heads and waterproofed capes brought from saddle gear wrapped around them, the men of the cadre drew slowly ahead of the lumbering carriage.

Rolfe sat holding Angeline against him, staring out at the rain, idly stroking her hair that flowed over his arm. On the finger of the hand that cupped her shoulder gleamed the old, soft gold of his wolf's head ring. They were safe and dry inside the traveling carriage, stifled and entrapped in damp intimacy. He tilted his head to look down at her, a smile of wry enjoyment curving his mouth. With a finger, he brushed away a lingering raindrop caught on the tips of her lashes. She swept them upward to gaze at him, and was ensnared in the turquoise light of his eyes. With a soft exclamation, he bent his head and pressed his lips to the sweet curves of her mouth. His fingers trailed along her cheek and downward to cup her breast.

Angeline felt the spread of treacherous longing. She wanted, with a sudden intensity that frightened her, to be held closer against him. She turned her head on a gasp, wrenching her mouth from his. "Don't—they will see us."

"They won't, but even if they did, being men of understanding, they will look the other way."

"But—but it's broad daylight and—and you can't—"

"No?" His fingers were busy at the buttons of her jacket, stripping them from their holes with dexterity, avoiding her fending hands with ease.

"Rolfe, no. This isn't—it isn't proper!"

"What has propriety to do with us?"

What indeed? Angeline thought with fleeting bitterness, and then her protests were stopped by his lips, swamped in the rising tide of desire. The rain lashed the carriage roof, a muted obbligato that seemed to thrum in the blood. The cool, damp air pressed in upon them so that their two skins clung where they touched, as clammily adhesive as their clothing. He untied her jabot, throwing wide the lace-edged ends, and slipped the horn buttons of her shirtwaist free, revealing the pink-crested fullness of her breasts. His hands, then his mouth upon them

were warm and arousing in their exquisite gentleness.
She pressed close in the fevered quickening of her
response, felt his warm breath against her throat, heard
his husky whisper, "Angeline—"

He brushed the jacket lapels and open edges of
her shirtwaist wider, then, shifting slightly, reached
to catch the carriage robe in one corner of the seat,
spreading it over them. Beneath its cover, his hands
smoothed over her, kneading her back, caressing
the slender indentation of her waist, sliding over her
hips, drawing her closer and closer as if to imprint
the memory of her form upon his body. She felt his
hand slip along her thigh to the knee, gathering the
heavy velvet of her skirts, pushing them upward. He
unfastened his clothing, twisting free of his pantaloons,
then turning her toward him once more, drew her
knee over his flank and fitted her to him.

The carriage jounced and she thought she heard
his soft chuckle as she was shaken free of the seat,
supported solely in his arms, the movement flinging
her more closely upon him. Slowly she subsided
once more, but his clasp remained firm, retaining
in sensuous enjoyment that deep penetration. The
moments stretched as he allowed the rocking ride
slowly to heighten her enjoyment, then rising above
her, he positioned her hips on the edge of the seat,
thrusting into her with gathering rhythm.

At that moment, the carriage wheel dropped into
a hole like a coal pit. Angeline felt herself hurtled
forward, felt Rolfe's instant withdrawal that kept her
from being driven upon his unyielding manhood and
the twist of tempered steel muscles that permitted

him to catch her to him as he turned in midair to spare her his weight. Then, as with a teeth-jarring jolt their carriage wheel hit bottom and bounded out again, they were plunged toward the floor. His broad shoulders struck, thudding. As Angeline landed upon his chest, the air left his lungs in a breathless grunt, then his body began to shake. An instant of fear coursed along her veins before she realized he was laughing. Answering merriment bubbled up inside her and lying in a tangle of velvet skirts and pantaloons, of the petticoats and the other gown of gray faille that had slithered down onto them along with the soft and shimmering fur of the carriage robe, they gave way to mirth, full-throated and joyous.

"To make love Cossack-style, across a wooden saddle on a galloping horse, may take greater agility than I suspected," he said. Still smiling, he levered himself upward and swung her beneath him. Holding her soft, gray-green eyes with his brilliant blue gaze, he pressed into her once more.

It was a glorious flowering, an expanding magic that took them soaring, winged and wondrous creatures of the elements. It was shared bliss, a most perfect union of passionate flesh, a thing of aching content, intolerant of intrusion, needing nothing and no one else, the sum of the universe or close enough that any lack could not be discovered.

They lay still with their limbs entwined when the first pistol shot rang out.

Rolfe cursed fluently and with an edge of self-blame as he came up from the carriage floor. With unnoticing ease, he lifted Angeline to the seat, then

jerked on his pantaloons, buttoning them at the waist
even as he pushed open the door and swung out
with the panel from the moving carriage to see what
was happening ahead. By that time more shots had
exploded in the dull and rain-wet gloom. There was
the sound of shouts and hoarse screams as the cadre
opened fire from nearer at hand. Then came a double
thump on the carriage roof, as if something heavy had
fallen to it from the tree limbs overhead. Immediately,
Rolfe drew back to kick through the glass in the door.
Placing his foot in the opening thus made, using it as
a precarious perch, he vaulted to the roof.

The carriage picked up speed, rocking from side to
side as if the reins had been let fall. Angeline, doing up
her buttons in feverish haste as she was thrown back
and forth, could hear the sound of grunts and curses
overhead and blows landed as men strained together.
It would be Gustave and Rolfe, she knew, against
whoever it was that had attacked in this woodland
ambush. Then there were horsemen riding beside the
swaying vehicle, reaching for the cheek straps of the
horses, swarming upward.

"Take the bloody bastards alive! Any man jack who
does us out of our ransom is a dead 'un."

Hard on the yell, there came the concussion of a
shot from the roof above. The struggling ceased, and
as the carriage came finally to a jiggling halt, the body
of a man plunged with boneless grace from the top,
falling past the window to the ground.

"Rolfe!" Angeline screamed, swinging wide the
door, scrambling out. She jumped to the ground and
ran to where he had fallen, going down on her knees

beside him. He lay face-down and she turned him with urgent hands. His eyes were closed, his face pale and still as the rain fell upon his colorless lips. Above one ear blood wetted the fine gilt of his hair and there was a raw and skinless patch across his face where he had struck the ground. That was not all. On the white of his uniform tunic, just above the waist, was an obscene crimson blossom of blood with a torn and fragmented center.

The fighting died away. A man rode up, scattering muddy water before him. His voice rough, he cursed the men now clambering down from the top of the carriage. Dismounting, he walked up to the man who held the still smoking pistol and knocked him sprawling to the ground with one hamlike fist.

"Goddamn ye for a sniveling fool and a coward to boot! If you've killed him, I'll have your lights for dice and your gizzard for a tobacco pouch!"

Wheeling around, the man who was obviously the leader of the attackers moved to stand over Angeline where she knelt beside Rolfe.

"Is he daid, then?"

His words were so thick with the accents of Scotland that it was a moment before Angeline understood. She removed her hand from where she had placed it over Rolfe's heart inside his tunic. "No, not yet. If—if he could be put into the carriage…?"

The Scotsman stood with his hands on his hips, a massive square-built man with a head of shaggy brown hair, a reddish-brown beard, and tobacco-brown eyes. He took in her disheveled appearance with a frowning abstraction, then with his thick brows drawn together in puzzlement, weighed her cultured accents, the delicate oval of her face. He shrugged. "Aye, and he can."

He bawled an order over his shoulder, and a handful of men came forward. As Angeline stepped aside to allow them to lift Rolfe into the carriage, she flung a quick look toward the road ahead. At first glance, it appeared the wounded lay everywhere. Then she saw that the disarmed men of the cadre were being held stretched on the ground, each with at least three men around him with pistol or long rifle in their fists. Though Gustave had blood running into his one good eye from a cut slanting across his forehead, Meyer grimaced with a shoulder wound, and Oscar seemed to have reinjured his wrist, they were all at least alive.

The same could not be said of the attackers. In a circle around where the cadre must have held their last position, fallen men were stacked like cordwood with a few that still lived moaning and mouthing curses among them. It appeared that a force of near forty, outnumbering Rolfe's *garde du corps* more than seven to one, had come down upon them. In the open road, taken by surprise, they had not had a chance, though they had given a good accounting of themselves. If there had been the least cover, any pretense of a defensible position, it was doubtful they could have been taken at all.

"Will you be getting in then?"

Angeline swung around as the words were addressed to her. She found the Scots leader holding the door of the carriage, waiting for her to enter. Inside, Rolfe lay upon the forward seat with a dark stain spreading like spilled wine from his side onto the maroon velvet. It crossed her mind to ask where they were to be taken, what was to be done with them, but she swallowed the question. There were some things it was as well not to know in advance. As the leader put his hand on her elbow to urge her inside, she snatched her arm away and, sending him a cold glance, climbed unaided into the carriage.

The vehicle jerked into motion. She steadied herself, going to one knee on the floor. With her mouth set in grim lines, she took up the mutilated underdress she had removed so short a time ago and began to rip the bottom flounces from it for bandaging. As they passed the place where the men of the cadre had lain, she saw they were being prodded to their feet and shoved toward horses, while the others of the outlaw clan slung their dead comrades across empty saddles. Turning her head to catch the last glimpse of the men, she saw Leopold swing angrily upon the man poking a pistol between his shoulders; saw Meyer reach to place a hand on the arm of Rolfe's cousin, urging him to caution. There was time for no more. Bending over Rolfe, she began to unbutton his tunic.

After a time, they turned into a muddy track so narrow that the branches of the trees scraped along the body of the carriage, poking in at the broken window. As they bumped along, lurching into holes and out again, Rolfe stirred. A low sound came from his throat, then his lids lifted. He stared at Angeline until lucidity gathered in his turquoise eyes. His voice soft, he said, "Pride before a fall—I was going to guard you."

"There were too many of them and they were waiting for us."

"Yes. What herald do you think announced our coming?"

There could be only one, and yet it seemed so farfetched an idea that she refused to speak of it. "How do you feel?"

A glint ousted the pain in his eyes for a moment. "Trussed up and modycoddled, and with Thor's own hammer in my head. If this is how your concussion took you three days ago, then I apologize abjectly for the carriage ride."

"You have lost a great deal of blood, and I think someone must have struck you as you began to fall after you were shot."

"Dastardly. One must wonder why they didn't finish the job."

His detachment was disturbing. "I gather the reason has to do with money, a ransom to be paid for you—and the others."

"Then," he said, letting his eyelids fall, "there can be no doubt of a gala welcome."

A short time later, the carriage drew up before a long, dogtrot cabin built of gray cypress logs with cypress shingles on the roof and a mud-daub chimney at each end pouring forth gray plumes of smoke. There were two others just like it flanking it on either side and a collection of barns and animal pens in the rear. They had been challenged some distance down the road from what was apparently the outlaws' stronghold. The guards that stood with long rifles cradled in their arms on the porch of the cabin made the place seem like an armed camp. To add to the effect, a pack of mangy dogs poured from around the

cabin and through the long open hall that bisected it.
Curs of enormous size and no certain breed, brown,
dun, and dirty yellow, set up a barking with lifted
napes and ferocious bared teeth that made it dangerous
to get down from the carriage.

The dogs were quieted by a roared command and
a few well-place kicks, though they still circled the
strange vehicle, sniffing at the door and lifting their
legs against the wheels. The men of the cadre were
dragged down from their horses and marched up the
steps into the dogtrot hall of the house. Rolfe pushed
to a sitting position with one arm clamped to his side.
Brushing aside Angeline's protests, he waited until she
had alighted, then stepped down from the carriage
without aid.

The effort was costly, judging from his pallor, a
feat of will rather than strength. As he stood swaying
slightly, the Scotsman who was the leader swung from
where he was watching the cadre shepherded inside
and strode toward them.

"Ye dinna look good, Your Highness. I am sorry
for the error that brought ye low, but had ye not put
up such a fight, ye'd not be in the shape ye are now."

There were growls from the other outlaws leading
the horses carrying the dead toward a burying ground
marked with crude wooden crosses, but the broad
man with the thick accent paid no heed.

"I assume," Rolfe said with polite irony, "that you
have a name?"

"That I do. I am the McCullough, leader of this
fine outlaw clan. Will ye come inside out of the wet
and take ye'r ease?"

Rolfe inclined his head, and the Scotsman, attempting to match the graceful gesture, returned a clumsy bow. That his order was couched as a request was a tribute to that indefinable sense of power that emanated from the Prince of Ruthenia even in his present condition.

"Your hospitality is overwhelming," Rolfe murmured. With Angeline at his side, he climbed the steps slowly, ducking under the silver streams of rain that ran from the roof. There was a chill, damp breeze blowing down the dogtrot. On it came the smell of woodsmoke and the odor of putrid decay from the green animal pelts that hung on stretchers along the mud-and-moss-chinked walls, vying for decorative effect with deer antlers, bear claws, and a string of cow bells that served apparently as a method of warning. Rich and lustrous even in the gray weather were the skins of bear, wolf, fox, mink, raccoon, possum, and an occasional beaver.

As they paused, the McCullough strode forward to usher them into the right-hand portion of the house, following on the heels of Rolfe's guard. At that moment, the door that led into the left side swung open and an Indian girl dressed in homespun and calico, though with her braids as silken and black as a crow's wing hanging beside her face, stepped out. Behind her there was a flurry of skirts, a drift of perfume, and then the crude doorway was filled by a woman. She wore yellow silk trimmed with black lace and held a shawl of Indian cashmere around her shoulders that was embroidered in every hue of the rainbow. There were jewels at her neck and on her arms and fingers, and satin slippers with small paste buckles gleaming below the hem of her gown.

"Claire!" Angeline exclaimed.

Her cousin was staring beyond her, beyond Rolfe to the men being herded into the opposite room, the members of the cadre. Her face was pale and as she turned back it seemed she collected her thoughts with an effort. "My dear Angeline," her cousin said in wonder, "I didn't know you would be with Rolfe, though *Maman* said he had you."

Angeline watched Claire send a glance to the man at her side, dropping him a curtsey tinged with mockery. Taking a deep breath, she said, "It was you that set these men on us, wasn't it? Though how you knew—"

"How did I know you were behind me? A guess, *chère*. *Maman* said you could not—you would not—be able to withstand the questioning you must be subjected to for long, and that I must get away as soon as arrangements could be made. Knowing something of Rolfe, I was inclined to agree. I did not expect him, in all truth, to be so close behind."

"Ye told me they were only hours back on ye'r trail," the McCullough growled.

Claire shrugged. "You were becoming somewhat… heated. I thought—"

"Ye thought to be rid of me long enough to wiggle yer way out of here and, at the same time, use me to take His Highness here off yer scent—if I understand the right of what's going on. It didn't work then, did it?"

There was a flash of rage in Claire's eyes as she rounded on him. "I didn't know I would be held at knife point by your savage paramour. She was quite vile, you know. I swear I am black and blue from her pinching at me, something for which I have sworn she will pay!"

"I'd be advising ye not to tangle with her. She's a wildcat," McCullough observed.

"Oh, I have no intention of coming to blows with her. There are other ways."

"That is something we'll be seeing about, just as by and by we will look into why ye thought to send me out after a will-o'-the-wisp. Like as not he's not even a real prince and ye have lost six good men for me for nothing."

As the other man was speaking, Angeline felt Rolfe's hand on her shoulder, the touch without weight, as if he sought no more than balance. The fact that he would reach out even for that much was an indication of the greatness of his need. Her voice low, she said, "For now, could we go inside?"

Rolfe crossed the common room where a fire blazed on the hearth, ducked his head to enter the bedchamber that opened from it, and reached the crude wooden bedstead that, with a stool and primitive wooden washstand, was the only furniture in the room. He sat down upon the rough quilts that covered the cornshuck mattress before he lost consciousness, keeling slowly over onto the rock-hard pillows.

The McCullough offered his service to put him to bed, but Angeline refused. She wanted no rough handling to start Rolfe's wounds bleeding again when she had managed to staunch them so short a time ago. The outlaw went away then, presumably to see to his prisoners, while the cadre gathered in one end of the common room beyond. In his stead, he sent the Indian girl who proved quiet-footed and silently competent.

They removed Rolfe's mud-caked and damp uniform and, dragging the quilts from under him, covered him to the chin. Angeline requested that all their belongings be brought from the carriage, among them the small wooden box that contained the sleeping powders Rolfe had found for her. Mixing some with water to give to him when next he roused, she sat down on the stool beside the bed to wait. The Indian girl took his uniform and bore it away to soak the bloodstains.

Time crept past. It might have been a half hour, it might have been longer, when Rolfe moved his head on his coarse sacking pillowcase and opened his eyes. Angeline rose to her feet at once and reached for the medicine that would ease his pain.

"Here," she said, slipping her hand beneath his head. "Drink."

"What is it?"

She told him, surprised at how vital his voice sounded despite its low timbre.

He met her gaze, his own bright. "I am to be lulled and supine, drugged to the eyebrows like a collicky, unweaned babe? Take it away."

"It's only what you gave to me."

"You had no need of rational, or even irrational, faculties."

"Had I not? I was a prisoner then—"

"Just as I am now? You may as well say it as imply it."

"I didn't mean that, not entirely."

"Never use half-measures, dear Angeline. Tell me I am helpless, completely at your mercy, and that of our Scots friend."

"Yes, and are likely to remain so if you refuse the help you need to make yourself well!" she declared, aware of an ache between her shoulders as she leaned over him.

"There, that's the spirit," he said with soft irony. "Will you also bid me to pen a note to my father asking for a patent on the royal treasury to gain my release? He wouldn't thank you, nor can you expect docility and tender complaisance from him any more than from me."

"What are you afraid of? That you will be unable to order and lead with your senses dulled? You cannot do that now. That you will lose control of your guard? You do not have it. That while you sleep events will take place of which you have no knowledge? You cannot prevent it."

"And now you will say that all this being true, I might as well accept the surcease you offer?"

"Yes, why not?"

His mouth curved in a smile that did not reach his eyes. "Did you resent so much being my prisoner that you must now make me yours?"

The charge took her breath away. She stared at him, searching in painful honesty to discover if he was right. "Could it not be that I prefer you in rude health rather than weakly rude, knowing that your return to strength is my own best hope of getting out of this coil?"

"So sensible, but you do not answer my question."

"What does it matter now? We are here, and so is Claire. She cannot escape you since she is being held as surely as we are. There may be a way to win our release, but for the moment I cannot see it. Until I can—until you can—why will you not rest?"

His gaze, not quite focused, moved over her. "A fearless, temper-ridden harridan dispensing balm and myrrh with her coat unbuttoned. I think I prefer her to the wounded virgin and, strangely, trust her more."

He reached for the glass she held, drank the powder in water to the dregs, and lay back with his blue gaze resting on her face, his features pale beneath the bandage wrapped about his temples. Within minutes his eyes closed, the gold-tipped lashes lying still upon his cheeks as he slept.

Angeline stood for long, aching moments staring down at him with the glass forgotten in her numb fingers. Sighing at last, feeling as if she had fought a hard battle and won over enormous odds, she turned away to resume her seat upon the stool.

He was right, as acute as ever even in blinding pain and semiconsciousness. Her coat was unbuttoned. What must those who had seen her so, the McCullough, Claire, the members of the cadre, and all the others, have thought? A slattern, they would label her, or a slut, as had her aunt. It did not matter, and yet as she rebuttoned the short-waisted coat and the shirt under it with trembling fingers, she wished she could erase the impression and start anew.

It was Rolfe who had enticed her into such abandon, but she could not blame him. She had not protested overmuch, had, in fact, enjoyed the wantonness of that carriage escapade once her consent had been forced. She hardly knew herself these last few days. Deprived of the stability of her life with her aunt, cast loose in the world, she kept discovering new facets and flaws in her character.

The early-winter dark was closing in when a tap came on the door. Angeline came stiffly to her feet and went to open the panel. It was Leopold who stood outside, a worried frown between his eyes. To his anxious query concerning his cousin, Angeline gave the only reply she could, that Rolfe was sleeping and the bleeding had stopped.

"We have been talking among ourselves," Leopold said, his voice low. "It's possible that we could force our way out of here, though there are double guards at the doors and every window. We don't dare, however, so long as we cannot take Rolfe with us. Then there is the fact that Mademoiselle de Buys is here. The whole point of this journey was to find her, and there is no longer the need to search."

"Yes, I understand. I—I have seen a few wounds since I used to help my aunt in quarters with the slaves who were injured. The pistol ball glanced off his rib, tearing its way out the side, I think. The damage was extensive and it would be best not to move him for a few days. As for Claire, unless you could arrange that she come with us, I think Rolfe would prefer to remain where she is being held, at least as long as there is no real danger to any of us."

Leopold shook his dark head. "From what I can discover, this outlaw thinks we are all of nobility with families that can be milked like so many dairy cows.

No doubt the ignorant Scotsman thinks to set himself up as a laird on the gold he can extort. He will be disappointed, but it will take some time before he can be brought to realize it."

"Time," Angeline said, "is what we need."

Leopold stared down at her, his dark gaze flitting over her face. "You look tired, Mademoiselle. I would be happy to take your vigil while you rest."

"Later, perhaps," she answered, "not now."

It was instinct, she thought as she shut the door, that had dictated her reply. At the moment the offer was made she had not consciously considered the threat to Rolfe's life. Now, glancing toward the bed, she knew that it had been in the back of her mind. In his weakened state, he would be easy prey to a killer, if there was indeed one among them. He had not mentioned it when he had refused the sleeping draught she offered, and yet she wondered if that was not what had been at the root of his distrust. An unconscious man was without defense, and since she was the one who had given him the medicine, then she must stand guard. So long as she was there on watch, he would be safe.

The evening drew in. The backless stool was not the most comfortable perch. Angeline shifted upon it, staring about the room at the bare walls, two of which had windows, one opening onto the dogtrot, the other onto the rear of the house, both covered by thick wooden shutters. She rose now and then to pace the floor, stooping to straighten the bedcovers that Rolfe disarranged in his restless turning, checking his bandages to be certain that no bright-red blood appeared, placing her hand upon his forehead to try it for fever. As dark fell, the heat of his skin grew. Once or twice he muttered in his sleep, the words slurred and indecipherable. He tried to throw off the quilts that covered him, tried to swing his legs from the bed and rise. Coaxing, whispering, pressing him back, Angeline kept him on the cornshuck mattress, though it was not easy.

A meal of squirrel stew and cornbread was brought to her along with a tallow candle against the darkness. She tried to wake Rolfe to persuade him to eat, but it was impossible. He hovered on the edge of delirium, thrashing so that once he knocked the spoon from her hand. She ate a few mouthfuls herself, then set the tray to one side.

A little later she noticed a tremor in the quilt that lay across his chest. His body was like a furnace, flushed and radiating heat, and yet he was convulsed with chill. With no fireplace to provide warmth and with the door into the common room closed, the damp cold of the room had increased as the evening advanced. Angeline herself was all too aware of the numbing discomfort. She warmed her hands over the candle flame, but its greasy smoke was sinking lower and lower.

Beyond the small room, the house was quiet. Her back ached and the vague pain in her skull that grew steadily more virulent was a reminder that it had not been too long since she herself had been hovering in the same stupor that gripped Rolfe.

Something had to be done. It was dangerous for Rolfe's fever to go so high. There were measures that could be taken—sponging with cool water, wrapping him in wet sheets—but she hesitated. Such drastic treatment might not be necessary yet, and he would be enraged if she tried to order it for him. The responsibility, then, was the most pressing thing. She longed for someone to ask for advice, someone to help her make the difficult decision.

She suddenly remembered Rolfe's scathing allusion to Meyer's skill at bone-setting when Oscar had been injured. She stood staring at the rough, unplaned log walls of the room, wondering if the big man were asleep, wondering if he would mind being called on for his opinion, if his own injuries would allow it, trying to think if it would be best to go in search of him now or wait until morning. Moving to the bed, she reached to touch the backs of her fingers to Rolfe's gold-stubbled cheek.

As if the touch, slight though it was, awakened the sense of danger that slumbered inside him, he stirred, his eyes snapping open. Fever bright, they narrowed on Angeline as she stood over him in the wavering light of the candle. Alert if tenuous recognition pervaded their stillness, along with a cobalt shimmer of discernment.

"Angeline," he whispered, "don't fret. You can do nothing."

"I can call Meyer. Perhaps there is something he—"

"If I had thought so, I would have asked for his services before now."

"But your fever—"

"—will leave me when I am healed. Do not fret. If you feel the need to be martyred rather than molested, then share my bed."

"I would disturb you."

"So you would, but that is something else you can do nothing about. Come."

He drew aside the quilt, waiting. The need to do as he suggested, leaving his well-being in his own hands, was nigh irresistible. But she managed it with only the greatest effort. "I think you need a physician."

"I did not bring you with me to be my nursemaid."

"I'm not trying to be one," she answered with a shade of temper, "but someone has to look after you."

"Permit me to know what I require, and what I do not. For the moment it is your warm body beside me, instead of a ministering angel, cold and concerned."

His voice was a harassed husk of sound. To argue with him would only deplete his dwindling reserve of strength. Her movement stiff, Angeline drew off the coat of her habit, the shirtwaist, and the heavy velvet skirt, placing them over the quilts as extra cover. Clad only in her chemise, she slid into the bed. His arm closed over her, drawing her nearer as he turned, so that she was held with her back to him, molded to the curve of his body, partaking of its furnace heat. She shivered a little at the sudden contrast with her own chilled limbs, and she felt an answering convulsive shudder run over his frame. His restlessness grew less, as if assuaged by her nearness. By slow degrees he was still, his grasp growing slack, until he slept once more.

Angeline lay still, feeling his warmth seeping into her flesh, penetrating to the bone. He was a strange man, Rolfe of Ruthenia. Unconventional, steel-willed, single-minded, of biting intelligence and mellifluous wit; he was secure within himself and therefore fearful of neither man nor the misfortune caused by a distracted God. There seemed no chinks in his armor except possibly, though not certainly, the approval of his father and a fierce and intuitive passion. By these attributes then he commanded the admiration, as Gustave had said, of his countrymen, the loyalty of his followers, the love of women.

The love of some women, of course, not all. She, by the grace of *le bon Dieu*, was unaffected. The disturbance of the senses she felt when she was near him was caused by anger and distrust and an understandable disquiet toward the man who had awakened her to the knowledge of her own physical responses. The fact that he found her attractive, even desirable for the moment, only added to her confusion. It would be folly to mistake her natural reaction to what had happened for anything more enduring. She would not be so stupid. She could not.

Soon he would be well, would discover from Claire what he wished to know, and would then arrange his freedom. He would take ship for his homeland, sailing out of her life. Nothing could change that, nothing hold him. Not that she wanted to do so, not at all. The burning salt tears she was forced to swallow were a sign merely of the distress of the last few days. It was imbecilic to consider that they might indicate anything else.

Twelve

MORNING CAME AFTER A DISTURBED NIGHT. DURING the long hours Angeline was jerked from troubled slumber by distant shouts and angry voices, the barking of dogs, the sound of a wild pig beneath the cabin, and the creaking of the log house in the cold wind that sprang up when the rain stopped. She felt worse than when she had got into bed, if such a thing were possible. Rolfe, from his surly comments when she inquired how he felt, was in the same state. The fever lingered. His lips were dry and cracked. He took the water and the second sleeping powder that she offered, but his very lack of protest was disturbing.

When he had drifted into sleep once more, Angeline donned the gray gown sprigged with lilacs that Rolfe had bought for her and let herself out of the bedchamber. Crossing the common room where men still lay rolled in quilts, she went in search of the outlaw leader who called himself the McCullough.

She found him at the breakfast table. He sat eating buttered biscuits and smoked pork with Claire at his side picking at what appeared to be a piece of heavy cake. Ranged along the rough board were Meyer and Leopold, as well as several of the outlaw clan. They looked up as Angeline approached the Scotsman.

"Good morning to ye!" the McCullough called at his most jovial, "And how is His Highness this morning?"

"That is what I wish to speak to you about," Angeline answered.

He gave a grunt in acknowledgment as he tore at a piece of ham with gusto. She had his attention, however, as well as that of Claire and the others at the table.

"He is not at all well. If he could have the services of a surgeon?"

"My good girl," the Scotsman said, lowering his meat, swallowing hugely, "there is nae such a person within fifty miles, and if there was he would nae be for venturing into No Man's Land, devil take the fee."

Angeline flung out a hand in appeal. "What do you do when a man is shot?"

"He gets well by hisself, or with such help as Morning Star here can be persuaded tae give him." He nodded in the direction of the Indian girl who was just rising from in front of the fireplace where she had taken a heavy cast-iron skillet from the coals, dumping more biscuits onto a wooden platter set ready to one side. Angeline looked at the girl and got an impassive stare in return.

"Will I be sending her to yon prince again?" the McCullough inquired in heavy irony.

Meyer cleared his throat, entering the conversation. "I think it would be more fitting if the members of the guard cared for Rolfe. I will claim the honor of looking after his injuries."

Angeline turned toward the broad-shouldered man, meeting his gray eyes. "For myself, I would be relieved, but I must warn you, I'm not certain he will allow it."

Meyer smiled. "If he can prevent it, then he has little use for a surgeon."

She did not like the idea of Rolfe being forced to receive attention he did not want, but something had to be done. She could only agree.

"Good," the McCullough said, slapping the table with the palm of his hand. "Now that we have settled that, will ye join us for breakfast? I am sure yer cousin here would be glad of the company."

Angeline glanced at Claire. The red-haired girl was trying futilely to keep her hand from being captured under the massive paw of the man at the head of the table. Catching her look, the Scotsman laughed.

"Ye be surprised I know the relationship? 'Tis simple, the finding out of these things. To begin with, I have eyes in my head tae see how much alike ye be. And then, Claire told me about it, and a deal else, during the night."

Angeline remembered the shouting and cries she had heard through her fitful sleep. From the mulish outrage she saw now on Claire's face, she was certain it had been her cousin and the outlaw leader in argument. What else had occurred between them? Her mind shied away from imagining it, despite the fatuous, well-pleased expression that hovered about the McCullough this morning as he allowed his gaze to roam over his captive companion.

Her voice stiff, Angeline said, "Thank you, but I will have a tray in my chamber."

"Ye'll have to get it yourself, then," came the answer. "Morning Star has tae much work on her hands to be traipsing around with trays for people able tae tend themselves."

"Certainly." As Angeline swung from the table, Meyer came to his feet, as did Leopold. They caught up with her in the open dogtrot. Frowning in concern, Meyer asked deliberate questions concerning the site and size of the wounds his half-brother had suffered. As they spoke, they moved on toward the bedchamber.

Rolfe's head injury was troublesome, but unlikely to become more serious. It was his side that worried her. The pistol ball had torn its way through, exiting at the back. The problem was being certain that it had carried with it all the bits of material from the jagged hole in his shirt, and that it had not been contaminated with dirt or the spattering muddy rain. Fever with a wound was a sign of the healing process, and therefore nothing unusual, but it carried its own danger should it go too high or last overlong. The things Meyer wanted to know and his comments on the answers given were comforting because they showed a superior understanding of medical matters.

As they crossed the common room of the section of the house given over to the prince and the cadre, Oscar and Oswald looked up from a game they were playing with a pack of greasy cards. Throwing them down, they thumped Gustave, still snoring, awake. While he tugged on his boots, the twins rose and came to stand just inside the bedchamber door as Angeline and Meyer entered.

Rolfe had roused in her absence and pushed himself up in the bed. The look in his eyes was overbright but lucid with irritation. "An invasion in force? Flattering, but unnecessary. You would be better employed, all, in surveying this rustic stronghold and its defenses."

"I only wanted to be sure you are well," Meyer said, coming to a halt.

"Behold me, blithe and bonny," his leader said with stringent force, "and then depart."

"I will do that, if you will let me look at your wound."

"I dislike denying privileges, but I prefer some privacy."

Meyer's face tightened. "We are dependent on you, Rolfe. If anything should happen—"

"Spare me your infinite patience. It won't help, and I'll have none of it."

"Be reasonable, I beg. Your wounds—"

"—are an inconvenience, but not a danger. As for reason, what need have I of it? I am the future King of Ruthenia."

It was said with irony and a certain bitter humor. The tone was somehow more affecting than a plea for sympathy would have been. He was alone, as was all royalty, and with no trust for any man, no matter how much he might require it.

Angeline moved forward, her hands clasped at her waist. "Meyer may be able to help you. You must let him."

"I need no help," Rolfe said, turning his brilliant turquoise gaze upon her. "I desire nothing, need nothing from anyone, least of all from an intermediary all lovely, spurious concern and tearful entreaty. You may leave with the others."

It was banishment for Angeline, for them all, even Gustave who had come to stand with his hands braced in the doorway. So long as Rolfe had the strength to defy them there was nothing they could do except obey his order.

Leaving the bedchamber, Angeline walked to stand before the fire in the common room, holding her hands out to the blaze. Meyer joined her, and Leopold, after closing the bedchamber door, moved toward them down the room.

"I could have told you," Rolfe's cousin said, "that he would let no one tend him. He's always been like that."

Meyer sighed. "He's a stubborn man."

"He likes to think himself invincible, and he very nearly is," Leopold said, then flung a quick smile at Gustave as the older man gave a grunt that might have meant anything.

"He's a man like any other," Meyer answered. "I don't think he fears the cauterization his wounds require to seal them from infection. Pride is his ultimate sin, pride too great to accept the aid he needs."

Leopold flung a quick look at Angeline, who had made a small sound of distress. There was a reflection of her horror in his own eyes at the thought of Rolfe's side being seared twice front and back, with white-hot metal in the act of cauterization. He glanced back at Meyer, his expression shuttered. "I don't think it's pride so much as preservation and ingrained personal dignity. Whatever the reasons, we are stalemated for now. I am going to see about the horses, if I can persuade our guard to trust me beyond the breakfast room."

"There's breakfast?" Oswald inquired as Leopold started toward the door. "Lead me to it."

"And me," Oscar added.

"I wouldn't mind a bit of something," Gustave said, though there was heaviness in his tone.

They went out, leaving Angeline with Meyer. They were challenged by the sentries. A short discussion could be heard, and then their footsteps receded. The fire crackled below the rough wooden mantelpiece. Meyer moved to where his bedroll lay on the floor and began to pick it up, folding the quilts and stacking them back into a crude hidebound trunk that sat against the wall beside a homemade settle.

After a moment he spoke. "I am sorry about your cousin. No matter what her connection with Maximilian's death, I would not wish her present position upon any woman."

"Her position?"

"As the mistress, if her place can be dignified by such a title, of our friend the McCullough."

"You—you think that is what she has become?"

"I know it. The man made it painfully obvious at the breakfast table before you came, a means of warning all and sundry away from his preserve, I imagine."

Angeline had little doubt that he was right. To be discussing such a subject openly with a man was strange. Her tone was strained as she said, "Poor Claire."

"It seems to be your cousin's fate to meet men who want nothing else of her. Maximilian was a bit more polished, I'm sure, but the end result was the same. How she could have expected otherwise is the question. She must have known, if she had used her head, that he could offer no more."

"Claire has never been known for studying the consequences of—of doing what she wants."

"What she pleases, you mean? A less headstrong girl would have recognized that Maximilian was bound to look to the royal families of Europe for a bride. His position demanded it, to say nothing of his father."

"Yes, it does seem obvious." It was also obvious that Meyer meant to bring that fact to her own attention as it applied to Rolfe. It was kind of him to be concerned, but the idea had hardly failed to occur to her. The only problem was that in her own situation, it made no difference. She had no choice except to stay with Rolfe.

"I am sorry for Mademoiselle de Buys. I wish there was something I could do, or that the guard could do, but I don't see what it might be. Our Scots host is unlikely to listen to a request, however politely worded, that he cease to molest the lady, and we have no weapons to put force behind it."

"I'm sure Claire doesn't expect it," Angeline answered, frowning into the fire.

She was wrong. Less than a half-hour later Claire sought her out. Meyer had been summoned by the McCullough, presumably for questioning concerning the prospect of ransom. Angeline sat alone in the common room, fighting the impulse to creep to the door of the bedchamber and peep inside. Only the thought of the biting things Rolfe might say if he saw her were a deterrent. She looked up as her cousin swept into the room with the ends of her shawl flying and her mouth set in a tight crimson line.

"You have got to do something!" Claire exclaimed. "If that oaf touches me again, I'll go mad with disgust!"

"You—you mean the McCullough?"

"Who else? He paws me like a clumsy bear after honey, kissing me until I can't breathe. He is a bull of a man, brutal, never satisfied, and worst of all, I am positive he went last night from my bed directly to that of his sneaking, savage darling, Morning Star!"

"I know it must be dreadful for you," Angeline said, "but I don't see—"

"Dreadful? You can't begin to guess—or can you? I suppose you think what I am enduring is fair enough after *Maman* and I left you to Rolfe? I might have known you would see it that way!"

"I didn't say that."

"You didn't have to! I can see it in your eyes. You were never very good at hiding your feelings." Claire flung back her head with its high-piled fiery curls and stood waiting for Angeline to deny it.

"You must think what you will," she replied, "but I am distressed that this is the result of your flight."

"In other words, it's all my own fault," Claire accused, her tone bitter. "My fault my driver was killed, my fault I was taken."

"I won't deny that, though it doesn't make me any less concerned."

"Noble," Claire said with a hollow laugh as she swung about to pace the room. "I can assure you that unless Rolfe was quite inhuman you were a thousand times better off than I was last night. I was ravished, there can be no other word for it! My clothes were torn from me and I was forced to lie under that strutting, rutting Scotsman while he took exactly what he wanted. I will make him sorry for it if it takes my last breath, but first I have got to get away."

"I think all of us would like to do the last."

"Are you sure? I would have thought Rolfe was happy. He has chased me down at last, hasn't he?" She whirled around, her green eyes glittering.

"He is in no condition to rejoice over it."

"You mean he is seriously ill? How inconvenient. I was sure that he could be depended on to win free, especially for the right prize."

"You mean—?"

"For the information he wants, of course," Claire said impatiently, though her manner was more subdued.

"You know something about Maximilian's death?" It did not require as great a reshuffling of her ideas of her cousin as might have been expected.

"Is that so surprising? I was there," Claire reminded her, a peculiar smile twisting her lovely lips.

"You never said anything the night of the soirée."

"*Maman*, my dear mother, was in the room. It is best not to disillusion the woman who bore you if it can be helped."

The cynicism of that remark chilled Angeline. Though she had a fair idea of at least a portion of the situation to which her cousin referred, her position as Max's mistress, she could not say so. "What do you mean?"

The other girl shrugged. "Does it matter? All that was a long time ago now. We must think what we are to do about the present."

"I told you—"

"Yes, yes, I know, but there must be something that can be done. If I must act on my own, then I will have to find this Scotsman's weak spot. He is worried about his men, I think, and about his position here in this godforsaken wilderness. He commands an armed camp—did you notice?—something that isn't necessary out of fear of the law. From what I heard him say to one of his men, I think he is involved in a feud with another outlaw, a rival band. How lovely it would be if he and his men were overrun by this other group of felons, whoever they may be."

"Where would that leave us?" Angeline asked with asperity.

"What difference as long as the McCullough suffers? But surely we can make our escape in the confusion?"

"There is no guarantee that if we do not the other outlaws will extend better treatment."

"We must take our chances."

"Not with an injured man who cannot defend himself," Angeline protested.

"Can he not? That must be distressing for Rolfe, a novel situation. I don't doubt he is hard to live with. No wonder you are sitting out here."

"Really, Claire," Angeline said with heat, "that is none of your affair. But I tell you to your face, I will have none of your scheming, even if by some means you could arrange to have an attack mounted. It's ridiculous, as you would know if you thought about it."

"Oh, I may not have to take a hand in it at all. From what I understand, they have been waiting for a raid these many days. All I need to do is provide distraction at the right time, and watch for the correct moment to dispense with the McCullough's hospitality. After all, what have I to lose?"

"It's insane, Claire," Angeline insisted, but the other girl, pacing up and down the floor of rough puncheons, paid no attention.

For the remainder of the day no sound came from the bedchamber where Rolfe lay. Angeline stayed where she was, refusing the noon meal from lack of hunger, though for long afterward she wondered if she should fetch water or broth for Rolfe. He could not go on as he was, she knew. Toward evening, however, Gustave ventured to open the door of the sickroom a crack. Rolfe was sleeping, he said, and volunteering Leopold and himself to keep watch in her place, he sent Angeline to the quarters across the dogtrot to partake of supper.

The meal was not quite ready. Angeline, standing in the doorway, weighed the choice of sitting at the long eating table with the McCullough and several of his men or returning to the dogtrot, where the other members of the cadre were engaged in card games and a contest with their guards that involved spitting tobacco juice into the yard. There was one other choice. Though Claire was nowhere in sight, the Indian girl was busy at the fireplace, lifting pot lids to stir, basting meat roasting on a spit, mixing the inevitable cornbread in a great wooden bowl. With a lift of her chin, Angeline ignored the McCullough's bow of welcome and went to stand beside the Indian girl, offering her help with a warm smile as she took the basting ladle from her hand. Morning Star stared at her for a brief moment, a weighing look in her deep brown-black eyes, then with a nod she relinquished the ladle. She watched Angeline pour the drippings over the meat, gently turning the spit, then satisfied that the chore was in competent hands, she turned away.

The men gathered with shouts, coarse jests, and voracious appetites. There was a great deal of rivalry, only half friendly, between the cadre and the men of the outlaw clan. It appeared that by common consent, or perhaps by agreement between them she had not witnessed, Rolfe's guard had set themselves to gain the regard and lull the watchfulness of their captors. They had not been particularly successful so far, but the stratagem seemed sound under the circumstances.

The single men of the clan took their meals with their leader. The men who had wives, or at any rate women to take care of their needs, kept for the most part to the other log cabins that straggled around the main house. During the day, Angeline had heard the noises of children at play, babies crying, all the sounds of a small village. What would happen to these dependents if the camp were attacked? she wondered. And what maggot of stupidity or arrogance possessed the men to subject their families to the danger?

Claire, when she arrived, was a beacon that drew the eyes of every man at the table. She wore chartreuse velvet with a short spencer jacket of orange satin and her hair was dressed *à la Tite*, as if she had spent the afternoon doing nothing except preparing her toilette as for some grand occasion. It was some time before Angeline realized that she herself was just as much an object of attention. However, the speculative stares of the men resting on her hair, sliding over her face flushed with heat from the fire to the circumspect neckline of her gown and her ringless fingers, were enough to destroy her desire for food. Even the McCullough himself bent his tobacco-brown gaze upon her in narrow, admiring appraisal as he shoveled beans into his mouth.

The situation was not helped by Meyer and Oscar sitting on either side of her, bristling in her defense. As if to surround her with an aura of protection, Meyer reached often to place some juicy tidbit on her plate, leaned close to speak to her in low tones, and touched her arm to draw her attention, smiling into her gray-green eyes.

Claire watched the byplay with derision curling her lips. Crumbling the cornbread in her long white fingers, she turned her emerald stare upon a bearded outlaw with one ear, the other having been bitten off in a no-holds-barred fight. A short time later the one-eared man came to his feet with a bellow and charged into the man beside him. As they fell to the floor punching, gouging, and kicking, Claire watched with disdain, though there was avid excitement behind her dropped lashes.

No one else paid over much notice until a knife blade flashed silver in the lamplight. The McCullough growled an order then, at the same time slanting a look at Claire that boded no good for her. She only smiled, and turned to watch as a second knife flipped through the air to stand quivering with its point in the puncheon floor in reach of the one-eared outlaw.

The two men circled, grinning. They lunged and jabbed with grunts and curses, doing little damage. Sweat broke out on their faces, trickling, dampening their shirts of homespun, permeating the smoky air in the close room with its acrid, animalistic odor. There was a quick pass and blood appeared in a rent in the sleeve of the bearded, one-eared man. His face twisted with pain, he stepped into the guard of his opponent, slashing with set teeth. The other man cried out, and his knife dropped with a clang to the floor as he stood holding his arm with blood dripping from his fingers, one of which had been hacked away.

"Crude and clumsy," Claire said in tones bell-like with contempt. "Any one of the men with the prince could have done it in half the time, and with more finesse. I am not certain that Prince Rolfe, as ill as he is, could not have dispatched both without disturbing his bandages. If this is the quality of fighting men you have around you, I'm not surprised you have to stoop to ambushing women."

"Ye think so?" the McCullough growled.

"I know so."

"Maybe it should be put to the test?" he suggested.

Claire lifted a brow, her pose regal. "Who am I to say? You must amuse yourself as you see fit."

"It will nae be for my amusement only," the outlaw leader said, his tobacco-brown gaze shrewd as he studied the woman beside him. "Still and all, I hae a mind to see what kind of men these overdressed fops come here from the old country be."

The men of the cadre present glanced at one another. There was no reluctance in their eyes, only wariness at the turn things had taken and a certain anticipation of a break in their passive roles as prisoners.

"A true test should also include their prowess with swords and pistols, should it not?" Claire inquired in silken innocence.

Hearing it, Angeline knew suddenly that the other girl hoped to provide the members of the cadre the means to effect their escape, and hers. What Claire did not realize was that their loyalty to the prince would not let them leave him. Glancing at the McCullough, she thought the outlaw leader was not fooled by Claire's ploy. His face was sour as he looked from his new mistress to those of his men at the table who were shouting and hooting their readiness to refute the slur cast upon them. The only question was how confident the Scotsman was that he could control the situation—and the men of the prince once they had weapons in their hands. Abruptly he brought the flat of his hand crashing down on the tabletop. "There's nae room in here. Bring the lamps and we'll take the meet outside."

They crowded into the dogtrot, shouting and laughing and passing demijohns of raw corn whiskey from hand to hand. Dogs yelped as they were chased into the yard, women complained, and bets were passed. A wild smell came from the pelts on the walls and the unwashed bodies packed at either end of the open space. The wind whipped the smoke that rose from the whale oil lanterns and made the flames sputter so that the wavering light cast odd shadows over the log walls and ceiling beams. The lantern glow played among the shovels and picks, the wagon rims and plowshares, woven baskets and sacks of weevilly seed and dried fruit that hung from the exposed rafters overhead. It also shone on the faces, reckless and ready, of the challenged outlaws, and glittered in Claire's excited emerald eyes.

They chose to compete with pistols first. A piece of split cypress shingle painted with a crude bull's eye was set up as the target. It struck Angeline that there was in the atmosphere some of the same violent good humor that had been evident the night she had held the playing card for Rolfe's shots. And then she saw the outlaw guards, more than a dozen in number, file down the dogtrot, taking up positions along its length, each man armed with a long rifle primed and ready to fire.

A chill moved over her. Suddenly, she could not bear to stand watching among the close-pressed bodies. She pushed her way through the crowd toward the side of the house where Rolfe lay. At the entrance she saw Gustave in close conversation with Leopold. Rolfe was alone then. Brushing past them she thrust inside the common room, then came up short.

The door to Rolfe's bedchamber stood open. The light from a single candle left burning on the mantel streamed into the darkened room. It illuminated the figure of a man just inside. He stood unmoving, his attention on the man in the bed. As Angeline started forward he spun around, dropping into a crouch.

It was Oswald. Recognizing her, he straightened, a self-conscious grin moving across his thin features. He came toward her then, his voice low as he spoke. "I wanted to check on Rolfe in case the noise outside disturbed him."

Angeline gave a nod, though she could not seem to make herself relax. "I hardly see how it can do otherwise when the shooting starts."

"It seems a pity."

"You mean he is still asleep?"

Before Oswald could answer a voice hoarsely caustic issued from the room he had just left. "No, nor am I like to be so long as hordes of the heavy-footed hold concourse just outside and conspirators whisper in the gloom. Either go and stop the din or else come and give me reason for it, but refrain from behaving as if before a sepulcher."

Angeline moved into the bedchamber at once. Oswald lingered long enough to fetch the candle before following. Placing the wooden candlestand on the stool where the rays would not glare into Rolfe's eyes, he began a trenchant, if detailed, report of what was occurring.

When he had finished, Rolfe lay staring at him with the fathomless expression that suggested swift and cogent thought. "The chances for success?"

"Minuscule to nonexistent."

"Your recommendation?"

"Wait for better odds, when you will be in our vanguard," Oswald said promptly.

"No thought of my circumstances weighted your decision, I trust. Five men free of unnatural fetters are much more of an asset to a beleaguered commander than the same loyal force in bonds."

"Doubtless, but the McCullough is expecting some sort of sophisticated knavery. As grating as it may be to disappoint him, I fear we must. He will be less vigilant another time."

"You intend then to lull him with your decadence? Or will you inspire him with awe for your skill?"

"Both, I think," Oswald said, and smiled.

There was neither trust nor mistrust implicit in the exchange, only a certain respect on both sides. Angeline could not prevent herself from watching Oswald closely as he said his goodnights and went away to join the others. His reason for being there might be just as he had said, and then again, it might not. No one was exempt from suspicion.

When she turned back, Rolfe lay with his eyes closed. His breathing was quick and shallow, as if the brief conversation had been a great effort. His fever still burned unchecked; the signs of it were in his cracked lips, his features refined to something near fragility with a sunken look under the high Slavic cheekbones, and the scabbed dryness of the scratches and scrapes standing out on his skin. His hands lay still on the coverlet, the strong, tapering fingers relaxed, and the gold of his wolf's head ring shining dully in the lamplight. If he was aware she had not left the room, he gave no sign, not even where she came to stand beside the bed. She wondered if he had slid gently into semiconsciousness, and was nearly sure of it when he did not stir as a light tap came on the door.

It was Morning Star. She carried a small, steaming iron kettle by its bail in one hand, the aroma rising from it pungent and strong. In the other, she held a knife of lethal sharpness.

"You are a woman of heart, not like the other," the Indian girl said. "I will help with your man."

Angeline paused, considering. Meyer, for all his touted skill, had not offered any medicinal means of improving the condition of the prince, doubtless because there had been no time to think of bringing such curatives in their hasty flight. What did that leave? Cauterizing the wounds as he had suggested, a course that would be a shock in itself.

"I am not certain he will permit it," Angeline said with steadfast frankness.

"He will not refuse you," came the answer.

Angeline was not so sure. It was a relief then that braving the test proved unnecessary. Rolfe did not move sinew or muscle as she drew back the covers, nor did the fringe of gold-tipped lashes that rested on his cheeks flutter as she pressed the cold steel of the knife blade to the flat expanse of his belly before sliding it upward to slit the bandage bound tightly about his waist. The cloth was stuck to the gaping, swollen edges of the wounds, both in the front portion of his side and in the back where the ball had exited. She dampened it with liquid from the pot Morning Star had brought, and with painstaking slowness pried it free.

The Indian girl instructed her in how to apply the stewed herbs. Angeline dipped a spoonful dripping from the pot, testing for heat since she did not want to scald Rolfe. Taking a deep breath, she laid the rusty green mess over the first of the holes in his side.

A shiver, an involuntary spasm of the muscles, ran over his frame, then subsided. With Morning Star's help, she was able to turn him slightly to reach the second wound, from which angry red streaks angled toward his back. The primitive poultice was bound to him with clean strips of bandaging and he was covered once more. They turned their attention then to his head injury, removing the soiled strip of underdress that covered it, washing the groove with the still warm herb water, scrubbing the rust-red of old, dried blood from the soft golden strands of his hair. As they worked, they heard the crashing explosion of gunfire, and later, the clash of swords, the weapons of the cadre. So absorbed in what she was doing was Angeline that she scarcely noticed.

At last the Indian girl took up her heavy pot and, promising to return in the morning to see if more was necessary, went away. Angeline took a length of gray but clean toweling and, leaning carefully over the bed, began to brush dry the bright blond waves where they had been left wet.

"Stuffed and dressed with vegetables, roasting like a suckling pig in my own heat. What comes next—the sauce?"

Angeline jumped. She had been so certain he was unconscious that the shock of hearing him speak was like a numbing poison running along her nerves. Made stupid by surprise, she said, "You are awake!"

"To my sorrow."

"But—but you let me care for your wounds!"

He opened his eyes, his smile fever-bright. "You were so anxious to do something, and it seemed... a harmless enough indulgence."

"So kind of you," she exclaimed, her lips tightening.

"Have I offended you?" he inquired, his tone not quite steady. "Now why? I have—never objected to any attention you chose to—pay me."

"I have not paid you any!"

"Can I be blamed for enjoying the novelty then?"

"You are delirious," she snapped.

"With joy?"

Ignoring his soft murmur, she said, "What if I had decided to—to slit your gullet?"

"Crude, too crude. Your vengeance, I think, would be a softer, more deadly kind, scented, searing, and indefensible."

Mollified against her will, though determined not to let him know, Angeline swung to mix another of the sleeping powders in water. Thrusting it toward him, she said, "Here, go to sleep."

He made no move to take it. "Harmless sleep that deadens the senses and unravels the threads of strain. Do I dare?"

"Your gullet is safe. You must."

He closed his eyes. "The noise outside has stopped. The contest is over."

"Would you like to know who won?"

"The cadre, if I know the men I have trained, and if they did not—the news—can wait."

His voice sank to a whisper. It was not sleep that robbed it of strength, however, but weakness. For the same reason, he had not reached to take the powder she held. With a quiet imprecation for her own failure to understand, Angeline leaned to slip her hand beneath his head. His eyes fluttered open and, holding her gray-green gaze, he drank.

Within minutes his chest was stirring with the quiet rhythm of benign slumber. This time it was real and deep. He did not rouse when, sometime after, the candle guttered out, dying in a shallow pool of grease, did not move as Angeline slid under the coverlet beside him, did not feel the hand she reached out to touch his hot forehead. She lay for hours, or so it seemed, unmoving, staring with burning eyes into the darkness. And slept finally with the tips of her fingers tangled in his hair.

The gray of early morning was in the room when she awoke. Rolfe was still deep in sleep, or if he was feigning the undreaming stillness it was a perfect counterfeit. She debated sponging his still hot body with water, but there was less than an inch left in the cracked ironstone pitcher. With the pitcher in her hand, she left the bedchamber and, crossing the empty common room, stepped out into the dogtrot of the house.

The McCullough, sitting in a chair tipped back against the wall with a hide seat still bearing the hair of the brindle cow who had supplied it, looked up. He let the front legs of his chair drop to the floor with a thud. "There ye are. I was wondering where ye got tae last night."

"I have a patient to take care of."

"How is he? Any chance the man'll be fit to be writing a letter today?"

"Very little," Angeline said, her voice sharp.

"I've had a thought, did I. It was mentioned that the French legation in New Orleans is for taking care of the business of Ruthenia in these United States, a courtesy like. I have been thinking 'twould be a fine thing if the letter yon bonny man writes was carried there. Mayhap I'd be for getting my gold and silver that much faster, then?"

"I wouldn't know."

"But the prince'd, I ken."

"You'll have to ask him," she answered, making as if to move past.

He caught her arm. "That I will, and I'll be looking tae it wi' joy. They do say, his men, that he's a brae one with pistols, his sword, even hand-to-hand fightin', better than they be."

"And they are better than you and your men?" she inquired sweetly.

"Better than the knuckle haids that ride wi' me, any by. My own skill I have nae tested, though I'm no green hand when it comes tae using a pistol, or cutlass for the matter. I sailed a year or two with Lafitte before yon fracas at New Orleans. When 'twas over I took my pardon from 'Ol' Hickory' and made for land."

"Perhaps when he is well, if he lingers that long with you, you will have the opportunity to see for yourself what he can do."

"I'd like that, I would. 'Twould be a fine thing to see his style. Aye, a fine thing."

"Yes," Angeline said, turning her wrist, trying to break his hold. "If you will let me go, I have to see to him."

"Ah, and what a bonny nursemaid you be, fair enough tae make a man take tae his bed. Ye be different from yon Claire, witch that she is, scratchin' and bitin' and yellin' fit tae bring the roof down. Ye be a quiet one, but deep, wi' eyes tae soothe a man and make his spirit lie, even while you raise his blood to boilin'. That's what makes ye the special woman tae His Highness then. I make no doot."

"I asked you to let me go," Angeline said, setting her feet to resist the slow and steady pull he exerted on her wrist. "You have two women. Isn't that enough?"

"I had two, right enough, but now there be only one."

"What?" she said, going still as visions of Claire killed by this man, or perhaps taking her own life, flashed through her mind.

"Morning Star is gone. I had tae put her frae me for the sake of yon witch. 'Twas a wager, she backin' the prince's men and me my own. She won, so my Mornin' Star was put out. She tried to knife me, she did, the Indian hellcat, and I had to clip her one on the chin. Eve' then she near unmanned me kicking and squirming whilst I threw her on a horse."

"And now you have no one to cook your breakfast? How terrible for you." Her sympathy carried a mocking note.

"Claire does nae cook," he agreed simply.

"You should have thought of that before you agreed to the wager!"

"Oh, aye, but then I was sure of winnin', and the forfeit I asked for was worth the chance."

She opened her mouth to ask what that was, then, catching the lascivious glint in his eye, shut her lips again. "You must apply to one of the other women."

"Aye, I could do that, but I'd have to tae wait till she finished with her own cookin'."

"Too bad." Twisting her wrist downward abruptly, she won free. As she dived for the door, the McCullough surged to his feet with a force that overturned his chair, and clamped a hand on her arm so she was brought swinging around against him.

"Let her go!"

It was Meyer who spoke, coming from the back of the house, just moving up the steps into the dogtrot. Behind him were ranged Gustave and Oswald. Loose-limbed and athletic, they were unarmed, but still a powerful force for one man to face alone.

The McCullough dropped her arm as if he had been stung. "Noo then," he said, rubbing his palm on the seat of his homespun breeches. "I was nae going to hurt her. She's like the honey that draws the bees, standin' there so sweet and fine I could nae resist like. 'Twas ye men I was waitin' for all along. I hae a proposition you mon want to pay heed tae."

"We are listening." Meyer glanced at Angeline with a faint tilt of his head toward the door. She needed no further suggestion. Moving quickly, she stepped around the outlaw leader and entered the other side of the house, where on a bench near the fireplace sat a bucket of water drawn from the well at the back. Filling her pitcher, she turned once more toward the dogtrot. Through the open doorway she could hear the McCullough saying something about the cadre helping to train his men.

"If I had fifty the likes of ye three, I could own No Man's Land; ferry crossin', roads, tradin' posts, and all. I'd be that rich I'd ne'er need to be robbin' anymore, except mayhap to keep my hand in. And best o' all, that snake-mean Spanisher that is set himself up against me would have nae more chance than a backslid whore at a meetin' of shoutin' preachers!"

The first thing that Angeline saw as she came into the bedchamber was the glisten of beads of perspiration

standing across Rolfe's upper lip, lying in the hollows
beneath his eyes, and trickling slowly along his hairline
to soak the pillow on which he lay. His hair was dark
gold with it and the sheets were drenched. It gleamed
along the muscles of his arms and shone across the
planes of his torso where he had pushed away the
cover in his restless discomfort.

She stood with tears rising in her throat and her
hand pressed to her mouth, then when that brief
flood of emotion had passed she swung away. The
danger now was a chill from lying half-drowned in
the morning coolness. He needed sponging from
head to foot, the bedclothes changed, and something
nourishing, like hot broth, poured into him. She had
to have help and with Morning Star gone it would
have to be one of Rolfe's guard, preferably the first
one she came across.

Oscar and Oswald, their faces scrubbed and high-
colored, as if they had been performing their morning
toilettes in a water pail, had joined the others. The five
of them, with the McCullough, were still gathered in
a group, talking with quick gestures, interrupting each
other. They looked up, an inquiry on every face, as
she came so impetuously from the common room out
into the dogtrot.

Before she could speak, there came a hail from the
front of the house and a pair of riders trotted into
view. On a third horse between them sat a man with
his head down. There was a bruise like a purple smear
across one cheek and his arms were tied behind his
back. He was hatless, his fine dark hair lifting gently in
the morning breeze. The first rays of the sun slanting

across his features caught the olive tint shadowing his skin, the thin mustache that outlined his lip. With his black eyes dazed, he stared at the group of people standing in the dogtrot, and then his glance caught and held upon Angeline. His lips formed her name, though he made no sound. Abruptly, he laughed.

It was André.

Thirteen

IN THE DAYS THAT FOLLOWED, ROLFE SLEPT, WOKE TO take broth and Burgundy, then slept again. A portion of his care was taken over by the cadre, who sat with him in pairs for his protection and their own satisfaction. Only at night was he left alone with Angeline. During the daylight hours, he was restless, but when darkness fell, he lay quiet, sleeping undisturbed by the firing of pistols in endless competition, the music of jew's harp, fiddle, and guitar, or the bawling of a herd of cattle driven into the outlaw stronghold under cover of night.

Released from the sickroom by day, Angeline was able to speak briefly with André. His presence was explained simply. He had set out on the trail of Angeline's abductors and been caught in the same net that had dragged them in. The bruise to his face was fading, but the blow to his ego would take longer to recover. He had thought to rescue her, and merely wound up looking ridiculous. So far, he was stubbornly holding out against the efforts to make him give his surname and the direction of his nearest relatives, but he knew well enough that it was only a matter of time before he would be forced to capitulate. Low in spirit, he could see no way that Angeline might be wrested from the outlaw McCullough, even if she could be taken from Rolfe and the men of his guard.

"Angeline?" he said one day as he sat watching while she chopped beef and threw it into water seasoned with salt and red peppers, beef from the cattle stolen by the clan.

She sent him a smiling glance. "Yes?"

"Are you certain you want to be rescued?"

"What a thing to ask!" Angeline stared at him with her knife held in the air, too startled to be offended.

"I beg your pardon," he said, keeping his voice low, "but I think our... friendship in the past gives me the right. You are Rolfe's mistress, are you not?"

"Certainly not!"

"How can you deny it, when you tend him like a devoted wife and share his bed?"

She lowered her gaze, taking the fat from a chunk of beef with great care. "He has been very ill."

He made a quick gesture of dismissal, as if the state of Rolfe's health made no difference. "I realize you were forced in the beginning, but I wonder if I were to ask you to come away with me now, would you do it?"

"We would not be allowed to go."

"But if we were?" he insisted.

"It would not be fair to you, to put you in that kind of danger, to saddle you with the responsibility for my welfare."

"That is my worry."

She raised her soft gray-green gaze at last. Her tone held pain and a trace of dismay as she said, "I couldn't leave him, not while I'm needed."

The bruise on his face had turned yellow. Now the skin around it took on the same hue. "I understand. You will be with him permanently, then?"

"Are you trying to ask if we are to be wed? The answer is no, we are not. I have been warned that it is impossible, and I accept that."

"Warned?" he exclaimed, his color returning in a rush. "You mean that petty princeling dared—"

"It was not the prince," she said quickly.

"Then who?"

"Does it matter?" The rising timbre and strain edging her voice carried their own appeal.

He did not ignore it, and yet he gave her more than one peculiar glance as he spoke of other things. It was a relief when Oscar came to bear him off to the shooting range that had been set up behind the barn.

There was some awkwardness between André and herself when next they met, but it soon passed. By degrees, they attained something of their old friendliness. He was more careful than the other members of the cadre to help her with the heavy work of bringing in wood and water, more apt to notice when she was tired. She discovered, in fact, that he kept close watch on her always, particularly in that moment at the end of the day when she went into the room she shared with Rolfe and closed the door. At those times, his face would take on a bleak hardness that made him look older than his years, and in his eyes would be the opaque glaze of suppressed fury.

Despite his anger toward the man who led the cadre, as the days slipped away it was not long before André was drawn into the fearsome game Rolfe's men were playing with the outlaws. Learning to shoot, to wield a sword for another purpose besides a show of valor on the dueling field, he grew more adept at parroting the imperial maxims handed down by the cadre's leader than all the others. His prowess improved so rapidly that he was easily able to outperform the majority of the outlaws that had been taken on as pupils, and he was only slightly less able than the members of the *garde du corps* themselves. As he attained excellence, and with it self-confidence, his respect for the man behind the training grew in spite of himself, regardless of the fact that he never spoke directly to Rolfe if he could prevent it.

André was not the only one to benefit. More and more, the men of the cadre found an outlet for their energy in the physical exercise of competition. It helped to take their minds from the stalemate they were in, far from the places of their births. It helped also to broaden their own range of skills. Fighting with broad-bladed hunting knives, or in rough-and-tumble, no-holds-barred contests that might end with eyes gouged out and ears chewed from their heads, was foreign to them in many ways. The agility, strength, and quick thinking needed to emerge supreme were not, however. Before long, the cadre was able to fend off punishment in those barbaric competitions as well, and even to give it. Meyer, in particular, showed an affinity for the long-bladed knife with its thick hilt and vicious, honed edge.

The men were able to use the knife for its proper
purpose at least once. A hunting expedition was
mounted in search of wild boar. The animals, the
descendants of pigs left to run free in the woods and
to live on acorns, nuts, roots, and berries, were hunted
down with dogs. They were dispatched by shots from
the long rifles, then at each kill a man had to go forward
to cut the throat of the dying animal or else thrust a
knife blade through the heart of the beast to let the
excess blood drain away so the meat would be edible.

The portion of the pork allotted to the McCullough
and his prisoners was no small one. It was Angeline's lot
to cut it up and cover it with salt to preserve it before
it was hung in the smoke house for further curing. She
was aided in this task by André and Oscar, and also by
Meyer. It was a laborious and messy job, though the
smell of pork chops gently frying, to go with beaten
biscuits for supper, made it seem worthwhile.

By slow degrees, a major portion of the cooking
had become her responsibility. Someone had to see
that clean, healthy dishes were prepared for Rolfe, and
while she was stirring his soups and stews it seemed
not much more trouble to throw something into the
pots over the fire to feed the others.

The McCullough, for some reason, appeared to take
her efforts as a personal compliment. As his tobacco-
brown eyes rested upon her there was a look of
complacency in them that grated on Angeline's nerves.
More than once she had to sidestep his grasping hands
as she passed near him. He pinched her one day before
she could avoid him, a mistake since she held a full
pot of hot coffee at the time. As she swung around by

sheer reflex action in her embarrassed and astonished wrath, the pot tipped and the scalding brew cascaded in a stream of steaming brown into his lap. Yelling, cursing as he jumped around holding the front of his breeches out from his body, he sent her a look of irascible accusation, but he had dared do no more since Oscar, gleefully amused, was present at the time, as well as Claire.

It was to her cousin, Angeline thought, that she owed her greatest relief from the McCullough's clumsy attentions. Despise him though she might, Claire seemed to grow daily more protective of her position as the outlaw's woman. It represented security, freedom from the lust barely contained in the other men of the clan, who came and went like hungry wolves, yellow-eyed and subdued, but with menace in their loose smiles.

One day Angeline came upon Claire standing with her back against the wall, surrounded by five or six of the outlaws like a doe at bay. Claire, stark gladness in her emerald eyes, moved from among them at Angeline's call, but the glance she threw backward was apologetic, almost caressing.

The two of them stopped for a moment outside the kitchen door. Claire put a hand on Angeline's arm, her voice low, tentative as she said, "Angeline, *chére*, do you ever feel… wicked, as if you must invite a man, any man to lie with you? Does the need of it rise inside you like an illness until you can think of nothing else? Does it seem that only in a man's arms you can forget, find atonement for the pain inside you as he gives you both pleasure and punishment?"

It was raining, the wet, gray streams running from the cypress shingles of the roof. The chill dampness pervaded the air as the muffled drumming closed out other sounds. Angeline stared at her cousin, arrested by the shading of self-loathing in her voice, the haunted look in her eyes.

She answered at last. "I—I have felt... desire for... with one man."

"Only desire? And with your prince, I suppose?" Claire's mouth curved in a weary smile. "That isn't what I meant, though I supposed that men, even princes, being what they are, you may come to feel something similar in time."

"Claire—"

"Spare me your pity; it is the ultimate insult. I know well enough that by my deeds I have blighted my life, and yours. Women are what they are, also. Did you know it? Why don't you hate me? That would be more bearable."

"I might hate you if I thought you were at fault."

Claire laughed, a hollow sound. "How do you know I'm not?"

"You could not be, it's too monstrous," Angeline said, though doubt echoed in her mind.

"Is it? What I would not give to be so certain again, so positive of right and wrong."

In a rush Angeline asked, "What happened with Maximilian? Can you tell me?"

"Max?" Claire said as if the name had a bitter taste in her mouth. "I loved him, that is the important thing. Everything else is... ugly past the telling."

A door opened on the other side of the dogtrot and

Oscar stepped out. Claire stiffened, then swung away, letting herself into the kitchen.

The quietest member of the cadre moved to stand at Angeline's side. "You look distressed. Is something wrong?"

Angeline gave him a fixed smile. "Nothing, and everything."

Rolfe's failure to rebound from the effects of his wounds once the fever was past, his meekness in accepting the gruels and possets she made, his lack of vitality, were a source of constant worry. He had lost quite a lot of blood, of course, and the ravages of fever were enough to weaken the strongest constitution, but for some reason Angeline had expected him to be less vulnerable than other men. Ridiculous, naturally.

The gash across his head had healed to a long, crusted scab, but it was possible that it had been more serious than had at first been thought. Or could it be that the depression of the spirits brought on by his untenable captivity made him careless of regaining his health? She would have thought he would be anxious to get well in order to force his release. While he was confined to his bed with doubt of his recovery hanging like a funeral vestment over the outlaw camp, at least the McCullough made no further demands of him for a letter requesting ransom of his father, the king.

Once she stopped just outside the bedchamber door where Rolfe lay, the better to adjust the tray she carried. From inside she thought she heard his voice raised in its old, baffling insouciance, lilting in poetic meter as he spoke to Gustave and Leopold, who sat with him. So startled was she that the dishes she held clattered together. When she pushed inside however, he lay still with his hands folded in listless repose upon the coverlet while Gustave swung rather shamefacedly to greet her with one hand held stiffly at his side, almost behind his back. There was a definite aroma of food in the room.

"What is that you have there?" She stared pointedly at Gustave.

"Now, Angeline, *meine liebe*," he began to protest.

"Are you hiding something?"

The one-eyed veteran sighed. "Only a bit of the turkey left from dinner."

What he brought forth was a full quarter of the bird, one of several wild turkeys bagged the day before.

"Something to tide you over until the next meal, I suppose?"

"You—you might say so," Gustave mumbled, sending Leopold a fierce glance from the corner of his eye.

"No doubt you thought the sight of you chewing such a morsel would tempt Rolfe's appetite?" she suggested, disappointment giving her tone a flicking note of sarcasm.

"Yes—well, perhaps 'twas a foolish idea." He looked to his leader in harried appeal but Rolfe only returned a limpid stare, one corner of his mouth quirked in what might have been amusement.

"That being the case, you can remove yourself and your meal!"

He obeyed with alacrity, but even as he went she was puzzled by the hilarity lingering in Leopold's eyes and the set look on Rolfe's face as he watched Gustave bear the offending roast turkey from the room.

There was another incident. One day while the cadre was out hunting, Angeline built up the fire in the common room to a roaring blaze and, dragging a wooden tub on to the hearth, poured into it water she had heated to boiling. She proceeded to take a long, soaking bath, even washing her hair after a fashion with the harsh, jellylike lye soap that was the only kind available. Scrubbed, marvelously refreshed, rosily flushed from the hot water, she wrapped a length of thin gray toweling around herself and moved into the bedchamber to search for a comb. After she found a wooden strip with wide, hand-carved teeth, she stood before the small, polished steel mirror over the washstand, drawing it with difficulty through the wet, tangled mass of her hair. As she leaned to one side to draw the length of her tresses over one shoulder, the toweling slipped, unfurling slowly, exposing the creamy, pink-tinted curves of her body as it dropped to the floor.

From the direction of the bed there came the sound of a sharp indrawn breath. She was sure of it. And yet when she turned to glance at him, Rolfe lay with his eyes closed and his hair glinting golden against the pillow.

That night, however, he lay on the far edge of the bed in unyielding stiffness, making no move to touch her or draw her nearer as he often had done even in the fever of delirium. As she turned restlessly, half asleep, her ankle brushed against him on the mattress and the tension leaped to palpable heights. In the brief contact she had felt the rigidity of his muscles. It crossed her mind to question why, but there was something in the

silence pulled taut between them that made it seem a
dangerous undertaking. He was not ill. His breathing
was deep and even, rigorously controlled. It was not
the pain of his wound that troubled him, for lately as
he turned he had ceased to favor or protect his side.

A vagrant idea came to her, but she dismissed it.
Why should he yearn for her, or yearning, fail to reach
out and take what he wanted? When, tired from the
exertion of the day, she slept at last, Rolfe still had not
relaxed, but lay staring into the dark.

Perhaps four days later the cadre, with André
among them, went hunting yet again, a night hunt
into the midnight hours. There had been a fox raiding
among the chickens, those that roosted at night in
the makeshift henhouse instead of flapping up to the
treetops where it was safe.

The men waited under cover until the alarmed
cackle of the chickens signaled the return of the
fox. From snatches of conversation she had heard,
Angeline thought no one expected to come up with
the fox quickly. A major part of the enjoyment of the
outing was, apparently, to build a large fire and sit
around it drinking while listening to the loosed dogs
giving chase with bugling voices carried on the wind.
Then, racing to their horses, the men tore out after
the swift-running hounds holding torches streaming
smoke while demijohns of whiskey bounced against
their saddle cloths.

Despite the attraction of the hunt, the outlaw
stronghold was not left unguarded. The McCullough
himself stayed behind, as did those whose turn it was
to watch over the roads leading to the house and most

of the men with families. The McCullough encour-
aged the men of Rolfe's guard to go; it would be an
experience they would long remember, he said, one
nae to be missed, this New World method of hunting
the fox.

The hour grew late. Angeline sat in the empty
common room, huddled into a corner of the rough
settle, staring into the fire. She wished for something
to read, a piece of needlework, anything to occupy
her hands and her mind. It seemed sometimes as if her
thoughts, endlessly repeating themselves, had worn
a groove in her brain from which it was impossible
to divert them. Going over the same ground again
and yet again, she could find nothing she might have
done differently, nothing that would have affected the
outcome of the past, nothing she might do in the future
that would guarantee happiness for the remainder of
her life. To dwell upon her circumstances was morbid,
but without any distraction, inescapable.

Behind her, the door leading to the dogtrot
creaked open. She lifted her head, turning to see
the McCullough closing the panel behind him. He
came toward her with sureness in his stride and a
satisfied smile curving his mouth, half hidden in his
bushy beard.

"There ye be, me dear girl. It's long I've waited
tae be alone with ye. Now that yon witch Claire is
sleeping and the others chasing a will-o'-the-wisp in
the swamps, let's make best use of the time we have."

Angeline came to her feet in slow-rising alarm.
"What are you talking about?"

"Ye ken well that I hae wanted ye. Women always

ken these things." There shone in his tobacco-brown eyes confidence and uncomplicated lust.

"But I don't want you!"

"Is it a game ye be playin'? Ye ken well that ye'd be better off with me than yon prince. I can protect ye, and he canna." His voice and accent thickened with emotion.

Angeline backed away from his slow advance, rounding the end of the settle, putting it between them. "What—what of Claire?"

"Aye, she be a problem, but I ken how to handle bitches such as her. To rule them, a man must never turn his back and be ever ready with a touch of the whip. So long as they ken who is master they make no trouble."

"You have her! What can you want with me?"

"Ah, you're that soft and sweet, that fine and beautiful and loving that you haunt a man, like a woman in a dream, or like the angel you are named. Dinna send me away."

His words were coaxing, and it might have been that he meant them, but the expression on his face was crafty as he circled the settle. He stalked her with swinging arms, the bulge in the front of his breeches making his rampant desire for her all too evident.

"This—this is foolish," she said, trying for a tone of reason. "I must ask you to leave me in peace, or else I will call out."

"Call for Prince Rolfe, maybe? Do that, if you like. He should be no more trouble to me, nor help to you, than a gnat."

With quick darting glances she searched the room for a weapon, saw one in the iron poker leaning against the fireplace. "The others, his men, will not let you get away with it."

"They are nae here."

Hard on the words, he lunged for her. She ducked and twisted, eluding his grasping hands to dive for the poker. The iron bar was heavy as she swung it, whirling back on him. He gave a yelp as the poker scraped his paunch, then with a mighty curse, he reached out on her backswing, clamping a hand around the soot-blackened end. He wrenched it from her grasp and, mouthing an oath, flung it with a clattering clang against the wall. The soot on his hands was smeared on the sleeve of her gray gown as he grabbed for her, dragging her against him. She kicked and wrenched away, but her struggles seemed only to excite him.

With crushing strength, he pulled her toward the corner where a pallet, one of those used by the cadre, was spread.

"No," Angeline panted, "no!"

"Don't make such a to-do," he growled as he sent her sprawling, flinging himself to his knees beside her. He tugged the suspenders from his shoulders, grinning. "It only takes a minute, and you mon like it."

He threw himself across her then, his beard rasping her face as he sought her lips. Soot blackened her clothing with telltale handprints as he pawed over her, squeezing the soft globe of one breast. Fury and pain burst inside her, and with raking nails she reached for his eyes.

He jerked his head back, snatching for her wrists, hunching himself upward to throw a knee across her thighs, to prevent her from kicking away from him. Her hands were numb from his grip, and with sickness rising from the pit of her stomach, she felt his hot, wet lips slide across her cheek.

Abruptly he gave a strangled cry as his body froze into immobility. Angeline, her breath catching on a gasp, slid from his grip that was suddenly lax, shuddering as she pushed away from him. Only then did she open her eyes.

Resting on one knee at the edge of the pallet with his forearm propped across his thigh was Rolfe. He wore only a pair of pantaloons hastily donned and a white swath of bandaging about his waist. In his hand, the point pressing into the McCullough's bull-like neck so that a bright drop of blood welled around it, was a long-bladed hunting knife. He was pale, but his hand was steady, and in his face there was a deadly calm.

"What shall it be?" he asked, his tone soft. "A pig's death, merciful and without a squeal, or swinish and undeserved life?"

The question was meant for her; the McCullough realized it before she did. "Angeline," he groaned, "for the love of God—"

"You will address her," Rolfe said tightly, "as Mademoiselle Fortin."

"Anything," the outlaw leader agreed, adding hastily as the knife point sank deeper, "Mademoiselle—Fortin."

"Don't," she said sharply, mistrusting the set purpose of Rolfe's face. "Don't kill him."

He sent her a piercing look. "Why didn't you scream, call out for me?"

"I had no breath to spare, and—and I didn't know it would do any good."

There was a tense moment while the McCullough shut his eyes tightly and sweat beaded his forehead, trickling down his nose. Gripping the knife hilt, Rolfe's brown hand was white around the knuckles. Angeline held her breath. Then as the knife was withdrawn with sudden decision a silent sigh left her.

Rolfe came smoothly to his feet and, transferring the knife to his left hand, reached to give his right to Angeline. He drew her with surprising strength to stand beside him. Staring down at the outlaw leader, he said, "Get up."

The face of the McCullough darkened now that his danger was past. "Ye fooled me, didn't ye? Ye pulled a sly one on us all with yer swilling of pap and dying airs. It will nae help ye."

As the Scotsman came up from the floor, his hand brushed the top of his boot and a knife leaped suddenly into his palm. Instantly Rolfe whirled Angeline behind him, dropping into a knife fighter's crouch. Seeing it, a smile of pleasure made a rent in the McCullough's beard.

"No," Angeline whispered, tightness like a fist gathering in her chest. Immediately, she lifted her fingers to her lips to press back protests. The two men paid no heed as they circled, watching for an opening.

"Ye be a bonny man," the McCullough rasped. "But ye canna beat me at this game, for 'tis mine."

"In Ruthenia, the gypsies can teach the art of wielding a blade to woodcarvers—and in my peach-down days I had a gypsy groom who taught me to ride, to call horses with a soundless whistle, and a few other bits that served to keep me alive and himself, therefore, employed. It may be I know a trick or two that will surprise you."

"Ye be a sick'un, just getting yer strength back from a hole blowed through the side of ye. Would you risk another for the sake of a few minutes gone with your woman, the taking of something she will never miss?"

"The lady's favors are mine by fief and her consent, and like a miser guarding gold, I would miss any loss from the close-hoarded riches."

"Pretty words," the McCullough sneered. "Shall we see if ye can back 'em up?"

Each man's blade flashed in the firelight, the blue gleams running to the wickedly sharp points. They gripped them with the edge up so that a quick thrust would tear through muscle and viscera to cause the most injury. There was enjoyment and a certain anticipation in the McCullough's face, as if this were a contest that suited him. He feinted with a lunging jab, testing the guard of his opponent, his eyes brightly watchful. Rolfe avoided the attack with ease. In his face was total concentration, a narrowing of the senses to the flicker and play of the knife the other man held, but no wariness and no sign of weakness.

Of the two men, Rolfe was taller with a longer reach and smooth, gliding muscles. There was power in the McCullough's squat shape, however, and knotted strength in his thick thighs, shoulders, and arms. To balance the lightning intelligence of the other man, the outlaw brought craftiness to the match.

The McCullough's smile of confidence grew wider

as Rolfe failed to attack. Again and again, he stepped into the defense of the prince, the gleaming arc of his knife swing coming within a hair's breadth of Rolfe's bandaged chest. But Rolfe gave ground without being touched, and without the tremendous effort of the McCullough that brought sweat streaming from him, pouring into his eyes, glistening in his beard, and wetting his shirt.

Watching with her breath caught achingly in her throat, Angeline thought that it was no part of the outlaw leader's plan to kill Rolfe, that he wanted merely to disable him so that he could have both Angeline and the prospect of a fortune in ransom. As for Rolfe, it was difficult to tell his purpose or even to discover if he had one beyond staying alive. He recoiled again and again, his movements like oiled satin, his turquoise gaze suspended in watchfulness.

Confidence burgeoned in the outlaw leader. A laugh rasped in his chest and he began to toss his heavy knife from hand to hand as if tempting Rolfe to make a move while it hung in the air. They circled, their glances clashing, the sound of their breathing harsh. The scuffle of their feet on the rough puncheon floor had an odd, hypnotic rhythm. A sheen of perspiration appeared on Rolfe's brow and gleamed along his arms, catching the fluttering orange fireglow. And then the Scotsman's knife flashed shimmering blue in his left hand, driving for a spot in Rolfe's side, the site of his injury.

There seemed no way to stop it, no way to avoid the blow. Rolfe appeared off guard, seemed caught by the trick in timing since any attack would have been expected while the knife was in his opponent's right hand. A growl of satisfaction began in the McCullough's throat.

It ceased abruptly as Rolfe parried with the skill of a swordsman, catching the knife with a sliding snick, deflecting it and carrying past the straight, unguarded blade to carve away the skin on the tops of the outlaw leader's fingers. The Scotsman yelped, cursing, dragging himself back with a wrenching effort, flinging his knife to his right hand, recovering his guard even while he pressed his cut fingers to the linsey-woolsey of his breeches to staunch the flow of blood. His smile was gone.

"You left yourself open just then," Rolfe chided gently. "A gypsy would have gutted you like a fish. Take care."

"I'll take care—of ye!"

With narrow-eyed cunning he stalked Rolfe then, trying one wily stratagem after another, less concerned now with what injury he might do his opponent than with his growing thirst for revenge. Rolfe matched each maneuver with the appropriate countermeasure, conserving his strength with economy of motion, waiting for the next, balanced and alert. And each time he explained in careful, polished phrases how the other man had erred, though the one mistake he failed to point out, one Angeline grew aware of herself, was the McCullough's habit of looking fixedly at the point of his attack each time a second before he struck.

With every failure, every continuing moment of futile exercise against a man supposed to be ill, before the woman for whom he fought, the Scotsman's control grew less. His temper surged so that he gritted his teeth, gripping his knife with a hand slippery with sweat. His movements became erratic and wild, more desperate to stop the all-too-accurate taunts, to reach and disable the elusive prince. He ceased to think in his flailing rage, which was his most grave mistake.

The McCullough made a pouncing swing with all his strength behind it. Grunting out a curse as he missed yet again, he came back with a slashing backhand that would have sliced through bone had it landed. It did not land. As the fury of his blow sent his knife hand wide, Rolfe stepped forward in a flurry of motion, snatching the outlaw's arm, twisting it, and, in the same split second, hooking his right leg behind the McCullough's knee. The Scotsman went down with a rattling crash. He started to bellow, then fell suddenly silent as he looked up to find Rolfe kneeling before him once more with his knife point balanced delicately against the hard-beating jugular in his throat.

The McCullough, not a stupid man, let his fingers unclench and, scarcely breathing, allowed the knife he held to fall with a thud to the floor.

"Terms," Rolfe said, his tone light, "are in order."

A measure of sanity crept into the Scotsman's eyes. "If I yell, there will be twenty men in here to skin ye like a wolf and throw the leavings to the dogs."

"Twenty men to see you die."

"After the ruckus, they mon be coming already."

"I doubt they would risk intruding on what they doubtless have reason to believe is your pleasure, however rough." The whiplash sting of those words were a reminder that Rolfe had not forgotten the attentions the man on the floor had been pressing upon Angeline. "But even if they would come, even if I should be taken, it would not profit you. Let us talk then of wolves who when their leader falls devour him in their greedy hunger—"

The McCullough went still. "Ye be right, damn ye. If my men see me like this, my life would nae be worth a Doe dollar."

A Doe dollar, Angeline had heard said, was counterfeit money made by a man of that name, a fancy coin the size of the scarce Mexican silver dollars, though more ornately engraved and clad with a thin coating of silver over the base metal. Acceptable tender inside the strip, they were worthless outside it.

"I am happy you take my point."

"I take it," the McCullough growled, "but even if I be struck down, ye canna escape with nothing but the pigsticker in your hand. My men would shoot you down before you had made three steps."

"That is doubtless true, or would be if they saw me. What I require from you instead, then, is your word of honor, not as the man you are now but as the one you used to be, that henceforth Angeline stands in no danger of being molested by you."

There was a brief struggle mirrored on the face of the outlaw leader before he spoke. "Ye would take it—my word?"

"I would."

"Ye have it then, the word of the McCullough."

"And if you break faith," Angeline struck in, "by look, word, or deed, I will make certain that your men know how easily you were bested by Rolfe."

"I'll nae gi' up my ransom," the McCullough warned with stubborn, frank cunning.

"As to that, we will see," Rolfe replied.

"It's a fine, hard pair ye be. I feel lucky to be let go with my skin, that is if I am to be let get up from here?"

Rolfe rose and stepped back, allowing the McCullough to heave himself to his feet. The outlaw leader gave a hitch to his pants, drawing breath with a snorting sound as if he had, until that moment, been chary of inhaling too deeply. His brown gaze met that of Rolfe with a shading of defiance, as if waiting for some sign of the triumph from the other man.

"I bid you good night," Rolfe said, inclining his golden head.

The Scotsman gave a short nod. "I'll nae be forgetting this."

"I trust not."

"I suppose, and if I did, ye would be ready to repeat the lesson."

"You misjudge me," Rolfe murmured. "I never waste time on measures that have been proven ineffective."

"Huh," the McCullough grunted, and, striding to the door, pulled it open. Looking back with the harried expression of a man who has given house room to a rattlesnake, he bobbed his head in a nod and stepped through, closing the panel quickly behind him.

Angeline swung on Rolfe with a frown between her brows. "You could have used him as a hostage, a shield to protect you while you forced your way through the guard around the camp."

"There is no guarantee that he would have had value as a shield. The men on guard might have considered his death a small enough price to pay to keep their hold on the fortune I represent. More than that, I have no way of knowing where the men of the cadre are just now, no way of preventing them from riding back in to face the vengeance of those I might have flouted. For yet another reason, there is no purpose for me in going without Claire, and in such a ticklish situation, I could not depend upon her cooperation. Finally, there is you, my sweet Angeline. To put you at risk, venturing greater injury than already inflicted, is something I cannot do. Nor could I leave you behind."

"I am sorry if I am a handicap!" Angeline turned swiftly from him to hide her confusion, feeling behind her eyes the prickling of tears she would not acknowledge.

"You misunderstand me."

The quiet flick of his voice was enough to make her hesitate. "What is there to understand?"

"That you are too necessary to me for the weight of your safety ever to be a burden."

Whirling back to face him, she caught her breath. She wanted to explore the declaration he had made, to define its limits exactly, and yet doubt restrained her. That she meant something to him she could accept, but that it went any deeper than desire, an attraction of the senses with overtones of compassion and perhaps remorse, was questionable. In defense against her need to know, as much as against him, she lashed out.

"If your concern for me is so great, why did you keep your recovery from me? Why did you keep me hovering over you like a nervous nursemaid with her first charge, boiling endless gruels and broths that I suppose you poured straight into the slop jar!"

"No, no," he said, amusement lurking in his eyes. "I drank them every one."

"And had Gustave smuggle food for you from the kitchen, like that roasted turkey I caught him passing to you!"

"Now there was a sacrifice, letting him take it away untasted."

"But you trusted him, and Leopold too, since he was there that day. I expect every man of your guard knows, and has been laughing at me behind my back for being fool enough to worry over you long after the danger was past." She clenched her fists, crying out, "Why?"

He slipped the knife into the waistband of his pantaloons, moving toward her, catching her arms in a light clasp. "Because you were the one the McCullough was watching, the one they all were watching. I could not be sure that, knowing the need was past, you would still cosset me and brew my possets and, with your look of aggravated anxiety at my lack of progress, keep them off guard."

"What should it matter, any of it, so long as you were still a captive." Against her will she felt herself bending.

"If I could regain my full strength without them being aware, then any ruse chosen to make good our escape would have had a better chance of success."

"But so much wasted time! I thought you were anxious to speak to Claire, to learn of how your brother was killed?"

"Do you think that your cousin would have told me what I wanted to know had I confronted her? I don't, and in the present situation, under the

McCullough's gentle protection, there is no way she can be forced. I have had the cadre speak to her individually, to gain some idea of what approach might meet with success."

"And you discovered," Angeline said slowly, compelled by the memory of a conversation with Claire, "that the most likely avenue was one paved with gold?"

"You know your cousin well."

"Yes." She lowered her gray-green gaze to his chin, which was faintly stubbled in gold. "Now the McCullough knows the deception, and it was all for nothing."

"A careful campaign gone for naught," he agreed, "but I am not sorry."

She looked up, startled. "You're not?"

"As much as I enjoyed having you hover," he said, his voice carrying a warmth that set the blood racing in her veins, "being an invalid had its drawbacks, not the least of them being the dilemma of how to convince you I was lingering at death's door while making violent love to you. Never, I pledge you my word, has my self-control been so tested. A man can sleep only so much as a safeguard from boredom, endure the company of men only so long with a lovely woman near at hand, always out of reach. Another day and I would have feigned delirium as an excuse to hold you."

"I might have been too frightened to respond," she said, her lashes veiling her expression though she could not prevent the hint of a smile that indented the corner of her mouth.

"And what of now?" he queried, then sought his answer not in words but by setting his mouth to hers.

The touch ran like wildfire along her veins. Animosity, doubt, the niggling hurt of exclusion were forgotten in the surge of rapture that consumed her. With a faint sound of despairing surrender, she spread the palms of her hands over his chest, sliding them upward, clasping her fingers behind his head as she pressed closer against him. His kiss deepened, tasting, probing. His chest swelled with the content of a man long starved, and he drew her more firmly against him, his hold tightening, one hand smoothing down to span her hips as if he would imprint the memory of her tender curves upon his body.

The pallet, rumpled but softer than the wood floor, still lay in the corner. He guided her toward it with caressing urgency. Dropping to one knee, he drew her down beside him until she lay full-length. He hovered above her, bending to brush the trembling softness of her lips with his own, his hands cupping the swell of her breast that strained against the material of her gown. With gentle insistence, he turned her to her stomach then, working quickly at the buttons of the closing that confined her, stopping as if compelled to trail his lips over the smooth, white skin of her back.

Stripping gown and underdress from her arms, pushing them downward over her hips and off, he lowered himself beside her. He pulled her against him, nestling her form into the curve of his body with her back to him so the bare skin of their upper bodies touched with a heated, fusing sensation. He breathed deeply of the warm scent of her hair, whispering her name against her temple, before brushing the shining length from her shoulder to press his questing mouth to the tender turn of her neck. She felt then the gentle nip of his teeth, following the turn of her shoulder so that she writhed against him with protesting, entranced laughter caught in her throat, her being suspended in senseless, unthinking joy.

Never could she remember feeling so alive to tactile sensation, to the faint rasp of the hair upon his chest, the firm yet smooth surface of his lips, the board hardness of his muscles in restraint, and his bold need of her that he would not permit to interfere with either her pleasure or that which he took in the slow exploration of the rounded softness of her body. Her chest rose and fell with the quickening of her breath. With melting languor she molded herself to him, permitting him willing and unashamed access. Blindly she turned her head. Holding her to him, he captured once more the passion-flavored sweetness of her mouth. His lips still upon hers, he released his grasp to work at the fastenings of his pantaloons.

It was at that instant that the muffled thudding of gunfire, like a nearing storm, came to them. Hard upon it came the sound of a horse ridden fast. The rider was shouting, his voice thin and carrying with excitement. As he clattered into the yard, the cowbells strung in the dogtrot outside jangled out an alarm.

It was only then that Angeline could make out the warning the rider yelled. "Raid! It's a raid!"

Long before the words became clear Rolfe had rolled from her with a wrenching movement, doing up his pantaloons in haste. "This," he grated, "is getting to be a habit."

Pausing long enough to pull Angeline to her feet and help her slip into her underdress and gown, he gave her a quick, hard kiss. Then with a long and unfathomable stare, he was gone out the door.

Angeline straightened her clothing as best she could, twisting her arms behind her to reach the buttons, her fingers clumsy in her haste and disturbance. She was just finishing when the door eased open and Claire swung inside. She came toward Angeline, her emerald eyes bright and her hair lying like a fiery-red cloak around her shoulders. That she had just come from her bed was plain, for she wore no more than a wisp of tissue-thin, flesh-pink French silk that left her arms and the voluptuous curves of her breasts bare while permitting the shadowy outline of her body to be seen through its fine weave.

"This is our chance, Angeline. We can get away now, if we try."

"Get away? You mean go out there—into that?" She waved her hand toward the front of the house where the crash of shots being exchanged had increased in volume until it sounded like a major battle, the noise so deafening she had to raise her voice to a shout.

"Yes!" Claire cried, coming closer. "If we go out the back they will never miss us, not with so much to occupy them. We can contact the man who leads the attack. Surely he can be persuaded to give us escort home?"

"Why would you think so?" Angeline exclaimed. "He may be worse than the McCullough."

"He could not be! But I know why you hesitate. I saw Rolfe miraculously arisen from his sick bed. You see him whole and hale again and, like a lovesick convent miss yearning after an altar boy, you cannot bear to be parted from him." The girl's sneering voice was vicious in her frustration.

"That's not true! I think it's mad to go blindly into something you know nothing about. From what I have heard of these other outlaws, they are the most despicable kind of thieves and murderers."

"And who told you? The McCullough, I make no doubt. And why should he be impartial toward his enemies?" Claire flung up her head, shaking back her mane of hair. "But I won't stay here like a rat in a trap any longer, waiting for the catch to spring at the beck and call of that backwoods lout! I'm getting out of here. Stay or not, as you please!"

As Claire whirled toward the door, it burst open and four men with the McCullough at their head pushed inside. The outlaw leader jerked his head toward the bedchamber door, pushing the two women in that direction with a scoop of one arm before he turned toward the shuttered window at the front of the common room. Already his men had the gun slits in the wood frames open and were sending shots from their long rifles flashing into the darkness, taking turns shooting and falling back, kneeling to reload.

Choking a little from the acrid powder smoke already swirling blue in the room, Angeline moved ahead of Claire into the bedchamber. With the door closed behind them, she turned toward the other girl, her face mirroring her gladness that the situation had been taken out of their hands.

Her relief was short-lived. Claire stood in the center of the room with her hands on her hips and her beautiful mouth set in mutinous lines. She stared around her, wasting no more than a glance on the bed where Rolfe had lain, her gaze settling on the window that opened on the rear of the house. Shooting a look of defiance at Angeline, she moved to it, releasing the latch of the shutter, flinging it wide.

"Claire, no," Angeline said, coming to her side in a rush, reaching to catch her arm.

The other girl turned, her face set and her emerald eyes dark with angry desperation. "I've got to go, don't you understand? I—I'm afraid to stay, Angeline, so afraid!"

"Of Rolfe? I have his promise he will not harm you."

"Rolfe? No—yes. You don't know the danger and there's no time to explain. Come with me, now."

"It's madness, I can't."

"Then let me go!" The other girl shook her off and boosted herself to the windowsill, swinging her legs over.

"No, wait—" Angeline grabbed for her again, but Claire pushed herself out the window, the fall breaking the grip on her arm as she plunged into darkness. "Come back," Angeline called, but received no answer.

She hesitated no more than a moment. The drop was longer than she expected and she stumbled to her knees as she struck the ground. She crouched there, searching the midnight dark for her cousin, listening, trying to hear over the sounds of the fight that raged in front of the outlaw stronghold. Claire must have run toward the sound, for Angeline could see nothing of her.

A scream, full-throated and vibrant with terror, pierced the night. Without thinking, Angeline surged to her feet and ran toward the sound. Rounding the corner of the house, she saw the pale blur of Claire's nightgown, saw her struggling between two shadowy figures. There was the sound of ripping silk and her cousin screamed again.

Angeline never reached her. Rough hands caught her from behind, bruising her arms, twisting in her hair so that her head was snapped back on the stem of her neck. She fought, kicking, reaching back to claw in an eruption of rage for the stupidity of what was happening to her. She heard the grunted curses of the men who held her, smelled their foul breath and sickening body odor, saw on the edge of her vision the fist drawn back to strike. And then pain burst along the side of her head and the night darkness, soft and placating, closed in upon her.

Sobs. Moans. A ceaseless noise in a peculiar repeated cadence accompanied by grunts in another voice. A snapping, crackling noise. The smell of woodsmoke and damp leaf mold. Cold. One side of her body was chilled, sensitive to the touch of a drifting wind, while the other knew a feeble warmth. There was dampness under her and the strong aroma of horses that had been ridden hard.

Some instinct of self-preservation warned her to lie still. Concentrating her senses, she discovered by degrees that she was lying on a horse blanket on the ground; there were the sharp proddings of sticks and twigs underneath her. Nearby was a roaring fire. It was a woman who cried out, and it was not herself. Claire, then.

By infinitesimal degrees, taking long minutes to accomplish it, she turned her head and opened her eyes to slits. She lay in a wooded clearing surrounded by the singing silence of a night forest that was illuminated only by the yellow, leaping flames of the fire. The curling smoke rising above it filtered through the canopy of the trees above. Five men could be counted at no great distance, clustered about the figure of a woman writhing on another horse blanket, her nightgown pushed above her waist to reveal her naked thighs gleaming in the firelight. One of the men, with his breeches about his ankles, crouched over her hunching, thrusting. Of the others, three stood to one side watching, calling a ribald comment now and then. The remaining man squatted with his clothing unfastened, holding Claire's wrists above her head.

"Hurry up there, Hoss; I'm 'bout like a rock and ready to go off like one of Ol' Hickory's cannons."

Her cousin was not fighting. It was easy to see that she was past that. Her moans had a hopeless timbre, blending pain and self-pity and something more that might have been self-hatred.

One of the men looked toward where Angeline lay. "Roust out the other one. We'll have a piece of her ass, too."

"She's still out. You shouldn't ought to have hit her so hard, Charlie. It'd shore be a waste of fine—"

Angeline closed her mind to the rest of it. The fourth man had finished and the fifth, panting like a dog, took his place. She allowed her eyelids to close, swallowing against sickness.

What could she do? She could think of nothing. She had no weapon and, though the longing to help Claire was like an ache inside her, against such odds her strength was as nothing. In truth, her own position was scarcely better. At any moment the men might grow impatient and drag her to lie beside Claire, unconscious or not.

Horses, ridden hard. The sound impinged on her awareness. From near at hand, the horses of the men around the fire nickered a greeting. A voice was raised in a shout. Through narrowed eyes, Angeline saw the mounts of a score of men jog into the light, coming to a trampling halt. A man stepped down and strode from among them; tall, cadaverously thin, with close-set eyes and a drooping, Spanish-style mustache that gave his mouth a cruel, downward turn. His dark hair was worn long, clubbed back with a leather thong in a mode long out of date. His coat was of bottle-green velvet with long tails that fell over a pair of leather breeches, much polished with wear, that left his knees bare above the cuffs of his high leather boots. At his waist in a sheath of worked leather he wore a dagger, the hilt chased with silver and gold. Cursing in accented English, he stepped to the fire and began to kick it apart.

"Bastardos! Sons of pigs! I might have known it was a woman. Because of your treacherous lust, we have been beaten by the braggart McCullough. And now you light a beacon to draw the Scots son of Satan after you."

"We needed a woman," one of the men whined. They backed away from Claire. The fifth man scrambled free, buttoning his breeches over his still-strutted manhood. Claire lay still, then reached to push at the hem of her nightgown, covering herself.

"Could you not have waited? A few minutes more, and we would have had all the women and the camp itself—the food, the horses, the stolen gold, plus the McCullough to dance upon the air at the end of a rope for our amusement."

"These two ran right into our arms."

"You did not have to leave us in the middle of the fight while you searched for a place to fling them to the ground. Fools! Traitors! I should have you shot."

The man known as Charlie doubled his fists, taking a step forward. "To hell with you! We got what we went after!"

"To hell with you, *mi compadre*," the outlaw leader returned, his voice soft. In a fluid motion, the dagger at his waist appeared in his hand. Almost before the eye could follow, he reversed it and sent it spinning end over end. It struck, vibrating. The man called Charlie gave a hoarse cry as he was flung backward, clutching at the hilt protruding from his chest above his heart. He fell, sprawling across Claire's legs and, shuddering violently, she kicked away from him, dragging herself to a sitting position.

Silence stretched taut in the woodland clearing, a ringing echo. The men near the dying fire hovered, waiting for the Spaniard's next move, their eyes wide.

Abruptly the outlaw laughed. He stepped to retrieve his knife, wiping it on his breech leg before thrusting it back into its sheath. Then as if suddenly noticing Angeline lying to one side, he swung in her direction.

She allowed her eyelids to fall shut. The footsteps, slow, deliberately measuring, approached, stopped beside her. The sense of being stared at, examined minutely as she lay helpless, was near unbearable. She wanted to jump to her feet, meeting him on his own level, or to scream and strike out. But she knew such a surrender to the irritation of her nerves would be disastrous. With set teeth, she forced herself to lie still, feigning unconsciousness even as, with a rustle of his clothing, the Spaniard sank to his haunches beside her. He picked up one flaccid wrist.

"It may be that in taking this one you have done the bastard Scotsman a greater injury than you know, amigos. What is it with her?"

The answer came quickly, given in at least three voices.

"A pity. It would be… unfortunate if she is permanently injured."

The threat was there in the chill timbre of his voice. The four men left of those who had abducted her hastened to give their assurances, claiming the blow was no more than a tap. Almost as an afterthought, one of them observed, "There's a chance, Don Pedro, she could be 'possuming, jes' curled up, pretendin' to be daid so we'll leave her be."

"Ah, sleeping beauty," the Spaniard mused. "I wonder if she will awaken to me?"

Hard on the words, she was jerked into the outlaw's arms. His lips, thin, hard, and hot, tasting of tobacco, prickly with his mustache, descended upon hers. For a brief flicker of time, she was able to sustain her pose, and then as his tongue probed her lips, pointed, prising, revulsion rose inside her. With a gasp, she wrenched her mouth away, raising her hands to shove at him, pushing violently against the whipcord strength of his grasp.

Hoots of laughter and raucous calls rang out. "You got her, ol' son, now take her!"

The hard gaze of the Spanish outlaw bored into her wide, gray-green eyes. As suddenly as he had caught her to him, he let her go so that she fell back, catching herself on one elbow.

"She will have to wait until there is more safety—and leisure. Some things should not be rushed."

Fourteen

"Mount up, amigos. Let's ride!"

The journey was not one Angeline would care to remember. She rode behind the Spaniard with her arms encircling his waist and her wrists tied together before him. With an ache like the thrust of a knife into her brain, she tried to remain erect without touching him more than was necessary. The strain on her back and arms was too much. As she was pitched forward against his velvet-clad back again and again, she allowed herself to accept its support by degrees. She felt rather than heard his satisfied laugh. She was tempted to straighten once more if only to cause trouble, but it seemed a wanton waste of her remaining strength, a useless tempting of the illness hovering inside her.

They had left the dead man lying spread-eagled in the dirt beside the smoldering ruins of the fire, abandoned to the wolves and foxes. Again and again the brutal carelessness of the memory touched her, stifling hope.

She was cold. Her gown was damp from where she had lain on the horse blanket and she was without an outer wrap. The cold night air fanning past her as they rode penetrated to the bone so that she knew a debasing, unwilling gratitude for the warmth of the Spaniard's body. If she suffered discomfort, how much more must Claire feel, clad in the torn remnants of her thin silk nightgown? Her cousin was no more than a blur sagging behind another of the outlaws, though now and then above the sound of the pounding hooves she thought she heard her crying.

Angeline allowed her mind to wander, to question what Rolfe and the McCullough were doing at that moment, to wonder if the cadre had returned from the hunt, and if they were all now embarked on an even greater hunting excursion. She could not depend upon it. There was nothing to say that the McCullough would know where to find the Spanish outlaw's encampment, nothing to guarantee that he would reach it in time to aid her. She had only herself to turn to, and the weapons of wit and daring she possessed were woefully untested.

In contrast to the quarters of the Spaniard and his men, the stronghold of the McCullough was palatial. Angeline and Claire were pushed into a one-room cabin with exposed rafters, a dirt floor, a door in front and back, and log walls that were not only unplaned, but still had the bark upon them. In such surroundings, the three bedsteads of fine, hand-polished wood with turned posts and carved headboards were incongruous. Upon them were closely woven coverlets, fine quilts stitched with patience and skill, and monogrammed sheets, though all in a state of unsurpassed dinginess. Fine Brussels and Wilton carpets were ground into the dirt floor, while clustered near the mud-daubed fireplace were utensils of silver and brass and odd, chipped and cracked cups, saucers, and plates, that had once been pieces in sets of fine porcelain.

It was an instant before it came to Angeline that these were the spoils of the outlaws, the household goods of the settlers who had been murdered and robbed as they crossed No Man's Land. She felt a contraction in the pit of her stomach and, as her gaze fell on a carefully hand-carved cradle, she clenched her teeth against yet another wave of sickness. She and Claire were not the only females. A slatternly woman with a gray face and greasy brown strings of hair sat up in the bed farthest from the fireplace. In the dim light of the flickering fire her eyes were wide, with wildness in their depths, and her body was swollen by advanced pregnancy. Her mouth worked, but no sound issued from it, and she wiped saliva from its corner with a vague, backhanded gesture.

"Oh, God," Claire said in a strained whisper, and shuffled to the nearest bed to fling herself facedown upon it, burying her face in her arms. Angeline, her movements stiff and slow, sat down beside her, reaching to put a hand on her shoulder. Rippling shudders ran through the other girl, shaking the bed with their violence. Angeline was shocked at how thin Claire was, the bones sharp-edged beneath her skin. Leaning, she caught the edge of the covers, drawing them over her cousin, tucking them in tightly.

The Spanish leader shouted orders over his shoulder as he strode into the room. Behind him came a handful of his men: They crowded around the fire, rubbing their hands, lifting the lids of the pots, and hefting demijohns of raw spirits. A few nursed wounds wrapped in bloodstained, makeshift bandages. One growled something at the woman in the far bed and she scrambled up, blinking rapidly. With trembling haste, she ladled out servings of an unsavory mess from an iron pot hanging over the fire. It was wolfed down without ceremony and the last drops sopped up with pieces of heavy cornbread.

Angeline, sitting beside her cousin and trying to chafe some warmth back into her body, was aware of the glances the men cast in her direction. Though her skin contracted with gooseflesh and the muscles of her abdomen tightened, she did her best to appear unnoticing. The minutes passed. Claire was still shivering convulsively. To do nothing while waiting for some decision, some action by the men toward her, grew insupportable. Angeline shifted, her gaze going to one of the demijohns of whiskey. Setting her mouth in a firm line, she slid from the high bed to the floor, moving toward the group about the fireplace.

"May I have a cup of that?" she inquired in a low voice, indicating the jug with a brief gesture.

The Spaniard stared at her, slow amusement surfacing in his narrow eyes. "But of course, *señorita*."

Glancing around, Angeline took up a pewter pannikin and held it out while a short, balding man with two missing front teeth tipped the demijohn to fill it.

"Thank you." Turning, she moved back to the bed, where she helped Claire sit up, then held the pannikin while the other girl drank. Though her cousin choked on the raw liquor, it was a relief to see a faint shading of color return to her pallid cheeks.

"Will you take some for yourself, *señorita*?"

Angeline glanced at the Spanish leader, her expression wary. "I have sufficient here."

"You must have more. I, Don Pedro Alvarez y Cazrola, insist."

"Thank you, no."

"A woman of spirit, but caution. I am intrigued." The man leaned back where he sat in a Hepplewhite chair of exquisite workmanship and stretched his leather-clad legs before him. The men around the fireplace snickered, their eyes avid as they fastened on her.

It was, Angeline thought, to be a game of cat and mouse with her as the prey. She set the pannikin aside without answering as she pretended to be occupied in settling Claire beneath the covers once more. Claire, her green eyes enormous, stared up at her in sick distress.

"Leave your friend, *señorita*. Come to me."

Angeline flicked him a bare look. "She is my cousin."

"Leave your cousin, then. Come. Now."

She could ignore the command, requiring him to come after her and force her compliance, or she could obey. Rather than give him the opportunity to lay violent hands on her, she rose, moving toward him with proud grace. Stopping a few feet from his chair, she lifted her chin in challenge. "You wanted something?"

"To have a better look at you, certainly. How are you called?" His eyes were a pale brown, almost yellow, ringed with black like those of a bird of prey.

She told him, her tone as steady and without emotion as she could make it. She glanced at the others, then allowed her gaze to run over the utensils, the dishes and cutlery the men had been using, searching for a knife of any size or design, a weapon of any kind. There was nothing, no butcher knife, no carving knife, not even an iron basting spoon of a size and weight suitable for a club. Or was there? The Spaniard still wore at his waist the sheath that held his ornate dagger, and reposing in it was the weapon itself, the base of the blade dark with cried blood.

Don Pedro nodded to the balding man. "Where are your manners, Sanchez? Give the lady refreshment."

The man, grinning hugely, picked up a china cup without a handle, wiped it out with his finger, and tipped whiskey into it. Don Pedro took the cup, then held out his own beaker for a refill. Turning, he offered the cup to Angeline.

"You will drink with me, Angeline?"

It was not a request, despite the tone. Angeline took the proffered cup. "Why? Do you not have enough people to keep you company?"

"You mean my men? Ah, yes, but they are not so pleasant to look at as you."

"A drunken woman can hardly be pleasant company."

"You are wrong—they can be most merry. But you are cold and I desire you to be… warmer of blood."

"I would not depend on it. I might just as easily be sick, violently so."

A slow smile without warmth curled his thin lips. "Do you think to deter me by such predictions? It will take more than that."

There was still another effort to be made. "It would be better to use this," she said, indicating the liquid in her cup, "to treat the wounds of your men. I have some skill with healing. Perhaps I could see to their hurts?"

The outlaw leader tilted his head. "You would do that?"

"Yes, why not?"

"It is a generous offer, considering your circumstances."

"My circumstances have not yet been established." She gripped her hands together upon the cup, the broken stumps where there had been a handle cutting into her palm.

"You are mistaken."

She gave him back stare for stare, ignoring the pain in her hand and the pounding in her head. "Because of the McCullough? I am not, nor have I ever been, his woman, so there is no reason to seek your revenge through me. Until taken by your men, I was merely his prisoner."

"I am to believe this, when you have been staying under his roof? "

"He… had another woman who interested him more." There was no point in going into further detail. By an effort of will Angeline refrained from so much as the flick of an eyelash in Claire's direction.

The Spaniard jerked his head toward the bed. "That one? More fool, he."

He had made no attempt to lower his voice or to temper his disdain. Claire opened her eyes, frowning, then levered herself to one elbow. She reached for the pannikin Angeline had left nearby, and drained the remaining spirits in a single draught.

Her gray-green eyes dark, Angeline looked from the Spaniard to her cousin and back again. "I think not."

"I do. You are a virgin, then."

"That is none of your concern!" A dull flush rose to Angeline's hairline. She did not know which was more disturbing, the question or the casual manner in which it had been put to her.

"On the contrary. It is a matter of great interest to me."

"I fail to see it. Do you require my services—as a nurse for your men?"

He lifted a brow, but seemed in his confidence to be willing to let the moment pass. Taking out a dark Mexican cheroot, he lit it with a coal from the fire, letting the smoke drift from his lips. With an expansive gesture of one hand he said, "They will be grateful, I'm sure."

Steeling herself to the task, she heated water and sponged the furrows and gouges made by bullets that were presented to her. Most were fairly clean wounds of no great seriousness; those too incapacitated to ride had been left to the mercy of the McCullough.

As she moved about the room, she was aware of the gaze of the Spaniard upon her, his patience feline, his threat of possession made in the woodland clearing more disturbing than the McCullough's straightforward lust had ever been. The thought came to her that to thwart him could be a mistake, that she might well have to pay for every minute he was forced to wait.

There was one leg wound that required probing for the ball. The boy who had taken it was scarcely more than twenty, but he cursed with violence and incredible variety as she sought with the tip of a dull, much tarnished silver knife for the piece of lead.

"Here, *señorita*. Perhaps this will be better?"

It was Don Pedro, leaning against the bench on which the boy lay, offering his dagger on the palm of his hand. The smile he gave her was inscrutable. His voice was quiet, perfectly normal, attracting little attention from those around them. As he waited for her answer he drew a last time on the stub of his cheroot and threw it into the fire.

She reached out, closing her fingers on the slender hilt. The urge to spring, slashing at the man beside her was so great she felt faint for a moment and her head throbbed so she could scarcely see. Only the knowledge that it was a deliberate ploy, a teasing temptation from which he must be more than ready to defend himself, made her pause for thought. To use the knife against the Spaniard in a lunge for freedom would be suicidal. She could not hope to elude the dozen or so other men in the room, even if she could break past Don Pedro, and trying would leave her open to certain assault. He had chosen his stratagem well, and his hard laugh as she turned toward the boy on the bench proved that he knew it.

When the pistol ball was prised free of its fleshy bed, Angeline laid the knife down to cleanse the deep puncture. The Spaniard made no move to pick it up. He waited until the last knot was tied in the bandaging, then extended his hand.

"My weapon, *señorita*?"

"Permit me to clean it for you," she said, her voice coolly polite. Two could play at the game of nerves, as she had discovered with Rolfe. What she was gaining by her efforts, as she dipped the dagger in the water, scrubbing at the blood upon it, was time. There was also the matter of a possible sense of obligation from the men toward her. She did not actually think it would make a difference in either case, but it was all she could manage for now.

"There you are," she said, and placed the weapon gently in the Spaniard's hands. She raised her gray-green eyes to his, her expression limpid, guileless, with no hint of fearful shrinking.

A dog barked outside. A man got up, moved to the door, and opened it to look out. Claire started, swinging toward the movement almost as if she had been in a trance, unaware of what was happening around her. Her eyes focused on the open doorway, then closed again as the man slammed it shut.

"'Tain't nothin'," the outlaw said.

The pregnant woman had returned to her bed, where she had taken a zither from under the covers and begun to play. She continued now, picking out a soothing and amazingly delicate melody, the notes falling softly in the dimness. Three of the wounded who had thrown themselves down on the mattress beside the woman snored in whiskey-sodden exhaustion, undisturbed. Others had rolled up in blankets with their backs to the fire, though there were still a few who sat staring into the low-burning flames waiting their turn to take the watch.

"You did that very well, *mil gracias*," the Spaniard complimented Angeline.

She turned, dipping her hands into the pan of water she had been using before drying them on a rag that appeared to have once been a man's linen shirt. "Anyone could have done the same, even you."

He shrugged. "If it had pleased me. I do not expect such attention when I have been injured. Why should anyone else?"

"Are you a stoic, or is it just that you have been lucky enough to escape before now?"

"You feel sorry for my men?" he answered with a question, his voice low, almost purring. "It is time you extended your compassion to me."

She glanced at him in inquiry. "Have you been concealing a wound?"

"Concealing something, yes, though not an injury." The words were without mirth though there was enjoyment in his peculiar eyes.

His nearness was frightening, there could be no other word for it. Whether because of his sudden flash of murderous rage in the clearing, his callousness in leaving his injured behind, the evidence of his savage trade, or the calculated cruelty of his game with her, she was afraid as she had never been before. His lack of violence or passion toward her did nothing to still her apprehension. If anything, it made it worse, since she could not guess exactly what he intended, what he would do to her.

She stared at him like a bird hypnotized by a snake as he reached to take the drying rag from her hands, then closed his fingers upon her wrist. His touch was as hot and dry as a heated iron band, the look in his eyes searing. Tilting his head toward the one unoccupied bed left in the room he said, "Come."

He meant to have her there in that crowded room, in full view of the men left around the fire. He would strip her naked and make of it a display, a taunt for his men and a certain flaying of all that was most sensitive within her. The horror of it gripped her. She drew back, resistance in every line of her body, negation in her frozen face. And through it all she thought the Spaniard was pleased, even elated, by her lack of compliance.

The music of the zither quickened, twanging with discord and misstruck notes. The ropes of the bedstead where Claire rested creaked as she sat up, following Angeline's movements with staring eyes. Then in a rush, Claire was on her feet, standing on the mattress, her shadow cast by the faint fire glow looming statuesque and goddesslike on the walls. She laughed, a low sound that began in the back of her throat and grew in volume, becoming vigorous and alive, only slightly tinged with hysteria. With her eyes half closed, she began to slip the torn neckline of her nightgown open farther, letting the cap sleeves slide down her arms, exposing the rose-tipped fullness of her breasts. Swaying in a slow and vibrant dance, she let the flesh-colored silk glide lower, to her waist, to the slight curve of her belly, to her thighs where it clung for an instant, framing the shadowed triangle before slithering to a heap about her feet. She raised her hands to her hair then, spreading the fiery mass around her, self-absorbed, her emerald eyes glittering. Twisting, undulating, she thrust her hips forward in a lewd parody of the act of love.

The Spaniard halted, still holding Angeline. Behind him, she heard a man swallow audibly while another breathed a soft oath. The fire sputtered, flaring red-blue and orange. Outside the wind whined, and a dog barked once more, then was silent.

In abrupt fury, Don Pedro swung toward the woman who played, making a chopping motion with his hand. The music ceased as if severed from the strings of the zither by a knife.

Claire looked up, her mouth curving in a smile. Kicking from the nightgown, she stepped to the edge of the bed and jumped lightly to the floor. Stretching her arms out to the tall, thin Spaniard, she moved to him, twining them around his neck.

"Take me," she said, her voice low and trembling, tears shimmering in her eyes. "Take me now."

"Claire, no," Angeline breathed, warned by some hint of uncaring desperation in the timbre of the other girl's voice. Was it perverted passion, an inability to bear seeing Angeline favored that drove Claire, or the desire to spare her cousin, giving her an opportunity to win release while the Spaniard was distracted? Angeline did not know.

"Are you jealous, little cousin," Claire murmured. "Don't be. Your time will come."

Don Pedro released Angeline, catching Claire's arms in a grip that made her wince and the color drain from her face. He dragged her down, giving her a hard shake that made her head jerk back and forth. "Go back to bed."

"Don't—don't you want me?" the other girl whimpered.

"No."

The rejection was savage, deliberate. As Claire slumped, he dropped her arms as if touching her was beneath him. And yet there shone in his eyes the light of rapacious enjoyment, dangerous anticipation. He reached then for Angeline's wrist, at the same time shooting out a hand to give Claire a shove before him. "We will, I think, use this bed, all three."

His words barely had time to register in Angeline's mind before Claire spun, snarling like a cat, to leap upon him. Her arms clamped around his neck, her legs about his thighs, and her nails sank into him with maniacal force.

"The knife, the knife," she panted, and opening her lips, she sank her teeth into the Spaniard's neck.

There was no time to think, only time to act. Angeline sprang to catch the hilt of the dagger, dragging it free of its sheath at Don Pedro's side. She whirled away then as the Spaniard sent Claire sprawling. Angeline came up against the cradle in the corner, catching herself in time to see her cousin gather her feet under her in a crouch with the cloak of her hair covering her nakedness and blood around her lovely mouth. Her cousin glared with emerald malevolence at the man who stood holding his neck, then transferred her gaze to Angeline.

"Why didn't you kill him?"

"Because—" she began, then stopped as the Spaniard cut across her words.

"Because unlike a bitch such as you who only thinks with what is between her legs, she knew it would be useless." He swung toward Angeline then, advancing with slow steps, his hand extended palm upward. "Give it to me. Return my blade once more and you shall be mine alone. Make me take it and you will know every man here who is able before this night is over. You will become like Alice there in the corner, a female thing used by all. This I swear."

"Oh, Angeline," Claire whispered despairingly as her gaze moved around the room to the men who hovered, half in, half out of their seats.

It was obvious where the sensible course lay. Hadn't she discerned that already? And yet Angeline, watching his grimly sure advance, weighing the heavy gold and silver hilt in her hand, knew she could not be sensible, could not give up the weapon another time. As he neared, her grip on it tightened. She could feel hardness congealing inside her, sense the darkness of terrible resolve closing in on her mind. She took a deep breath, her gray-green eyes steady.

He was supremely confident, and why not? Hadn't she relinquished the advantage she held without a murmur? He came closer, reaching, triumph already rising in his starved falcon's eyes.

She slashed out, holding the blade as she had seen Rolfe do only hours before, stretching with the full weight of her body toward the narrow, unprotected span of his belly.

He caught the blow on his forearm, driving her hand upward, but not before the knife sheared through flesh, cutting to the bone and glancing off to rip its way across muscle and vein. Vicious fury leaped into his thin face and he swung his hand, smashing it against the side of her face, knocking her backward. She slammed against the wall, the knife flying from her hand. With blood dripping from his left arm, the Spaniard scooped up the dagger, coming after her with bared yellow teeth and murder in his narrow gaze.

Gathering herself, Angeline ducked away, diving to put the cradle, crazily rocking, between them. Don Pedro put his hand on it dashing the lightweight piece to the floor, stepping around it as the woman called Alice moaned and scrambled from the bed, going to her knees in awkward haste to examine the cradle, pawing at the soft blue bedding that had spilled from it.

Angeline skipped backward. A man near the fire stretched out a hand to grab her, then dropped it as the Spaniard snarled an order.

"Desist, imbecile! She is mine, and mine will be the pleasure of vengeance."

That did not keep the men from moving to bar the front door as she circled toward it. She was driven then toward the bed where Alice had lain. On a fragile cherrywood table beside it sat a teapot and an assortment of cups. She snatched at them, throwing them as fast as she could pick them up. One glanced off his cheekbone, leaving a bruise he seemed hardly to feel, the others he avoided with ease. But she had tarried too long. With long gliding steps he cut off her retreat, forcing her into the corner. Spinning, she set her foot to the bottom rail of the bed and vaulted to its sagging surface. As Don Pedro lunged for her, she swung a pillow into his face, following it with the covers, hastily dragged free. He stabbed the pillow to throw it aside, sending feathers, smelly and suffocating, floating in the air, but was tangled for an instant in the smothering coverlets. She jumped over the end of the bed in scrabbling desperation, half-tripping on her skirts, snagging splinters in her hands from the rough floor as she landed. Pushing erect, she whirled from between the footboard of the bed and the one opposite in the right-hand corner.

"Angeline—Angeline—Angeline—" Claire gasped, rocking back and forth, her eyes wide and dark with horror. The sound, with the sobbing cries of Alice and the coarse shouts and suggestions of the men, made a confusing chorus. Angeline edged with skimming steps toward her cousin, taking care not to turn her gaze even the fraction of an inch toward the back door. Even so, Don Pedro saw her objective and flung himself in that direction, reaching it before she could dodge around Claire. Teetering on one foot, she changed directions. It was then that her cousin, gathering herself, pushed to her feet. They blundered together with stunning force and, before she could recover, Angeline fell hard, raking fingers sinking into her hair, pulling, snatching her into an embrace with the coppery smell and sick feel of blood.

"Now," Don Pedro said in sibilant tones against her ear, his chest heaving with the quickness of his breathing, "I will show you how a *puta* who resorts to the knife is treated."

With the red glow of pain behind her eyes, she was dragged to the nearest bed and thrown face-down across its footboard. The carved wood caught her across the pelvis, her feet left the floor and she lay stunned with her face buried in the mattress. A weight descended across her shoulders. She felt a sting at the nape of her neck, then heard the dry whine of splitting cloth.

He was cutting her gown from her. As she shrank with a gasp from the slicing blade, she felt the give of her underdress also, sensed the chill draft of air moving over her bare back. A hand closed over her hip, kneading, squeezing. She felt the tight pull at the high waistline as the dagger reached the thicknesses of cloth gathered there. In an instant she would be obscenely exposed and vulnerable, helpless to avoid the vengeance he would take, no matter its form. She writhed, kicking, turning her head to drag air into her lungs, aware all the while of every hissing breath of excitement the Spaniard drew.

A rending crash shattered the night. The back door of the cabin flew open, crashing against the wall, hanging from one leather hinge. As Don Pedro released her with virulent Spanish invective, Angeline twisted, wrenching, dragging herself over on the mattress, turning to see. The door opening was filled with men, a phalanx of white and gold with pistols in their hands, backed by rough men carrying long rifles. They were led by a powerful, grim-faced figure with blond shining hair and slitted turquoise eyes.

"Rolfe," she breathed.

With startled yells, the men around the fire came to their feet, scattering, reaching for weapons. Claire swayed where she stood and, as if suddenly aware of her nakedness, crossed her arms over her body. From the front of the cabin came the sound of gunfire in the deep night darkness.

Rolfe came to an abrupt halt, his expression impassive though his gaze quartered the room in a single sweep, taking in the situation before settling on Angeline.

Relief, wanton and wild, ran along her veins. It gave her the strength, when the Spaniard leaped for her, to tear from his grasp, rolling, sliding over the bed, plunging to the floor with her slit gown twisted around her, before she hurled herself toward Rolfe. She came up hard against him. He caught her, holding her in the protective curve of his arm while gunshots crashed around them, underscored by the thud of flesh on flesh as the McCullough's men closed in. Claire, her face dazed, stumbled toward Angeline and Rolfe.

Balked of one prey, Don Pedro settled for another. He swooped to snare the other girl from behind, using her unclothed body as warm and tender cover. Claire cried out once, then was silent as tears of despair welled into her eyes. "Remain there, *amigo*," the Spaniard said with soft malevolence, unerringly recognizing Rolfe as the man in authority. "This woman means less than nothing to me—a useless one, much used, without pride or feeling behind the empty eyes. Lay hand on me, and I will slit her throat as easily as a cook wringing the neck of a pullet."

The members of the cadre had not joined in the general melee beyond exchanging a shot or two. Now Meyer, with André, impetuous in his excitement, beside him, moved as if to attack. Don Pedro's grip on the knife tightened, and the blade glittered as he lifted it nearer the smooth, exposed line of Claire's neck.

"Hold!" Rolfe said, the command sharp and certain.

Stillness descended. The Spaniard's men inside the cabin had been subdued, though in the uneasy quiet could be heard still the shouts and explosions of the battle being waged outside. André and the cadre stood in arrested poses, watching as Don Pedro, dragging Claire with him, inched toward the front door.

There was nothing that could be done. In the arm of the man who held her, Angeline could sense the tension stretching taut through muscles and sinew, evidence of the impotent, unbelieving fury with which Rolfe watched Claire escaping him yet again.

The Spaniard wrenched open the door and, with a sneering smile lifting the drooping corners of his mustache, said, "Follow me, *amigos*, and you will find the woman lying dead in the road."

He stepped through the door. They heard his booted treads along with the scuffling of Claire's bare feet. There were shouts and shots, a strangled yell, and then the thud of hoofbeats, fading.

They reached the front door in time to add their firepower to that of the McCullough's men, and to come to the aid of the Scotsman himself, who had been pinned down by vicious crossfire behind a woodpile. Their added weight put the Spaniard's men to rout. Leaderless and facing superior odds, they took to their horses and flogged pell-mell down the road in the direction Don Pedro had taken.

❧

"Victory in war," Rolfe said, standing over the prostrate form of the McCullough where he lay on a horse blanket beside the campfire, "is the claim of the fool with more men and arms than his enemy."

"Ye call me a fool to my face and think to get away with it because ye ken I owe ye a debt," the McCullough growled. "I have said I'll give up claim to the ransom due me on ye and yer men, and even on yon André Delacroix, in exchange for the saving of my hide and head, but ye needn't think I'll be taking yer insults lying down!"

"How else?" Rolfe quipped, lifting a brow, smiling slightly as he stared down at the outlaw.

In answer, the McCullough could only glare. He squirmed and winced while Angeline applied a bandage to his knee. He had been shot during the last flurry of the fighting, the pistol ball tearing a furrow, chipping the bone. He grunted now. "All the same, we sent them running like whipped curs, with their tails between their legs."

"Yes, and with Claire over the saddlebow of the most rabid of them all."

"'Tis a pity." The lack of regret in the McCullough's voice was as obvious as the look of spurious concern he sent Angeline.

"It's more than a pity. It means the whole operation of rescue will have to be mounted again—and the Spanish outlaw defeated, for good."

"For the sake of that woman?"

"Exactly," Rolfe answered, going smoothly on, "and for your own peace. You must know as well as I that though you have made ashes of the Spaniard's rooftree and set his livestock roaming to the four winds, it will require less than a month for him to rebuild his shelter and steal sufficient food to sustain himself while he raids in your territory once more."

"That's so, damn his eyes!"

"Then what have you gained?"

The McCullough snorted. "I ken ye now, ye wily devil. Ye only want my men to aid you in bringing back the woman, though what ye can want with her when ye have Angeline, here, is more than I can see."

"Why, her domestic talents, of course," Rolfe answered, his eyes wide with mocking innocence. The Scotsman snorted once more, turning away.

It had been necessary to make camp a few short miles from the inferno that had been the Spaniard's stronghold. Not only were the wounded in need of treatment, the men were exhausted, and the horses that had brought them so far during the long night also needed rest. Meyer, Oscar, and André had helped with the injured, and now the McCullough's outlaws and Rolfe's guard, both the original cadre and its newly adopted Louisiana member, all lay rolled in blankets around the fire. The Scotsman had insisted on being the last to receive attention, and would trust no one except Angeline to touch his knee. She had not minded; it was better to be busy. The last thing she wanted was leisure to think, to remember.

As she finished with the outlaw leader, Rolfe was at her side, placing his hand under her elbow to help her to her feet.

"Could I be having a drink of water?" the McCullough asked, rolling to his side, his cunning brown gaze bent upon her.

Before she could reply, Rolfe said, "If you can get it for yourself. Angeline has done enough."

"Enough for everybody but ye, I'll wager," the other man called as they turned away.

Though the lines about Rolfe's eyes tightened, he made no answer. He led her from the fire toward a shallow depression in the ground where blankets had been spread, a patch of gray in the predawn dimness. A man groaned as they stepped among the sleeping figures, and Alice, brought with them in trembling terror, reached out moaning to clutch at the empty cradle beside her for comfort.

The man's cloak that had been found for Angeline against the damp cold and to cover the rent in the back of her dress dragged over the ground as she walked, catching on twigs and spiked sweet gum balls. As she gathered the folds around her, she wondered if Claire had been given anything with which to clothe her nakedness, if she were still alive, still with Don Pedro, or if she had been cast aside once her usefulness was at an end. Oswald and Gustave had been sent to track the outlaws on just that chance. Their orders were to keep well back, to be wary of ambuscades, and to make no attempt at rescue that might endanger Claire's life.

It seemed little enough, that discreet surveillance. Though Angeline could see nothing more that might be done, she felt as if she had abandoned her cousin. To be traveling in the opposite direction seemed wrong, a betrayal. She could not wait there alone of course, nor could she blame Rolfe and the others. Their hands were chained as surely by their concern for Claire's safety as by steel fetters. The Spaniard would be on guard against just such a daring raid as had wrested Angeline from him and destroyed his base. Time must elapse before he could be caught off guard again, time during which he must be allowed to think that Claire had little worth to the McCullough and those who

rode with him, time to lessen his wariness and make
him believe that no one cared whether he returned to
the site of his burned-out cabin or stayed concealed in
some damp and snake-infested canebrake. How long
that might be, no one could say.

Moments after she had stretched out under the
blankets, Angeline began to shiver. The trembling
seemed to come from inside in radiating waves. It
was not the cold, she knew; she was warm enough
with Rolfe beside her, near but not quite touching.
The cause was reaction to the events of the night, a
sheer physical response to the fear and humiliation of
what had happened, one suppressed until this moment
when all was done and her duties ended.

She thought that after a moment it must go away,
but it did not. The shudders rippled through her until
her teeth chattered and she felt as if her body was
being drawn like a bow.

"Angeline——" Rolfe whispered, shifting under the
blankets, placing his hand lightly on her shoulder.
"What is it?"

To turn to him was difficult, not least because she
did not know what he thought of her capture by the
Spaniard, or the scene he had so fortuitously interrupted. In the end it did not matter, for her need was
greater than her apprehension.

"Hold me," she breathed, her voice a shaken husk
of sound. "Please hold me."

He gathered her in his arms, drawing her against
him, his hands gently easing her hair from where it
was caught under her shoulder, smoothing it down
her back. There was comfort without passion in his

encircling embrace, in the brush of his lips across her brow, in the words he spoke soft and low.

"Peace, sweet Angeline. Release your hold on remembered dread and banish the phantoms of the night. I have you safe and will not let you go, not even in the final morning of life, nor will I ask of you what you cannot give. Trust me, then, and forgive me, that what I have done in the past awakens inside you an echo of the treatment meted out to you this night. Take my love for buckler and shield, and with it vanquish the scaly dragons of the mind, sustaining... peace."

The words penetrated slowly, and when they reached the center of her being, she was still. She breathed deeply, evenly, once, twice, three times, feeling the steady pound of his heart beneath her cheek as she was held against him, wrapped in the heat of his body and the warm male smell of him. When she spoke, her voice was quiet, detached. "Love?"

"I would give it to you polished and shining, set with seals and tasseled ribbons if I could. Failing that, will you accept it, tarnished by the past and unadorned, unwieldy with its great size?"

"Oh, Rolfe," she said, swallowing against a weak and salty rising of tears. "It would be unfair if—if the words were said from remorse, for recompense."

"Never," he answered simply.

"Still, I cannot accept it—unless you will take my love for you in return."

She had not known she would say the words. They seemed to rise of their own accord to her lips, to have been waiting inside her, well rehearsed, for countless days, perhaps months, years, even all her life.

"I could wish," he said softly, "for no more perfect exchange."

And still his clasp was without that vibrant tension that communicates desire. The lack was disturbing in view of the warm and giving sensation she felt flowing in her veins.

She stirred, tilting her head back, trying to see his face. He watched her, she knew, though she could discern no more than the outline of his face, a faint sheen in the darkness of his eyes mirroring the graying light of the dawn. Gathering her courage, she lifted her hand, laying the fingers lightly along his cheek, trailing them down the strong angle of his jaw to the taut tendons of his neck. She drew his head down then, and brushed her parted lips across the firm and sensitive contours of his mouth. He accepted her kiss, prolonging it for the space of a heartbeat past the instant when she began to draw back. Silence hovered between them as he breathed with steady control, once in, once out.

"We rest here only until good light. Sleep now."

The terseness of his words was an indication, despite outward appearance, of his lack of repose. "And if I cannot?"

"You must."

She lowered her lashes, one finger tracing the convolutions of his ear, her voice low and musical as she said: "Must I?"

"It would aid my resolve."

"Not to—to ask more than I can give? But what if it is I who ask?"

"Angeline, I am only a man."

"You are a prince who will one day be king and subject to the canons of the office, among which is included, unless tradition is different in Ruthenia, that of... *noblesse oblige.*"

His breath left him in a soundless laugh. It quivered still in his voice as he spoke. "Angeline beyond price, I would willingly oblige you if it were not for exhausting your strength."

"That need not concern you."

"How can it not? Anything that affects you concerns me."

"My... need to be held, to be loved, as well?"

"Tenacious and brazen, are you not?" he inquired, his tone deep.

"Do you mind?"

"It is my delight. Lie still then, hoarding your strength, and permit me to love you in princely, if far from noble, fashion."

His expertise, royal or not, was equaled only by his concentration. He undressed her with many caresses, each accompanied by the sensuous play of words weaving a paean to the tender symmetry of her body, the pearl smoothness of her skin, the fragrance of her hair and exhalations of her very pores; to rapture taken, given, shared. With gentle insistence, he evoked her murmured response, requiring her to reveal the sites of her greatest pleasure, the rhythm of their voices twining, joining in soft and flowing harmony. He sought, it seemed, to find the entrance to her soul, but would not enter unless tendered the key by her own complaisant will.

He touched her breasts with moist fire and spanned

the slender indentation of her waist with his callused swordsman's hands. The velvet-skinned flatness of her abdomen enticed him lower and he lingered, brushing the sensitive surface to tingling tautness with his lips. He parted her thighs, exploring their fine-veined sides, trailing downward to the touchy, ticklish area of her knees while with his warm palm he cupped the center of her body and being.

Angeline was no longer cold, no longer isolated with self-inflicted responsibilities. She was suffused with fire, her skin glowing, her mind without moorings, awash in perilous languor. As he substituted the heated adhesion of his mouth for his hand, she drew swift breath, touching the soft waves of his hair in entreaty and benediction, uncertain, as she was transported in ecstasy, which was paramount.

Her senses expanded, her muscles grew stiff with the tension of desire. Her breathing quickened, banishing lassitude for an ascension toward ravishing, turbulent bliss. She reached it, that trembling paroxysm of pure sensation. Before it subsided, he removed his clothing, shifting to lie beside her, at a slight angle. Placing one of her legs across his narrow waist, he drew her close against him, easing into her in a liquid and searing slide of delight. She touched his face, smoothing the tips of her fingers down his neck to his shoulder. Her voice soft, with a catch in its timbre, she said, "Rolfe, oh Rolfe."

"Can you endure being taxed again, and tumbled withal?" His firm hand was spread over her breast, the palm pressed to the jarring of her heart.

"I could not endure denial," she whispered.

There was no chance of it. Once more the tumult came with gathered strength and thrusting tempo, a wild and escalating explosion, a ravaging of the senses vivid and pulsating. It flowed, surging between them, shared glory. There was nothing except this, no reality, no past or future. The increasing dawn brought creeping fingers of light, forcing the retreat of shadows, slanting, reflecting silvered and golden in their eyes as they lay entwined. And in their locked glances it could illuminate no trace of darkness, only bright and surfeited joy.

Fifteen

"I'M A LONG-TAILED, CAT-EYED SON OF THE SWAMPLAND! My daddy was a grizzly bear and my mama part panther and part eagle. I can ride an alligator like a short-legged horse, run a buffalo into the ground, and use the mighty Mississippi for my spittoon from right here. Come out of there and get whupped! Yahoo!"

The yell split the morning. Angeline looked up from the rent seam in the shirt she was mending, one of the many rips and tears garnered by Rolfe and the cadre in the past days of intense preparation following the raid. Supper bubbled over the fire in the McCullough's stronghold, while men sprawled everywhere, drinking, playing cards, and moaning over their sore muscles.

"What the devil?" the McCullough exclaimed, jumping out of his chair, cursing as he bumped his sore knee on the table leg. "That sounds like—"

Rolfe, his turquoise gaze alert, paused in the cleaning of his Manton pistol while the other fell silent.

"You coming out, you mangy, flea-bitten mountain-bald Scotsman, or do I have to come in and get you?"

"By Gawd!" A grin cut through the McCullough's beard before he began to limp in haste toward the door. Several of the others pushed to their feet and crowded after him. Angeline set her sewing to one side and, with Rolfe beside her, followed more slowly.

A young giant of a man sat his horse before the steps leading into the dogtrot of the house. He was well dressed in a tailcoat of fine gray wool, a cream waistcoat embroidered with black silk, and buff breeches tucked into gleaming, calf-high riding boots. As he caught sight of Angeline he doffed a beaver hat, uncovering hair of reddish-blond above a broad, tanned face with even features and dark-gray eyes.

"Mademoiselle Fortin," he said, surprise in his voice.

"Mr. Bowie," she replied, smiling.

"You once called me Jim," he rallied her before slanting a hard glance at the McCullough. "May I inquire how you come to be here?"

There was a marked contrast between his quiet, well-mannered tones and the raucous yell of moments before, in typical backwoodsman's or river boatman's greeting to a fellow.

"Now Jim, don't you be climbing on yer high horse," the Scotsman intervened hastily. "I can explain."

"It might be as well if you did. I have been acquainted with Mademoiselle Fortin for some time, our families being neighbors, so to speak, near St. Martinville until my father took it into his head last year to light out for less crowded territory. I don't take it kindly, finding a lady of her stamp here in this Godless place with the likes of you."

The McCullough accepted the last with no show
of ill will. "I'll gi' ye the story in the house then, if
ye'll step down and come in. You there, Jack, take
his horse!"

Jim Bowie got down with a muscled grace rare
in so large a man. Tucking his hat under his arm, he
moved to Angeline and took her hand, bowing over
it. The glance he threw at Rolfe, who stood with his
arm possessively at her waist, was even less friendly
than had been his tone to the Scotsman.

The two men were near equal in force of personality, though Bowie had a minor advantage in height
and weight. It was age that made Rolfe the more
commanding of the two, he being perhaps four or five
years above Bowie's twenty-four; age, and the indefinable superiority that wide experience brings. He with-
stood the younger man's scrutiny with narrow-eyed
patience, inclining his head civilly as the McCullough
rushed to make rough and ready introductions.

"A prince," Jim grunted. "You are far from home.
I wonder what brings you to our country?"

"A private matter."

"It must be pressing to lead you to so isolated a spot."

"Yes." Rolfe's voice was even, unencouraging.

"No doubt you will be glad to depart?"

"I can't agree. It has, so far, been a fascinating
interlude, one I would not have missed."

"I trust you will feel the same—when you do finally
leave us."

Rolfe inclined his head once more. "It seems likely."

There was an undercurrent to their exchange of
pleasantries that disturbed Angeline. Nor was she

soothed by the appearance of André then, coming forward to claim acquaintance with Jim from his St. Martinville days, shaking hands.

"It's good to see you here," André said, his smile faint, but satisfaction in his tone.

"And you," Jim replied with an almost imperceptible nod in Angeline's direction.

André grimaced. "It's little enough, being here. Sometimes all a man can do is wait."

The McCullough, tired of being left out, interrupted. "Enough blather on the doorsteps! Come in, Jim, come in, and we'll find something to drink."

They turned into the house, the guest of honor pausing to allow Angeline to go before him. At the doorway, she looked back to see Rolfe standing where she had left him, watching Jim Bowie and André. On his chiseled features rested a frown of wary concentration.

As the men settled down to talk, Angeline moved about, setting the evening meal on the table. Jim was in No Man's Land, he said, to buy up acreage. He and his brothers, Rezin and John, were involved in land speculation. There were strong rumors of a treaty to be signed between the United States and whoever was in power in the country across the Sabine River—either Spain or the revolutionary elements of Mexico, none could say which from one day to the next—to make the river the boundary separating the two countries. With that treaty in effect, the American Army would be authorized to move into the neutral strip and clean out the nests of bandits. Once the area was made safe for settlement, land values would rise, and the men who had holdings in there would stand to make fortunes.

"Ah, man," the McCullough jeered, "they have been saying such things for these eight years and more, since General Hampton sent his lieutenants, by name McGee and Zebulon Pike, in '12. They burned me out three times at least, but they have nae cleaned me out yet. It's a faradiddle, and ye'll lose yer hard-earned silver, me lad. Take it from me!"

"I think not," Jim Bowie answered. "Were I you, McCullough, I'd be thinking of some way to convince the soldiers at Fort Claiborne I was an honest man, or else making tracks into Texas."

"Texas, is it? I think you tried that last year, with that crazy fool, Long. What was it ye were going to do, the two of ye, take the Tejas country for the U.S., sending to Galvez Town with offers for the pirate Lafitte to make him an admiral in the Texas Navy? Look what came of that!"

"We got thrashed and sent running home, I know. Still, it was a good fight with a worthwhile aim. Texas should be part of the United States and, God willing, shall be one of these days. I would do the same again."

"Ye'll get yourself killed, like as not," the McCullough growled. "If it's a fight ye be itching for, I've got one for ye."

Jim had always been a man of chivalrous impulses. When he heard of Claire's plight and her relation-ship to Angeline, he was more than ready to join the battle that loomed. He had never met Claire; she had been in France during the time of the Bowie family's residence near St. Martinville. But he knew of Don Pedro by reputation, and at the thought of a gently bred woman in his hands a grim light sprang into his gray eyes.

Despite the Scotsman's explanations, there was no lessening of the suspicion with which Bowie surveyed Rolfe. Later, as Angeline was clearing the table, the big man picked up the heavy iron stewpot, bringing it to where she was stacking dishes beside the pan of hot water on the wash bench.

"Tell me quickly," he said, leaning to set the pot down, "are you here of your own will?"

It was little wonder that he should ask, since the McCullough had been, under Rolfe's penetrating gaze, deliberately vague about her part in Rolfe's interest in Claire. Angeline hesitated, remembering her parting with her aunt, the lack of alternatives, the dictates of her own heart.

"Yes," she said.

"I take leave to doubt it. That you, of all women, should be traveling with this man, living with him, I find incredible."

His attitude was both balm and bitter medicine. Jim had been used to walking with her now and then, giving her his escort along the wooded path between the convent school and her aunt's house. There had been a time when she had suspected him of lying in wait for her at the road; he had appeared too often, leading his horse behind him, for it to have been otherwise. Then he had moved away with his family. There had been rumors that he had become involved with the smuggling of slaves from Lafitte's compound at Galvez Town, pirated slaves taken from ships at sea into Spanish Texas through that lawless port of entry, and then brought into the United States illegally through the back door of the No Man's Land. She had never believed it, until now. Why else should Jim be on such friendly terms with the man who manifestly controlled the entrances and exits of the neutral strip?

"I cannot help that. People's lives change, they change themselves."

"Not you. I want to talk to you, Angeline."

She forced a smile. "There is nothing to be said. Ask André. He will tell you how it is with me, then perhaps you will understand."

"I'll do that," he said, then after a silent moment, went on. "Still, I would like to help you. If there is aught I can do, you have only to command me."

"There is nothing," she answered, her voice not quite steady.

"You were living with your aunt in St. Martinville, I think. Perhaps I could return you to her? I would be happy—" As she shook her head, he stopped, then tried again. "A message, then? I will see that she gets anything you might care to write, or deliver a spoken greeting in person."

Should she send news of Claire to Madame de Buys? It might be kindest to refrain, waiting until some definite word of her was received, or until she was safe. "Thank you, Jim. I appreciate the offer, but no."

There was no time for more. Oscar and André arrived at her elbows, each bearing a stack of plates. It was so novel a development that she looked in surprise to the table. There, Rolfe, with his quick and acerbic tongue, was organizing a cleaning brigade, directing disgruntled and suddenly clumsy outlaws in taking plates and bowls to the wash bench. He met her gaze over the long, scrap-strewn trestle table, his bright blue eyes unsmiling as he watched the results of his industry—which was to separate Angeline neatly from the man who had sought her out.

It was not to be expected that the animosity, covert though it was, would escape the McCullough. He studied the two men, a crafty look in his brown eyes. Nothing could have exceeded his affability as he drew both into a discussion of the differences between hunting in Europe and in the young United States, of the habits of different animals and their species and plentitude, of methods and of weapons.

"Show Prince Rolfe your knife, Jim," he said, his smile showing yellow teeth.

"My knife?" Bowie took it from a sheath at his side that was half-hidden by the tail of his coat. Flipping it in his hand so that the razor-sharp edge caught the light in a silver blur, he let the haft fall with a solid smack in his palm.

"May I?" Rolfe inquired, his gaze intent on the knife, his interest patent as he held out his hand.

"Of course." Jim reversed it and passed it over.

It was a unique weapon. To the lethal, eighteen-inch-long butchering knife of the frontier had been welded a crosspiece between hilt and blade to prevent the hand from slipping down onto the cutting edge. The blade itself had a slope from midway along the top to the tip, and was sharpened also for the last inch or so of this upper ridge to make a point.

Rolfe weighed the knife in his hand, tossing it to feel the balance. "A superior weapon, rather like a *cinquedea*, a type of short sword with a quillon or crossbar. The workmanship is good, but not so fine as in the crafting of swords."

"It was made for me out of an old rasp by the Negro blacksmith on my father's plantation," Jim drawled. "I intend to have it copied if I ever run across a man I think can do a better job."

The McCullough nodded, his gaze bright as he looked from one man to the other. "When it comes to using it, there's none better than Jim, here. Ye be a fair man in a knife fight yerself, Yer Highness, but here's the man who can beat ye."

Angeline, rubbing goose grease into her hands where they had been reddened by the harsh lye soap of the dish water, went still, her breath caught in her chest. It was a challenge couched in banter, one Rolfe in his pride might feel compelled to accept. To do so was a greater danger than he could know, for it was rumored that even at his young age Jim had killed more than one man in knife fights. And yet to refuse would be to lose the respect of the outlaws and, possibly, that of his own men.

Rolfe glanced at Bowie, who was staring at the Scotsman with a frown between his gray eyes. "A useful skill, doubtless, in this place, at this time."

"Ye fancy yerself as a master, or at least the men who ride at yer back give ye that title. Have ye nae desire to test yer skill against Jim here, the local champion?"

"For your delectation?" Rolfe inquired. "As much as it pains me to disoblige my host, I see no reason to provide such entertainment—or to pander to your hope of revenge."

"Ye're afraid ye'll be bested!" the outlaw leader declared, growing red in the face at the exposure of his base motive and the reference to the fight between Rolfe and himself.

"The possibility always exists."

"But what a contest 'twould be! Ye owe it to yerselves to find out which is the better man."

Rolfe, a faint smile in his dark-blue eyes, looked to Jim Bowie. "Shall we slit and slice each other standing toe to toe? Lacking rancor or reason, shall we seek to spill life's blood for the sake of laurel leaves out of season?"

"I have no quarrel with you," Jim said, his gaze level, "and seek none." He looked then toward the McCullough, a warning in his stern features. "The only fight I am interested in is with the Spaniard, Don Pedro."

Bowie's announcement was greeted with cheers and whistles and much back-slapping. He would be a formidable ally, all agreed. And at once they settled in conclave, scraping chairs and rattling maps, forming plans that required only one thing: the discovery of the hiding place of the Spanish outlaw and his men.

Angeline was not left out of the planning, but neither was she included. She picked up her mending, but could not settle to it. Oddly restless, she wandered about the room, adding a log to the fire, sweeping up the trash around the hearth, dipping a drink of water from the bucket at one end of the wash bench. The air in the room was thick with the smells of food, woodsmoke, liquor from the demijohn being passed around, fresh-filled spittoons, and unwashed men. As the flames in the soot-blackened fireplace leaped higher, increasing the heat in the room, the odors strengthened.

Angeline moved to the door, opening it a thin crack. The air that seeped through was so fresh that she swung it wider, stepping outside and closing the panel behind her. The coolness of the night air was welcome. Folding her arms over her chest, she moved down the dark dogtrot to the front steps. For long moments she stood there, staring out into the blackness. Lifting her gaze, she watched a single star shining like an icy beacon through the interwoven limbs of the trees.

And then from not far away, a man coughed, a sentry on duty. The tenuous peace was broken. With a deep-drawn breath, she swung back toward the room she had left.

Light shafted into the dogtrot as the door opened, and in a wafting of loud voices and curls of smoke, a man came out. It was Meyer, his square shoulders blocking the light for an instant before he pushed the door to behind him.

"You will freeze out here," he said, his tone laden with concern.

"It isn't that cold," she answered.

"We don't want you to take sick. It would be too much on top of everything else that has happened to you." He stripped off the white coat of his uniform and, before she could protest, swung it around her shoulders.

The warmth enveloped her along with a hint of the smells she had left behind in the common room.

When she would have removed the coat, however, his hands holding the lapels prevented her. "Perhaps—I had better go inside after all."

"In a moment. I have been wanting to speak to you, Angeline, for several days, but with Rolfe and the others staying so close there has been no opportunity."

"What is it?" she said as he hesitated.

He released the coat and, propping one hand on the wall above her, leaned closer. "I have been watching you since Rolfe brought you to us. I have only admiration for the way you have behaved in a trying period, the way you have adapted to your situation. So often I have felt such compassion for you, I cannot begin to tell you."

"It is kind of you, but—"

"No, let me finish. You are so strong within yourself, and yet so fragile. I have wanted to protect you. More than that, I have longed to have the right to keep you safe, now and always. You—you know what I am, the king's bastard; still, I am not without a certain standing and influence in Ruthenia. As my wife, you would have a place at court, the respect—"

"Your wife?" Her head came up. "You are asking me to marry you?"

"What else? Did you think I was suggesting you leave Rolfe for the same kind of arrangement with me that you hold with him? I would not so insult you."

"I—I am sorry, but you must admit that you have given me no reason to think otherwise; indeed, no reason to expect anything from you."

"The circumstances are somewhat unusual. Rolfe will not thank me for interfering in his private affairs, and he is both my commanding officer and my prince, as well as my half-brother. But my deep concern for your welfare will not let me be silent."

"You speak of compassion and admiration, but no more?"

"There have been marriages of great happiness based on less. However, if it is love you require, that also I can give."

She stared at him looming over her in the darkness, caught in the snare of her own tangled thoughts and emotions. He was offering security, respectability, belonging. How could she refuse? And yet measured against the passion and joy she had known with Rolfe, it seemed without substance or value. She could find no acceptance within her mind. "Meyer, I can't— think you mean it. You hardly know me, or I you."

"I know all that is necessary, but you can hardly be expected to accept that. I don't require that you leave Rolfe and cleave to me now. In truth, I'm not sure he would allow it. But later, when this venture is done, I will be there waiting, and I will ask again."

It was plain that he expected Rolfe to desert her sometime, somehow, and that he wanted to cushion her aloneness. She should be grateful, but felt instead a paralyzing and painful anger. At the sound of a door opening, she swung her head to see Rolfe emerge from the common room. He came toward them with the controlled power of the wolf for which he was named and with his hair glinting gold in the lamplight behind him.

"Your turn at duty," he said to Meyer, the words soft and trenchant.

"Yes, of course." Meyer's tone was stiff as he straightened, turning away.

"Wait," Rolfe commanded. "Your jacket?"

He slipped it from Angeline's shoulders and threw it to Meyer, who swung back to catch it. The glances of the two men locked for an instant, then Meyer gave a curt nod and moved away down the dogtrot and into the night. Rolfe closed his hand around Angeline's arm, turning her toward the side of the house where their bedchamber lay.

"Shall we retire for the night?"

With a chill moving over her that had nothing to do with the loss of Meyer's jacket, Angeline allowed herself to be led across the cold and empty front room and into the bedchamber she shared with Rolfe. He pushed the door shut, then leaned against it, watching as she moved into the room. Under his hard gaze, she felt awkward as she went to the bed, fumblingly turning down the coverlet.

"Such a plentitude of suitors," he said. "They spring up like the progeny of dragon's teeth, offering—what? Succor and the trappings of honor, the two things for which your heart pines?"

She paused in the act of fluffing a pillow. Without looking at him, she asked, "Does it trouble you?"

"No, no. It is *fort amusant* in a puerile yet tragic fashion."

"I am glad you are entertained," she answered, lifting a brow, her gray-green gaze level and tinged with hauteur as she looked at him.

"Was that the purpose? You might have warned me. I would have trotted out a jealous rage by way of appreciation. As it is, I have nothing to offer for your amusement in return. Will you forgive me?"

"No."

The word hung between them, cutting through pretense, ignoring misunderstanding, standing as a simple affirmation of the fact that she preferred a display of jealousy, was not, in fact, disconcerted by the one to which he was subjecting her.

A crack of laughter burst from him. The hard line between his eyes dissolved before, just as abruptly, he sobered. "Will there be more?"

"Suitors? I cannot say."

"You would be better off, doubtless, with any one of them."

She pursed her lips, sending him a glance from under her lashes, pretending to consider. "Do you think so?"

"I know so," he answered, moving toward her, his turquoise eyes bright. "But if by chance any one of them looks like convincing you, I will give you his bones carved for hairpins and his teeth strung with knots as rosary beads for your prayers. Only in that way will he come close to you."

As a declaration, it brought a certain violent satisfaction, but it was no commitment, no promise of lifelong happiness, no proposal of marriage.

She would have told him of Jim Bowie's suggestion that he take her back to her aunt, and of Meyer's amazing promise to ask for her hand again when Rolfe relinquished it. However, he had given her no opening and she had not wanted to force one. That would have been too much like parading her conquests, as if challenging him to make her his own avowal. If she could have it at all, she did not care to have it that way.

What was it he had said? He would give her his love polished and shining, set with seals and tasseled ribbons if he could? Had he meant then that he would have married her by contract pressed with official seals and ribbons if such a thing were possible? Had he been saying, in his own oblique way, that he wished her to be his wife, and would have it so if circumstances permitted?

What were the circumstances? The traditions of royalty interbreeding with royalty to keep the blood-lines tinted purest azure? Such things no longer accounted for much in the New World, but were of great import still in Europe. No doubt his father, the king, expected him to take a princess to wife. No doubt, too, the marriage that had resulted in the births of Maximilian and Rolfe had been just such a one. Otherwise, why would it have been necessary to bring Meyer's mother to court in that underhanded, face-saving arranged marriage?

No, she must not expect marriage from the future King of Ruthenia. But what course could she take as a substitute?

Angeline lay in bed staring into the darkness above her, her mind endlessly turning. Beside her, Rolfe lay still, but there was a taut-stretched feeling in the air that let her know he was not sleeping. He seemed to have retreated into himself, and Angeline was aware of coolness in her own mind along with nebulous anger and dread. If she were honest with herself, she would have to admit there was another reason why she had not forced the various proposals made to her upon Rolfe's notice. There was always the chance that, had he known of them, he might have sent her away for her own good, or else pressed her with his implacable will to accept Meyer in order to be free of the responsibility for her. There was every indication that, if he so desired, he might even have enjoyed an arrangement such as his father had before him, with his paramour married but available for his convenience; certainly it was doubtful that Meyer would have demurred.

No. She would not think such things. That way lay the same cynicism and despair that had driven Claire, the same self-disgust that made her cousin count her favors and her life as worthless. It was a pitfall she must and would avoid, for no one could degrade her unless she allowed it, and that she would not.

Claire. What was happening to her cousin at that moment? Where was she in the cool and damp night? What pain and humiliation was she enduring while the men who planned her rescue sat back waiting, watching, talking, doing little? Oh, there were scouts sent out to search and to listen to rumors, primed for care and in disguise so as not to endanger Claire. Among them were members of the cadre, especially Gustave and Oswald who were chastened at the ease with which the Spaniard had eluded them, that first night, vanishing with his captive and his men into the virgin forest. But the search effort was so little that it might well be too late. Her cousin, Angeline thought, had not been wholly responsible for her

actions when she was first captured. How long could
her sanity survive the treatment to which she had been
subjected and which she must still be suffering? How
long would it be before she became like Alice, living
in mindless terror, suspicious of every touch, shivering
at any raised voice.

Now and then, since her return to the McCullough's
camp, Angeline had allowed herself to remember the
night she and Claire were taken. Was the danger in
which her cousin was trapped now greater or lesser
than the danger that she had fled? She had assumed
at the time that it was Rolfe that Claire had feared,
his trap that she had spoken of, and yet her cousin
had not said so. Angeline could not rid herself of the
feeling now that the omission was deliberate. Who, or
what, had so inspired Claire with terror that she had
risked leaving the relative safety of the outlaw leader's
protection for the dubious chance of escape with the
Spaniard and his men?

Though Angeline flung herself from side to side all
the night, seeking an answer through the labyrinth of
her memory, when morning came she was no closer
to understanding.

On the fifth day after the return to the McCullough's
camp, the Indian woman Morning Star put in an
appearance. She sat upon her horse on the winding,
muddy track, waiting while the sentries brought word
of her arrival to the Scotsman. The outlaw leader
hemmed and hawed and scratched his head, but finally
permitted her to approach while he went out to meet
her. What she said to him, or he to her, was unknown
since they spoke in a quick and rough Indian tongue,

but the outcome of the matter was that Morning Star slid down from her horse and, with impassive face but light step, entered the house. She went straight to the kitchen arranged around the fireplace, where she tasted the dishes Angeline had prepared, sniffing cautiously at the ladle each time before she brought it to her lips. She threw nothing out, but Angeline had the impression that it was due to the Indian woman's respect for food, rather than any compliment to her own cooking skill.

Morning Star had been ensconced in what she obviously considered to be her rightful place in the McCullough's bed and before his hearth for some days when sightings of the Spaniard began to be rumored. He had crossed the Sabine at the ferry on the old Camino Real, barely evading a patrol of soldiers from Camp Sabine. On the Arroyo Hondo, a woman had been brutally raped and her husband killed by men who rode with a mean-tempered Spaniard who kept a half-naked woman with red hair roped to his side. A woman at Grand Ecore had given his description while telling of how two of her best horses and thirty head of longhorn cattle had been taken, and news of raids had been brought from Los Adais, an ancient town not far from Natchitoches that had been settled by Spanish priests.

Finally came the news for which they had all been waiting. Don Pedro was found; his new headquarters had been established at the edge of the swamplands of Bayou Pierre, where he had taken over an abandoned homestead. His stronghold was stout and foursquare, as if he did not intend to be put easily to rout again.

His trail had ranged wide, covering much of the neutral strip. That he had been located at last was pure chance. Gustave, leaving off his uniform in order to be less conspicuous, had been diligently combing the woods with one of the McCullough's men as a guide. They had stopped to water their horses and buy a packet of food from a woman in the small town on the bank of Bayou Pierre. They had seen a man who looked familiar; it was a part of the oldest cadre member's training in the mercenary armies of Europe to remember men and be always on the lookout for enemies. Following the quarry, they had come upon the outlaw encampment. Taking note of the number of men, the size of the homestead, means of access to it, and the number of doors and windows, they had hastened back to the McCullough stronghold with the information.

The news set the men to hollering, shooting off guns, and pounding each other on the back in their exuberance. Still, it was twenty-four hours before the plans so painstakingly worked out over the past few days could be put into operation. There were only a few who knew the exact destination or the strategy that would be employed once they arrived. Regardless, the anticipation was felt by everyone, from the wives and children of the outlaws to Rolfe himself. One result was an increase in the consumption of drink. The men became boisterous and overloud, playing practical jokes on each other as they cleaned their weapons, dragged out rain capes against the gathering clouds that darkened the skies as dusk fell, and gambled among themselves. Rolfe remained outwardly calm, but the slicing edge of his tongue was felt by any man caught unprepared, anyone who failed to answer quickly and accurately any query put to him.

To escape the noise and the nauseating smells of liquor, food, and masculine excitement on one hand, and the irritating efficiency of the preparations for an expedition in which she had no part on the other, Angeline swung a cloak around her shoulders and let herself out of the house. She moved quickly along the dogtrot and into the yard. A cur growled, raising his hackles, then was silent as she spoke to him and he caught her familiar scent.

Evening was fast approaching, but at some distance down the track that led to the house she could see the white gleam of a uniform tunic. Taking a deep breath of the dew-laden air, she drew her cloak closer and stepped out in that direction.

It was Oscar who stood in the gloom beneath a leafless black gum tree, taking his turn at sentry with a long rifle held in the crook of his arm. He smiled as she approached.

"Mademoiselle Angeline, have you come to relieve my tedium? There is naught out here except rabbits nibbling dogwood seedling while keeping a wary eye out for the dogs, and I am forbidden my guitar by common sense as well as Rolfe's edict."

"Have you tired so soon of our flora and fauna?" She leaned against the tree trunk beside him, bracing her back upon the rough bark.

"I have studied every bare twig in sight, but there is little to be learned at this season, and night is falling now."

"Perhaps you will still be with us when spring comes, only short weeks away now. There will be shrubs and bulbs in flower in the dooryard gardens, and soon the wild plums and cherries will bloom."

"I have noted the swelling buds and tips of green here and there, changes that had occurred since we came, and miraculous ones for February. However, if we are successful on the morrow, I am afraid we will be gone before the full glory can be seen."

"Back to Ruthenia? Will you be glad?"

"Here or there, it's all the same to me. My brother and I follow Rolfe. His joys are our joys, his sorrows ours also, and where he chances to stay, there is home."

The simple declaration was so moving that her voice was husky as she spoke. "There will be problems to be faced in Ruthenia, I think."

"This is true, more problems even than here."

"How can you say so?"

"The king is there," he answered, then flung her a quick glance as if wishing he could take back the words.

"Gustave has spoken of the strained relationship between Rolfe and his father," she said, seeking to soothe his fears.

"And did he mention that it is the king who most wishes our prince dead?"

Angeline stared at him. "Surely you are mistaken. Even if he thought him the cause of Maximilian's death, that would be unnatural."

"I tell you, no. He had ever a greater love for his eldest son, and with Max's death, he has become mad, a condition fed by the rumors about the palace of Rolfe's involvement. It would not be surprising to me to discover that the assassin who has dogged our footsteps is in the pay of the king."

"But—it's barbaric! Surely Rolfe would be accused of the crime, given a trial?"

"That would be to parade the family pride before the world. No, it would suit the king better if it were settled quietly, and out of the country."

The words, spoken so gently, were all the more frightening for their tone of reason. "But who would accept such a commission?"

"There are always those ready to do the bidding of royalty. The inducement would be strong—wealth or, more likely, the high honors that the king can bestow. Then if a man were wily, there would be the weapon for gain by blackmail, of having murdered for the king."

"Only think, Oscar, if Rolfe were killed, there would be no direct heir to the throne!"

"What matters that? The king has always maintained that Rolfe was unfit compared to Max, a charge both unfair and untrue, but impossible to disprove. That being the case, why, it will satisfy the tyrant well enough for his nephew Leopold to ascend to his throne instead. It may, in fact, be a source of pleasure to him to prevent Rolfe from taking his place as the people have made plain they wish."

She frowned in thought, hesitated, then finally spoke. "But if it is the king's assassin who has dogged Rolfe's footsteps, trying to arrange his death, and not the same man who killed his brother, then—who did kill Max?"

"Who can say? It may have been a suicide. Or it could have been a jealous husband, a jilted woman— even Claire herself."

"You can't be serious!"

"Stranger things have happened. She didn't die, and she seems fearful beyond the ordinary."

He was right, and yet Angeline could not convince herself that he had the answer. There remained one other possibility. It flashed across her consciousness with the fiery brilliance of a shooting star and faded just as quickly. It was that the king was correct; that Rolfe in a moment of uncontrolled fury had indeed murdered his brother. She did not believe it, would not, and so with supreme will banished it.

They spoke of other things in wandering and fitful bursts, but between them, like a red-hot coal evilly gleaming, was the thought of the king sending someone after Rolfe, his own son. She did not like to consider that it could actually be so, but wasn't it true that the first attempt on his life had been made outside the palace after an unsuccessful attempt to see his father?

As for the hired assassin, wouldn't the most efficient choice available, the one likeliest to catch Rolfe off guard, be one of his own men? Loyalty, camaraderie, fidelity, all these could be found wanting in the balance against the prospect of preferment and riches. Knowing these things, as surely he must, how then could Rolfe trust anyone? How could he hope that even if he discovered his brother's killer it would make a difference? Reason would not gain the respect of a man so lost to fatherly affection and decency as to try to kill his son, nor would it elicit the love heaped upon Maximilian, deferred for Rolfe these many years. The long chase might be for nothing then, a useless and dangerous risk.

Sixteen

THEY RODE OUT JUST AFTER NOON OF THE FOLLOWING day. Rolfe and the McCullough were in the forefront, with the cadre, including André shoulder to shoulder with Oscar and Oswald, leading the force of outlaws that straggled behind. The men shouted and whistled as they trotted away from the encampment. Even the members of the guard seemed happy to be active once more, calling out to each other in their exuberance. Only Rolfe was grim of face and manner, staring ahead with no pleasure at the prospect of the fight.

He had kissed Angeline good-bye, a brief and hard farewell peculiarly without words. She had stared at him, her chest too constricted to speak, drowning in the infinite turquoise depths of his eyes. Then he had turned away, mounting swiftly, sitting his horse with the light catching dark-golden gleams in his hair even in the grayness of the day. He had lifted his hand in command, and they had swept from the yard, going in a clatter of horses' hooves and thrown clods of mud. The hoofbeats grew distant and were heard no more.

The rain, as silent and heavy as the tears of old grief, began within the hour. She lit the lamps against the gloom. Evening drew in early. It seemed odd to be there alone, without the constant coming and going of the men, their tracking in and out with muddy feet, their demands and appetites. Angeline sat before the fire, staring into the flames, making little attempt to discipline the thoughts running through her mind. She felt lethargic, weighted with dread allied to a burgeoning ache in the region of her heart.

How had it come about that the safety of one man could so affect her? She had not meant it to happen. The days had passed, and the nights, and she had been enthralled. What, now, would come of it?

It was time that she thought seriously of what she must do. Avoiding the issue, putting it off, would no longer suffice. But what were the choices open to her? Even if Claire were rescued, she was not certain that her aunt would receive her back into her home. And if she did, only a living death awaited her, so lost to reputation was she after this escapade. That being so, Jim Bowie's offer of escort required careful thought.

There was Meyer's proposal. The image of the intimacies that becoming his wife conjured up was daunting. Could she endure a loveless union stiff with protocol and gratitude, near Rolfe but separate from him? Could she endure Ruthenia, so far from everything familiar since birth, without the *raison d'être* of a passionate attachment? And would not the taint of having been Rolfe's mistress follow her even there, clouding the future though they never spoke to one another again after the shores of Louisiana dropped from sight?

It might be better for her peace of mind and future happiness if she spoke, instead, to André. He had tried several times in the last week to have private words with her, but had always been prevented. Knowing how blameless she had been in her fall from virtue, would he, perhaps, renew his avowal of affection? Did she want him to? Did he deserve to be burdened with a woman who had little more than liking to offer in return? Could he be happy with her when the memory of her association with Rolfe would always lie between them? She would be able to stay in Louisiana, among people who spoke her own language and kept the same customs, and yet what good was that if happiness eluded her?

There were other alternatives. Mother Theresa, if she could not offer her a place at the convent school for fear of the displeasure of the parents of the students, might suggest another religious house that would take her in. Failing that, she might find work as a seamstress or governess, though how she would live until then, and how she would acquire a position without past experience or references attesting to her high moral character, were questions she could not answer.

It seemed imperative to do something, or at least to plan. There was no permanency with Rolfe; that fact had been brought home to her in these last days of coolness between them. Her well-being rested upon nothing more tangible than his desire for her. If that should fade, then she would be bereft, alone without friends in a strange country. She put no faith in the assertion made by Gustave—or was it Meyer?—that Rolfe would make a settlement upon her at their parting. Such promises had little meaning, she expected, and in any case, she wanted nothing from him. Pride might be an expensive commodity in her situation, but it was all she had, and she refused to relinquish her self-respect so that he might have a free conscience.

A rattling crash shattered her reverie. She sat up, listening. It seemed she could hear Morning Star moving about on the other side of the dogtrot, in the area around the fireplace kitchen. A solid thump, as of something heavy dropping to the floor, confirmed it. Was the Indian woman preparing a meal for the returning warriors? If so, it would be some time before they would be there to eat it. It might be as well to offer aid, instead of sitting there moping, riding her thoughts in circles that went nowhere. It was possible she might also save the kitchenware at the same time.

The Indian girl had her back to the door as Angeline pushed it open. She was taking skillets and pans from the dish shelf and putting them into a sack that lay on the floor beside her. Those that did not suit her requirements, she tossed to one side. A large wooden bowl with a crack down one side was sent flying against the wall as Angeline watched.

"What are you doing?" she asked, her tone sharp with outraged surprise.

Morning Star swung around with the bail of an iron stewpot in her hand and her brown eyes defiant. "I am taking what is mine."

"Yours? All this?" Angeline waved her hand at the tin plates pulled out and stacked ready, the sacks of flour and meal, coffee and beans that were set to one side.

"Mine, by right. I brought cattle to the McCullough when I came to him from my tribe, also furs and baskets and beaded leather that he sold. Once before he sent me away with nothing. Now I will have everything."

"I can't let you do that. The men must have food when they return"

"I say to you, take a portion for yourself and go. There is no reason to linger." The smile in the Indian woman's dark eyes was not pleasant.

Angeline was aware of a prickling along her nerves. She frowned. "What can you mean? There is as much reason as ever was. I can't go."

"Stay, and you will be alone, you and the other women who are used by the cruel white men. Because you have smiled and worked beside me like a sister of the blood, I tell you. It is best to go, now."

"What is it? What have you done?" Angeline took a step toward the other girl, but Morning Star stepped back, scooping into her sack the foodstuffs she had gathered.

"I? Nothing, except carry a message to the Spaniards. It was not so great a thing and gave me pleasure. Even now, the one known as Don Pedro waits while the McCullough rides toward him."

"What—what of the others?" The question was a useless husk of sound, for she already knew.

"The trap," Morning Star said, "has a wide mouth. But why should you care, if those who will die are the men who took you from your people against your will?"

Angeline moved swiftly forward, leaning with both hands on the table as the Indian girl retreated. "Who? Who asked you to take the message?"

Morning Star tilted her head. "The one who understood my hate, having seen its blackness so often before."

"But his name?" Angeline cried.

"What do I know, or care, so long as he pointed out to me the way of my revenge?"

"At least tell me if he was one of the men with the prince?" Morning Star was edging toward the door and she followed after her.

"Men come and go here. I do not know them all, nor do I wish to, for it is not the place of a woman to look them in the face. Farewell, Angeline. I go now."

She was gone like a wraith, flitting down the dogtrot, fading into the gathering rain-gray evening. There came the muffled beat of hooves, and then silence. Angeline stood with her hands tightly clasped together and her teeth set in her bottom lip. Her thoughts were in chaos, while her scalp prickled with horror. A trap, well baited, and with the Spaniard set to spring it. At that moment, Rolfe and the others were riding toward it, confident, unaware.

How long had it been since they had left? An hour, perhaps? More? They had expected to be at the Spaniard's as night fell, a sortie under cover of darkness. The rain created an artificial dimness, belying the hours still left of the waning day.

Angeline drew a deep breath as she felt her resolve growing, then in sudden decision, she dived for the door. Flinging herself across the dogtrot, she pushed into the common room, jerked down her cloak from a peg in the wall, and whipped out again. Throwing it around her as she ran, she made for the stables.

A chestnut mare pricked her ears forward as she saw Angeline. It was no trouble to saddle her, though Angeline gritted her teeth at the delay. Leading the horse finally out into the misting rain, she stepped to her back, settled in the Spanish-style saddle, and dug in her heels. The mare whinnied in surprise, throwing up her head, but then she stretched into a run, pounding from the yard down the winding track that led through No Man's Land.

Angeline knew where to go and what roads to take to get there, for she had heard Gustave's report to Rolfe. What she had not expected were the myriad trails and dim paths that meandered back and forth over the main road; military highways, Indian trails, and animals' pathways. The gradual loss of light did not help matters, nor did the lack of houses or other travelers along that back road. There was no one she could ask for directions, no one to inquire of for news of a party of men who had passed along the way ahead of her.

The miles thudded away beneath the mare's hooves, speeding by in a blur of dark tree limbs and tangled, wet undergrowth. She splashed through deep, clinging ruts in sandy roadbeds and forded creeks and bayous swollen with the recent rains. Now and then, she stopped to search for tracks of the horsemen ahead of her, but the rain had washed them away so that only now and then was she able to discern the splattered indentations, like fingerprints in melted butter.

She grew tired, her leg muscles hard with cramp and her fingers crooked like those of an ancient crone around the reins. Still, she did not stop. The mare's breathing grew labored and she faltered, and Angeline pulled her up to let her drink at a spring-fed stream, but then, despite the foam that clotted her sides and the steam rising in the cool air from her sweat-streaked coat, she pushed the horse onward. She could afford rest for neither herself nor her mount; in this race, the penalty for failure to reach the finish was too great. Narrowing her eyes, she stared with burning intentness through the gathering shadows, willing night to hold off, praying that Rolfe and the McCullough and those who rode with them had tarried, that they were behind time.

She did not feel the wind that lashed her face, or the rain that stung her cheeks. Her cloak became sodden, dragging at her shoulders, slapping against the mare's rippling flank. The pounding of her own mount's hoofbeats thudded in her brain, drowning cut other sound, echoing back from the far-stretching woods. The sound of firing, muffled and distant, was like a counterpoint, repeating the same drumming with sharp emphasis.

No, no, no, was the silent cry that rose in her mind, though she did not slacken pace. Leaning low over the horse's neck, she put her head down, urging, asking for the last, straining effort of which the mare was capable. She gave it, carrying Angeline nearer and nearer the shooting. There was one final explosion close enough to hear the whine of the ricochet, then all was quiet.

It would be foolhardy to ride straight into the homestead. A few yards more and Angeline drew in the mare, then got down and led her into the woods.

She forced her way through the wet undergrowth beneath the dripping trees, her every tread bringing forth the odors of wood's mold, decaying leaves, and night dankness. She tied the mare to a sapling when she was well out of sight of the road, then pressed on toward the glow of a lamp she could just glimpse through the trees.

Light poured in golden rectangles from the windows of a double-pen log cabin. It slid across a wide porch and into the yard where it glanced over the bodies of men sprawled with arms outspread in death. It picked up butternut-brown and faded red, linsey-woolsey gray and blue so dark with rain-wet it was nearly black. And off to one side, glimmering softly, was a splotch of purest white, though the identity of the man who wore it could not be seen.

A shot splatted in the damp night, coming from the dark line of a gully that lay to one side of the cabin. It was answered from nearer at hand where a grove of evergreen cedars stood, their low branches creating a black retreat. Inside the double-pen log structure, the figure of a man moved, jumping up quickly to fire from the window toward the cedars. He drew no return shots, however.

From where she stood, it seemed to Angeline that the Spaniard had left one or two men in the lighted cabin as decoys while stationing his main force in the gully. When Rolfe and the others had moved in on the homestead, they had been cut down as they came into the light, like waterfowl against a sunset. Collecting their men, Rolfe and the McCullough had taken cover in the cedar thicket. At least she thought, she prayed, Rolfe was among them. That still figure lying in the muddy yard looked too slim to be the Prince of Ruthenia, but the impression might well be a trick of the uncertain light. A pistol belched flame from the gully, and in the cedars a man gave a moaning scream, proof of the inadequacy of the protection of the trees. The cadre and the clan did not dare move for fear of the lamplight striking through the branches giving them away, while Don Pedro and his followers could lie hidden and pick them off with ease.

Where, in that scene of straining senses and mud-splattered death, was Claire? Was she in the cabin, one of the decoys enticing Rolfe and the others to come and get her? Or did she lie in the rain-washed gully with Don Pedro, a hostage for his safety if anything should go wrong? One thing was almost certain: she was not with the men in the cedars.

What was Rolfe going to do? For some reason it did not occur to her to expect decisive action from anyone else, not the McCullough, not even Jim Bowie. With her hands clenched on her skirts, she studied the alternatives, few and dangerous though they were.

He could charge the gully, trusting to the superior skill with weapons of the cadre and the men trained by them to overcome the advantage of the Spaniard's position. To risk it, however, he would have to be willing to take the inevitable losses. He could retreat to the horses left some yards away, but to do so he would have to leave the protecting darkness of the cedars, with the carnage likely to be as great as in a frontal attack. Last of all, he could in some way persuade Don Pedro to make a sally into the open, mounting an assault against the cedars.

Hard on the last thought came a call in a voice deep and whetted with mockery. "My Spanish friend, I compliment you on your perspicacity, though your marksmanship deserves none."

"It will serve to end your life, *amigo*!" came the reply.

"Hope is a fine thing, even a necessity for a man cowering in a ditch with mud plastered on his belly and rain trickling in his ears. Could I offer you an umbrella oiled with fragrant cedar, prickly but a fine protection for your powder? Don't tarry, now, or you may be disarmed by feeble rain, and that would be a pity."

As the words, flowing, effortlessly carrying, came from the cedars, relief poured over Angeline. "Rolfe," she whispered, and without warning she dropped to her knees in the wet leaves as her legs refused to support her. Tears rose into her eyes, and with a fierce gesture, she used the heel of her hand to wipe them away, the better to see.

The insults, gently acid on one side and returned with rising irritation on the other, continued. Now and then a shot rang out, always answered. In the small periods of quiet, Angeline heard cows bellowing as if disturbed, coming from somewhere to the rear of the cabin. No doubt there was a settler somewhere bitterly cursing the outlaws.

The idea came slowly, in bits and pieces. The Spaniard did not know she was there. If she could make some noise, create a diversion, he might be distracted enough for Rolfe to launch an attack. She had no weapon, had not thought, in her hurry, to provide herself with pistol or rifle, was not certain there had been a spare of any kind left. She had nothing with which to make a noise, nothing to bang or clatter. She could scream and yell, but any effect she might have would not be longlasting. It would help if she could even put out the light inside the cabin, but to approach close enough to throw sticks or broken limbs at the lamp was much too risky, and there were no stones in the soft alluvial soil. Moreover, if she were caught, the plight of Rolfe and the cadre would be worse, for it was possible they would be forced to greater risk for her sake.

What then could she do? The greatest need was for some way to flush Don Pedro out of the gully. One rider on a horse would hardly make them stir. What was needed was a host of mounted men sweeping down in a body from behind. As she knelt there in frowning concentration, a cow lowed again. Angeline blinked, then a slow smile curved her lips. With a soft exclamation of satisfaction, she scrambled to her feet and set off with hurried stealth for the place where she had tied the mare.

Leading the horse, she circled through the woods, stumbling, running headlong into vines and tree limbs in her breathless haste, giving a wide berth to the head of the gully, where the Spaniard and his men lay. The lighted cabin, gleaming through the woods, made a useful beacon for her circuitous route. Keeping it always on her right, she came at last to the rear of the homestead.

The cows were being held in a pole pen made of peeled saplings stuck into the ground and lashed together with rope. It sagged here and there, but was

stout enough to keep in check the score or so of cattle
that surged from one side to the other in their crazed
fear. Their feet made sucking sounds in the mud they
had churned into a bog. Their lowing had a desperate
sound, and in the darkness the smooth clicking of
their long horns as they milled together made an
ominous rattle.

The gate was made of poles tied together in a large
rectangle and looped from its outside post to the
pole of the fence for a closure. Moving as quietly as
possible, Angeline pulled herself into the saddle, then
leaned to draw the rope loop over the post. The gate
swung wide, its weathered poles creaking loud enough
to split the night apart.

The cattle needed no further prodding. It was all
Angeline's mare could do to dance out of their way
as they surged through the opening. Once in the
clear, they bolted with Angeline riding at their head,
raising her voice in a hoarse shout to swerve them in
the direction she wanted them to go. The mare, as if
sensing her desire, headed off the hulking cow that
thundered at the head of the herd, turning her toward
the right side of the house. They spilled around the
corner at a loping run, bellowing with walled eyes,
their trampling hooves shaking the ground as they
pounded straight for the gully where Don Pedro and
his men lay.

Exultation lifted Angeline's heart as she rode. She
wished there had been some way that she could have
warned Rolfe and the others, though even so, she had
little doubt that they could and would use the situation
that was developing. A hundred feet from the gully,

she drew the mare in, turning her, letting the galloping cattle pour past. Only then did she notice the winded wheeze in the gallant horse's breathing, feel the trembling that ran over her. She slid down, drawing the reins over her head, smoothing her drooping neck.

Intent on the mare, she did not see the first panic among the men of the Spaniard, though she heard their yells. When she spun around, it was to see the cows stumbling down the sides of the deep wash, trying to leap across it, bawling as they fell. The Spaniard and his men swarmed forth with curses and superstitious terror, their pistols blazing as they splashed through the falling rain toward the men erupting from the dark ambuscade of the cedars.

The two forces clashed like iron and anvil, with shouts and oaths and groaning grunts, fighting hand to hand as pistol and rifle were discharged with no time to reload. They swayed and weaved in the drenched lamplight that slithered along the barrels of rifles used as clubs and the blades of lethal, snicking knives. The clash was bloody, but brief. Within minutes the cows had run bellowing into the night, those not bawling with broken legs in the ditch, and the defeated Spaniard and those of his men still left alive were stretched out, bound hand and foot, across the comparative dryness of the rough floor of the porch.

Rolfe, his bare head shining wet in the lamplight, moved across the yard to where the white-uniformed figure lay. He went to one knee and with a gentle hand reached to grasp the shoulder, pulling, rolling the man to his back. Boneless and without grace in death,

Oscar stared upward with sightless eyes. His sandy hair fell lankly away from his thin young face, dripping cold rainwater. The bandage of his injured wrist was brown with mud, and his slender musician's hands were cupped and lax, so that the pistol he held had fallen away. The front and side of his uniform were no longer white, but glistened wet and red.

"Hail the young warriors," Rolfe said, his voice ragged, almost inaudible. "They spend themselves for honor and fruitless causes, for country and sometimes for worthless men, but not for love. They hone their bodies and brains and conquer boundless realms of fear, but not for love."

"He loved you," Angeline said, moving with slow steps to stand at his shoulder.

He turned his head to stare up at her, his turquoise eyes dazed in his inward search for blame. "I should have said, for the love of women. Hail, too, our defending angel, wet, worn, and draggle-tailed, infinitely welcome. What the hell are you doing here?"

"I came to warn you, too late." Though she was blinded by tears and could not bear to glance toward the face of the dead boy lying beside them, she was satisfied. For an instant there had been something near to death in Rolfe's features too, a gray agony of remorse that might seek any means to avoid the unyielding responsibility for the loss of Oscar's life. With his anger had come acceptance, and enough forgiveness for himself that he was able to turn to the responsibility for her presence as well.

"And were those your sweet tones we heard, driving Zeus' red-horned cattle, wreaking godlike justice?"

"I did what I could." Glancing around, she saw Jim Bowie leaning his long frame against a post of the porch, cradling a rifle in the crook of his arm as he kept watch over the captured outlaws. Off to one side she glimpsed Oscar's twin, a pistol in his hand and his face twisted with enraged grief, start toward Don Pedro; saw Gustave and Leopold step to his side to stop him, holding his arms, talking in quiet voices. Meyer was binding a flesh wound in the upper arm of a man who sat coatless and shirtless on the steps of the porch. It was only after a second look that she recognized the injured man as André, so drawn and white was his face and so rain-plastered his hair.

"You might have been killed," Rolfe said, rising to stand beside her, the words stark and unadorned.

She swung back, her gray-green eyes enormous in the pale oval of her face. "So might you."

"I am better equipped for defense, while you—"

"While I have only my wits and a fortunate star? What does it matter? I am here." She wanted to be held close, to be warmed and made to know she was safe. She understood his sense of guilt and driving duty, also his irritation that she had risked so much for his sake, but understanding was no comfort.

"Don't be impertinent to the teacher," he said softly. "Beyond my jittery qualms concerning your safety, I require to know what foul whisper, what perfidious plot, made it necessary for you to come here at all?"

She opened her mouth to tell him, but abruptly he caught her arm, tuning her toward the warmth and protection of the cabin. Once inside, he went to the hearth, where with his swift and precise efficiency, he put wood on the dying embers. As they flared into life-giving warmth, he stripped a blanket from the bed and, removing her sodden cloak, bundled her into its folds and pressed her into a seat before the fire. Only then would he allow her to speak.

As the heat penetrated her clammy clothing, reaching her chilled skin, Angeline shuddered, but she would not allow the tremor to be heard in her voice. The effort to prevent it was exhausting, but her tale was short.

"You are certain Morning Star gave no hint of who might have made her his go-between?" he asked, frowning into the fire, scarcely aware of its radiating heat for all the move he made toward it.

"Certain, and I have had much time to consider it on the ride here."

It was a moment before he spoke, then his words seemed to have nothing to do with the subject under discussion. "Oscar's wound was to the side, his right side, and only slightly to the front."

Angeline stared at him. The puzzlement slowly cleared from her face to be replaced by sick horror. The Spaniard and his men had been in the gully to the left of the cabin as the cadre closed in. Rolfe's trained men would not have done so in a mass, but in several smaller groups, probably from different directions. Oscar had been in the party making a near frontal attack, judging from where he fell. That meant that somehow in the confusion of the charge and the springing of the trap, Oscar had been shot by one of their own men. With reluctance she forced herself to the second conclusion: it had not been an accident.

Did Rolfe suspect? The dark pain in the depths of his eyes was its own answer. He knew, and scourged himself with the knowledge. Had Oscar been mistaken for him in the darkness? Or had it been deliberate, for some reason that escaped detection, something Oscar had known, or guessed, or seen that he had not recognized himself?

Angeline looked up, Oscar's theory of an assassin hired by the king pounding in her mind. At the braced expression of Rolfe's face, she shut her lips. He had enough to contend with for the moment without being forced to confront the fact that his own father might be happy to see him die. He had cared for her in the midst of this desperate attack, had offered her warmth and covering and opened to her the recesses of his mind. She could not repay the boon by inflicting such a mental wound, not now.

Instead, she said, "What of Claire?"

"A fine point. Let us see what our Spanish friend has to say."

If Don Pedro thought to barter for his life with the information he held, then he was given little satisfaction. Rolfe would strike no bargain and said so. It was the McCullough who held the key to the Spaniard's life or death; for himself, Rolfe said, he had jurisdiction only over his comfort.

To see the warrior prince extract the information he desired from the hardened Spanish outlaw was enough to make Angeline realize, if she hadn't before, the extreme delicacy with which he had treated her, the exquisite self-control it had taken to do so. He had no need for such things with the man who had abducted Claire and, in an excess of acid rage, he cast them aside.

Don Pedro, screaming curses and maledictions, broke in a mercifully short time. Claire, he said, had quickly become a burden. At Los Adais she had been traded for a horse and bridle to a man who saw her on the street. The man, a gambler by profession, had no home. It was thought he was on his way to Natchitoches, though for what reason only God could tell.

Events moved with oiled swiftness then. Oscar was interred by the light of a lantern, the muddy grave marked by a hastily constructed cross. Rolfe and the cadre raided the supplies of the Spaniard and slipped what they needed into their saddle pouches. Jim Bowie, free now that the fight was over and anxious to be on his way, offered to act as their guide to Natchitoches and was accepted with a bow and a handshake. André was delegated to return with Angeline to the outlaw stronghold, setting out at once, while the McCullough and his men would follow more slowly. The reason for the latter plan was unstated, though it seemed obvious that something must be done with the men still tied up on the porch.

Angeline was at least partially dry after turning before the fire like a roast on a spit, being excluded by custom and Rolfe's order from the services for Oscar. As the men stood ready, she got to her feet and set the blanket aside to take up her cloak that had been spread to dry. Rolfe turned and came toward her, a gutta-percha-coated cape in his hands. As he neared, he swirled it around her shoulders.

"I can't take this," she said, lifting it with a suddenly nerveless grip. "You'll get wet."

"Not I. It was Oscar's and he will not be needing it. Nor is there need to be squeamish—it was discarded before the firing started."

She met his gaze without flinching, her face set. "I—I wish you would let me come with you to Natchitoches."

"Claire's presence may be no more than a chimera, long-legged and frolicsome, leading us ever onward. What will you wager on the chance?"

"But Don Pedro swore—"

"The oath of a dead man and, by the McCullough's reckoning, one who has no hope of paradise. Besides, it is too long and tiring a ride, with no rest for the night."

"If you can make it, so can I."

"Can you, sweet Angeline, all heart and no heeding? Can you?"

For a brief flicker of time there was in his gaze a softness that caressed her sore spirit. "I could try."

"You could, but I cannot allow it. Go with André. It will be best for now."

There was no relenting in his features. After a moment, she nodded. He held her gaze for eternal seconds, lingering on the tender curves of her mouth as men milled around them, warming themselves at the fire, searching for food and drink, pulling on raingear and gloves. Abruptly he moved toward her and, sweeping her against him, took her lips with his warm, firm mouth. His uniform coat was damp, its buttons cold, but there was about him the freshness of the wet night and his own vibrant male heat. His kiss was possessive, flavored with a hint of despair. It seemed, as he released her, that there was reluctance in the corded strength of his arms, that it required an effort of will for him to step back, turn away.

And then in a few quiet phrases he gathered his men. They erupted from the cabin, carrying Angeline and André with them. The horses were led up. Gustave gave her a boost into the saddle. She sat with slack reins, waiting until André, with his arm in a makeshift sling, had mounted, then sat as the cadre swung astride around her. Was there some signal between André and Rolfe she did not see, some instruction she had not heard? It did not matter. Her former suitor leaned to catch her bridle, leading her out of the melee, away from the cadre and their shouted good-byes, away from the curses and moans of the Spaniard's men as they were bustled to their feet and dragged from the porch, away from the McCullough's clan who were already throwing ropes over the limbs of venerable live oak trees.

She looked back over her shoulder to where Rolfe sat his horse, oblivious of the noise and confusion, the look on his face absorbed as he stared after her. Then as she watched, Meyer reached out to touch his arm. He whipped around sharply before collecting himself, gathering his reins. The *garde du corps*, only four in number now, swung in a body with Rolfe at their head and Jim Bowie cantering up beside him. They straightened like a flock of geese setting a northward course in the spring, riding in the direction opposite to hers. Their rain capes glimmered an instant in rain-slashed darkness, then they were lost to sight.

Angeline faced forward. As the minutes passed and the space between herself and Rolfe of Ruthenia widened, she felt drawn, carrying the ache of unshed tears in her throat and tightness in her chest. It was as if an unseen line connected her to the man riding away, one being pulled more taut with every yard that separated them, one being tested, one that could and would break. It came, with snapping, tearing agony, and she let the tears slide down her cheeks, mingling with the falling rain.

Beside her, André was a moving shadow. Their horses' hooves splashed and thudded in the mud of the road. Against the hood of her cape she could hear the quiet spatter of the falling rain. She was glad of the covering night, the wet weather, and their swift travel that prevented conversation. She could not have spoken. In her mind she lived once again the moments of her farewell to Rolfe and the cadre, and try though she might, she could discover nothing to prove that it was not final.

Seventeen

SMOKE SPIRALED UPWARD IN SLOW EDDIES FROM THE burned-out rubble, blending with the gray light of morning. Women, their faces red with weeping and heat, straggled here and there, trying to salvage something, anything from the charred, wet ruin. Children sat in huddled groups under the scorched trees, though one girl with black braids hanging down her back and a missing front tooth drew water at the well. The earthenware pitcher she poured it into appeared to be the only unbroken household item in sight.

Angeline and André sat their horses, staring around them at what had been the McCullough's stronghold. Of the houses and outbuildings, not a one stood; all had been burned to the ground. There was no livestock of any kind in view, with the exception of a banty rooster, scratching where the stable had stood, his bedraggled plumage rust and green in the growing daylight. Twisting in his saddle, André beckoned a towheaded youngster forward.

"'Twere them thieving Indians," the boy said when questioned. "They come in the middle of the night, the kin of the McCullough's woman. What they didn't burn, they run off or tore up. Ma says we'll have to go somewhere else, least-ways, till the cabins can be built back."

The boy caught the penny André threw him and ran off with it clutched tightly in his fist. The man beside her said quietly, "Well, Angeline?"

She summoned a smile as she met his dark-brown gaze. "If by that you mean to ask what I am going to do, I don't know."

"You agree that it alters matters then? You cannot live outside like an animal."

"No doubt the McCullough will find shelter, perhaps even the homestead we left last night."

"Yes, and take these women and children there where the men they defeated are hanging like so much rotten fruit from the trees? That is, of course, unless in a moment of distraction they forgot to put the torch to the house."

Angeline's brows drew together. The vision André had conjured up was all too likely. "What else is there?"

"You can come with me, to New Orleans, to my mother."

By now Madame Delacroix would be in the city by the river, enjoying the winter season. She always closed up her house near St. Martinville the last of January and made the trek, taking with her wagonloads of silver, china, and crystal, of wardrobe trunks, bedding, feather mattresses, and special pillows, hogsheads of hams, sides of beef, preserved figs, apples, peaches, and pears, plus jellies too numerous to mention. All this just as if her house on the Rue St. Anne was not

well supplied with food and other comforts, and kept
well aired, swept to shining cleanliness in expectation
of her arrival.

"It—it is kind of you to ask, but unnecessary."

"For whom? It is necessary to me! I love you,
Angeline, and I want to take care of you. I bleed
inside to see you like this, with no one, no place to
go, lacking a decent change of clothing. Come with
me, I beg of you!"

"I could not impose," she said in distress, looking
away to where a woman swooped on a piece of blackened ham, her shrieks of triumph drawing the others
so they came running, stumbling over smoking trash.

"It would be no imposition. My mother would take
care of you and enjoy doing it, especially if you were
to be her daughter-in-law."

She swang back to face him. "You would marry
me? Now?"

"It is my dearest wish."

Yet another proposal. How very fragile she must
seem to awaken such a protective instinct in men,
or else how forlorn. She did not feel fragile within
herself. She felt vital and strong, despite her weariness
at the moment. Only Rolfe had withheld the protection of his name. Only Rolfe.

"Think, Angeline, *ma chère*," he went on when
she did not respond. "What if Prince Rolfe does not
return for you? What if—what if there is a child?"

She lifted her chin, faint color appearing on her
cheekbones. "What if there is?"

"It will be mine in name and affection for your sake.
I will never—this I swear—reproach you or regret it."

"You are too kind, André. I can't—"

"Kind?" he exclaimed in outrage. "I suit myself and pray you will agree! I have always valued your friendship and admired your courage, your gentleness and beauty. But never until I saw you rise above the degrading conditions of the last weeks did I realize how dear you are to me."

Angeline scarcely heard his declaration. There could be a child. She had lost count of the days and weeks, but she knew that her monthly courses had come last some two weeks before Madame Delacroix's soirée. When she had thought of it, she had been glad not to be troubled here, where it would have been so difficult to manage. Still, there had always been the fear, gnawing and constant, at the back of her mind. Lately she had begun to be bothered by odors, brushed by just a trace of nausea at odd hours. There were other signs, small but telling.

What was she to do, then? Go heaven knows where with the McCullough when he arrived hard on their heels, trusting that Rolfe would find her, and do so before the Scotsman decided to brave the danger and complete the ravishment that had been interrupted? Rolfe, she thought, trusted to the McCullough's fear of reprisal and André's presence to prevent the recurrence, but if she refused André, what reason would he have to stay?

She pushed her hood away from her face, raking back her hair with her fingers in a weary gesture. "Could we get down for now? I feel the need to walk, and it may help the ache I have in my head."

"Why didn't you mention it before?" he asked in concern as he dismounted, moving to give her his good arm to help her from the saddle. "The horses need rest anyway, as well as water and a chance to crop. I don't suppose we can expect anything except the water. I will bring that to you."

She walked toward the women, speaking to one or two of those she had become acquainted with during her stay. They seemed wary of her after her disappearance, and resentful that she had taken part in the events of the night while they had been left behind. She satisfied their curiosity over what had happened, then seeing André walking in her direction, carrying the silver cup of the pocket flask from his saddle pouch, she broke off and moved to meet him.

He passed her the cup. At her frowning glance of inquiry over the cloudy liquid it contained, he said, "Powders for your headache. I'll bring fresh water when you have taken it."

Holding her breath, Angeline took a swallow, shuddering at the bitterness. "Isn't it a little strong?"

"Could be, but it is the dosage recommended—for my arm, you know." He patted the neck of the horse that cropped nearby. "Rolfe gave it to Meyer for me, so there can be no harm."

"I suppose not," she said doubtfully. Steeling herself, she drank down the contents and handed the cup to him. As he took it, he sent a quick, searching glance down the road in the direction they had come, a harried expression on his face.

Watching him, she said, "Maybe you had better have some too."

"Yes, in a moment." Turning, he strode quickly back to the well. She saw him glance at the pitcher the black-haired girl had used, but since it had become the community drinking vessel, he merely returned with his silver cup full once more. When she had drained it again, he took it and rinsed it and, since the bucket had been emptied, drew a fresh supply before slaking his own thirst. If he took his own share of laudanum drops, she did not see him, and Angeline frowned, wondering if he had given her his only dose. To accept so many sacrifices on her account was worrisome. Meyer had given her his coat, Oscar his rain cape, and now—Oscar, quiet, gentle Oscar who made such beautiful gypsy music on his guitar; he had not needed his rain cape.

Her mind was wandering. Her legs felt leaden so that she had to lean against the split-rail fence. André seemed to be dawdling at the well, talking to the children, giving them pennies. Now he was coming, swaying a little as he walked. The trees behind him seemed to be swaying too, and the two half-grown boys who trailed after him, watching her with wide eyes. She took a step toward him, stumbled.

He caught her against him and half-led, half-carried her back to the fence. The two boys had brought the horses to stand, heads down snatching at tufts of grass, beside the railings.

"I am sorry, Angeline," André murmured. "There was no other way."

He picked her up then, grunting with the pain in his injured arm, giving slightly to it so that she almost fell and had to clutch the collar of his coat. Stepping to the middle rail of the fence, he used it like a mounting block, swinging both himself and his burden into the saddle. He settled her in front of him where she lay unmoving and without conscious will, her cheek resting against his chest. He kicked the horse into a tired canter and, as the rocking motion began, she let her weighted lashes fall and slept.

❧

The morning sunshine poured like golden syrup into the room. Its warmth had already begun to chase the coolness of the night away, though the small fire burning beneath the marble mantel was cheery and comforting. Angeline lay in the middle of a tester bed of rosewood carved with acanthus leaves in high relief. She was propped against a bolster covered with white lawn trimmed in lace, and surrounded by fat pillows trimmed with satin, crochet work, and embroidery. To one side, a tray of highly polished silver sat on a lap table of mahogany; upon it were a chocolate pot of rose-sprigged china holding its steaming, aromatic brew, a single cup and saucer, a plate of warm croissants covered by a linen napkin of drawn work, and a small bouquet of narcissus in a silver holder. The perfume of the flowers mingled with that of the chocolate, wafting through the room, teasing the senses. There was also an undercurrent of potpourri from an opaline glass jar that sat on the mantel, warmed by the heat of the fire.

She stretched and reached for the chocolate pot, pouring a rich brown stream into the cup. She had never been so pampered in her life, not even when she was ill. From the comforts and indulgences lavished upon her by the Delacroix household, one would have thought that she was an invalid at the very least. For three days now, she had not been allowed to rise from her bed. She had been provided with the latest fashion journals from Paris, novels between marble and onyx covers, and innumerable small dishes and treats to tempt her appetite. Her hostess visited now and again, but for the most part she had been left alone to rest and recover.

At first, she had been too weary to do other than sink into the blessedly soothing luxury. So spent had she been that she had not even protested at being bathed like a baby and having her hair washed and combed by Helene Delacroix's lady's maid. The haze of fatigue had in some ways been merciful. She could scarcely remember the long journey that had brought her to New Orleans. By the time she had slept off the effects of the headache powder, she had been nearly twelve hours away from No Man's Land, rocking along in the bed of a wagon André had managed to borrow. He had refused flatly to turn around, and she had felt so ill that when she had tried to get out of the wagon she had staggered and would have fallen headlong if he had not caught her.

They had traveled on through the night into the next day, though André's eyes were red-rimmed and his face haggard. Finally they had stopped at a plantation. The people were unknown to André, but they had provided food and shelter in the strangers' room built on one end of the house for just such visitors as they were, a common occurrence on the lonely road. André had slept outside, rolled in a quilt under the wagon, while Angeline had taken the bed. What their host thought of the arrangement they did not know, for they had been up and gone at first light. By then, Angeline had felt less unwell, but so dispirited that it had not seemed to matter where she went, or with whom.

The one thing that remained in her mind was the moment when, days later, they had come to the Delacroix town house and been shown into the presence of Madame Helene, André's mother. The look of scandalized horror that had appeared on that intensely modish lady's face had been scalding. Her concern, it seemed, was not with convention but for the bedraggled appearance that Angeline presented with her much-worn gray gown, crumpled cloak, and undressed hair, and for André's stained, rumpled unkemptness. What if some of her friends had witnessed their entrance in such a state? Or their arrival in a vehicle so hideous? *Tiens*, it was not to be thought of! It was only later that she noticed the sling on the arm of her only son and began to demand what they were doing there, and in such a condition.

Angeline sipped her chocolate, letting her gaze move over the ecru moiré taffeta that covered the walls, the woodwork with its delicate shell and bellflower design, the window hangings of rose silk looped back with heavy tasseled cords and underhung with curtains of lace as fine as spider webs, the polished floors with their scattering of rugs in rose and cream and green. The house was an exquisite blend of Spanish design and French ornamentation. Fronting one of the most fashionable streets of the *Vieux Carré*, the "old square" at the center of the oldest section of

town, it had eight rooms, all opening into each other
for free ventilation, all located on the second floor
above the noise and dust of the street. The lower floors
were given over to slave quarters and storage rooms.
To the rear was a beautifully laid out courtyard in
the Moorish manner, with a fountain sparkling in the
middle, hedges of oleander and althea against the brick
walls, and beds of flowers outlined by brick paths.

The interior furnishings carried overtones of Paris,
however. In the room where she lay there was a
dressing table in one corner set about with a candlestand
of brass on one side and a Fragonard screen painted
with milkmaids and amorous goatherds on the other.
Its storage drawers were concealed by swaths and
swags of lace, and on its surface was a collection of
silver-topped jars, silver-handled brushes and combs,
and, in a silver frame, a miniature in pastels of André.

André. He had been kindness itself on the journey.
There had been nothing he would not do to secure
her comfort and peace of mind, nothing except
return her to the McCullough. Her resentment
had elicited no anger from him. He was apologetic,
but immovable. Neither tears nor threats had kept
him from doing what he thought was best. He was
troubled by her apathetic silence after the second
day and night of travel, but he did his best to appear
cheerful and unconcerned, though his arm must have
pained him dreadfully with the constant pulling of
driving the wagon.

There were times then and now when she had been
almost grateful to him for forcing the issue. Not that
she had forgiven him for drugging her, but the choice

had been so difficult that indecision had paralyzed her. To go with André was the alternative of intelligence, and yet she was not sure that she could ever have brought herself to it, to leaving Rolfe. He had sent her from him, it was true, with no word of when, or if, he would return for her. But neither had he said he would not.

The sound of a light tapping on the door was a relief, promising a distraction from the endless round of her thoughts. Turning toward the carved panel with its china handle, she called, "*Entrez!*"

Helene Delacroix swirled into the room in a dressing gown of blue velvet lined with peach silk, and with her hair covered by a charming cap of lawn and lace tied under one ear with blue ribbon. Behind her came her lady's maid bearing a pile of gowns draped over arms stuck out straight before her with all the care of a nurse with a new charge.

"*Bonjour, ma chère*! I trust you slept well?"

"Marvelously, yes." She had tossed for half the night, the result, she thought, of too many worries and too little exercise, but it would be impolite to complain.

"Ah, good. Perhaps you are rested enough to think of fashion then, yes?"

"I don't think—"

"But you must indulge me, *chère*. My daughter has never had the least idea of dressing and quite refuses to allow me to guide her. I so crave someone upon whom to impress my taste!"

"I have a gown to wear," Angeline said, smiling a little even so at Helene Delacroix's enthusiasm.

"That gray thing? It was suited only for the rubbish

heap, and that is where I put it—or had it put," she added with scrupulous honesty.

"You burned my gown?" Angeline demanded, her smile replaced by an incredulous frown.

"It was best, I do assure you. Anyone who saw you in it would take you for a penitent. That would never do. You must flaunt your unconcern without deigning to notice the whispers. That is the only way."

"It might be, if I intended to go out into society, but I have no desire——"

"Not go out? Fatal, *ma chère*, fatal! They will all know you have something to hide." As Madame Delacroix saw the expression on Angeline's face, she stopped herself with an exclamation of annoyance. "Ah, I did not mean to fling it at you in such a way. You must know, however, *chère*, that everyone is aware of your abduction by the prince. Why, few have talked of anything else since I came to town. It is the on-dit of the season!"

"Then assuredly I will not go out!" Angeline said, setting her cup down with a clatter, pushing away the tray in sudden loss of appetite.

"But you must! You cannot hide forever. I will give you my chaperonage and whisper to a few, only a few, that it is all a great exaggeration, that André, your so gallant cavalier, rode to the rescue in time. Then when the wedding banns are read, all will believe, for none will think that my son would take a soiled bride. A piece of silliness, of course, for why should he not if he loves you? But people require these charades."

Angeline looked up quickly. "Oh, no, Madame, you go too fast. That there is to be a wedding has not been agreed."

For a flashing instant, there was something like relief on the face of André's mother. It was erased by courtesy and concern. "But he has said it will be so, and truly, since he has told me something of your history, it appears it would be best."

"He takes too much upon himself."

"You must not blame him, for it was his affection for you that made him confide in me and request my help. He has always known what he wanted and, somehow, managed to get it."

"I don't doubt it," Angeline said, a wry smile curving her lips. "but I cannot allow him to arrange my life to suit himself."

Helene Delacroix's face was sober as she stared at Angeline. "What else can you do, *chère*? I don't think you realize how things will be if you do not. I will help all I can, but without the respectability of being wed, and that fairly quickly, I fear your life will be a misery."

"It cannot be helped."

Madame Delacroix stared at her for a long moment, then shrugged plump shoulders under her blue velvet. "I will leave it to you and André, but I warn you, he will not be easily dissuaded. For now, you cannot go naked about the house, whether you venture out or no. Will you look at what I have for you?"

So coaxing was her tone, so reasonable her attitude, that it seemed stupidly sulky to refuse. The maid, a Negro woman with a neat shape, a dazzling smile, and her hair covered by a cap only slightly less ornate than that of her mistress, moved toward the bed, placing the rainbow-hued pile of silk and velvet, satin and toile upon the bed. Noticing the array for the first time, Angeline exclaimed, "But there is so much!"

"Alas, yes," Helene said, her smile rueful. "I am become a trifle *embonpoint* this season. These gowns were made up in Paris to last year's measurements and, try though I might, I cannot insert myself into them. Ceci will not look at them, so would you?"

Ceci was André's sister, a good friend to Angeline though a year or two younger. "Is she here?"

"No. Was ever there a more provoking girl? She came down with the chicken pox two weeks before time to depart for town. Such a fright she gave us! It might have been smallpox, you know. She will remain at the plantation with her father for company until the scars are quite healed. It must be next year before she has her box at the opera, I fear. But enough. Come try the apple-green silk. It will, I think, be charming, and require the merest stitch here and there."

That description of the needed alterations was more than a bit optimistic, but within twenty-four hours Angeline was able to leave her room attired in regal simplicity, with a cinnamon-colored spencer over the apple green silk gown with its raised waistline and a heart-shaped neckline rising in the back to a standing collar that was trimmed in the same lace that edged the gigot sleeves. Her hair had been cut in the front so that modish curls clustered finely about her face, and on her feet were slippers of glove leather trimmed with cinnamon velvet bows. In an upstairs bedroom was a seamstress brought in to make over the other three ensembles Helene had insisted she must have, one in lavender and deep royal blue, another in rose

with a bonnet to match with plumes, and the last a
redingote pelisse of yellow striped faille with a collar
of Vandyked tulle.

Helene was in the morning room, Angeline was
told when she asked. It was her custom to tend to
her correspondence and keep the household accounts
there. At the door, Angeline knocked, then entered
with an exaggerated swirl of her skirts.

Madame Delacroix looked up from her writing desk
and put the quill pen she was using into an inkstand of
polished onyx. Her son, standing over her shoulder,
glanced up also, his face creasing into a slow smile.

"Charming," Helene said. "Is it not, André?"

"Delightful," he answered, clearing his throat of the
huskiness that had crept into it.

"I thank you both," Angeline replied, her own
tone bright as she recovered her poise. "What are you
doing, the two of you, with your heads together?"

"Well you may ask." Helene sent her son a quick
glance. "It concerns you, *chère*. I meant to ask your
permission before the missive was sent, but thought
first to consult with André concerning the wording. I
am writing, you see, to your aunt, to tell her of your
safe return."

"It… is kind of you, but will be a useless exercise,
I fear."

"So André tells me. Still, I cannot reconcile it with
my conscience to keep her in ignorance."

Could it be that Madame Delacroix hoped her aunt
would arrive to take Angeline off her hands before
she could succumb to André's persuasion? She could
not be blamed. It hurt to think so, however, since

there had been a time when the match had had her complete approval.

"You must do as you see fit," she replied.

"*Chère*, don't look so!" the older woman exclaimed. "Why, it would not surprise me to see Berthe de Buys driving into town within the week. You'll see!"

It did not happen. As if to distract Angeline from the lack of response from her relative, Madame Delacroix arranged expeditions to the shops that lined the streets beneath the houses of the French- and Spanish-speaking people of the *Vieux Carré*. There they bought handkerchief, scent, gloves, veils against the strengthening spring sunlight, under-dresses, and vetiver roots to lend their pleasant herblike fragrance to their clothing and keep mildew and moths away. She ordered the carriage and they drove into the section known as the Faubourg St. Mary where the English-speaking inhabitants of the town, being shunned by the Creoles of French and Spanish descent, had retreated to build their houses with Greek and Roman motifs. They walked along the levee and around the old *Place d' Armes*, the square before the Church of St. Louis, Helene nodding to acquaintances and stopping now and then to introduce her young friend, her manner calm, impervious to sudden stares and stammered responses.

On Sunday evening, they attended the *Théâtre d'Orleans*, where a Parisian diva with a vocal range nearly as impressive as her heaving white breasts held center stage as Rosina in a traveling performance of Rossini's new comic opera, *The Barber of Seville*. They were visited in their box during the intermission by a pair of elderly ladies of impressively aristocratic airs who had turned their gimlet glances upon Angeline rather than the diva's charms during the performance. They chatted for a few moments, asking Angeline easy, meaningless questions while missing nothing of her appearance, manners, or character. Graciously accepting an invitation to pay their dear friend Helene a visit the following day, they took their leave.

"Ah, *chère*," Madame Delacroix said on a happy sigh as she leaned back in her chair, "now we will see something. There are no more important a pair in New Orleans than those two, once attendants to Marie Antoinette herself. If they accept you, all will be well. If not, then we are lost."

Angeline was not certain she wished to be presented for evaluation like a horse in the arena or a slave on the block. The next morning she dressed in the gown of rose silk, and with a certain stiff-backed defensiveness, made her way to the *salle* where the two *grande dames* were being entertained.

They were there, their dark eyes like glass beads in the white-crêpe fineness of their faces. Helene, pouring orange-flower water from a silver carafe, directing a maid in the passing of small cakes topped with nougat and slivered almonds and candied violets, dark purple and glistening with sugar, indicated a chair near the ancient pair.

Ill at ease, Angeline could think of little to say in reply to their sharp queries, and all of Helene's frowns and nods of encouragement did nothing to help. Her hostess tried valiantly to distract them with a tale of a collision in the Mississippi River between a flatboat and one of the few paddlewheel steamers plying the river. They listened with glazed eyes and returned to the attack, their questions artless, never quite prying, but designed to foster confidences. Perhaps she was acquainted with the cathedral in the capital city of Ruthenia; doubtless the prince had mentioned it to her? The prince's mother was a fine woman, related to the Wittelsbachs of Munich, ruling family of Bavaria. Some said a cousin had been chosen from that branch of the royal family tree to be the bride of Maximilian. Were there plans now to confer the same girl upon Rolfe? She didn't know? How peculiar. It would be intriguing to hear what subjects she had discussed with the prince. The tastes and interests of such royal personages were apt to be unusual, not like other men, were they not?

Rude answers formed in Angeline's mind and had to be bitten back for fear of embarrassing Madame Delacroix. There were limits to her patience and diplomacy, no matter how necessary the approval of these women might be.

"Tell me, Mademoiselle Fortin, how did you find the conversation of the prince? Or did you, perhaps, not spend time in idle talk?"

For a moment Angeline could hear an echo of Rolfe's flowing phrases. "His conversation," she said slowly, "was seldom commonplace, or vicious. That is to say, he never made idle talk a snare for the unwary. What he wished to know, he asked, and if he received no answer to his liking, either sought another way to force the issue, or else was silent."

The allusion could not be mistaken. A small

gasp fluttered the air in the room. The elderly Frenchwoman drew back, her face stiff with affront. Her sister seemed petrified with disbelief.

At that moment the door opened. The Delacroix majordomo, brought from St. Martinville, the same who had announced Rolfe on the night of the soirée, trod forward, bowing. "Your pardon, Madame, but the prince is here."

"Oh," Helene said faintly. It was unnecessary to ask which prince. "I—I suppose you had better send him in."

"There is no need," Rolfe said, strolling through the door. "I take my reception for granted and trust you will forgive both the intrusion and the conceit."

There was a moment when, as his gaze swept the room, touching Angeline, he checked, paling. His glance shifted then, acknowledging Helene, assimilating the presence of the two elderly women, assessing them on the instant. Then he was lifting his hostess's hand, saluting the tips of her fingers with bent golden head, immaculate in his white uniform and carrying its cropped coat slashed with gold bars draped over one shoulder.

Angeline felt her heart pulsing in her throat, felt the blood leave her face and return with added heat. She clasped her hands tightly in her lap, aware too of the stares being bent upon her.

Rolfe was straightening, turning. "And may I be presented to these distinguished ladies?"

Helene rushed to comply with the request, her voice a trifle breathless as she added the two women's credentials as former members of the French court, ladies of the bedchamber who had barely escaped the Terror.

"Of course," Rolfe said, his smile warmly sympathetic as he bowed over the hand of first one, then the other. "One could not mistake the air. The fear can be conquered, can it not? But it is the illusions of order and safety and trust in men that cannot be regained, and the loss makes itself known."

"Exactly what I have said," the eldest of the two answered, her delight bringing a touch of pink to her white cheeks. "One can always identify another emigré. It is in the eyes."

"Or the faces, our maps limning past horror, past pleasure?"

"I trust not, your Highness!"

If she had been possessed of a fan, that aging doyenne of the French court would doubtless have fluttered it in the manner approved nearly fifty years before. As Angeline watched in disbelief, Rolfe seated himself between the elderly sisters and soon had them laughing and chatting like girls, telling of their hasty departure from Paris in a cabbage wagon, and reaching to touch his sleeve with their gloved fingers as if to be certain he was there beside them.

They were captivated as, with great adroitness and drawing-room finesse, Rolfe drew Helene and Angeline into the reminiscences and sprightly repartee. Soon the ladies seemed inclined to view everyone with the same bemused approbation.

During a lull, Rolfe looked to Helene. "I thought to find your son at home this morning?"

"André left the house a short time ago, intending to visit his tailor to make up the deficiencies of his wardrobe. Shall I send a servant after him?"

"I thank you, no. I will see him another time if, as I suspect, Mademoiselle Fortin can give me the information I seek. May we be private?"

"I... why, Your Highness, I..." Madame Delacroix floundered, plainly struggling between the inclination to allow so courtly and matter-of-fact an appeal and the certain knowledge that no young woman under her chaperonage should be permitted to be alone with a man.

"You must know, Your Highness," the elder of the sisters said, "that Madame Delacroix cannot grant what you ask. It would not, I fear, be proper."

"I must plead previous acquaintance with the young lady as a reason for exception—"

"*Mais oui*," the lady said, shrugging bony shoulders covered by black silk bombazine overlaid with lace, "we are aware. Still the appearance is everything, you understand?"

"Perhaps in this case," Rolfe persevered, his tone light though a frown made a slash between his brows of dark gold, "there could be a royal dispensation?"

"Ah, Your Highness, I was being harried in the gardens of the Tuileries by royal princes when you were no more than a cherubim among the angels. There is little you can claim in the way of prerogatives that would surprise—or shock—me. But this, regrettably, is not France—or Ruthenia."

Angeline was well aware that the inquiry after André was no more than a ruse. She had no wish to speak to Rolfe, in fact, mistrusted his urbanity and the smoothness of his request. Still less did she want to be alone with him. She cleared her throat, saying in stiff tones, "Perhaps we might step just to the end of the room for a few minutes?"

Rolfe was not pleased, but there was little he could do except follow her to the window alcove, draped in velvet and lace and shared by a marble nymph on a pedestal, that overlooked the rear courtyard of the Delacroix house.

His dark-blue gaze was upon her as she turned. "Assault, betrayal, and acid tittle-tattle. You have not had an easy time of it since you met me."

It was not what she had expected. "It doesn't matter. Did you find—"

"Of course it matters!" The suppressed violence of the words cut across her question. "It removes your free choice and forces you to the shrinking of a pariah for no fault or cause. Will you absolve me, all forgiving, now you are away from me? I prefer your blame with your presence."

"To what end?" she demanded. "A place in your baggage train? I am not suited to being a camp follower, always awaiting your return from the skirmish, not knowing to whom I will be passed if by chance you forget where you left me—or do not return." It was as plain a statement of her position as she could bring herself to make. That he understood it was evident from the sudden narrowing of his eyes.

"You have my bond."

"A bond of words?"

"What other is there, ever? The law and the Church give it sanctity in equal parts, but cannot create what isn't there."

She looked away, down into the courtyard where a maid had come out of the house and climbed onto a stool to dip water with a hollow gourd from the giant clay olla that stood just under the overhanging gallery of the kitchen wing. The girl went back inside. Angeline said, "André has asked me to marry him."

It was a moment before he spoke. "How noble of him."

"You needn't jeer!"

"Strangely enough, I was not. It is no mean tribute. Will you accept it?"

"I—have not given him my answer." Her reply was short, stifled.

"It is a solution with much to recommend it. He is of your background, your country, of sufficient means to assure your comfort; sober, intelligent, faithful, and he cares for you."

"A paragon, in fact," she said tonelessly.

"And if in spite of it I were to say: Come with me?"

His voice, quiet, deep, with its faint foreign lilt, seemed to touch a vibrating chord inside her as much as his words did. The urge to turn and fling herself into his arms, to let slip the moorings of the future and be guided only by whatever winds shaped his destiny, was like an ache inside her. Prudence and an odd, unformed fear dictated caution. "Where? Do you even know?"

"For the moment, the French legation. After that, Ruthenia."

"Have you found Claire?" She turned then, though she kept her back straight and her hands clasped together.

"We lost her trail in Natchitoches, but had confirmed information that she and her present paramour took passage aboard a steamboat with the intention of coming here, to New Orleans."

"So you took the first boat after her? No wonder you were so surprised to see me!" Her gray-green eyes mocked his concern for her present position.

"To discover you wrapped in silk and solicitude, receiving like a daughter of the house, was confounding, I admit. Otherwise, no. We retraced our footsteps, my guard and I, after parting with your friend, James Bowie, to the McCullough's desecrated homestead. There we were told that you had appeared, but had been carried away again over the cropper of your dark swain's gallant steed, all swoons and sighs."

"The last due to the effects of more of your powders, a trick which will require forgiveness if ever I become André's wife. "

He was quiet, his blue gaze watchful. "I see. Not a rescue, but another abduction?"

"With variations, and for the best of motives."

"Which have since impressed themselves upon you? I wonder if it would upset your plans if Delacroix were to receive further instruction in the conduct of an honorary member of the *garde du corps*?"

The color receded from her face as his meaning sank into her mind. "You wouldn't—" she began, but of course he would, without a qualm. She swallowed, then tried again. "Wouldn't that be somewhat hypocritical?"

"But," he answered with a slight smile, "so satisfactory."

"You are not my protector!"

"What an unfortunate choice of a word, my dear Angeline, and attached to a fallacy."

She reached out to touch his hand, her fingers cool

upon his warm skin. "Promise me you will not—will not harm André. If you mean to meet him on the dueling field, it—it would be exactly the kind of thing to cause more notoriety."

"Your sole consideration, of course?" There was no longer any amusement in his voice.

"I must think of it, since you will not," she returned, withdrawing her hand, warmed by the slow rise of anger for his detachment.

"It has been brought to my attention in force this morning, along with the solemn weight of responsibility. The question that remains is what method will be best to reinstate you, judicious neglect or flamboyant patronage? It would be of infinite aid if I could know what you desire. Or perhaps that knowledge would only be a handicap, and it will be better if I choose the best course, at least for one of us."

The sapphire hardness of his eyes was not reassuring. She was given no chance to question him, however. Helene came toward them down the room then, gay comments on her lips for the length of time their consultation was taking and the jealousy of her other guests.

"Forgive me, Madame Delacroix," Rolfe said, turning, reaching out to draw Angeline with him as he strolled to meet her. "I fear I cannot stay longer. When I arrived at the French legation last evening, I found a multitude of dispatches waiting, all requiring my attention but unforwarded for lack of an address. I must see to them at once."

"How disappointing," Helene cried. "We were depending on a long visit."

"Perhaps I can retrieve myself. The obligations of royalty are many and inescapable, among them the necessity of representing one's country. By my presence at the French legation I made my visit to your fair town official, and so the round of social duties began. If you care for such mincing and posturing, I hope I may persuade the other ladies present, and yourself, to accept the delivery of cards of invitation to a ball to be given in some few days. In that way I will also assure myself of deliverance from tedium for the occasion."

There were cries of pleasure from Helene and regal acceptances from the older ladies. Borne on a stream of facile compliments and meticulous courtesies, he left them. There was a vivacious discussion of the handsome features of the prince, his bearing, his address, his thoughtfulness, when the door closed upon him. Angeline took little part. So confused were her thoughts that the beaming smiles cast upon her by the former attendants to Marie Antoinette made little impression, and it was necessary for Helene to prompt her when it came time to say her good-byes.

❧

Three days later Madame de Buys' ancient Berlin traveling coach drew up in the street outside the Delacroix town house. Claire's mother had lost weight, appearing haggard and sallow of face. Her suffering had not improved her disposition. Wasting scant time on the formalities, making not a single reference to any obligation to Helene for taking in her niece, she gathered up Angeline and bundled the girl away to a house near the river, the home of Tante Berthe's widowed sister.

Located above a wine shop that was owned by the widow and rented out to a free man of color, the small, airless dwelling was permeated by the smell of liquor and dampness. It had five rooms, a *salle*, and a bedchamber fronting the street, and across the back, another bedchamber, a dining room, and a still room fitted out with shelves where food and other stores were kept. The back rooms opened out onto the rear gallery that overlooked a tiny courtyard, the one saving feature of the house. At some time a portion of the gallery had been taken in to form a tiny room for use by a maid-servant. Since the widow could no longer afford such a luxury, this room was allotted to Angeline. Though Madame de Buys had brought her maid Maria with her, she apparently preferred that the Frenchwoman share her bedchamber instead of Angeline.

The arrangement suited Angeline just as well. Little as her aunt had put herself out to show an amiable face to Helene Delacroix, she made even less effort toward Angeline. So austere was her manner, in fact, that Angeline was at a loss to know why she had bothered to come for her at all. She had thought seriously of refusing to make the move to the widow's house, so unwelcome did she appear, but it was impossible to take advantage of Helene Delacroix's hospitality any longer. Moreover, André, upon learning of Rolfe's presence in town, had begun to be importunate, demanding, pleading, accosting her wherever she turned as if he would wear her down by his persis-tence. To be away from him for a while, until she had made up her mind, would be a good thing.

Mercifully, Madame de Buys—or perhaps it was

Maria—had ordered Angeline's old clothing packed into a trunk and brought it along. With her own things restored to her, Angeline had tried to return the gowns that Helene had had fashioned for her. André's mother would have none of it. They were hers, she declared, and she would be most cruelly hurt if Angeline refused them.

Angeline was shaking out the lavender silk, hanging it in an outmoded bonnet-topped armoire when Madame de Buys entered the open doorway.

"I would like to speak to you," the older woman said without preamble.

"Yes?" Angeline did not pause in her task.

"I want you to know that I am not here in New Orleans for your sake. I had... other business to transact that required a visit. I thought it best to remove you from the Delacroix house before you caused a scandal there, too. André has made enough of a fool of himself over you, riding off like some knight in armor to save you."

"Prince Rolfe would, I'm sure, agree with you."

"You will refrain, if you please, from speaking that name in my presence. I abhor it, and wish to forget I ever heard it. My humiliation at his hands is an ordeal from which I may never recover, a blot of shame upon my very soul. All I require from you is silence on that and all subjects, silence and a chastened manner, if you can manage it. You will not flaunt yourself abroad, you will not receive visitors who may chance to call, you will not accept invitations. Not to put too fine a point on it, you will not leave this room without my express permission. There will, in the next few days, be ample time for thought. What I suggest you consider is the possibility of taking vows as a novice as soon as it may be arranged. That is all I have to say."

As her aunt began to swing around, Angeline asked, "Does your journey to town have anything to do with the possibility that Claire may be here?"

"What?" The other woman's voice was sharp, but not surprised.

"You did not ask after her, didn't even question whether she was dead or alive, or if I had seen her."

"My daughter—what she does, where she is, what I know of her—is none of your affair. You are as one dead to us, no longer of our family. You will do well to remember it."

Angeline lifted a brow. For some reason, the cold words the other woman spoke had little effect upon her. "If you intend to sever the relationship, then you must forfeit any authority over my actions you might have been presumed to have. You cannot expect me, then, to submit to your dictates."

Madame de Buys drew herself up. "We will see about that!"

"Yes," Angeline agreed.

Nevertheless, she did not leave her room in the days that followed. What point was there in it if there was nowhere she could go, no one to talk to, no one who would be even passingly civil? Tante Berthe's sister was an unfortunate creature, worn by poverty to a state of mean-spirited bitterness. Without ever having done more than set eyes upon Angeline, she was quite ready to accept everything her sister said of her, and to amplify her scorn in sycophantic appreciation for the improved meals her sister's presence brought, and the increased leisure. It was Maria who cleaned and who cooked in the outdoor kitchen, Maria who did the laundry and who took her basket to the French Market every morning to do the shopping; Maria who, when the others had eaten, brought Angeline a tray containing what was left.

At midmorning of the third day in the widow's house, Angeline was lying across her bed, staring up at the rough planking of the ceiling with its cracks stuffed with dried moss. She did not feel well, but neither did she feel unwell. It was as if she were in the grip of an unspecific malaise. Spineless, she castigated herself, and yet she could not force her mind to focus on the problem of what she was to do. It was as if she were caught in a net like a fish; the more she struggled, the more firmly she became entangled, and the more exhausted she grew. In some vague corner of her mind she recognized what was wrong, what caused her faint sense of illness, her tiredness, her tendency to drift into sleep. She refused to name it, for then the problems that beset her would become more acute, demanding concentration and action.

The sound of a door slamming drew her attention. So scarce was the activity around the widow's house that she stirred and got to her feet, moving to the only window in the room, it being a town ordinance that no window could overlook the private property of another person. Below, she saw Maria emerge from the bottom of the stairs that led down into the courtyard. She was wearing a cape and bonnet. She went toward the detached kitchen where she moved about in the shadowy interior, coming out minutes later with a basket over her arm. Angeline thought she was merely making ready to go to the market when just outside the kitchen door she stopped and adjusted a napkin that covered something she was carrying.

If she meant to buy food for the day's cooking, then the basket should have been empty. It appeared that the maid was taking food somewhere.

There was no time for questions of where, or to whom, or why. Angeline knew, and the moment the knowledge came, she whirled, snatching from the bed the shawl she had been using to cover her feet, fishing her slippers from under a chair, dragging them on even as she hopped toward the door. She slipped lightly along the gallery and tiptoed down the stairs. It was not that she was afraid of being stopped by Madame de Buys, but rather that she wanted to avoid the noise and shouting that such a confrontation would entail. She paused an instant to be sure that Maria had already let herself out of the gate at the side of the house, then moved forward, rounding the building, opening the wrought-iron grille, letting it close noiselessly behind her.

She could just see the gaunt figure of the maid hurrying down the street, dodging between a woman selling rice cakes called *tout chaud calas* from a tray and a young Creole gentleman twirling a silver-headed cane. Maria was heading toward the market on the square. Angeline stepped around a pair of nuns in flowing habits and moved after her.

The market was a narrow, open-air pavilion that extended for the better part of a block. Its nearness was announced by the babble of voices as the population of New Orleans—French, Spanish, Creole, English, German, Gaelic, Choctaw, Greek, Italian, Maltese, and the seamen of a half-dozen other nationalities— haggled back and forth over the wares on display. There were market boats moored along the levee of the river, come to bring fish and shellfish, venison, rabbits, squirrel, raccoons, opossums, and robins, black birds, pigeons, and the small plovers called *papabottes*, known for their aphrodisiac qualities among Creole gentlemen, plus vegetables tied in bundles or heaped in baskets, and exotic fruits from the West Indies. The Indians that squatted here and there offered pelts, woven baskets, wild pecans and chestnuts and black walnuts, and sassafras roots that would be pounded into filé powder for gumbo. Here and there was a sailor hawking parrots and small monkeys.

The buyers were gentlemen for the most part, marketing being considered too rough an occupa- tion for ladies, who would be forced to bargain with crude vendors and support the sight, occasionally, of a Choctaw brave covered only by an artfully draped blanket. Those women who did appear were always accompanied by a manservant to protect them and carry the items considered worthy of the home table. This especially applied to the elegantly dressed quadroon *plaçées*, the mistresses of men of wealth of the city, who might also have with them a maid whose sole duty was to ply a fan to keep the ever-present mosquitoes at bay.

Of the kaleidoscope of color and noise, of the smells of mud and decaying vegetation, of fresh greens and wet fur and onions, garlic, hot peppers, cloves, and allspice, Angeline took little notice. Her gaze was upon the fast-moving shape of the maid. She saw her stop beside a fresh-faced German woman selling golden cheese in round balls, saw a woman covered head to foot in a long cloak of cheap frieze work approach and take the basket. So intent was she on what was happening ahead of her that she did not notice the scrawny cat underfoot.

She stepped on it. The cat squawled. As Angeline jerked back, her elbow struck a pyramid of oranges, setting them to rolling, bouncing, falling everywhere. Two small boys hovering nearby scrambled for them. The vendor yelled and in a moment all was in an uproar. By the time peace had been restored both Maria and Claire were gone.

Had they seen her, or was it only caution that had made them vanish so quickly? But why was she still in hiding? Did she know Rolfe and the cadre were in New Orleans, or was it some other impulse of self-condemnation that kept Claire hidden? Fear or shame, what was the answer?

The urge to tell Rolfe what she had seen was so strong that Angeline stopped in the street, bemused at her own change of attitude. When had her faith become so implicit? If she could trust him in this, why not in the other, the matter of her future?

At the curious stare of a nursemaid leading a boy dressed in velvet knee breeches and carrying a hoop, she began to walk again, though with little idea of where she was going or why. Her footsteps took her past the Church of St. Louis and the garden of St. Anthony behind it. She walked with a sense of freedom, but also with perplexity and wonder at her own foolishness. There was no security anywhere. That which seemed to beckon in wedlock was an illusion; witness the widows of the world, alone and bereft. The only safety was in the citadel of oneself, from which fastness the disasters of the world could be countered with courage, whether for victory or defeat. Once that bastion was manned, it was fine to sally forth, to meet others in friendship and love. Those who were weak within themselves, those who crumbled at the first challenge and needed constant bolstering, were never able to savor the glory of standing alone, or meeting an adversary, male or female, on equal ground.

When next she noticed where she was, she stood in front of the French legation, a massive building of gray stone and plastered brick. There was a levee in progress, a morning reception of great ceremony. Liveried servants lined the portico steps, their gold buttons glittering in the spring sunlight. A line of carriages stretched for blocks, equipages that had not been used in many a day, while other guests less conscious of their dignity made their way to the front door on foot. Ladies in their most elegant morning costumes and men in cutaway coats with tails, high cravats, and embroidered waistcoats mounted the steps that led to a set of great double doors standing open to the street.

Inside could be seen the sparkle of chandeliers, the faint shimmer of silk wall hangings, the gleam of jewels and orders. There was a receiving line just beyond the doorway, its rank receding into the shadows so that it was difficult to make out those who were being honored, and yet the men who entered folded themselves in half in deep bows and the ladies sank into profound curtseys.

Who else would receive such obeisance except royalty? Who else could the levee be honoring except Rolfe?

Had she ever curtseyed to him in all the time she had known him? No, not even at their first meeting. The omission, suddenly, seemed telling. Pride—was that the reason? Stubbornness? Ignorance? There had been times, many times, when she had ceased to think of him as a prince at all. He had not minded, and yet it seemed a matter of importance. She did not belong. It made no difference how much she might long to tell the heir apparent to the throne of Ruthenia that she had made up her mind, that she wished to be with him—it would be a mistake.

There could be no happiness in such an arrangement for her, hovering always at the edge of his world, never a part of it. She would be too dependent upon him in all things, too much his mistress, not enough her own.

And when it was over, what then? If the rending pain she felt could come from the end of mere weeks of closeness, what would it be like to live separately, to sleep alone after months, even years?

No. It would be better to let it end. To choose the best course for him and for herself, instead of letting it be chosen for her.

Turning, she walked quickly away. In the wrenching finality of the moment, it was not strange, perhaps, that she did not think again of Claire.

Eighteen

THE DOOR OF ANGELINE'S TINY BEDCHAMBER SWUNG open. Maria stepped inside carrying a tray covered by a crumpled napkin. The widow and Madame de Buys kept country hours, sitting down to their dinner shortly after nightfall. Since it had now been dark for some time, Maria must have cleared away their dishes before she had deigned to bring Angeline her tray.

"Tsk," the maid said as she paused, "you should have lighted a candle. I might have broken my neck coming in here in the dark."

"There is nothing to see."

"Moping, are you? I suppose you think you should have been allowed to show yourself at the ball this evening?"

"Ball?" Angeline inquired. "This evening?"

"Certainly. Don't tell me you didn't know. There has been talk of little else since the day Madame returned the cards of invitation that came for the two of you. Why, even now she and her sister have gone to watch the guests arrive. Madame did not wish it, certainly—the less she sees of this prince the better.

But her sister is starved for such sights and insisted on going to stand and gawk."

Angeline watched as the angular woman set the tray down with a bang on a rickety side table. "I did receive an invitation?"

"I saw it myself, as well as any number of other missives inscribed with your name that have come in the last few days. The notes of hand were thrown into the fire, most of them. The invitation was only put back into the basket carried by the servant from the legation so that it might be returned, signifying that you would not be present."

"I would not have gone in any case," Angeline said wearily.

"Most wise, I'm sure," the maid sneered. "The ladies of New Orleans have been vying with each other in a most unseemly fashion to see who will wear the most fashionable and costly gown. The ball for the prince will be the event of the season, one talked of for years to come. Why, there were women on the fringes of New Orleans society, especially the *Americaines*, who were ready to kill or to prostitute themselves for one of the coveted cards of admittance."

Rolfe, it would seem, had made a favorable impression in the town in the week just past. She wondered how he had been spending his time, beyond the receptions and teas, the dinners and soirées that would have been arranged in his honor. Had he been searching for Claire as diligently as during those days at the hunting lodge, and with as little luck? It was doubtful that the information she had to impart would be of much help. Most likely, he had had a watch on the house for days; he would not leave uncovered so obvious a possibility as Claire contacting her mother. At least that was the argument she had used to convince herself the information she held was unimportant.

Angeline slanted a glance at the smug face of the maid as the woman leaned to strike tinder to light a candle. Would Maria have been left unaccounted for in the investigation? Her contact with Claire had been brief. It might have gone unnoticed in the bustle of the market, even if she had been followed by one of the cadre. It almost seemed that it must have been, for otherwise Claire would have been discovered, and there would have been some indication of it, some repercussion in the household of the widow.

She wished there was some way she could know for sure, some way she could send a message to Rolfe and have one in return. That was all she wanted, all that she could bear just now.

The maid went away, disappointed at Angeline's lack of response to her barbs, twitching her skirts as she closed the door behind her. Angeline pushed herself up from the bed. The food under the napkin, cold chicken and asparagus in a curdled sauce, was unappetizing. She felt, in fact, that to eat it might make her ill. There was a small glass of wine that she drank in slow sips before setting the tray outside the door.

Turning back into the room, she moved to the tiny mirror of polished steel that hung above the table that served as a washstand. In the flickering light of the candle, she looked better than she felt. There was

a bloom to her skin and secretive silver lights among
the copper flecks in her eyes. Her hair hung, aureoled
in golden candlelight, about her shoulders, cascading
down her back. In an effort to banish her depression,
she had heated water in the kitchen that afternoon
and toiled with it up the gallery stairs to her room so
that she might bathe and wash her hair. She made no
effort to put the shining mass up again once it was dry,
however, and she wore only a worn wrapper pulled
from her trunk.

A bell clanged at the gate that led to the rear courtyard, the only means of entrance to the widow's abode
since the street door on the lower floor led into the
wineshop. She paid little attention. Maria would attend
to it.

The tramp of booted feet on the gallery was her first
warning. They came nearer, purposeful and firm, their
thudding on the uneven floorboards testifying to the
fact that there was more than one man. Maria could be
heard protesting, her tones sharp and breathless. There
could be only one person whom they wished to see, for
they had surely been told the other ladies of the house
were out. If there had been a lock on the bedchamber's
flimsy door, Angeline would have turned it. As it was,
she could only draw her wrapper close around her and
face the panel.

It swung open. In a flare of white, Gustave, Meyer,
and Oswald marched inside, pushing Maria before
them. They stopped short, bowing with a clicking of
heels, though Gustave retained his grasp on the struggling Frenchwoman and Oswald carried a large and
ungainly ribbon-tied box under one arm.

"Forgive the intrusion, Mademoiselle," Meyer said. "We three may appear unlikely fairy godmothers, but we have come to see that you are transported to the ball."

A smile curved her lips, a smile of pleasure at the sight of them and of answering amusement for both the witticism and the cheerful anticipation she saw in their faces. "It is kind of you, but—"

"If you mean to refuse," Gustave said, "I would advise against it. If you will not come with us, then Rolfe himself will leave all the town fathers and their overdressed fraus, all the politicians and warriors who insist on telling him how they defeated the British here six years ago, to fetch you."

"His temper is... somewhat strained," Oswald said, his manner so quiet he might have been taken for his dead twin.

"That was none of my doing, but it doesn't alter the fact that I cannot come with you."

"You must."

"But I have nothing suitable to wear for such a grand occasion."

Oswald stepped forward and placed the box he carried on the bed. "Prince Rolfe anticipated such an objection. This was ordered to your measurements some days ago."

As Angeline made no move to open the box, Oswald swiftly pulled the bow loose and lifted the lid. Inside lay a gown of white tissue silk in a weave so fine it had the look of gossamer shot with spider web strands of copper. The bodice above the high waist was lightly embroidered with heavier handwork to make the collar stand above the deep *décolletage*. Stiffer embroidery still gave weight and grandeur to the train that fell from the waist to spread like a fan.

"I—I cannot accept it."

"And if you do," Maria sneered, "Madame will make you sorry."

Gustave gave the woman a shake. "You are the one who will be sorry if we hear again from you."

"Are you being coerced?" Meyer demanded. "We will deal with whomever has dared to hold you."

"It isn't that, exactly—"

"Then why do you hesitate? I must tell you that it would be of great help to Rolfe if you would appear. He would never ask for himself, you know, but it is being said that he took you from your home and did you great injury. If you were to be seen on terms of friendship with him, then the stories would be revealed as a fabrication."

Angeline held Meyer's gray gaze for a long moment. There was sympathy there, and a certain regret for the level of the appeal he had just made, as well as the necessity for it.

Gustave spoke then, his voice a deep rumble. "He misses you, *meine liebe*, and is determined to see you at least, if he can do no more. That is the long and short of it."

"The woman here will put up your hair, since she claims to be maid to your aunt," Oswald added. "Then we have a carriage waiting to take you swiftly to the legation."

"Please, no," she said, lifting a hand to her eyes though even she recognized the uncertainty of the words.

"We have been instructed not to use force under the most severe penalty. But he will hold to no such prohibition himself, as you know." Meyer's words were soft, insidious.

She flung up her head. "All right then, if Maria will dress my hair, I will go."

"She will call upon her skill as never before," Gustave promised. "That, or else tend the weeds that grow on the bottom of the Mississippi River…"

The threat and the look of calm menace that went with it were powerful incentives. Maria dressed Angeline's hair in a coronet of shining curls that sat regally upon her well-shaped head. She then assisted her into the gown of silk and copper thread, rolled silk stockings up her legs, and knelt to place upon her feet the white kid slippers with copper embroidery found in the bottom of the box. To Angeline's expression of appreciation she made no reply, but after handing her a pair of long gloves, waited until she had pulled them on to do the buttons. With that, the maid went from the room to inform the men waiting outside that Angeline was ready.

Carrying her train over her arm, Angeline went down the stairs ahead of the men. She was handed into the carriage that waited, a low-slung equipage picked out in gold, its flowing, Parisian lines suggesting it was the official vehicle of the French legation. Meyer, Gustave, and Oswald swung into their saddles and, as the carriage began to move, took their places around it like so many outriders in a guard of honor.

In a short time they were driving up before the building that housed the legation. Whale-oil lanterns stood out from the wall in brass holders on either side of the doorway, to light the way of the arriving guests up the steps. The windows were golden squares of molten brightness, spilling into the night, framing the people who milled about inside. The sprightly sounds of French horn, violin, harp and pianoforte hung in the air and two young black serving boys jigged to the music on the banquette, or sidewalk, in front of the building.

A ripple of comment and admiration ran over the gaping crowd as Angeline alighted from the carriage. For an instant she wondered if her aunt was among those gathered to view the spectacle, then dismissed it as unimportant. She dropped her train, letting it glide behind her, as she ascended to the double front doors on Meyer's arm. They opened to admit her, and she was inside, smiling as her name was given to the French Consul and his lady wife, smiling and dropping into a curtsey of unstudied grace as Rolfe took her hand, smiling as she met Leopold's dark and serious eyes. Then, with the receiving line behind her, she could breathe again. Though Rolfe had spoken her name, had pressed her hand, she had not raised her gaze higher than the blue ribbon with its jeweled order that slashed his chest.

She was a fool. With his rapier judgment he would guess something was wrong. She must use every weapon of feminine guile and instinct she possessed to keep him from the truth. What purpose would it serve to have him know how much she longed to be with him? What good would come of having him discover that she was to have his child? Neither piece of information would gladden him. The last was her burden, and hers alone.

"You seem flushed," Meyer said. "I fear we rushed you. Would you care for something to drink? There is warm negus and iced champagne, plus the orange-flower water that seems to be the favorite beverage of the ladies of New Orleans."

"Thank you—the last, I think," she replied, and stood looking around her as he went to get it.

To say that the women of New Orleans had come in their finest was no exaggeration. There were gowns of Oriental silk and Lyons velvet sewn with lace and jewels, gowns trimmed with fur and lined with satin, gowns of brocade and brocatelle. The light of two thousand candles glittered in the diamonds that sparkled at their necks and wrists and in their ears. The multicolored flash and gleam of emeralds, rubies, and sapphires played over the walls, while the fragrance of expensive perfume wafted over the gathering like incense in a cathedral.

"Here you are," Meyer said, at her side once more. She took the small glass from him, murmuring her thanks as she lifted it to her lips. The smell of the orange-flower water rose to her nostrils. Nausea struck at her like a hammer blow as she caught an aroma like that of laudanum, the sleeping powder André had given her and which had made her ill no great time ago. Like the drug, the beverage was derived from the fruit of the Oriental poppy. She might have known. Her aunt had always taken the drink for her nerves.

"What is it?" Meyer asked, moving to stand between her and the other guests, taking the glass from her shaking hand as she pressed the other to her mouth.

"Nothing," she gasped with a shake of her head. "It will pass."

"Are you certain?"

She nodded, managing a smile, letting her hand fall to her side as the spasm relented. Still, she did not think Meyer was convinced. His gray gaze was considering as he surveyed the softness of her eyes, her skin with its peach flush despite her moment of illness, and the blue-veined whiteness of her breasts swelling against the low bodice of her gown.

She glanced about for some subject with which to distract him and saw the receiving line breaking up and Rolfe moving around the room in the tow of the consul's wife. As the royal guest of honor bowed to those the lady chose to distinguish with conversation, the order he wore swung on its cerulean ribbon, catching the light. It was a Maltese cross of enamel and gold set with diamonds, sapphires, and rubies.

"Tell me of the order Rolfe wears," she said. "What does it signify?"

Meyer turned to look at the man and the emblem he wore. "It is an order instituted by the present king's great-grandfather in 1726, awarded for valor to those who lead men in battle to protect the soil of Ruthenia. It was given Rolfe for his part in turning back border raiders during a small disagreement with our neighbors to the north some years ago." He paused, then went on. "It was Max who insisted on the presentation. Their father—our father—would have ignored the incident, especially since Max, along

on the same sortie, saw no action and so was ineligible
for a like honor."

"He... must be proud to wear it."

"There is nothing, I think, that he values more,"
Meyer agreed.

As they spoke, Rolfe deftly detached himself
from the lead of the consul's wife and vanished.
Unconsciously Angeline searched the growing crowd
for the glimmer of white and gold.

"Imperious and beguiling, a vision to stun the mind
and banish sight, unsurpassed in this room, this town,
on this continent or any other. Will you lead the
dancing with me, fair Angeline?"

He spoke from behind her. It was not the best time
to face the challenge that was Rolfe, and yet it had
to be done. She turned, summoning a smile, forcing
lightness to match his tone to her own voice.

"Willingly, but I thought you would be fated to
lead out your hostess?"

"Her teeth protrude and her gown has been worn
before on a night of surpassing warmth, I would judge.
I prefer to show my paces, if I must, with you."

His turquoise eyes were a little too bright. He had
been drinking, and his mood was as joyous and reckless as on the night he had won and lost the women
provided by M'sieur de la Chaise and shot against
Oscar for the favors of an Acadian girl. She must bear
in mind, however, that drinking did nothing to dull
his wits.

"That is proving my lack of ill will with a
vengeance, don't you think? Why not post a placard
admitting that I was your willing mistress?"

"Why not? Except it would be a lie."

"What does that matter to these people when it is what they prefer to think?"

"Disillusioned, sweet Angeline? That was never my purpose, insofar as I had one. But give me your hand and I will endeavor, with decorum and punctilious politeness, to hand them reason to consider that I am but trying to repair a wrong through clouds of boredom."

She allowed him to lead her out and, indeed, his manner could not be faulted. His attention was upon the crowd that lined the floor waiting for him to begin the dancing. He inclined his head to first one side and then another, his expression distant, detached, and when he swung her into the steps of a lilting waltz, his grasp was as impersonal as if she had been a sister ten years his junior.

It was an oddly deflating experience. Still, as she watched the determined vacuity of his features, her lips curved in involuntary amusement. The wide swing in her emotions was such a surprise that she shook her head unconsciously.

"What? The pretense doesn't meet with your approval?" he inquired, glancing down at her.

"No, for I have no part. If yours is to be bored, then what must I be?"

"Awed?" he suggested, the picture of innocence.

"I think not!"

"Gratified?"

She sent him a smoldering look. "No."

"Is there no pleasing you? What say you to infatuated?"

"Somehow, it doesn't suit," she answered even more tartly.

"It suits me. One thing is certainly forbidden, and that is scowling at me."

"I was not!"

"You were, and most unsettling it is. Do I have a spot on my collar?"

"You know very well you don't!"

"I know I pay Sarus an exorbitant sum to make certain of it. He has rejoined me, by the way."

"That should make him happy."

"Ecstatic. I have heard nothing from him except complaints for the mistreatment of the uniform I had with me on my sojourn in No Man's Land. I think he misses having feminine garments to launder, however, for he asked particularly for news of you."

His hold had become a trifle closer. She threw him an uneasy glance. "Such daily attention is no longer necessary, though you may tell him with my compliments that I am well. On the subject of clothing, I should thank you for the gown I am wearing. It was most thoughtful of you to order such a beautiful creation."

"It is a magnificent gown, though it was only passable until you donned it," he parried conventionally before continuing in a sharper tone. "You accepted similar items from André Delacroix, so it is no great matter."

She drew back, a frown gathering in her gray-green eyes. "From his mother whom I have known since childhood—a different thing."

"Deny, if you can, that they were given for his sake."

"Perhaps in part, but not entirely. And you aren't supposed to make such accusations!"

He lifted a brow. "I have ever had the best of intentions. Would you care for that as my epitaph?"

"There's no need to go to such extremes!"

The smile he gave her was of heart-stopping brilliance. "There has been nothing of a lesser nature between us."

This was dangerous ground. It was an instant before she could gather her wits enough to discover another, safer subject. "There—there is something I must tell you. I saw Claire."

"Where?" His gaze rested on her face, and traces of warmth remained in his eyes.

She told him, more certain than before that it was of minor importance to him, that he must have his own sources of information.

"It is a pity that you lost her among the turnips and turning fish. Was she alone?"

"So far as I could tell, yes."

He nodded, though without conviction. "I prefer that you not go trailing after your aunt's maid again. This is no game of 'I Spy' we are playing, no contest of delicious danger. Claire's life will be forfeit if the wrong person finds her first, as will yours, lovely Angeline, if you get in the way. I fear that keeping you close to me would inscribe for you a warrant of death, while my greatest torment is the fear that in some way you will place yourself in jeopardy while you are apart from me."

She had been wrong; it was important. But the intriguing intimation, one she hardly dared believe, was that Claire and the information she held were not so paramount as she herself.

Before she could question it, the music ended. His dark blue gaze held hers, then he turned with her hand on his arm and led her to where Helene Delacroix stood with the two elderly ladies of the ancient régime whom Angeline had met at her house. Lifting her hand, Rolfe turned it to press a kiss in the palm, then bowed and walked away.

"How marvelous you look tonight," Helene said, her voice cool. "It is plain that at least one gentleman also thinks so. The prince was captivated!"

The younger of the two elderly women sighed, clasping gnarled hands in lace mitts. "It was most affecting, the way he ravished you with his eyes."

"I—I'm sure he did no such thing," Angeline protested.

"Not everyone is as observant as we who have seen the two of you together before," the older sister assured her. "You need not be vexed."

"You don't understand!"

"There is not the least need to explain, *ma chère*," the older woman said, touching her arm with a fan with yellowed ivory sticks. "I have not been so entertained, or so carried back to my youth, in years. To transgress with such a one is the merest *bagatelle*, of no great moment—except to oneself perhaps. All must be forgiven these royal rogues and the women who have the good fortune to catch their eye." A distant memory flickered across her face, then was gone as she went briskly on. "And so I shall tell anyone who chances to speak ill of you in my presence. 'Twill be spite that is the cause, I make no doubt, and jealousy!"

André joined them then, and with conspiratorial glances between the older women, the subject was dropped. When the music began again, André was prompt in asking her to take the floor, and there seemed no reason to refuse.

"You went away without saying good-bye," he said after they were well away from his mother and her friends.

"I know, and I'm sorry, but my aunt came for me."

"She blames you, I think, for Claire's disappearance. Has she been treating you well?"

"Well enough." There was no need to inflict her problems upon him, especially if she meant to withhold from him the right to redress them.

"I take leave to doubt it! I have been told repeatedly that you were not at home when I know it isn't true, but let it go." His brown eyes were serious as he stared down at her. "I must speak to you. There is a matter still unsettled between us, an urgent one, at least to me."

"I didn't know you had called," was all she could find to say.

"My letters were not answered as well."

"I never saw them."

"If you will see me, I will force my way in. Your aunt cannot keep you a prisoner."

He was mistaking her distraction for encouragement. "No, but in truth, André, though your concern is comforting, I am not sure I can give you the answer you want."

"I ask little of you."

"I know," she answered, her eyes dark with compassion as she stared up into his face with its olive skin and the thin mustache outlining the smiling curve of his mouth, "but you deserve so much more."

The cadre closed in then, a wall of sheltering white, isolating her. As they led her through dance after dance, while of royal necessity Rolfe twirled the wives of dignitaries about the room, she wondered more than once if their gallantry was the result of their concern for her or their commander's orders. Gustave, red of face but light on his feet, swept her through a country dance. A stately waltz was Meyer's choice. Leopold executed the steps of a quadrille with exactness and style and a certain quicksilver charm. Oswald bowed before her for a court dance rather like the old minuet, come back into fashion since the return of the Bourbons to the throne. His manner was quiet, and like all the others, he wore a black band on his white sleeve. Still, he was courteous and considerate, with a hint of warmth in his mien that made him startling in his resemblance to Oscar. It almost seemed, Angeline thought, glancing at him from the corner of her eye, that it might have been Oswald who had perished, so changed was Oscar's twin.

Such reflections occupied her mind, serving to keep her from following Rolfe's movements too closely, or from dwelling overmuch on her own queasiness. After a time it passed, though for the remainder of the evening she resolutely refused anything to drink. Rolfe, she noticed, did not.

"He has been like this," Meyer said beside her, "since the day after we reached New Orleans, the day he began to read the dispatches that waited him here. It could be he has reason. I did not see what was in them, but I'm told a number were from his father castigating him for avoiding his duties, while others were from the minister of finance concerning expenses, and still others were from the foreign secretary regarding the possibility of a betrothal to a Bavarian princess."

"Enough to try the temper of any man," she managed with a great effort, "but doubly so for one with a mission such as Rolfe's."

"I couldn't agree more. His energy is awesome. Not only has he slept little in the pressure of his search for your cousin, he has been constantly entertained, constantly available to every sweet-seller and dressmaker who might have information to impart. In addition, he has made excellent progress in consolidating relations between his country and your own and, as if that weren't enough, drafted replies to every communication that he received."

"He... does seem to have a genius for organization."

"And for doing without rest or repose, something that worries those of us who are close to him, especially now, when we are so near to seeing an end to our visit here."

"He has news of Claire?" she asked quickly.

"He is being cautious about it, and who can blame him? But I think it possible, even probable."

"If that's so, why has he done nothing?"

"Who can say? It may be that he means to make certain of her this time, and will not risk flushing the quarry before he is ready to pounce."

Or it could be, Angeline thought even as she nodded her understanding, that, trusting no one, he meant to keep them all guessing.

Near the time for the last dance before the midnight collation known as supper, Rolfe came toward her. He took her hand and led her out onto the floor, and in the midst of dozens of other laughing, chatting couples, drew her into his arms to the strains of a waltz from the court of Vienna. He did not speak as he held her, but there was nothing impersonal in his clasp. It was as if he embraced her, careless now of appearances. His face was grave, his attention reserved for her alone, dismissing all others. And it seemed that in his single-minded solemnity there was something of a silent farewell.

His arms were a strong haven as he guided her, whirling down the room. Angeline felt warm and protected, moving in perfect union, enclosed in intimacy. With every nerve in her body, she was aware of him, of the virile glide of his muscled form, the power that he held in leash. Her heartbeat drummed in her ears and her body was suffused with the tingling tension of longing while the ache of tears constricted her throat. She found herself thinking of the night they had met, and of his ruthless persecution of her upon the dance floor. How different was the gentle control which he used with her now, but how much she would have preferred the other if it had meant they could be together always.

She had come to think that his purpose in bringing her here this evening was as he had hinted at Helene's house a week before, in some sense to re-establish her in her community, to repair the damage he had so unwittingly done. She honored him for it, though she had every reason to fear that the effort would be useless.

"Have you had enough of twangs and scrapings and the heavy-footed? I must stay to the end, capering goatishly, dutifully, awash in gall-flavored champagne, but I will send you home whenever you wish it."

She was tired, and it would be best if she took her leave now with pride and decorum instead of staying to follow his progress around the room with burning eyes until she was forced to go. "Yes," she said, her voice low. "I have had enough."

Meyer rode in the carriage with her, a quiet presence leaning against the squabs of the seat. He made little attempt at conversation for the first few blocks. Finally he turned his head, watching her profile outlined against the light of the lamp that burned outside the carriage door.

"I wonder if you have given thought to my suggestion made some weeks ago?" he asked, his voice coming low and almost pensive from the dim corner where he sat.

"I wondered if you had not forgotten it yourself, or else wished it unmade," she answered.

"How could I? But there have been other problems, other considerations for you, such as your elopement, if I may call it that, with young Delacroix."

"Yes, I was not accusing you of—of laggardness. Indeed, you could hardly be blamed for having doubts. Perhaps I should have said at once that I have considered your offer, but cannot accept it." When after some moments he had made no reply she asked, "Have I offended you? It was not my intention, I assure you. I will always be grateful for your concern, and for your attempt to remedy my peculiar condition. I only regret that I cannot think throwing myself upon your goodwill is a useful solution. I am persuaded neither of us would be happy."

He reached out as if he would touch her, perhaps take her in his arms, then as the carriage began to slow to a halt and Leopold, on horseback, came even with the window, he drew back. "I am sorry, even desolate, that your decision was not favorable. I have wished that events might have been different, different in so many ways."

"If events had been different, then we would not be the same people," she said.

"Yes," he answered, his tone stiff as he sat forward to open the carriage door.

There was no one to aid her in removing her finery, no one to unfasten her gloves, no one to remove the heavy train, no one to slip the dozens of small pearl buttons down the back of her gown from their loops. Madame de Buys and her sister had returned, for she had seen a light in the *salle*. It had been snuffed immediately, as if to prevent her intrusion.

She did as best she might alone, twisting and turning until finally she stepped out of the gown and put it away in the armoire. After donning a worn nightgown, she took the pins from her hair, letting it fall free. Then she pulled her brush through the thick, curling curtain, easing her tension as she eased the soreness that had been caused by the pull of the dressed weight of hair upon her scalp. When it hung straight and shining around her, she blew out the candle and got into the narrow bed.

She did not expect to sleep. Her tiredness was of the spirit and impossible to judge. One moment she lay staring into the dark, the next she had dropped into oblivion.

She came awake in a rush. Lying perfectly still, she stared around her. The hour was late, for the night was still dark, without a vestige of moonlight, or even starshine.

What had awakened her, she could not tell, but the nerves of her skin jangled a warning. Slowly, inescapably, she became aware that she was not alone. She could not tell how she knew, but she was certain there was someone in the room with her.

Her breathing was shallow, her senses strained for a sound, a movement. The urge to fling herself from the bed, to run, was almost impossible to control. Her muscles stiffened with cramp. Time stretched. Somewhere a rooster crowed. A breeze rustled the vines in the courtyard so that they made a small scratching noise on the brick wall. Angeline moistened her lips.

"Tante Berthe?"

"Neither shuffling crone, nor thief in the night. It is only I."

His voice came from just inside the door. She turned toward the sound. "Rolfe!"

"Contain your glad welcome, if you can."

"Why—why are you here?" There was an undercurrent of derision in his voice that disturbed her. She sat up with a creak of bedropes, flinging her hair behind her back.

"For the same reason that a beggar approaches a shrine, in forlorn hope of benediction."

"You—you might have knocked!"

"And been turned away? The risk was too great to take."

From the shifting source of his voice she could tell that he had come closer, though she had not heard him move. A frisson ran over her that she recognized as trembling gladness. That he could arouse her to desire so easily, manipulating her emotions, tearing her apart by sending her away, then demanding her presence, forcing his way into her chamber, filled her with rage.

"I am turning you away now," she said, her voice firm. "I don't care who you are, you can't do this."

"I have done it, clambering your gates and climbing perilous steps past the lairs of the dragons. Having come so far, why should I leave without my reward?"

In his boundless effrontery, he was laughing at her. No doubt he was drunk still, too, and ready to throw what he might have gained for her that night to the winds for the sake of—what? A whim? A prank? Some senseless wager? The results mattered little; the fact that he would use her for his amusement fueled her ire.

"You will have to," she answered plainly.

"No soft welcome, sweet Angeline? No honeyed kisses to cherish? Once there were, only once, freely given, unsolicited. Must I live in haunted dreams of remembrance?"

A warm touch slid along her arm and she shied away. "The dream is that you are here now. Go away, and it will be as if you had never come."

"Go away and leave you sleeping, bundled in night air, unprotected and untouched? I am a man, no wraith to be banished on command. My need of you is a flame that singes my will and sears my heart, leading to this base and sneaking consummation."

She sensed the hardening in his tone and lunged away as he reached for her. With catlike quickness, she twisted over the opposite side of the bed where it was pushed nearly against the wall. As her feet touched the floor, she crouched, hearing the whisper of his booted footsteps on the floorcloth as he moved instinctively to cut her off from the door. Immediately she ducked under the high frame of the bed, rolling, feeling the coils of dust mice against her arms, coming silently to her feet on the other side.

She stood still with senses alert for the smallest sound, knowing he was doing the same. Closing her eyes, she opened them again, trying to pierce the Stygian blackness for the shimmer of white that was his uniform. It did no good. She clamped her teeth into her lip as the seconds passed. It was difficult to control her breathing for so long, and she was shivering with rage and strain and a peculiar excitement.

He had only to stay where he was to keep her a prisoner in the room. If she was to get past him, he must be persuaded to move. With exquisite care, she reached out until her hand touched the pillow on the bed. Her fingers closed on the linen casing and she lifted it, then with a wrenching twist, slung it into the far corner of the room, away from the door.

A floorboard creaked as he sprang toward the slithering thud of it striking the wall. Even before it fell to the floor, she was gliding around the bed, reaching toward the doorknob.

"A trick mossy and toothless with age," he said, close beside her, laughter vibrating in his voice.

"Try this one then," she grated, and with her clenched fist struck out straight toward that mocking voice.

He was not expecting it, that much was plain from his grunt of surprise. Still, he turned his head enough that her knuckles only grazed his mouth. It was the fury behind her blow that made him hesitate so that she was able to wrench open the door and slide through, whirling toward the stairs into the courtyard.

She heard his oath as he threw himself after her. It spurred her flying steps as she hurtled down the stairs with her hair streaming behind her shoulders and her nightgown caught up in one hand to keep it from tripping her. The stairs, none too stable, shook as he took them in hard, lithe bounds. He was closing in on her, though she dared not look back as her bare feet sought the worn treads. If she could make it to the bottom, there would be more room, more places to hide.

A hand clamped on her shoulder. She felt herself pitching forward. A scream rose in her throat, cut off as an arm of steel snaked around her waist, cutting her in two. Thrown off balance, his booted heel slipped and he clattered and thumped downward before clutching the old, groaning railing to stop them. As they came to a halt, Angeline was wrenched back against him, turned in his arms even as she fell so that he cushioned her landing with his own muscled length. She lay still, with her head against his shoulder, panting, feeling the hard jarring of his heart.

"Are you all right?" he asked in low-voiced concern as his hands moved over her.

Her eyes closed, she waited for some hint of pain or cramping, some deep internal ache. There was none. "I think so."

The tension of his hold eased. She thought she felt the brush of his lips against her hair. "Dangerous and fleet, it seems you have learned too well in your time with me."

"Not well enough to defeat you."

"Who can say? If this is my victory, then where is its joy?"

"Did I hurt you?" She could not prevent the question.

"I will carry the scar always." His touch had ceased to search for injury, becoming soothing, caressing as it smoothed over the curve of her hip to the indentation of her waist and upward to cup the full globe of her breast.

She shifted, tilting her head back, trying to see his face, but it was no more than a dark blur above her. Her anger drained away, leaving confused desolation. She raised her hand to touch his mouth, encountering the wet trickle of blood at one corner. "Only a small one."

"No, a soul wound that will not heal, more baneful than a father's hatred or the swift, unnecessary death of a young warrior. Not fatal, though enduring its rack I might prefer it to be."

It was not his fault that his bloodlines were royal, that the unscalable wall of duty and honor stood between them made more massive by his self-inflicted responsibilities. He had sought to extend to her his protection and aid where another man of his position would have left her to suffer alone. If he had come to her now careless of the consequences for her, he had given no more thought to those for himself. And if he had been amused by her reaction to his invasion of her room, that brief diversion was gone, leaving nothing but the timbre of raw anguish.

"Will you let me tend it?" she asked.

"How? With swabbings of bitter words? A scourge of sorrows?"

"With the laurels you were seeking, with love, with—joy."

His breath left him. He lay unmoving. Finally, as if the words were drawn from him against his will he asked, "At what cost?"

"It will not be counted, nor could it be, ever."

"A gift of tears?" His voice was soft, tentative.

She had not realized she was crying. She whispered, "Salt, they say, is beneficial."

"Sacramental," he said, touching his fingertips to the wetness that ran slowly from her eyes, touching his forehead, his heart, his shoulders in a cross of blessing, "but if mending is a means of forgetting, I will not accept it."

"No, no," she said, a catch in her voice. "Let me live with you in memory, if in no other place."

"Forever, I plight thee my troth, without abeyance, without end."

He placed his fingers along the tender line of her jaw then, lifting her chin to take her lips with his own. The taste of blood and tears mingled on their tongues, cementing the bond. The kiss deepened, became more passionate. Angeline strained against him, turning to slide her hands upward, clasping her arms around the strong column of his neck. Her breasts pressed, flattened against his chest. Fueled by despair, she felt the swift rise of ardor. It burned inside her with such desperate need that she wanted to be a part of him, to make him a part of herself. She curled her fingers into the gold silk of his hair, a soft murmur like pain in her throat.

His mouth bruised hers, slanting, burning. His arms tightened, crushing her to him as if the pain could assuage the deeper ache inside them. Lost in their towering need, they had no thought for where they were, no sense of the discomfort of the stairs on which they lay. Absorbed, enthralled, they defied time and place, searching for the boundless rapture of the present.

Rolfe smoothed his hand down the small of her back, spreading his fingers over the swell of her hips, pressing her to the lower part of his body. His grasp moved lower, kneading her thigh, drawing her nightgown upward to uncover her knees, pushing it higher still as he touched cool, bare skin. Like a tender marauder, he explored the curves and hollows of her body so that she gasped, aware of the melting fullness of her innermost being, the suffusing heat of her blood.

She loosened her clasped hands and trailed her fingers to the buttons that held his coat, slipping them free. She pressed her hand to his chest through the heavy linen of his shirt, sliding it downward to the fastening of his pantaloons. He released her hand then to whip over his head the wide blue ribbon and the glittering order suspended from it, to strip off his coat and fold it for a cushion that he eased beneath her. In a few quick moves, he rid himself of shirt and pantaloons and, taking the hem of her nightgown, peeled it off over her head. Like a magnet and iron they came together again, he supporting her in his arms, taking the edge of the steps against his hard form.

He bent his head to trace a warm, wet path around her breast with his tongue, circling to the taut peak. She trailed the tips of her nails along his side and down his flank, wending over that hard surface to the front where the crisp triangle of hair that began on his broad chest ended, where sprang the incredibly silken length of his manhood.

"Angeline," he breathed, "angel of mercy, mistress of my heart, will you bid me enter, or shall we prolong the sweet agony until, blind and mute, I am only fit for begging with a bowl?"

"Never mute, never, never mute, for that would be to have only half of you, and for this night I would have you whole."

He raised himself above her and, parting her thighs, pressed deep into her. She caught her breath, spreading her palms wide over his chest, sliding them to the lean, muscle-padded expanse of his waist where she clenched her hands, drawing him deeper and deeper within her.

He whispered her name, brushing her eyelids with his lips, tasting the sweetness of her mouth once more. Then in rising-and-falling tumult, intent and powerful, he swept her with him into ecstasy. With tightly closed eyes, she reveled in the impact of his thrusts, felt the mounting pleasure of them vibrating through him, knew her own trembling, sensual enjoyment of his desire for her. There was no recess of her being he did not plumb, no fastness left unbreached. She gave herself without stint, rising against him, taking him, enclosing him in vibrant, pulsing heat. So intense was the rapture that the sudden spiraling apex of it ran like the shock of ground lightning along her nerves. She cried out and his hold tightened.

Buoyantly they soared, bound, locked together in elemental splendor. On the razor edge of perception, the sensation was so intense it hovered near pain, so immense it filled the world, leaving no room for anyone, anything except the two of them. Clothed in magical and godlike divinity, exulting, they bade the perilous future come forth, to spill its riches, rendering a lifetime of happiness and sweet content in a few brief moments.

"Rejoice with me, my lovely love," he said, his voice ragged against her hair, "haven and heaven, it is all we are allowed."

He plunged into her a final time, then gathered her to him. Their chests heaved with their breathing, finally slowing; their skin, warm and damply glowing, began to cool. The jubilation that was a cover for their anguish ebbed.

Angeline became aware of the hard edge of the steps cutting into her shoulders, of her weight that must be pressing it even deeper into Rolfe, of her ankle caught between the balusters of the railing. A cool night wind brushed her shoulder, the turn of her hip. She shivered.

The man who held her made a sound between a groan and a hollow laugh. He pushed himself to one knee and reached to pull their scattered clothing together, dropping it into her lap. Bending, he scooped her into his arms and rose with her against his chest, mounting the stairs with slow steps.

They were near the top when candlelight fell in a yellow shaft from the back bedchamber window. The door that opened from it onto the gallery swung wide, and Tante Berthe, with a wrapper of puce and blue muslin over her squat form and her gray hair trailing in a plait down her back, moved to block their way.

"Well!" she said, tight-lipped as her gaze fell on Angeline lying naked in Rolfe's arms. If his similar state of undress troubled her, she gave no sign. Her black stare was triumphant, as if she felt she held some advantage in her covered state.

"I bid you *bon soir*, Madame," he said politely.

The woman ignored the greeting. A sneer curved her lips as she met Angeline's dark gray-green eyes. "I thought I heard a bitch in heat!"

Rolfe, regal and cutting, clothed or unclothed, lifted a brow. "Snufflings from your own dreams, doubtless."

As intended, the scathing rejoinder drew attention from Angeline to the man who held her. Madame de Buys drew herself up, rage in her face as she glared at Rolfe. "I demand you leave."

"Demand," he said softly, succinctly, "and be damned."

"This is not to be borne! I will not have such behavior under my sister's roof!"

"Who will stop me? But perhaps you are piqued from jealousy? Shall I, to make amends, send for Meyer, or Leopold, or even—Oswald?"

That Berthe de Buys remembered the men who had undressed her on the unforgettable night she was taken was plain from the way she shrank back at the mention of them. "You—you wouldn't!"

"Gentle woman, dear relative of Angeline's who has cared for her so lovingly, tell me why I should not?"

Angeline, hearing the phrases freighted with incisive scorn, could almost feel sorry for her aunt.

Madame de Buys gave him a look of fearful anger, then scuttled back into her bedchamber and slammed the door. Rolfe moved on, reaching Angeline's room in a few strides, shouldering inside, placing her on the narrow bed. He swung to close the door, then returned, lifting one knee to the bed, sweeping their clothing to the floor, lowering himself and turning to pull her against him. He drew the covers up over them, tucking them in at her back.

With her cheek upon his shoulder, her body pressed to his warm length, enwrapped in his vital heat, she grew calm, warm. She spread her hands upon his chest, turning her face into the curve of his neck where his strong-surging life's blood pulsed.

Time was fleeting. Soon it would be morning. He shifted, his hold tightening. She slid her fingers to caress the firm turn of his jaw, lifting her lips in invitation, one he was not slow to accept.

And so, with soft words, with sweet, tender ingenuity and savage delight, they regaled each other, cavorting in mindless bliss. Still they could not hold fast to the night and at last, aching and replete, bodies entwined and hands clasped, they slept while dawn seeped into the room.

The day was bright with sunshine of liquid gold when Angeline awoke. It shone upon the order of valor of Ruthenia on its ribbon of cerulean blue that lay winking in cold and careless brilliance, placed carefully upon the pillow next to hers. She was alone.

Nineteen

THE OUTDOOR KITCHEN OF THE WIDOW'S HOUSE smelled of damp and mildew and the crumbling plaster that was falling away from the soft bricks of the inside walls. The stale odors of cooking lingered also, along with the sour smell of dishwater, scummed with soap, left from the washing up of the noon meal. Angeline had not been hungry at lunch, when morning sickness held her in its grip, but now as the afternoon advanced she was ravenous.

She lifted the lid of a pot of fish stew, cold and with a coating of grease. Shuddering, she replaced it. A dish of eels received the same treatment. A crusty loaf of bread was acceptable, however, as were a chunk of cheese and a few boiled shrimp. With these in her hand, she started back toward the outside stairs.

She was halfway up when her aunt emerged from her room and started down. The older woman was dressed for an outing with a short cape about her shoulders, a basket on her arm, and a bonnet pulled close around her face. Perhaps it was the bonnet's brim that prevented her from noticing Angeline until they were both on the stairs. Then again, it could have been willful spite, for as she neared her niece the stout, older woman set her face and brushed past her, taking up most of the width of the narrow staircase, nearly pushing Angeline over the railing. Continuing down the steps and along the walk toward the gate that led to the street, she did not look back. Angeline stared after her aunt with a grim light in her gray-green eyes. It was hurtful to be blamed so unjustly for Claire's misfortune, and irritating to have her existence ignored. Still there was gratification in the other woman's silence. It seemed Tante Berthe did not dare insult her; that much she owed to Rolfe.

Beyond her attitude, there was something about her aunt that disturbed Angeline. In the flare of distress and anger, it was moments before she recognized what it was. Her aunt was not dressed in her usual rich style. She was, in fact, wearing Maria's cape and bonnet and carrying the maid's market basket.

Tante Berthe was going to see Claire. She knew exactly where to find her; what could be plainer? No doubt she had thought to slip out unnoticed, had not expected to see Angeline out of her room where she had been lying all day. Did she, in her arrogance, think she could not be identified in Maria's clothing? It was ludicrous on the surface, she was so stout and her maid so thin, and yet little attention was paid to servants or slaves in their comings and goings, unless one were watching for them.

Was Rolfe watching? She wished she knew, wished she had some idea of what he was doing to find Claire. He had told her not to follow Maria again. Why, unless her cousin's hiding place was known? Unless he had preferred that Angeline not become embroiled in the affair again?

He had not, of course, mentioned following her aunt. She hesitated, then descended the stairs again, taking a few steps along the path. If she discovered Claire's whereabouts it would not be just to inform Rolfe. She wanted to see her, to know how she was faring, if she was all right. She wanted to talk to her. There were so many questions that required answers. It was terrible to leave her alone and afraid. She thought of her the last time she had seen her, naked in the Spaniard's arms, wild-eyed with terror, and suddenly she was running, throwing down the food she carried, letting herself out the gate.

The streets were nearly empty as the afternoon waned. There was still a tendency in the *Vieux Carré* to keep to the old Spanish habit of the siesta, with shops closing for an hour or two, reopening later and keeping their doors wide until far into the evening. She could see her aunt ahead of her, walking quickly in the direction of the river.

Angeline followed more slowly. It was a warm day, bringing out the odors in the ditch that ran down the center of the street. A good rain was needed to wash the offal and slops, the garbage scraps and droppings of horses into the canals below the town, and from there into the river. There was some chance of it, for a gray bank of cloud was moving in from northwest, bringing with it a freshening wind. She had not stopped to find a wrap, but with luck she would not need one. The gown she was wearing, an old one of cream–and–rust–striped *cord du Roi*, had sleeves to the wrist and a high neckline inset with lawn to provide a fair amount of warmth. If rain began she would be protected by the galleries fronting the houses, supported by posts of wrought iron.

Tante Berthe avoided the levee market, turning down a street of houses backed up against the earthenworks that protected the town from the rampaging of the Mississippi in flood. Once the homes of the powerful and influential, they had gradually succumbed to the constant damp, the flooding, and the winds of hurricanes. The owners had moved to higher ground, leaving the buildings with their sagging floors and exposed brickwork to become coffeehouses, wine shops, and gaming hells, most with brothels above them. Here congregated the sailors from the docking ships, the river boat men who poled their craft upstream and, with the profits of an entire season in their pockets, looked around for a place to spend them. Here also came the young Creole bloods with money to spill from their white fingers and vast, if languid, inclinations toward dissipation.

There was hardly a day that went by that a dead body wasn't found in the alleys around the district, and many were the reports of mysterious splashes heard in the river behind the houses, and odd, bobbing shapes floating away. Only the year before a young man of good family, the son of a man who owned no less than three plantations worked by four thousand slaves, had disappeared. Some said he had been given drugged wine and put on board a ship bound around the horn to China, others that he had been robbed by thugs and sent the watery way of other drunks and derelicts.

The one certainty about the section was that it was no place for a woman to wander alone, not even one such as Madame de Buys. That she plodded farther and farther into it, a woman of her nervous sensibilities where such dangers were concerned, revealed her love for her daughter. It was also an indication of yet another reason for donning her maid's clothing. To be accosted in such a place would be terrible enough, but to be seen there by her friends would mean the greater terror of social ostracism.

The older woman turned sharply into an alley between two buildings. Angeline moved forward, stepping around three men who had taken the banquette for their game of cards. She passed the open door of a coffeehouse and a man called after her in drunken tones. Ignoring him, keeping her eye on the alleyway where her aunt had vanished, she moved on.

Abruptly a hand caught her arm. She was hauled around and pulled into an open doorway of a dim room with sawdust on the floor and the anise smell of absinthe hanging in the air. As she came to a halt, she jerked her arm free and swung to stare into the bearded face and tobacco-brown eyes of a man she had thought never to see again.

"Well, ye can never tell who ye'll be meeting on the streets of New Orleans," the McCullough drawled. "What a fine thing it is to be seeing ye again, Mademoiselle Fortin, me bonny girl."

"What—what are you doing here?" she asked, indignation strong in her voice.

"I might be asking ye the same. 'Tis no place for a woman the likes of ye, that I know. Where is your princely lover? Don't tell me he never caught up tae ye? I'll not be believing it, he was that anxious."

The instant suspicion that Rolfe had brought the McCullough with him was dismissed. "I have no idea where he is."

"Or he, ye, I'll be bound. I'll ask again, what are ye doing down here near the river, and where were ye going in such a tearing hurry?"

"I have business," she said shortly. "You haven't said why you are here, either."

"Oh, an itch for town living," he answered with a wink. "The neutral strip was getting too tame, and forbye, young Bowie may be right about the army moving in. There's been far and away tae many soldiers around of late tae suit me."

It did not ring true. "If you are looking for Rolfe, he can be found at the French legation."

"Nay, why should I be wanting to see His Highness? It's ye that I'm interested in, have been for some time, as well ye ken."

"You must excuse me, I can't stay. My—my meeting is an important one and time is pressing."

He reached out to catch her wrist as she made to slip past him. "It wouldn't have anything to do with a bed upstairs, would it? If so, I would be that pleased tae pay ye a visit."

"No, it would not!" she exclaimed, snatching her hand free, a flush of anger on her cheekbones.

"Are ye with the Frenchy, Delacroix, then? Is he the one waiting for ye?"

"It's none of your business who I am with, and I have no time to discuss it." Ducking under his arm as he tried to bar her way once more, she dived through the door and into the street. As she hurried away, she thought the McCullough followed her out the door to stand staring after her. To her relief, he did not come any farther.

She passed the alley her aunt had taken, glancing down it in as casual a fashion as she could. At the next dim and narrow pathway between the houses, she swung into it herself, moving quickly to the end. That the McCullough must have noted her turning could not be helped and, in fact, mattered little so long as he did not try to stop her again.

Despite that bit of bravado, as she emerged in the area behind the houses, she found herself shaking. She stopped for a moment, taking a deep breath, trying to collect herself. It was a coincidence, the McCullough being there, nothing more. It had nothing to do with Claire. It was natural, given the circumstances, that they should gravitate to the same area.

Looking around her, she saw the rise of the levee covered with rank winter grass and topped by the dark-green, leafless, and thorny thickets of mock oranges. One or two of the houses had small gardens in the rear protected by walls of brick, but most had only blank ground where lines of clothes, mostly sheets, flapped and piles of rubbish drew flies and prowling cats. Built shoulder to shoulder, the houses seemed to be leaning together for support, their rear galleries, overlooking the river, tipped at alarming angles. Compared to the general air of decay, the gutters along the rooflines were in good repair, leading to vast cisterns built of wooden slats like whiskey barrels and standing on tall frameworks of posts. Another thing in excellent repair were the stairs that led downward from the upper floors.

Tante Berthe was nowhere to be seen. The only person in sight was a mulatto maid who had stepped out onto a gallery to shake out a duster. She gave it a final flip, sending a fog of dust into the air, then went back inside, slamming the door.

Of the houses standing in ranks up and down the river, her aunt might have entered any one. With no idea of which she might have chosen, Angeline could go no farther. Stepping into the shadow cast by a nearby cistern, she prepared to wait.

Was she being foolhardy, venturing this far to see a cousin who cared little for her, who had not made the slightest effort to see her, much less save her, when she herself was being held by a man against her will? There was nothing to say that Claire was in that situation now, of course. Surely if she was, her mother would have made some move before now to remove her from it? Still, Angeline did not understand why Claire had not been shifted from this place to the widow's house with her mother. Perhaps she had thought she would be too easy to find there, or maybe Tante Berthe's sister had objected? Or, having reached a refuge, perhaps Claire had been reluctant to leave it again?

There was every possibility that it would not be long before she herself would be needing some such harbor. She could not think that her aunt would allow her to remain in her vicinity when it was discovered that she was *enceinte*. Her mind trod the same paths it had taken so often before when she tried to plan for the future. The urge to tell Rolfe, placing the weight of the problem on his broad shoulders, accepting whatever arrangements he might make for her, was strong. Only the thought of his father's solution in a like situation—marrying his paramour off to another man—stopped her.

Somewhere a door latch clicked. A woman moved out onto a balcony three houses down, a woman in cape and bonnet. Angeline drew back as her aunt descended the back stairs and, pulling on her gloves, turned into the alley through which she had come.

She had not stayed long, not above a half-hour. Angeline gave her time to reach the street, then moved from her place of concealment and approached the back stairs from which the older woman had emerged. She climbed upward with quick, light steps. Before the door, she paused, then taking a deep breath, she turned the handle and pushed inside.

She was in a small, dark stair hall. Directly in front of her, a staircase with an ornate turned rail descended to the lower floor, while other doors opened from it on either side. From below came the rumble of male voices, the clink of glasses, and the rattle of dice. By stepping forward, she could just see a table covered with green baize on which cards were being dealt as men with stacks of gold coins at their elbows sat gathering them into their hands at leisure.

The wall hangings of green silk in the stair hall showed the brown circles of water damage, the gold leaf that picked out the carvings of the banister railing had flaked into scaliness, and the Brussels carpet that

centered the hall floor had seen the tramp of many
feet and few beatings upon a line. The place had the
tawdry elegance associated with the class of establish-
ment known as a gaming hell, an impression verified
by its smells of liquor and snuff, tobacco, dust, and an
odd scent rather like flowers left too long in a vase.
Angeline lifted a brow. She had heard of such places,
though of course she had never seen one. She closed
the back door behind her.

Now that she was here, she had little idea of what
to do. She was reluctant to just start opening doors,
looking into rooms. On the other hand, it did not
seem wise to descend to the gaming room below
and inquire for Claire. She could not stand dithering,
waiting for her cousin to appear of her own accord.
With stiff muscles, she stepped to the nearest door
to the right, turned the handle, and pushed it open a
crack. When no sound issued out of it, she swung the
panel wider.

It was a bedchamber with hangings of deep-blue
velvet that were gray with dust in the folds, a cracked
china pitcher, bowl, slop jar, and *pot de chambre*, all
painted with blue roses, the first two items sitting on
a cheap pine table. There was also a spindly bed and
armoire of the Directoire period sitting upon a floor
cloth of black and white woven squares. The bed, with
its great swag of mosquito netting hanging in rags about
the thin posts that supported the tester, was empty.

"*Bonjour*, Mademoiselle, or is it Madame?"

Angeline whirled to face a tall, thin Frenchman
with a mustache, a narrow, pointed beard, and the
coldest black eyes she had ever encountered. He stood

in the doorway, having just left a room on the opposite side of the hall.

"*Bonjour*," she replied automatically while her mind raced, trying to anticipate this man's next question.

"Do you require a position, or are you one of the young matrons of our fair metropolis who favor something a bit more exciting in the afternoon than they receive at night from their husbands?"

She was not prepared for anything of that nature.

"No, no. I—I've come to visit my cousin, Claire de Buys."

"Our lovely Claire?" The man's eyes narrowed as he stepped into the room, inspecting her slowly from the top of her head to the tips of her slippers just visible beneath her unfashionably long skirts. "Yes, one sees the resemblance."

"She is here? I can see her?"

He shrugged. "It's all one to me whether she entertains men, women, or cur dogs, so long as I make money. But there was something—ah!"

Hard on his exclamation, there was a movement inside the room across the hall. A woman appeared in the doorway. She wore a dressing gown composed of layer upon layer of white taffeta edged with lace and lined with silk. Tied with an emerald ribbon, it fell open in the front, clearly revealing the slender white body, thin to emaciation, underneath.

"Etienne," she said, "I thought—Angeline!"

"Claire, I—" Angeline started forward only to find her way blocked by the man Etienne, who must be the gambler who had bought Claire from the Spaniard. He gave her a rough push so she stumbled backward into the bedchamber behind her. Reaching for the door, he pulled it shut in her face. As she grabbed for the handle, she heard, in disbelief, the sound of a key turning in the lock.

"Claire!" she called, pounding on the panel, rattling the handle. "Claire?"

From outside came the sound of a scuffle and a woman's protesting voice. The crack of a slap rang out, followed by weeping. Another door slammed. Footsteps could be heard descending the stairs at a quick tempo, then everything was quiet.

Stupid, stupid, stupid to have walked so blindly into something she knew nothing about. She paced up and down the room, beating her hands together in self-contempt. She might have known it would not be so easy, though why her aunt had passed in and out unscathed she could not imagine.

What was going to happen to her? Tales of young women silly enough to be taken up outside their houses, girls who had run away from convent school or who had been put out of their homes for reasons of misbehavior returned to her. Her aunt had been fond of dwelling on the things that could happen to such willful innocents. She had taken great pleasure in describing the beatings, the starvation, the drugs that were used to force such females into selling their bodies. The object lesson had been plain, even then, but she might discover the truth of it now.

Claire, though her face had looked ravaged, did not appear to have been mistreated. A picture of her cousin swaying in the firelight, standing on the bed in the Spaniard's stronghold, wantonly, lewdly offering herself to Don Pedro, returned to Angeline. She dismissed it with a determined shake of her head. She had merely been trying to distract the Spaniard, that was all.

Braving the dust and the spider webs that lurked under the velvet window hangings, Angeline discovered that the windows had been nailed shut. Whether to keep women in or to prevent the male clients from absconding without paying made no difference. She could not have jumped from such a height in any case, and the sheets on the bed were so spotted with gray mildew it was doubtful they would have supported her weight if she had used them for a knotted ladder.

She could smash the windows with the china pitcher if need be, but both glass sashes faced the river and there would be no one to hear or, hearing, act on her cries. There was a candle on a small table near the bed, but no tinder box with which to start a fire that might draw attention.

What was left except pacing and borrowing a few of Rolfe's more spectacular oaths, her mouth twisting in a smile as she said them so that she might not dwell too heavily on what was going to happen.

Time passed. Now and then she went to the door and beat upon it, calling, but if anyone heard her, there was no sign. The daylight faded. Darkness thickened in the room. Rain began to fall, drumming on the roof, splattering dully against the window glass.

Sitting on the edge of the bed, Angeline let her shoulders sag. Maria would discover she was gone when she brought her dinner tray in another hour or two. It was unlikely she would give the alarm, though she might inform her aunt. Even so, little would be done. They would think she had gone to Rolfe, or failing that, to Helene Delacroix. It might be days before they discovered their mistake, and even then, neither of them was likely to do anything about it.

Rolfe would search, diligently, exhaustively, but how could she reasonably expect him to trace her to this obscure place?

In the darkness, with the rain lashing against the walls of the strange house, she listened to the firm beating of her own heart in her ears and thought of the child she carried. It made her vulnerable in a way she had never been before. A threat to her was also a threat to it. To protect it she would do anything. Anything. Nothing must be allowed to dislodge it from its soft, warm hold. Soon, it would be all she had, all she would ever have.

Light, inching forward as it was carried, framing the door, sliding under it, heralded someone's approach. The key scraped. The door swung wide and a lamp was lifted high as two men stepped inside, its rays searching out, finding Angeline there in the dark room. One was tall and thin, his face outlined by mustache and beard. The other was big and broad; the light caught a pale gleam in his hair.

"Yes, that is she," Meyer said. "I am in your debt."

Something passed between the two men; there came the click of coins. "I thank you, M'sieur," the gambler called Etienne murmured, and passing the lamp into the keeping of the other man, he bowed and walked away.

Angeline got to her feet, a smile beginning as she moved toward the door and the tall man who filled it. "I'm so glad to see you! Is Rolfe coming?"

The bastard son of the king of Ruthenia stepped inside, closing the panel behind him, setting the lamp on a table near the door. "Oh, yes, he will come—now."

The malignant satisfaction in his quiet tones was like a blow in the face. She stopped. "He… knows I am here?"

"He will, soon."

"That man will send a message, I suppose, just as he sent one to you?"

"Clever, but then cleverness is one of your many charms."

She lifted a brow, ignoring the compliment. She felt as if a great weight on her chest was making it hard to breathe, even harder to speak. The doubt that ate into her mind was virulent, growing. "What I don't understand is why it was necessary to keep me here at all, and why he thought you might be interested, or, suspecting it, how he knew you?"

"I see no reason why your curiosity should not be rewarded. He knew me because when I traced Claire to his abode here just yesterday, I made it my business to gain his acquaintance. As to the purpose of my interest, that did not trouble his mind, so long as the reward for bringing you to my notice was high enough. In keeping you here, he showed great presence of mind, a quick cunning that is not unusual in one of his stripe. That you came at all was an unexpected piece of luck. I quite expected that you would have to be enticed with a missive from Claire. The only delay in the negotiations with our friend with the beard was his reluctance to lose the lovely Claire's services. I had every reason to think that his scruples could have been overcome for the right price."

"You mean that you…"

"Your cousin has been a liability for some time."

Angeline stared at him, at the satisfaction on his broad face, the smile of malicious triumph that curved his mouth. "You—you are the one she was afraid of, the one she has been running from since she left Ruthenia."

"That may be, but what of you, Angeline, my dear? Are you afraid? Don't you want to know why I set my dogs on you?"

Her gray-green eyes were wide as she stared at him. She licked her lips. "It seems plain enough. If you are the one whom Claire was running from, then you killed Maximilian and tried to kill her. It follows then that you are also the one who has tried to kill Rolfe. I mean nothing to you, therefore—"

"Oh, I wouldn't say that," he interrupted, a peculiar look in his opaque gray eyes.

She went on as if she had not heard. "Therefore, you think that because of my position as his woman while we were in No Man's Land he may be lured here."

"I not only think it, I know it."

She summoned a laugh, and was surprised at how easy it came. "That's nonsense. He has no more feeling for me than for Claire, whom he has scarcely set eyes on."

"How can you say so?" Meyer asked with a slow shake of his head. "I saw how he was with you there in the wilderness and also last night on the dance floor before what passes for the *crème de la crème* of New Orleans society. And later, as I followed him from the legation, I saw—or rather, heard—a most convincing portrayal of caring upon the back stairway of the house where you are staying with your aunt."

"How dare you!" she cried. She would have expected to feel the most burning shame at hearing such a thing spoken of, but instead she knew only rage at his profaning what had been a precious memory.

He laughed. "Seldom have I been more entertained. But after so vivid an experience, do you still think that the Prince of Ruthenia won't come, alone and unarmed as I will specify, if he thinks it will save you? He would do it for the least of his men, even for me. Why would he not be a thousand times more likely to run the risk for your sweet sake?"

"Another trap, like the one for Max baited with Claire, like the one the night the cadre and the clan attacked Don Pedro's camp?"

"Both well planned, but not favored by luck. This time will be different."

His confidence was supreme, quiet, bred of certain power. In an attempt to shake it she said, "You failed to kill Rolfe any number of times, in Ruthenia, at Le Havre, in New Orleans, at the hunting lodge. You couldn't even arrange for someone else, such as Don Pedro, to do it for you. And finally, when you fired on him in the dark in desperation, you shot the wrong man."

His eyes narrowed. "I once told you he was acute. He seems to have an instinct for danger that must always be taken into account. At the last moment, there before the ambuscade set by the Spaniard, he sensed something wrong and ordered a retreat, covering the others himself, before the advance was well begun. As for trying to kill him myself, no. I was too close to him and the rest of the cadre after that first abortive charge to make it feasible."

"But Oscar was not killed by Don Pedro or his men."

"A regrettable necessity, that, one which gave me no pleasure. But Oscar saw me with Morning Star and, if he had survived the fight, might have remembered it when the time came for a council of reckoning."

She swung around, suddenly unable to bear his calm, almost objective expression, as if the things he had done and those he meant to do were perfectly reasonable. She took three steps, then stood still. "If you killed Oscar for what he knew—"

"You are as quick as our prince, in your own way. Why didn't you accept my offer of marriage? I would have seen you had no regrets. You would have been comfortable, honored. I would not even have exacted revenge for the inconvenience you caused by pulling Rolfe from the funeral pyre I had built for him, or for flushing the Spanish cowards from their ditch—except the child you carry, Rolfe's bastard, would have died at birth. Tragic, but there would have been others."

"You know." Her face was so stiff with horror that it was difficult to form the two words.

"How should I not, I who have been watching for signs as closely as any midwife, even to hanging about as Sarus did your laundry and, later, inspecting the things you hung to dry. I was not certain until the night of the ball. No medical training is needed to recognize the sickness that comes and goes, with some women in the morning, with some at odd hours, with odd odors."

"And now?" she asked, the words forced from her.

"And now I will have the pleasure of you I have been denied, something long anticipated, I assure you. I have ever enjoyed possessing those things that have belonged to my brothers, even those they have discarded."

The deliberation of the words, their cold pleasure, made her heart beat with sickening thuds. There was a greater fear, however, hovering at the fringe of thought. He could not let her live, not knowing what she did.

To test the theory she said, "After which, when Rolfe comes and you have settled with him, I will... disappear."

"It is not the solution I would have chosen, but one that seems necessary. You cannot be allowed to tell of this night. I will need the sympathy and support of the cadre when I return to my country."

She whirled. "Do you honestly think they will let Rolfe come here without weapons with which to defend himself, without his guard?"

"If he requests it, they will, and he will request it."

"For my sake."

He inclined his head. "He is being told at this moment, you see, that you will be released unharmed, without knowing who was your captor, when he is under lock and key."

"No," she whispered, her eyes dilating as the full implication of his words struck. "No. No!"

She started forward, lunging for the door. He swung to catch her, clamping hard fingers on her forearm, swinging her around, dodging his head back as she struck out at him. A hard shove sent her sprawling, but she scrambled to her feet, backing away.

"Yes," he mocked as he moved after her, "and I will make very sure that before he dies he knows it has been for nothing."

"You have misjudged him. He won't step into your trap so meekly. He will defeat you yet."

He moved slowly after her. "That may be, but it won't help you. Nothing can help you."

She came up against the post of the bed and slid to one side without taking her eyes from the hard smile that creased his face. The small table holding the china pitcher and bowl was near. Veering toward it, she snatched the pitcher's handle and threw it at Meyer's head with all her strength. He ducked and the pitcher struck the floor, scattering pieces of china and dead spiders and flies from inside the vessel. The bowl followed quick and hard. He sidestepped it, but the heavy piece of china bounded from his shoulder. An exclamation broke from him. Flushed, his eyes congealing to gray agate, he came on.

Whirling, Angeline overturned the table, giving it a wrenching shove, leaping behind it as it clattered against his shins, dodging away from his reaching, clutching hands.

She was not quick enough. He caught the fullness of her skirts, dragging her off balance. She careened into him, falling. As she struck the floor, flinging out a hand to catch herself, her fingers sliced across a piece of broken china. Despite the shaft of pain that ran along her hand and up her arm, she clutched the shard, coming up with it in her hand, swinging at his face as he dragged her into his arms.

A long, red gash was scored along his cheek. He ground out an oath and, touching a hand to the blood that gushed, brought it around in a vicious backhand slap. Her head snapped back as agony and rage exploded in her brain. His hand clamped on her wrist and twisted cruelly so that the piece of china clattered to the floor. Swinging her around, he half-lifted, half-threw her across the bed. She hit the mattress with a hard jounce of the bed ropes and lay still, stunned.

"I think," he growled, "that I will teach you a trick or two Rolfe may have neglected, a lesson in humiliation."

Angeline gasped as he rolled her to her stomach, one hand pressing upon her hips. He gave a short laugh, vaulting up on the mattress, landing heavily beside her.

A bed rope gave with a groaning snap. The mattress tilted, sliding toward the center. The frame of the bed creaked as the four tall posts leaned inward. Dust sifted from the bed hangings as they jerked and flapped. Angeline could feel herself slipping, rolling. It was reflex action that made her draw her knees up just as her weight brought her sliding down on top of him.

Her knee struck his groin. He made a strangled sound, his hold going slack before he gave her a violent shove from him. She used the impetus to grab the side of the mattress, pulling herself up, scrabbling from the bed. She dived for the door, wrenching at the handle. As it came open, she heard the thud of a plunging footstep behind her, and the panel was slammed shut again. He caught her and slung around so she caromed off the wall with stunning impact. Then he was upon her, his hard hands ripping at the lawn of her neckline, tugging at the *cord du Roi*. As it held, he thrust his fingers into her bodice, closing them on her soft, white breast, squeezing so that a cry was torn from her throat. His left hand he sank into her hair, twisting in the silken knot at the nape of her neck, dragging her head back as pins shifted and slid.

His open mouth, hot and sour, covered hers, his tongue probing and thick as he tried her set lips. Revulsion and anguish washed over her so that she heaved, as tears ran from her eyes.

Cursing, he drew back, hauling her toward the bed with its caved-in mattress, holding her with one hand twisted behind her back so that her shoulder seemed parted from the socket as he dragged the top mattress to the floor. He forced her down upon it, dropping beside her.

She was no match for his enormous strength or his ferocity. She recognized that fact in dark agony as, straddling her body, he ripped at the hooks that held her gown. Fleetingly it came to her that her first night with Rolfe had been a dream of careful seduction compared to this brutal assault, or to the like punishment she had taken at the hands of Don Pedro. Rolfe, Rolfe, she cried silently as she felt cool air against her bare back.

Meyer released her wrist, his nails raking her arms as he dragged the sleeves down, exposing the upper part of her body. Rising to one knee, he closed his hands on her skirts, pulling them upward, digging his fingers into her tender flesh so that she twisted and turned under him like an animal in a trap. She bit her lips to keep from crying out, aware with cringing senses of the hard bulge that he drove with pumping motions against her hip. Her breath came in panting gasps and at the edge of her vision was a red haze.

He fumbled at his clothing. With the last vestige of her strength, she heaved under him. He fell across her, grappling with her to pinion her arms, thrusting his knee between her legs. She was crushed beneath him, unable to move, unable to breathe. There was a ringing in her ears above which could be heard the hard pulsing of her heartbeat. The lamplight seemed to be fading, extinguished by mists of gritty and dirty gray.

A crash resounded as the door was flung open. Abruptly she could breathe as Meyer slewed around. There was a flash of white, then it was as if he were picked up bodily and flung across the room. Rolfe, the planes of his face bronzed by the lamplight, set like a mask, moved after him with dangerous agility. He carried no weapon. With bare hands he reached once more for his half-brother.

There was a flurry of movement in the doorway. Angeline, shaking her head to clear her vision, saw the thin, bearded face of Etienne, and with him a burly, half-bald thug carrying a cudgel.

Angeline levered herself to one elbow. Her voice no more than a croak, she cried, "Rolfe, look out—"

It was too late. Even as he turned, the bald man brought the thick stick down in a whistling arc. It struck Rolfe at the base of his skull, just behind his ear. He went down like a deer shot on the run, keeling forward, unconscious before he struck the floor.

"Again," Meyer said, pushing himself up, his face twisted as he held his hand to his nose, which streamed blood. "Hit him again."

The bald man complied, a glancing blow that split the skin in a jagged streak, leaving a fast-spreading glint of red in the gold of his hair.

On his feet, Meyer stepped to Rolfe and kicked him once, twice, in the belly. He glared down at him a moment in vindictive triumph, then looked to Angeline, who was covering herself in trembling haste, stumbling from the mattress to fall to her knees beside Rolfe. His voice thick, he said, "You I will attend later, when I've done something about this bleeding—and when we have an audience to appreciate the spectacle. That is, of course, if he revives enough to care, or revives at all."

Etienne held the door for Meyer, then waited until the bald man was through it before exiting himself and pulling it shut. The key scraped in the lock and was withdrawn.

Angeline ripped the sheet from the mattress as she lifted Rolfe's head and eased it onto her knee. There was a large lump behind his ear, but the skin was unbroken where he was struck first. Blood ran from the second wound in a stream, matting his hair, dripping onto her skirts and the floor cloth. She tore a strip from the sheet and, folding it into a pad, pressed it to the wound, then wrapped a second strip around it.

His pallor was frightening, nearly a match for the dingy sheet around his head. His gold-tipped lashes were still, the firm lines of his mouth relaxed so that he looked young and defenseless. There was a split in his lip where she had hit him the night before. The sight of it hurt her more than his other injuries. Cradling his head in her lap, wiping at the blood that darkened his hair, she sat unmoving as the minutes passed.

The flame on the wick of the whale-oil lamp fluttered. Angeline raised her head to stare at it. Little noise penetrated to this room. The house might have been empty for all she could tell. No, there was a faint rumble of voices. She tensed, half expecting them to stop outside the door of the room. When they came no closer, died away, she relaxed once more.

When would Meyer return? Her mind shied away from the thought and of what would happen then. There was nothing she could do, nothing anyone could do. That Rolfe had come, ready to exchange himself for her, trying to save her, filled her with love and despair. A noble gesture it might be, but it was for nothing. And yet, given the steadfastness of his nature, his unflinching acceptance of responsibility, what else could he have done?

The waste, the terrible waste. That he should have to die in so contemptible a fashion, in so mean a place, far from the court of his father where he should have held a glittering place, was unbearable. That he should have been lured here because of her was the final twist of the knife blade inside her. Salt tears brimmed in her eyes and fell, splashing warm and wet upon his face. She did not notice.

"A lachrymose angel," came a rustling whisper, "all woe and lamentations—flattering, but not reassuring."

She caught her breath, smiling with a shake of her head that sent more tears showering. "No. I'm sorry."

"The apologies are mine. I have no knack for the rescue of maidens in distress—not Claire, not you. Heroic gestures are well enough, but something more is required."

"You—you stopped him," she said, her voice low.

"For how long?" The bitter twist of his mouth showed plainly how well he could guess at the course of events while he lay insensible.

She returned his gaze without evasion, though her lashes were spiked with tears and there was a bruise, livid and purple, beneath the fragile skin of her cheek. "Not long."

"God," he breathed, his features contorting. "For involving you in this coil I should be flayed alive and fed to the swine." He reached up to touch the shining auburn swath of hair that had slipped to spill over her shoulder, his hand not quite steady. "You have been both victim and bright-burnished goal of us all, even Meyer, especially Meyer. To see you like this is so—"

"I am well enough," she said, unable to bear the quiet assessment, the flow of words that might become a litany of riches that must ever be denied. "What of you? Can you stand?"

A shimmer of amusement came and went in his eyes. "A practical angel. You would save the man yet another time, and leave the spirit faltering?"

"I have a tendency to think the first is more important."

"With such an accolade, how can I not do as I am bid?"

The shattering of glass drowned his words. Rolfe flung himself upright in a smooth reflex of trained muscles, then stood swaying so that he had to snatch at the sagging bedpost close by. If the threat had been borne out, he might have faced it with the strength of necessity; instead, only a horse-shoe clanged across the floor, coming to rest against Angeline's slipper. It lay there, dark with rust, incongruous among the slivers of broken glass and smashed china that littered the floor cloth.

Angeline picked up the horseshoe and, stiff from sitting so long in one position and the punishment she had taken, hobbled to the window. A man stood below. For a moment, she could not make out his features, then as he stepped back into the lamplight falling from the window, she recognized the McCullough.

"Good, I have the right room, then. I thought it, frae the noise earlier."

Before she could speak, Rolfe was at her side. "McCullough, a weapon?"

"Thought as how ye might like some such." From his belt he took a pistol and, waiting until Rolfe had reached through the broken pane, cast it upward. Powder and shot followed, with finally the wheeling glitter of a knife.

"I thank you, my friend," Rolfe said.

"Ye saved my life. Tae return the favor is the least I can do, or so I thought when I heard how yon man of yours had offered pay to my men for yer scalp. Thought I'd take a hand in the game."

"Consider the debt canceled."

"Hold your whist, I'm coming in. Ye may have the ordering of yer own clan, but nae my own, not now. We'll nae be for lying back while ye be killed, ye and the lass."

Rolfe nodded, his attention on the pistol he was loading with speed after thrusting the knife into his waistband. "Tell Gustave he and the others are released, the agreement broken. There are hired thugs such as your men, guards—"

There was no time for more. Footsteps were heard outside in the hall. The doorknob rattled as the key was turned and the panel swung inward.

Meyer surged into the room with Etienne behind him. His eyes widened as he saw Rolfe on his feet, saw the leveled pistol in his hand. He came to an abrupt halt. His lashes flickered downward to shield his expression before, sidestepping, he revealed Etienne with a pistol cocked and ready in his fist. The thin man brought the weapon up a fraction.

Suddenly Meyer shot out his hand in a fierce staying gesture, his gaze on the pistol Rolfe held. It had not wavered but still pointed straight at him.

It was a standoff. Angeline was still, hardly daring to breathe. She looked from Meyer to Rolfe and saw, for the first time, a fleeting resemblance in their tight-lipped determination.

"What now, dear brother, sharer of swaddling and fatherly scorn? What will you do?"

Meyer's face hardened at the soft-voiced jibe. "Withdraw, I think, and allow the fire already set to roast you, while keeping watch on the window lest you choose a quicker death."

The grip of Rolfe's hand on the pistol tightened so that his knuckles blanched and the light glinted gold on his wolf's head ring. "And what of Angeline? To sear so fair a form would be madness."

"Do you offer her to me, when not so long ago you wanted nothing more than to wrest her away? Death is not, then, preferable to dishonor? For I would dishonor her, you know, thoroughly—"

"No!" Angeline exclaimed, instinctively moving closer to Rolfe.

"She is reluctant," Meyer sneered. "Would you advise her to be accommodating, to study my wishes, my—desires, in the hope that I may keep her with me? I would have to hold her a prisoner since she will know your fate. A wearisome pleasure, but you know something of that, do you not? I might do it, if only to permit you the supreme sacrifice. I do salute you. So many men would rather see the woman they loved shrivel and smoke-blacken before their eyes than permit it."

"No," Angeline said again. "He would kill me."

Meyer smiled. "There is that chance."

Rolfe was silent, his turquoise eyes reflecting strained balancing of his thoughts. Into that moment of quiet came the click of a woman's heeled slippers and the rustle of skirts. Claire, wearing still the dressing gown of white taffeta, appeared in the hall beyond the doorway.

"What is it, Etienne? I heard shots and I smell smoke, I'm sure—"

She stopped and suddenly all were aware of the exchange of gunfire from the street below. Angeline met her cousin's eyes across the space that separated them, saw Claire's face blanch with shock as she looked from her and Rolfe to Etienne.

"You said she was gone," she cried, her voice rising. "You said she went away." As the man shrugged with a glance at Meyer, she turned on him. "Not again, Meyer! I won't be a part of it, not this time!"

"I think," Rolfe's half-brother said in a mockery of chivalry, "that it is time the ladies left us. What say you, my Prince?"

"Go with him," Rolfe said without looking at Angeline, his voice low.

"I won't." She lifted her chin, her gray-green eyes both pleading and defiant.

His gaze was darkly blue as he faced her. "Though I treasure the resolve and would ask nothing more than to let death find me in your arms, I cannot accept so sweet and solacing a pillow."

With his left hand, he caught her shoulder, pulling her around, placing his fingers in the center of her back to push her forward. He gave her the impetus, but the impulse to carry it further came from inside, borne of impotent rage and hate and fear. She launched herself at the man with the gun, trusting that he might think her only running, uncontrolled, toward freedom, uncaring if he did not, disdainful of the consequences. Her fingers were curled into claws, reaching for the pistol, knocking it aside, stretching like a female bird of prey for his eyes.

Etienne screamed. The pistol clattered to the floor. Meyer bent swiftly to pick it up. Angeline swung, saw Claire with thinned lips and wild eyes launch herself in attack, grappling with the gray-eyed man. The thundering concussion of a shot bloomed beside her. Claire made a small, wheezing sound, her mouth open, her eyes staring in shocked surprise. She sagged, falling, the ruffles of her wrapper stained red.

Rolfe could not use his pistol for fear of hitting Angeline or her cousin. Angeline heard the rush of his advance in frantic joy. Then a hard arm snaked around her neck and she was dragged back, choking, against Meyer while he leaned to snatch a knife from the top of his boot. It flashed before her eyes with a gleam of blue fire and the edge was laid against her throat.

"Stop," Meyer said at her ear.

It seemed as if Rolfe could not stay the hard, springing fury of his charge. Pale and panting, he was within inches of them when he wrenched his muscles into stillness.

"Etienne," Meyer said, satisfaction in his tone, "take his pistol."

Rolfe barely flicked the other man a glance. "I wouldn't try it. You are expendable, and he will not give up his protection at this range should I decide to eliminate you."

The man called Etienne hesitated, and in that instant Rolfe took the knife from his own waistband, holding it loosely in his left hand.

"You fool," Meyer spat at Etienne, his hold tightening so that Angeline could hardly breathe.

Rolfe, his bright blue gaze on the arm that constricted Angeline's throat, said, "What now, dear brother, fulsome in threats and endlessly nimble in clearing your way? Spill so much as a drop of Angeline's blood and I will carve my initials into your backbone and make a whistle of your clavicle. Cut deeper, and there is nothing on this mean and musty little earth that can save you—nothing."

It was flamboyant but a promise, deadly serious. Meyer knew it, for the pressure of his arm eased and his chest rose and fell in quick succession. He did not speak. Angeline's mind flitted to the cabin of the Spaniard when Claire had been held as she was now. There had been no countermeasure possible then, across the width of the cabin, no vicious test of nerves and will. Claire lay just behind her now. She had made no sound, had not moved since she had dropped to the floor. Angeline ached with the impossibility of seeing to her. She might be bleeding to death even then. Etienne had barely glanced in her direction. Now he was backing slowly away.

"Your henchman is leaving," Rolfe mocked as the bearded Frenchman's footsteps quickened and the man spun around, heading for the door that led to the back gallery. "Now it is only you and I—and Angeline. Folly come forth, I have a proposition. I will put aside my pistol if you will release Angeline. Then if you care to match your skill with a blade against mine, I will give you leave to hack and slash at me in fair competition."

"You need not indulge me," Meyer said.

"Oh, but isn't it what you wanted, what you have always wanted? Your need to trounce me has been obvious for some time. No one else in the cadre had so great an inclination. Why else do you think I refused to let anyone face me, except to prevent the bitterness defeat would bring? Come, now is your chance."

"The defeat and the bitterness would have been yours."

"Prove it," Rolfe challenged. "You have such a need to excel in something, do you not? My prowess has always been the touchstone, the mark which you chose for your target. Max's position and my repute, for good or ill, and of course our women—these things you craved. Take them now, if you can."

"Put down your pistol then."

Rolfe laughed. "Shall I also bare my breast to your first great swiping blow? Release Angeline, and I will comply."

"Your word?" There was trust mixed with the contempt in the inquiry.

"Sworn on holy relics and our father's throne? Whatever pleases you, you have it."

A protest rose in Angeline's throat and she choked it back. She must not distract Rolfe, must do nothing to affect the fine balance of the decision he was forcing. By slow degrees, she felt the muscles of Meyer's arm shift, loosening his hold. The knife moved out and away as his arms opened. She drew a deep, steadying breath and, at a gesture from Rolfe, stepped from Meyer, coming up against the door frame.

His movements deliberate, Rolfe turned to place his pistol on the table just inside the room, next to the lamp. Then, as Meyer backed into the open stair hall, he eased past Angeline, past Claire lying on the floor, his intent blue gaze never wavering from his half-brother.

It was difficult to tell looking at Rolfe, how much or how little the blows to his head had affected him. He moved with sureness and control, but there was a line between his eyes that might have been concentration or a throbbing ache in his brain. More, it was no great time since he had been shot in No Man's Land, a further drain on his stamina. Meyer, on the other hand, was as rigorously fit as the cadre was required to be, unharmed despite the ravages he had caused. That he realized it was in the sneering confidence of his slight smile as he removed his coat.

When they were well past, moving into the center of the open hall, Angeline went to her knees beside Claire. Reaching out her hand, she placed it on the white-taffeta-covered chest, all the while knowing the gesture was useless. There was no movement, not the slightest rise and fall of breathing or tremor of heartbeat. Her cousin's eyes were wide and staring, and across their green surface, like frost on still water, was the glazing of death.

Angeline glanced at Rolfe with tears rising in her eyes. His gaze was upon her and with a quick shake of her head, she came to her feet. He looked to Meyer, transferring the knife he held to his right hand.

"Another victim claimed, dear brother, beauty soft and defenseless destroyed. Does it give you pride?"

Meyer flung his coat over the stair railing, tested the edge of his blade with his thumb. "You speak of Claire? You need shed no tears for her. She killed Max, you know, as surely as if she had held the pistol to his skull."

"Out of love denied?"

"Out of the hate and thirst for vengeance of love offered and spurned. He had set her aside, paid her off with a few baubles. It was foolish of her to expect anything else, but, expecting it, she was enraged when it was withheld."

Without warning, Meyer whirled and lunged. His knife blade whipped past Rolfe's shirtfront as he leaped back, slicing air with a vicious whine. Rolfe gave a short laugh as he twisted away out of range, and Meyer, his face grim, dropped into a crouch and moved after him.

"From the tenor of his letters while I was afield," Rolfe said, circling to prevent Meyer from driving him toward the staircase, "I would have sworn Max was besotted."

"He was, until the rumors began. He was a fastidious man and a proud one. He liked to think that no other man had ridden the mare of his choosing."

Their feet made a scuffling sound on the dirt-encrusted carpet. Meyer's steps ruffled the surface as he sidled, searching for an advantage.

"The lady," Rolfe said quietly, "did not strike me as being stupid enough to allow herself to be mounted."

"No, but there were hints, subtle suggestions, careful observations—"

"Yours?" Rolfe mocked, dancing back at a sudden slashing blow, the movement easy, almost negligent, as if only half his attention were upon the deadly contest.

Meyer frowned. His tone carried a bite as he answered his half-brother's query. "They were true enough, later, between the time of her dismissal and the time he died."

"You caused a rift between Max and Claire and, when it was accomplished, seduced her, fired her rage, persuaded her to revenge, and showed her the way. Then, when she went to Max and smiled her way into his bed a final time, you came upon them, shot Max,

and would have killed Claire in the attempt to make
it appear a murder-suicide had your aim been surer."

The light in the stair hall was dim, coming from
a small bracket lamp pinned to the wall on the
landing just above. The knives the men held were
lethal, darting shadows that flashed points of fire as
they caught the feeble illumination. The two men
were well matched in size and reach, though Meyer
was heavier, without the suppleness of body and
lithe economy of movement Rolfe brought to the
dangerous duel. With her heart in her throat and a
pounding ache in her head, Angeline watched, unable
to look away even as a fusillade of shots echoed up the
stairs from below, along with a vaporish gray coil of
smoke and distant cries of "Fire! Fire!"

When Meyer made no reply, Rolfe went on. "In
the meantime, you had been whispering in the king's
ear, busy rumormonger that you are, telling him of the
jealousy and ambition of his second son. A fine cover
should anything go wrong. So well did it succeed
that you kept the murder-suicide for the public but
reserved the other for the private delectation of our
father in the hope that royal justice, swift and without
appeal, would remove me from your path."

In a flurry of motion, Rolfe sprang, his blade
homing for Meyer's heart. The other man plunged
aside but not far enough. A rent appeared in the
linen of his shirt before, as Meyer began a delayed
riposte, ·Rolfe recoiled. A red stain appeared at
Meyer's side. He grunted, his words hurried as
he replied, finally, "Most astute, but then I never
expected you to be misled."

"But Claire did not die," Rolfe went on, his voice incisive. "She had to be silenced and, the moment she realized how she had been duped, she knew it. She ran for her mother and home, with me after her and you in my train, with, I doubt it not, a dispensation from the king appointing you my executioner."

"Ah, yes, but the affections of the people made it necessary to move with caution, to arrange for your demise first, if possible in an accidental fashion, and to blacken your character later when it had been accomplished."

"Beyond that, there was the cadre to consider?"

"The cadre, yes, any one of whom might be expected to strike in retaliation for your death without bothering to glance at a dispensation, regardless of whose name and seals graced the bottom."

The strained jostling for position, the feinting and swift withdrawals brought the memory of Rolfe's fight with the McCullough shafting into Angeline's mind. The man he faced now was a more dangerous opponent by far because he made no unnecessary moves, intent on one thing only, the death of his adversary.

What had become of the Scotsman? Were he and his men the cause of the firing? It did not matter. Nothing mattered except the slicing flash of the knives, the harsh breathing of the men, and their voices, as probing and malignant as the blades they wielded.

"Such paradigms of plotting, such sneaking purveying of scandals and midnight eruptions of spite designed to accomplish my demise, added to a trio of useless deaths. Why?"

"Why? But you know. I wanted what you had, you and Max. And I intend to get it."

In the murky dimness, perspiration beaded the faces of the men, dampening their clothing. The gold of Rolfe's hair was dark with it, and his face was flushed. When next he spoke there was a ragged edge to the words.

"How? Child of love, you lack the legitimacy that is the sole requirement of an heir apparent."

"Influence will do as well. I will be an indispensable counselor, appointed—"

"—but not anointed. What will happen when the king dies, as he must?"

Had Rolfe forgotten the stairs in his quest for the truth? They loomed behind him, a well of roiling smoke underlit by the flicker of flames and sending up waves of heat like the maw of Hell. The firing had stopped, and the crackling of spreading fire could be heard plainly.

"Leopold is next in line, after you," Meyer said.

"A reluctant king with an aversion to crowns."

"Did you ever think otherwise? His care of you has been touching. He will be grieved that it was unsuccessful, but will make a fair and biddable ruler with me behind him to guide and correct."

The stairwell was close, too close. Rolfe was being driven toward it by a series of hard, powerful jabs that he, nearing exhaustion, could not counter beyond retreating before them. Angeline's eyes widened as Rolfe made no move to avoid the peril. A warning crowded into her brain, but she checked it, fearful that one brief second of distraction could bring death.

Meyer, as if sensing Rolfe's fatigue and his own advantage, pressed harder. He seemed to swell, dominating the match, his blows sharper, harder, more difficult to parry or evade. He exuded power and confidence, despite the small wound he had received. Bull-like in his strength, he was pitted against the flagging will of the injured wolf.

Gathering himself, Meyer attacked with charging fury. Rolfe gave way. He stepped back within inches of the top step. Angeline cried out, running forward. It was too late. He teetered, slipped, fell, twisting to jump at the last moment.

Meyer growled, a sound of exultation as he leaped after him, knife poised for the final thrust. Then that deep-voiced sound turned to a hoarse scream as he saw the trap laid ready for him. Rolfe, his agility abruptly returning, directed by clear and cogent intent, had come to rest a few steps below with his weapon in his fist. Rising from a crouch, he spun to allow the force of the other man's attack to slide past him. Before Meyer could catch himself, the winking blue steel of Rolfe's blade ripped into his belly, sinking deep. It was immediately withdrawn so that Meyer plunged downward, catching at the railing to stay his fall, tearing loose a baluster that he clutched in his hand as he bounced to a halt halfway down the flight. His knife, released from nerveless fingers, clanged after him. A few quick steps and Rolfe had picked it up, standing above the injured man with a weapon in each fist.

Fresh air wafted through the stair hall, coming from the door that led to the back gallery. Dazed, Angeline swung to see the McCullough, with Leopold beside him, standing not ten feet away. The clothing of the two men was charred as if from contact with flame, and Leopold's uniform was streaked with smoke and soot. How long they had been there she could not have said, but from the grim look on Leopold's face she thought it long enough. The McCullough spat on the floor in triumph and swung toward the open back door. A moment later he could be heard yelling at his men, calling Gustave and Oswald.

"Some dreams are more accessible than others," Rolfe said, his tone weary, "some visions more splendid. And some stink of rot and decay, a carcass supporting the worms of greed and malice, needful of destroying."

Meyer struggled upward, flinging away the baluster, clamping a hand to his abdomen, the fingers glinting ruby red and wet, his face twisted with pain and rage highlighted by the leaping flames below him. "I would have had it all," he said thickly, "if not for you."

Above them, Leopold stepped to the railing, the pistol he held swinging at his side and sick contempt in his eyes as he stared down at Meyer. "No. There would have been no place for you at my court, not for the man who held back during the attack upon the Spaniard's camp, keeping well out of danger, or for the one who, when Rolfe was shot by the McCullough's men, stood staring, doing nothing. I knew not whether you were callous, a coward, or worse, but you would not have been among counselors I might have accepted."

"Fool," Meyer gasped, his gray eyes cold as he stared up at him. "You could still be king if you choose. You have only to—to kill one man, and the weapon is in your hand. Use it quickly, and—and there will be no need to speak of what might have been."

"One man, and also one woman," Leopold said.

"Both then, what of it," Meyer grated. "Or shall I... help... you after all... my future king? You take one... I the other."

Sticky with his own blood, his fingers groped his waistband and brought out a pocket pistol. Its gold chasing gleamed in the gloom of the swirling smoke. Her eyes smarting, Angeline stared at it for the space of a heartbeat, sensing also the moment when with a swift movement Leopold lifted the weapon weighting his hand. At such point-blank range, neither man could miss.

The concussion of the shot reverberated in the close space, a thunderous explosion, a flame that lit the scene with the yellow light of flashing powder. The ball whined, singing, flying straight and true with the skilled marksmanship drilled into the cadre with relentless practice and hearings of scorn and praise. It found its mark.

Meyer was flung backward, toppling, falling like an oak diseased to the heart, struck down by the clean fury of a spring storm. Leopold had made his choice.

Twenty

"MADEMOISELLE FORTIN, A MESSENGER FOR YOU."

Maria stood at the door of the small *salle*. Her tones were subdued and overlaid with a new respect. Angeline looked up from where she sat at a small writing table, penning notes of acknowledgment for condolences. It was a task that had occupied her for the better part of the morning, one thrust upon her by her aunt. Tante Berthe had been prostrate, with her sister in close attendance, since the news of Claire's death had been brought to her three nights ago.

Angeline had arranged for the removal of Claire's charred body from the burned-out shell of the gaming house, for the burial afterward, for the *requiem* mass for her soul. She had ordered the clocks stopped at the time of death, the mirrors turned to the walls, the black crêpe hung upon the doors, and the preparation of food and drink for those who came to call. She had received the visitors in the *salle*, explaining away her aunt's inability to be present, turning away questions, oblivious of the strange glances that rested upon her.

Angeline got to her feet, shaking out the folds of her gown hastily dyed the black of mourning. "Send him in, if you please, Maria."

The Negro manservant wore the blue and gold of the French legation livery. In his hand he carried a small basket lined with satin, which he presented to Angeline. A card bearing her name lay on top of a small pile. With a smile and a request to Maria to provide the man refreshment, she took the card in slim fingers that had a slight tremor, and opened it.

The honor of your presence is requested—

The words blurred before her eyes. It was a farewell dinner for Prince Rolfe of Ruthenia. She cleared her throat. "The—the prince leaves soon?"

"Yes, Mademoiselle. I have been instructed to say that it will be a small gathering out of respect for the bereavement of the prince on the death of his half-brother."

It was an effort to force herself to refold the note and place it back into the basket. "As you see," she said, indicating her own black with a small gesture, "I am in mourning myself. It would not be fitting that I attend."

The man once more removed the folded square with its fine calligraphy, placing it on the edge of the writing table. "I have also been instructed, by the prince himself, not to accept a refusal from you, Mademoiselle."

"Oh, but you must."

"I cannot."

The man bowed and, turning, went quickly from the room. The door closed behind him. Somewhere near, she heard Maria speak to him, doubtless inviting him to partake of a small glass of *bière* Creole.

She sat down again, staring at the white square. She had deliberately closed her mind to what had happened, using the duties that had devolved upon her in the widow's house to stave off the horror of that evening. The gaming house, with its wood tinder-dry with age, had gone up like a paper spill in a draft. They had barely gotten out before the second floor collapsed. Three other houses in the same row had burned before the flames had been checked by the rain and the late-arriving fire companies. Rolfe and what remained of the cadre, the McCullough and his men, had helped to fight the fire, along with half the men and boys of New Orleans. Afterward, Rolfe had escorted Angeline to the widow's house and, giving her into Maria's hands with swift and pungent orders to see that she was cared for, had closeted himself with Madame de Buys, there to impart the news of Claire's death. In the time since, Gustave and Oswald had come to call, their gazes upon her measuring, as if they might be expected to make a report upon their return to the legation. André had also been to the house, sitting for a few minutes each time, speaking of commonplaces, of anything and everything except the time she had spent with the cadre. Of Rolfe she had seen nothing.

She was aware that he was as involved in the inescapable processes attending a death as she was herself, if not more so. And he had other obligations far surpassing her own. She had heard there had even been a deputation of town officials who had waited upon him to offer their appreciation for his part in preventing the spread of fire, the great terror of New Orleans that had struck more than once in the past.

It had seemed to her that her association with the prince was finally at an end, her dismissal accomplished. In a way, it had been a relief to have it over, though the sudden shafting pain of it brought tears rising to her eyes at odd hours of the day and night.

Because of the intolerable ache of remembrance, she had shut from her mind also the memory of the other events she had lived through in the past weeks. They flooded in upon her now, etched indelibly in fear and in passion, in pleasure and grief. Searching among them, she shied away from thinking of the night she had been abducted by Rolfe and what had followed, turning instead to the afternoon that Meyer had allowed her to escape from the hunting lodge. She had thought it prompted by chivalry at the time, but knew instead that it had been only a means of removing her from Rolfe's grasp before she told him what Meyer did not want him to know: the hiding place of her cousin.

It was Meyer who had drugged Rolfe the night of the fire, doubtless slipping into Rolfe's food some medicament from the stores he kept as physician to the cadre. A man of weaker constitution might have been killed by the overdose alone, an outcome Meyer must have hoped for as he was tardy in answering her alarm even though his room was only a step across the hallway.

Later during the melee with the men of St. Martinville after the midnight visit to the convent, she was sure that her mount had been struck to make it

rear, and that a blow to her own knee had loosened
her seat in the saddle, causing her fall. Meyer had
been close at hand, riding just behind her, but what
threat had she been to him then? None, unless he
thought she might know the relatives in Natchitoches
toward whom Claire was even then advancing and
had sensed her weakening toward Rolfe. Or might it
not have been an impulse of vengeance for her part
in his humiliating trial by staffs and resulting defeat by
the cadre, or for leading Rolfe to the convent where
Claire had been hidden away?

There was no question of why he had approached
her at the McCullough's stronghold. Because of
Rolfe's intensifying interest, he had conceived a
passion for her that he thought to satisfy while also
gaining control of the child he suspected she might
be carrying.

It seemed so simple now. Why had she not seen it?
The answer was, it was difficult to see an enemy in a
man who wore the face of a friend. How much harder
must it have been for Rolfe who had played with him
as a boy, shared with him their father's disdain and
neglect, trained with him and fought beside him as
members in an elite corps.

From what had been said, she thought that Rolfe and
the cadre, with Meyer among them, had been in and
out of Ruthenia during the months of Claire's affair with
Max. Hadn't Rolfe said he had seen her once or twice at
a distance? Their jauntings back and forth over Europe
had been at that time for pleasure, so far as she could
tell; if Meyer had returned to Ruthenia alone in that
period he must have been secretive about it. Certainly,

he had waited most carefully, until Rolfe was within the borders of the country himself, before he had carried out his plan to remove Max. That had been a necessary point since he meant to implicate his half-brother.

And he had succeeded. There was the dispensation from the king, freeing Meyer from blame should Rolfe be killed. Was it still among Meyer's papers, or had it been found and destroyed? Or perhaps, in a gesture of bitter pride, been left intact to be returned to Meyer's nearest relative, his father, the king?

She reached out to touch the corner of the invitation inscribed with her name. Rolfe was leaving, returning to his homeland. When he reached it, would he be forced to appear before his father, to account for Meyer's death? Would the king accept the truth from his second son, even with Leopold as witness? And what would happen then? More wandering over Europe, searching for a cause? Or would he be welcomed as the heir, dressed in jewels and velvets, paraded before the people and pelted with flowers as a Bavarian princess became his bride?

She would not go. She would not say farewell before a score of people with a smile like a mask congealed upon her face and her knees too shaky to allow her to curtsey. She did not want to see Gustave ill at ease in his best uniform, Leopold standing back in prickly pride, or Oswald quietly observant, so like Oscar. She preferred them as she had seen them last, exhausted from fighting the fire, but with their exhilaration at winning over it, and at having Rolfe safe with them once more, shining on their sweat-and-soot-streaked faces. She preferred the farewell that

Rolfe had made her in those midnight hours before Claire had been found, a farewell of close-held kisses, quicksilver endearments, and golden phrases of love that would ring in her mind until death stopped their sweet resonance. No, she would not go.

But she did. It was fear that he would send the cadre for her as he'd done before, fear that he might come himself, that made her take from her trunk a gown of silver-gray silk, never worn because of its somberness. It had been Claire's, donned once for the death of a great-uncle just before she was sent to France. As Maria dressed her hair for the dinner, Angeline sat staring into the mirror at the gray silk with its frosting of lace at the low neckline and upon the small puffed sleeves, thinking of her cousin.

Claire had loved Max, she knew, though perhaps the other girl had not understood how much until he was dead. The emotion she felt for him had been bound up with pride and conceit and an overweening certainty of the high position she would hold when they were married. When she had been dismissed, her vanity had demanded reprisal. Left alone, she would have raged and stormed and destroyed crockery, but with Meyer to encourage and direct her feelings of ill usage, the consequences had been more than she could bear. The danger and degradation that had followed had been enough to drive her to madness, and yet, at the end, she had fought to help Angeline, to prevent Meyer from accomplishing the purpose that he had used her to begin.

Another reason for her decision to venture the dinner had been a note from Helene Delacroix saying

she and André had received an invitation and would
be delighted to take her in their carriage. With that
promise of support, she might endure the trial.

There was a subdued air about the French legation.
No lights burned in the main reception rooms, no
liveried footmen stood on the steps waiting to hand
guests from the carriages. The door was opened to
Angeline, with André and Helene close behind her,
by the butler who took their wraps and escorted them
with quiet ceremony to the *salle*.

Perhaps a score of people were gathered in the long,
elegant room with its gilt mirrors, curved and carved
rococo furnishings, and shimmering brocade hangings.
Governor Villère was in attendance, as was the mayor
and his wife, and one or two other dignitaries. Jim
Bowie stood in a corner talking to Gustave, and as
Angeline came into the room, he lifted his glass to her
in a silent toast. Upon the settee in skirts of midnight-
blue satin edged with swansdown was the operatic diva
who had thrilled New Orleans in *The Barber of Seville*,
invited, so Helene Delacroix had said as they rode in
the carriage, to entertain them after dinner. Leopold
and Gustave stood behind the diva, their heavy banter
with her made up for the most part of compliments
while they leaned to view the bountiful charms shown
to advantage by her extreme *décolletage*. Oswald,
looking harassed, was playing the gallant to the consul's
wife, while Rolfe stood with the lady's husband and
the governor.

Magnificent in dress uniform, with an order or two
pinned to his breast, he caught her eye from across
the room, smiling a little, his turquoise gaze keen,

only returning his attention to the two men as the governor tapped his arm to make a point. To Angeline he seemed tired, and somehow incomplete without his wide blue ribbon of the order of valor across his chest. Her fingers tightened on the reticule that she had kept with her. Then Oswald was coming forward, Helene made a brittle and amusing comment, and the moment passed.

The diva, the wives of the consul and the mayor, Helene, and Angeline were the only females present. Therefore, when dinner was announced a short time later, the table was more than a bit uneven. The repast was a long one with interminable courses. Onion soup was set before Angeline, followed by oysters *en brochette*, *daube glace*, wild roast turkey stuffed with oysters and pecans, and a dish of *grillades* of veal. The meal was finished with a dessert of *tarte aux pêches* and a selection of cheeses, brandied nuts, and dried figs. Though the food was excellently prepared and beautifully served, she pushed it about on her plate while trying to make conversation with André on one side and the mayor on the other. She prevented herself from constantly watching Rolfe by concentrating instead on the *piece of montée de nougat* in the center of the table, formed in the shape of a Maltese cross that was melting under the heat of the candles in the chandelier overhead, running into the sugared fruits that surrounded it on its silver dish.

When the meal was at an end, the ladies were escorted from the dining salon and the older women seated with every attention to their comfort while they waited for the diva to make ready to sing.

Angeline stood with Oswald while André went to fetch his mother's shawl from where Helene had left it on her chair at the table. She looked around her for a place to sit that would be neither too close to the singer and the places of honor arranged for the dignitaries, nor too near Madame Helene, who had a tendency to chatter through such entertainments. Oswald was pointing out a chair to one side when he stopped abruptly and turned away. Angeline swung to discover the reason and found Rolfe at her side.

"A dove in gray plumage, mournful and infinitely dear. How have you fared?"

"Well enough. And you?" she managed to answer, her gaze moving to the shining gold waves that she knew covered the long gash in his scalp.

"I comb my hair with care and lie abed in the afternoon in a darkened room, longing for the bedraggled dryad of the wilderness to come to me. I would roam the streets raving for her except I fear that those of the cadre who remain would restrain me bodily. Not for my health, you perceive, but for exposing you to the titterings of the town."

"You have been ill?"

A shadow of annoyance crossed his face, as if he regretted speaking of it. "Gustave will tell you I am harder of head than most. It is of no moment."

"Don't listen to him, *meine liebe*," said Gustave, who had approached to stand beside them. "It is a revival of the concussion from the head wound taken during the capture by the McCullough clan. The blow in the gaming house brought it on again."

"Thank you, Gustave," Rolfe said, his voice soft, though carrying a lethal sting and with it a dismissal. With a short nod, the mercenary moved away. Rolfe went on. "I must speak to you, Angeline."

She was able to judge the importance of the request by its starkness. She remembered, suddenly, Gustave's assurance when first they had met that she would not lose by her association with the prince, that she would be compensated when it ended.

"I... there is no need," she stammered. "You have discovered what you came to find out, and now you must go. I understand."

He studied the flush on her cheekbones and the hint of pain in her averted gaze. "Do you? Or is it the equivalent of a perfumed bauble with my name in cipher you expect, something like this?"

From a pocket he took a necklace. For an instant, Angeline stiffened, then she recognized the small perfume vial on a gold chain that Max had given to Claire, the vial Claire had given her as a gift that night at the convent.

"Where did you find it?"

"It was among the things Sarus brought from the lodge of M'sieur de la Chaise. Worthless, laden with events less than joyous, I thought still you might value it."

"Yes," she whispered and held out her hand that he might drop the chain and the vial of perfume, warm from contact with his body, into it. Pulling wide the top of her reticule, she slipped the necklace inside, then reached deeper to touch the silken ribbon within the small drawstring purse.

"And I brought this to return to you. It is a superior bauble, but one I cannot accept."

In her hand as she drew it out lay the Ruthenian order of valor on its blue streamer that he had left upon her pillow. His gaze was dark as he raised it from the order to her face. "Why?"

"Its value is too high."

"An impossibility." The words were curt.

"I will accept the compliment," she said, her voice low, "but you must take back what is yours by right of strength, courage, and deed."

"You are my courage, my strength, Angeline. Hear me—"

There was a commotion at the entrance beyond the *salle*. The butler entered the room in haste and moved to speak to the French consul. That gentleman turned at once to look at Rolfe, then with a brief word to the butler, moved quickly toward his guest of honor.

"Your Highness, a delegation to see you, just arrived by ship from Ruthenia."

Before the words had left his mouth, three men appeared in the doorway. Men of substance and noble bearing, they were dressed in black and their faces were grave. Coming to a halt before Rolfe, they made each a deep obeisance.

Watching them, Angeline thought for one strained moment they had come to arrest Rolfe, to take him back to face his father for the death of Max. Then, as she swung toward Rolfe, saw his face, the hardening of his gaze, the white line that appeared around his mouth, the rigidity of his erect bearing, she knew.

The eldest of the three men straightened first, spoke. "I regret to be the bearer of ill tidings, Prince Rolfe. It is my unpleasant duty to inform you, however, that your father, the king, is dead. We await your commands, Your Majesty."

Majesty, not Highness. Rolfe was now the king. The men of the delegation bowed once more, a deeper genuflection. There were outcries and oaths and gasps in the room, and then the others, the cadre, the consul and his lady, all were on their feet performing that traditionally recognized gesture of respect.

Angeline sank into a curtsey, rising as she felt a swift touch upon her shoulder. Lifting her gray-green gaze, liquid with compassion, she met that of the new King of Ruthenia, and saw there anger and frustrated pain.

"Perhaps I may suggest, Your Majesty," the consul said, "a room where you might withdraw for private conversation with these gentlemen?"

"Yes," Rolfe said, his tone distracted. Then, as the older man put a hand on his arm, indicating that he must precede them, he turned finally, repeating, "Yes."

It was André who came to Angeline, who took the order of valor from her numb fingers and tucked it back into the reticule that dangled from her arm, pulling the strings closed. He led her toward a chair to the side of the room as the diva, obeying a signal from the consul's wife, began an aria in fervent and rich voice.

The audience was restless, craning toward the room where Rolfe and the delegation were shut away, exchanging whispered comments. The greatest singer in the world could not have held their attention in competition with such events. After only three selections, their hostess rang for coffee and brandy. The diva, with ill grace, pleaded an early rehearsal and took her leave, though the others lingered on, eager to discuss the new development in the fascinating saga of the Balkan royalty in their midst. It seemed to Angeline that the only thing that might further their pleasure in the exercise was the absence of one of the principals in the drama, herself. But when she suggested to André that they leave, he shook his head decisively. Taking her hand and drawing it through his arm, he guided her to an alcove with a small, velvet-covered bench set into the niche.

"You must not run away," he said, positioning himself in front of her as she sank down upon the seat. "That would be to undo the good that has been done."

She smiled wearily. "I am grateful for your concern, André, but I care very little for such things anymore."

"They are important. Rolfe will return to his own country—unencumbered especially now, and you must remain here. As matters stand, there are whispers, but no one has, or will, turn their back on you in the street or refuse you invitations."

"For now, André, but in a few months, what then?"

"It should be better, for a new scandal will have come along to divert attention."

"Not if—if it is seen that I am to have a child."

"If—" His olive skin turned sallow, and he moved to sit on the bench next to her, reaching to place his hand over her cold fingers clasped in her lap. There was new determination in his tone as he began to speak, slowly at first, then more quickly.

"In time, when you are obviously *enceinte*, they will say nothing, for you will have been my wife for some months. We will go into the country, to the plantation. There is a woman there who is an excellent midwife. The last weeks will be spent in seclusion as is customary, and, if necessary, we will delay the announcement of the birth and the baptism of the infant."

"Oh, André, I didn't mean—"

"I know," he interrupted. "You have avoided my proposals often enough. This time I will not permit it. You will marry me as soon as it may be arranged."

It would be so easy. André would make a good husband. He would never, she was sure, reproach her or withhold his trust. In time, she would come to care for him for his generosity and steadfastness, if for no other reason.

"I can't let you make such a sacrifice," she said, her voice low.

"It will be no sacrifice, but an honor."

His brown eyes were soft, so very different from the brilliant and vibrant blue of Rolfe's. His emotions, his duties were simple. There would be no great mental stimulation in his company, but there would be ease; no great passion, but gentle pleasure.

"I would... try to make you happy."

"You have," he answered, and raised her hand to press his lips, prickly with the brush of his mustache, to her fingertips.

He drew her to her feet then, and led her down the room. "Listen, my friends, *Maman*," he called. "I am the most fortunate man in New Orleans. Angeline has just agreed to be my wife."

Helene Delacroix turned, her face mirroring her struggle between consternation and tearful gladness for her son's transparent satisfaction. It was not the reaction of her future mother-in-law that held Angeline's attention, however. It was that of the man just returning to the room.

As the announcement reached him, Rolfe came to a halt. For an instant he looked shattered. Then he was moving forward with easy grace, smiling, congratulating André with all cordiality.

"We sail within the week, the cadre and I," he said. "But before we go, I will give myself the gratification, my companion in misfortune, of seeing you wed."

The words were spoken to André as he gave him his hand, but his blue gaze stabbed briefly into Angeline's eyes, and she knew they were for her.

Why? Why was he doing it? Was it some subtle punishment, some further attempt to re-establish her by showing his indifference, some peculiar obligation to see her safely settled before he went away? Why would Rolfe insist on attending her marriage?

The question haunted her as she prepared for the ceremony in the Church of St. Louis. She had bathed in the early afternoon and washed her hair, allowing it to dry in the warm spring sun as she sat with eyes closed, willing herself to remain quiescent, unthinking. But as the hours sped and the time drew nearer, she could not restrain the vagrant wanderings of her mind.

She glanced at the gown laid out upon her bed, one of heavy ivory satin with matching underdress, a gift from André's mother that had been impossible to refuse. The exquisitely cut gown with its bell sleeves to the elbow, its high waist and flowing skirt, was beautiful, and in truth, she had nothing remotely as suitable. She would not like to embarrass André, and so she would wear it.

She would have preferred a quieter ceremony, perhaps in the country, at some small chapel with only herself and André, Helene, the priest, and, since he insisted, Rolfe in attendance. It was not to be. There were dozens of Delacroix relatives: grandparents, the aunts and uncles of two generations, and innumerable cousins of all degrees who must be included. It was André who had insisted that the affair be held at the church on the main square. He had not said so, but she thought he intended that no one should be able to say that there was anything the least secretive about their wedding.

Her own side of the church would be woefully empty. She had few relatives, and none in New Orleans other than Tante Berthe. Her aunt's sister, she thought, would have liked to attend, but would not say so. Tante Berthe herself, having arisen at last from her bed, was making preparations to return to St. Martinville. She had made it clear she did not mean to waste time hearing the vows of a niece she had come to hate. Without reservation, she blamed Angeline for her daughter's death, and would have liked to order her into the street if she had thought she could do so without retaliation.

No, Angeline must journey to the church alone in the Delacroix carriage. She would walk down the aisle on André's arm. Vows would be exchanged before the priest. They would sign the church register. Her flowers would be dispatched to the Delacroix tomb at the cemetery. They would return to the Delacroix town house for the wedding supper and remain there afterward for the five days of seclusion required by tradition. When that was at an end, they would journey to the plantation at St. Martinville and take up their lives in much the same way that they might have done if Rolfe of Ruthenia had never come to Louisiana.

Sighing, Angeline stood and, removing her wrapper, took up the underdress. Pulling it on over her head, she let the cool satin ripple down over her skin. Seating herself again, she rolled tubes of silk up her ankles and over her slender calves, fastening them at the knee with garters of embroidered satin. She stepped into her slippers then, and stood smoothing her hands over her waist. She was still slim, and would be for some weeks to come. There would be no bulges to give the wedding guests cause for gossip. Still, she felt as if her condition were branded upon her.

Dropping her hands abruptly, she moved to the small table that held the *corbeille de noce*, the nuptial basket sent by the prospective groom to the bride-to-be. Of white leghorn straw lined with satin and trimmed with lace and ribbon, it was a sumptuous offering, in marked contrast to the rather severe bracelet of rubies set in gold that André had presented to her as a token of their engagement.

The basket had arrived that morning by special messenger, a bit tardy, but then she had not expected one at all. When she had seen the items it contained— the finely worked gloves of white kid; the shawl of gossamer-fine weave, fringed and embroidered in

silk; the fan with sticks of gold and a delicate scene
after Watteau painted upon its spread; the parure of
diamonds and topazes set in such exquisite workmanship of pure gold that it appeared fragile, set
with sunlight and moonglow; and finally the veil of
handmade Valenciennes lace as light and ethereal as
a spider web, brought from Europe at an incredible
cost—she had known why the betrothal offering was
late. André must have scoured the shops of New
Orleans for the contents of that basket, and spared no
expense in filling it.

The veil she would wear, draped over her hair,
falling past her shoulders to below her waist; so perfect
a complement to her gown could not be resisted.
The remaining articles would have to be packed in
her trunk for later use. It would be as well to do that
now, while she waited for Maria, who had promised
to come and help her into her gown and dress her hair
the moment she could escape from Madame de Buys.

At last she was ready. The carriage arrived. Angeline
descended the steps of the widow's house into the
courtyard with her bouquet of spirea and violets in her
hand and Maria carrying her trunk behind her. As she
emerged from the gate that led into the street, a liveried
servant stood ready to hand her into the waiting vehicle.
The door was closed upon her and her trunk swung up
behind. The carriage jerked forward. Angeline raised
her hand to Maria, left standing on the banquette, then
settled back upon the cushioned seat to compose herself
so that she might present the appearance of a serene
bride when she was set down before the church.

At the first crossroads past the widow's house, there

came the clatter of hooves from behind her. A white-uniformed figure rode into view, drawing even with the carriage window, and then another, and another. She sat up straight, but neither Gustave, Leopold, nor Oswald spared a glance for her as they stared straight ahead, sitting their horses as stiffly as if they served as an honor guard for royalty.

Then there came a fourth horseman into view. The door on the right side of the carriage was jerked open. The present and future king of Ruthenia easily made the complicated swing from horseback into the moving vehicle. He paused a moment, balanced in the open doorway, to give her a bright and mocking smile, then leaning to catch the swinging panel, he slammed it shut and threw himself down beside her.

She swept her satin skirts from under his booted feet, sending him a fulminating look. "What are you doing here?"

"Escorting the bride, an old Ruthenian custom."

For a wild instant she had thought—but no. She was grateful for the dimness that covered the swift rise of color to her hairline, the trembling of her fingers. In self-protection she exclaimed. "You are intoxicated!"

"With your beauty only. I have never been so sober in my life, a state I expect to be permanent."

"If—if this is meant to re-establish me, then I tell you to your face that it has all the earmarks of a libertine delivering his mistress in relief to his successor."

"Waspish, and with a tongue as bitter as aloes. If this is the kind of wife you will make, I pity your husband."

"It would be wasted! He will have no regrets."

"That is, of course, gratifying to hear."

"Why you should care, I can't imagine!"

His gaze grew pensive. "Like the man who planted flowers so rich in perfume that his neighbor suffocated from the scent, I feel in some sense responsible."

"If you mean to say that I will overpower André, it's ridiculous," she said, regaining control of her voice, striving for dangerous calm.

"I'm sure he will try to prevent it. The question is, can he? Or will he seek winding sheets instead of bed linen to find repose from his conjugal efforts?"

"This is outrageous!" she cried, abandoning restraint. "I suppose you think you would be a better match."

He turned his head on the squabs to look at her, the light of the carriage lamps catching a dark golden gleam in his hair. "Oh, yes, sweet Angeline. I am your mentor, your mate, your equal, the frayed and quivering string to your bow, the tempered sword for your soft and supple sheath, the enamored twin of your soul, half of your whole, a partnered swan who without you will die, singing."

Pain, white-hot and unrelenting, began near her heart and flared upward into the uttermost recesses of her mind. She could not speak, could not draw breath. It was only as the carriage slowed, drawing to a rattling halt before the church, that she was able to whisper, "Don't do this."

"I have done it," he answered. Gathering himself with the taut and effortless strength of the wolf for which he was named, he sprang down as the door was opened and waited to help her to alight.

André was nowhere to be seen, nor were the dozens

of carriages she had expected to be lining the streets around the square, bringing the relatives to march down the aisle behind the bridal pair. The doors of the church stood open with the glimmer of candlelight beckoning from inside. The aisle, hedged with dark and empty pews, stretched to the altar, where the white vestments of the priest shone. There was the smell of incense and burning wax, of dust and sweat ingrained into wood. There was the faint sheen of gilt on carved plaster saints, the fleshlike gleam of marble, the tracery of pierced and carved wood. Their footsteps, and those of the cadre behind them, were muffled, yet loud in the stillness.

For a brief space of time, Angeline permitted herself to dream. The man who walked beside her was vital and real, a man in whom emotions ran strong and deep. She could feel the corded muscle beneath the sleeves on which her fingers lay, feel her own response to the life force that burned so brightly within him. Then, ahead of them, André stepped from the shadows to stand at the altar, blocking their way.

Rolfe came to a halt within arm's reach of the other man. The two of them stared at each other, blue gaze clashing with brown. Tension vibrated between them like a strung wire. Angeline felt the arm under her fingers harden, saw André's hands curl into fists. With a swift drawn breath, she stepped forward, releasing Rolfe's arm, stretching out her hand to André.

It was a supreme act, the most of which she was capable, but she could not prevent the rise of desolation that came from inside, standing in her gray-green eyes. André saw it, and his face twisted. His fingers crushed hers, then though his eyes remained bleak, he smiled. Turning her gently, he carried her hand to his lips, then gave it back into Rolfe's keeping.

"As you asked," André said, "I watched her face as she came down the aisle. You were right. I relinquish her to you."

He stepped back and, turning, retreated quickly up the aisle. Angeline stood dazed, turning her head to look after him even as she was drawn forward toward the altar and the priest who waited.

The exchange of vows was brief, made longer only by the recitation of her Christian names and those of Rolfe she had never heard before, including his surname, one of the most illustrious in Europe. Then it was over, the register signed. They were outside the church, where the cadre, in boisterous, laughing gaiety, kissed her soundly before allowing Rolfe to place her in the carriage. Inside, she turned to him, staring at him. But it was only yards to the dock, and before she could find words to speak, they were stopping once more.

He swung her from the carriage into his arms, and strode with her up the wooden steps that led to the levee and across the gangplank onto the deck of the tall ship that waited. A whistle piped. Men bent themselves in half as they passed. Rolfe inclined his head, but did not stop.

He moved swiftly down the companionway and along a passage to where a pair of uniformed guards stood on either side of the doorway. They leaped to attention as they recognized Rolfe. One, a bit more observant than the other, jumped then to open the door and earned a rare smile for his pains.

The cabin was spacious, with paneled walls set with glowing whale-oil lamps in gimbals, a Turkey carpet underfoot, a bank of mullioned windows with a table and chairs of mahogany set beneath, and, at the opposite end, a great bed of state in mahogany picked out in gold upon the towering posts topped with ostrich plumes, and draped in blue velvet embroidered with the arms and insignia of the kings of Ruthenia. Rolfe stepped to the bed and placed her gently upon the coverlet. The side of the mattress sagged with his weight as he sat down beside her. He leaned over her, his arms braced on either side.

"I am sorry if this is not what you wanted. It was necessary to me. I could not bear to be apart from you, or to think of you as the wife of another man, bearing my child in repentant sorrow, shuffling it away in the pain of remembrance while you conceived and bore other children fathered by André. I had to have you with me, or go mad with longing and useless remorse."

She felt no surprise, only deep relief. "How did you know?"

"There was mystery in your eyes on the night of the ball, and sweet grief in your smile. Later, when I came to you, your breasts were ripe and full in my hands, and—"

"Yes," she said hastily, lowering her lashes before sweeping them upward again in a searching glance. "But if that is true, and if you felt yourself free to marry me, then why—?"

"Why did I not proclaim the coming union days ago and gather you beneath the mantle of my protection, bidding the trumpets sound? You would have become an official target and, if your secret became known, the guardian of my future heir—someone who must be removed as surely as I myself. Further, it would have presented you as a hostage for my presence, since where you were taken, I must go. I could not prevent the attacks upon myself. How could I safeguard you? It seemed you would be better apart from me, even if in my need for you I could not stop myself from nullifying the arrangement."

"Meyer guessed, and my use as a hostage was proven."

"Don't!" he said, his voice rough. "Think of Ruthenia under diamonds of ice and opals of snow instead, or else of shawls with fringes of silk, of fans of gold and rainbow hues, of sun-filled topazes and veilings of Valenciennes." He brushed aside the web of lace that covered her hair, finding the pins that held it in place, drawing it aside.

"The things in the *corbeille de noce*," she said in wonder. "You sent it! I thought André had run mad with the expense of filling it."

"And why should you not? He was the chosen groom, and, very nearly on that night when he dared to announce your coming marriage, the victim of the wrath of a new-minted king!"

"Instead, you congratulated him!"

"The most difficult words I have ever spoken. Tell me why they had to be dredged up with bile and spleen and bits of my heart just then? Why could you not have waited for my declaration, coming as surely as Orion follows Cassiopeia through the heavens, upon Meyer's death?"

"I couldn't know it would come. I had been told you were expected to marry among the royalty of Europe, that there was a Bavarian princess chosen by your father that you might reasonably be expected to accept for the sake of his approval."

"Sweet Angeline, I have long since grown past the need of any man's show of favor or sign of affection. As for taking a royal bride, Max might have complied, but what use have I for such a conceit? If I choose now to take a commoner to wife, who is to stop me? I am the king."

"But your children—"

"—will be born of love and grace."

"Nurtured on mare's milk and almonds," she said, stirred by a faint memory.

"Yes, and all the affection their father can spare from the hoard he keeps for their mother." He smiled into her eyes before he went on. "And if you are worried that they need hang their heads for the color of their blood, blue and bright red mingled to make royal purple, then think of Europe after the ravages of the Corsican Napoleon, who elevated himself and his plebeian family to the status of royalty overnight, setting his relatives upon half its tottering thrones."

"Why, yes," she said thoughtfully.

He lifted a brow. "Having said so much, permit me to ask why you are concerned, when in your family chart you hold the name of a Bourbon king?"

"It was Claire who made that claim, not I."

"The charts she flaunted in Ruthenia traced her father's line. You are the daughter of his sister—are you not?—which gives you the same regal lineage."

"I see," she said, pursing her lips, reaching out to touch with one finger the gold buttons of his uniform coat that hung within her reach. "You married me because I am suitable."

"God, no!" He caught her arms, dragging her upward, holding her so close that she could see the reflections of the lamp flames in the gimbal beside the bed glowing red in the depths of his eyes. "I married you to bind you to me beyond sundering, to honor a bond made in perfect communion beneath a wilderness sky, to offer you a surfeit of riches found in no storeroom, but in mind and body and heart, to seek in your arms the warm pulsing of life and receive the gift that cleanses and heals, but can also destroy—"

"I love you, Rolfe of Ruthenia, my king."

His words stopped in full spate. He whispered, "Yes, for that."

She clenched the braided and laced bars of his coat, twisting her hands into the cloth, and drew his head down until his lips touched hers. His arms closed around her with fierce strength as mouth to mouth he bore her down upon the bed. She pressed herself against him in trembling relief, in desire and passionate joy that caused her to swallow salt tears. His body against hers was warm and exciting, heavy and infinitely welcome. The ship slipped its moorings, drifting with the river, swinging to head downstream to the gulf and out to sea.

Spiteful and mean the world might be, with greed and malice and ugly death both in town and wilderness. But there were in the dusty march of days flashes of brilliance, sweet moments gilded with glory, snatched splendid and whole from the dreary parade.

So thinking, Angeline touched Rolfe's face. He drew back, the light in his turquoise eyes softly shining as he met her gray-green gaze. Then he took her lips again, his hands moving upon her. She thought no more.

About the Author

Since publishing her first book at age twenty-seven, *New York Times* bestselling and award-winning author Jennifer Blake has gone on to write over sixty historical and contemporary romances. She brings the seductive passion of the South to her stories, reflecting her seventh-generation Louisiana heritage. Jennifer lives with her husband in northern Louisiana.

FOR MORE FROM JENNIFER BLAKE,
READ ON FOR AN EXCERPT FROM

FIERCE
EDEN

THE GATHERING WAS SPARSE. AT THE BOARD OF Commandant Chepart, with its cloth of Flemish linen scattered with bread crumbs and ringed with spilled wine, there were a number of conspicuously empty chairs. It was not to be wondered at, of course, not when every day brought fresh rumors of unrest among the Indians. The village of the Natchez tribe was so close and tempers so uncertain that few cared to risk being caught on the road at dawn, should the evening be prolonged.

Elise Laffont had felt a qualm or two herself. She did not usually attend such affairs as the commandant's soirée, nor would she have this evening if it had not been most important. She had kept to herself during the past three years since her husband had died. Some considered it, she knew, a becoming show of grief and modesty in such a young widow. The truth was that she preferred her own company and had far too much to do managing the estate left to her for frivolous amusement to be an attraction.

From the head of the table came a roar of laughter.

Chepart, chuckling at his own joke, signaled the servant behind his chair to refill the glasses of his guests with the excellent Madeira that was to accompany the dessert course. The light of the candles in the crystal chandelier, hanging from the rough rafters overhead, gleamed among the waves of Elise's honey-brown hair, bright despite their dusting of white powder, as she turned her head to glance at her host. The warm amber of her eyes turned cool with the disdain that rose to her finely molded features.

Two places farther along the board, Madame Marie Doucet leaned across her husband to catch Elise's eye. Her plump face was alight with good-natured amusement and pleasure. "Commandant Chepart is quite the *bon vivant* tonight, is he not?"

"Certainly he thinks so," Elise said under her breath.

"What was that, *chère?* I didn't quite catch it."

The older woman had been quite pretty once, in a doll-like fashion. She had kept the quick coquettish mannerisms and light tone of voice despite the gray in her fading blond hair. She had been a good friend to Elise, however, in the past few years and a good neighbor who lived less than a third of a league away. Elise had learned to overlook much of the silliness for the sake of the kind heart underneath.

Elise shook her head in quick dismissal. "Nothing."

The commandant of Fort Rosalie, the representative of his Royal Majesty King Louis XV here in the wilderness known as Louisiana, was indeed given to good living. Elise, with a slight curl of her mouth, which was smooth and a trifle wide, thought that he was more of a *debauchee* than a *bon vivant*. Chepart had been a tankard friend of her husband. He and Vincent Laffont had spent many an evening drinking each other under the table and guffawing at crude stories. When her husband had had the consideration to drown himself while fishing on the Mississippi, the commandant had come to her. He had been all concern, most solicitous of her comfort and well-being; so solicitous in fact that he had pressed her down upon a settle and thrust his hand into her bodice to fondle her breasts. She had snatched a wooden knitting needle from the basket in the corner of the settle and done her best to skewer him with it, then had taken down Vincent's musket from over the fireplace and ordered the commandant from her property. When he had gone, she had cried for the first time since Vincent's death, tears of rage and disgust, and of gladness that she need never again submit to any man.

It was distressing, then, that she must now ask a favor of Commandant Chepart. She did not like to accept his hospitality, much less endure his company; still, she would do it until she had what she wanted from the fat fool.

She allowed her gaze to wander around the room, noting the jewel-colored Turkish rug underfoot, the silk hangings at the shuttered, glassless windows, the Watteau pastoral scene that hung above the enormous fireplace where red coals pulsed with fire and a black log smouldered. How out of place these things seemed in the simplicity of the house provided for the fort's commander. With the elaborate table setting and the ridiculous grandeur of the crystal chandelier that shed its light upon them, the furnishings were an indication of both the commandant's pretentious arrogance and his ambition. Chepart intended to use his office as a stepping-stone to greater things, perhaps an appointment at court, but in the meantime it pleased him to live in comfortable splendor, regardless of how his underhanded dealings with the commission merchants might affect supplies for the fort and the men who manned it.

What means could she use to persuade someone like Chepart to listen to her? She did not have the funds to offer him monetary inducement, and she refused to consider bartering that commodity she felt might interest him most: herself. But perhaps she was wrong in thinking that he would want something in return for what she would ask. It was not so great a request, not so unusual after all, however much it might mean to her. It would be no loss to the commandant to allow the prisoners now in the guardhouse at the fort to build a storage barn and poultry yard for her.

The men were not dangerous, being charged officially with nothing more serious than insubordination, for all of Chepart's railing about sedition and a blatant attempt to undermine his authority. The crime committed had been the spirited representation by these men, all of them officers of the fort, of the wisdom of preparing a defense against the coming Indian rising. That there was going to be one, they were positive. Their information had come straight from the Indian village of White Apple, from women who had heard it direct from Tattooed Arm, mother of the Great Sun who was the ruler of the Natchez.

Chepart had not been impressed by their source. He had declared that French soldiers should know better than to be swayed by their Indian whores and that his officers would learn better if he had to whip the skin from their backs to bring home the lesson. No puny Indian tribe would dare to challenge the might of France. Hadn't the diplomacy of the French governors of Louisiana always ensured amicable relations with their Indian allies? They were as children in the hands of men of intelligence and guile. Besides, no Indian chieftain would dare to order an attack knowing that the armed force of France would be turned against his people for such treachery.

In Elise's opinion, it was just such blatant disdain for the Natchez, just such lack of judgment in dealing with them, that was the reason for her pressing need for a barn and fenced yard. It was Chepart's bungling that had caused the recent unrest of the Indians, had turned them into marauders who took delight in carrying off her chickens and ducks, hogs and calves. Not that the Natchez had any great appreciation for property rights at the best of times, but everyone knew that their depredations in the last months were made from a sense of ill-usage and spite. And every day they became bolder.

Unconsciously Elise turned her amber gaze upon the corpulent figure of her host. Chepart, catching her eye, raised his glass to her. His expression held a hint of barely concealed lust as he surveyed her high-piled hair, the proud tilt of her chin and the determined self-possession of her features in the oval of her face. He lifted his hand to twist a curl of his long, full wig where it fell over his shoulder as he permitted his overwarm gaze to drop to the low bodice of her gold brocade gown that cupped the gentle swells of her breasts. His thick tongue came to lick his lips, leaving them wet.

Elise clenched her teeth, but could not prevent the shudder of repugnance that rippled through her. In sheer reaction, she covered herself as best she could by drawing up the edges of her shawl as if against a chill draft.

"Are you cold, my dear Madame Laffont?" Chepart called down the table, clapping his hands at the same time for a servant. "Now that we cannot allow!"

An African slave, little more than a boy, came running. The commandant gestured toward the fire and the boy went quickly to the hearth. At the same time, a serving woman emerged from the back of the house with a tray of cakes and custards. A small silence fell as the diners watched the mending of the fire and waited for their dessert to be placed before them. The only sound was the crash of logs being thrown on the hot coals and the crackling rush as they caught. The flames leaped up the chimney in a burst of yellow-orange light that chased the shadows from the corners of the room. The bright glow also penetrated, through a doorway that stood open, into the dimness of the connecting salon, a reception room with access to the outside.

A shrill scream shattered the quiet. "An Indian! Come to murder us!"

It was Madame Doucet, her eyes glassy with shock as she pointed with one trembling hand toward the

salon. Men surged to their feet, looking around
wildly. Women gasped and cried out, springing up to
clutch at their husbands. The serving woman threw
her tray into the air, then stood rooted as custard and
cake dishes crashed to the floor, scattering their sticky
contents over her feet. Chepart cursed, flinging down
his glass so that wine streamed across the table and
dripped like blood down the cloth to the floor. Elise
clutched at her shawl with white-knuckled hands as
she turned in the direction Madame Doucet indicated.

The Indian moved forward from the salon doorway
into the dining room with silent animal vigor, tall as
the Natchez were tall, magnificent in his sculptured
barbarian grace, infinitely savage. The firelight was
reflected in a copper shimmer from the muscled planes
of his chest that were shadowed by intricate lines of
tattooing unobscured by the faintest trace of body hair,
lines that gave mute evidence of his ability to bear
pain. The light also caught the beading that patterned
the white doeskin of the moccasins on his feet and the
breechclout that covered his loins, and shimmered in
the soft white nap of the cape of woven swansdown
that hung from his shoulders. More swan feathers
had been used to form the circlet that he wore on
the crown of his head in the fashion of the Natchez
males of royal birth, those of the Sun class. Just behind
that circlet was the knot of his hair where it had been
drawn up, the thick, black knot that offered an easy
hold for an enemy in deliberate scorn for any prowess
other than his own, one that would become a scalp
lock should that prowess fail. But his hairline had
not been plucked for a higher brow in the Natchez

fashion, and his eyes, watchful, dangerously opaque, were not black but gray.

"*Merde!*" the commandant exclaimed, the oath bursting from him in his relief. "It's Reynaud Chavalier!"

The fear that had gripped the men in the room dissolved into anger. Tight-lipped, they exchanged glances before turning back toward the intruder. The women sighed and whispered among themselves with nervous titters. Elise sat very still, staring in horrified fascination. She saw the man called Chavalier sweep the room with a glance that seemed to hold an edge of contempt, felt the glance touch her in stinging appraisal, pause, then move on as if there was nothing there to hold his interest.

Madame Doucet bent toward Elise over her husband's empty chair. "He's a half-breed," she said in a trilling undertone.

"I know," she replied.

She did know, as who did not? She had never met Reynaud Chavalier, but she had heard of him. He was the son of Robert Chavalier, Comte de Combourg, and the Natchez woman called Tattooed Arm, and the brother to the man now known as the Great Sun. He had been raised by the Indians until his thirteenth year. At that time he had been taken to France by his father, when the comte had returned to his native land after his service in Louisiana, to be educated. The old comte had died some years later, leaving Reynaud a sizable fortune and an immense tract of land on the west side of the Mississippi River. Reynaud had tarried in France to settle his father's affairs, which had included a French wife and a legitimate heir to the title and estates.

Then five years ago he had returned, melting into the wilderness of his holdings and dropping the mantle of civilization as easily as he had shed his satin small clothes. He spent most of his time on his lands across the river where it was rumored that he had entertained the governor and his entourage in great state on occasion. No one believed it. When he visited the Grand Village of the Natchez in the jurisdiction of the commandant of Fort Rosalie, he always wore the trappings of his mother's people.

Reynaud Chavalier surveyed the startled faces before him with grim impatience. He was here on a fool's errand he was certain, but it must be carried out. At last he swung toward the commandant, sketching a bow totally without subservience. "I give you good evening."

"What is the meaning of this intrusion?" Chepart blustered, snatching at the remnants of his self-possession as he jerked his napkin from his neck and flung it down on the table.

"I sent a request to see you this afternoon and was told I must wait on your convenience. Not wanting to trouble you while you were occupied with the weighty affairs of your office, I thought to seek you out during your leisure." The words were smooth, but carried the whiplash flick of irony.

"You thought to see me at a time when I would be less likely to have you thrown in the guardhouse for your impudence! I've half a mind to call my men—"

"Certainly, if it pleases you. I trust you will not be too disturbed if they fail to come."

Chepart gripped the table edge as he leaned forward, demanding, "What have you done?"

"Merely disarmed them."

His speech carried the cultured tones of Paris, his voice was deep and vibrant. If she closed her eyes, Elise thought, it would be possible to suppose that she was listening, at the very least, to a courtier, if not a member of the French nobility. She stared at the silver armbands that compressed the muscles of his upper arms, aware of a feeling of disturbance inside her that she did not like.

"How dare you!" Chepart demanded.

Irritation gathered inside Reynaud, combining with a hard anger as he regarded the corpulent and self-important fool before him. "Because I felt it necessary. It is of the utmost urgency that you listen without doing something so stupid as ordering yet another arrest. The lives of your command, the people you are here to protect, even those assembled in this room, depend on it."

Lessons in French

BY LAURA KINSALE
New York Times bestselling author

"An exquisite romance and an instant classic."
—Elizabeth Hoyt

HE'S EXACTLY THE KIND OF TROUBLE SHE CAN'T RESIST...

Trevelyan and Callie were childhood sweethearts with a taste for adventure. Until the fateful day her father drove Trevelyan away in disgrace. Nine long, lonely years later, Trevelyan returns, determined to sweep Callie into one last, fateful adventure, just for the two of them...

"Kinsale's delightful characters and delicious wit enliven this poignant tale...It will charm your heart!" *—Sabrina Jeffries*

"Laura Kinsale creates magic. Her characters live, breathe, charm, and seduce, and her writing is as delicious and perfectly served as wine in a crystal glass. When you're reading Kinsale, as with all great indulgences, it feels too good to stop." *—Lisa Kleypas*

978-1-4022-3701-0 • $7.99 U.S./$8.99 CAN

MIDSUMMER MOON

BY LAURA KINSALE

New York Times bestselling author

"The acknowledged master."
—*Albany Times-Union*

**IF HE REALLY LOVED HER,
WOULDN'T HE HELP HER REALIZE HER DREAM?**

When inventor Merlin Lambourne is endangered by Napoleon's advancing forces, Lord Ransom Falconer, in service of his government, comes to her rescue and falls under the spell of her beauty and absent-minded brilliance. But he is horrified by her dream of building a flying machine—and not only because he is determined to keep her safe.

"Laura Kinsale writes the kind of works that live in your heart." —Elizabeth Grayson

"A true storyteller, Laura Kinsale has managed to break all the rules of standard romance writing and come away shining."
—*San Diego Union-Tribune*

978-1-4022-4689-0 • $9.99 U.S./$11.99 CAN

THE
PRINCE
OF
MIDNIGHT

BY LAURA KINSALE

New York Times bestselling author

INTENT ON REVENGE, ALL SHE WANTS FROM
HIM IS TO LEARN HOW TO KILL

Lady Leigh Strachan has crossed all of France in search
of S.T. Maitland, nobleman, highwayman, and legendary
swordsman, once known as the Prince of Midnight. Now
he's hiding out in a crumbing castle with a tame wolf as his
only companion, trying to conceal his deafness and desperation. Leigh is terribly disappointed to find the man behind
the legend doesn't meet her expectations. But when they're
forced on a quest together, she discovers the dangerous and
vital man behind the mask, and he finds a way to touch her
ice cold heart.

978-1-4022-4686-9 • $9.99 U.S./$11.99 CAN

SEIZE THE FIRE

BY LAURA KINSALE

New York Times bestselling author

> "Magic and beauty flow from Laura Kinsale's pen." —*Romantic Times*

AN UNLIKELY PRINCESS SHIPWRECKED
WITH A WAR HERO WHO'S GOT HELL TO PAY

Her Serene Highness Olympia of Oriens—plump, demure, and idealistic—longs to return to her tiny, embattled land and lead her people to justice and freedom. Famous hero Captain Sheridan Drake, destitute and tormented by nightmares of the carnage he's seen, means only to rob and abandon her. What is Olympia to do with the tortured man behind the hero's façade? And how will they cope when their very survival depends on each other?

> "One of the best writers in the history of the romance genre." —*All About Romance*

978-1-4022-4683-8 • $9.99 U.S./$11.99 CAN

The WILDEST HEART

by Rosemary Rogers

Two destinies intertwined under the blazing New Mexico sun

When passionate, headstrong Lady Rowena Dangerfield travels to the savage New Mexico frontier to lay claim to her inheritance, she finally meets a man as strong as she is: Lucas Cord, a dark, dangerously handsome, half-Apache outlaw. Fighting scandal, treachery, and murder, Luke is determined to have Rowena for his own, and as their all-consuming passion mounts, no one is going to stop him...

WHAT READERS SAY:

"It makes you cry, it makes you wish, and it makes you dream. It's what a romance novel is all about."

"The Wildest Heart kept me captivated well beyond the last page..."

PRAISE FOR ROSEMARY ROGERS:

"The queen of historical romance."
—New York Times Book Review

"Her novels are filled with adventure, excitement, and, always, wildly tempestuous romance."
—Fort Worth Star-Telegram

978-1-4022-2274-0 · $7.99 U.S. / $9.99 CAN

My UNFAIR Lady

BY KATHRYNE KENNEDY

A WILD WEST BEAUTY TAKES VICTORIAN LONDON BY STORM

The impoverished Duke of Monchester despises the rich Americans who flock to London, seeking to buy their way into the ranks of the British peerage. Frontier-bred Summer Wine Lee has no interest in winning over London society— it's the New York bluebloods and her future mother-in-law she's determined to impress. She knows the cost of smoothing her rough-and-tumble frontier edges will be high. But she never imagined it might cost her heart...

"Kennedy is going places." —Romantic Times

"Kathryne Kennedy creates a unique, exquisite flavor that makes her romance a pure delight page after page, book after book." —Merrimon Book Reviews

"Kathryne Kennedy's computer must smolder from the power she creates in her stories! I simply cannot describe how awesome or how thrilling I found this novel to be." —Huntress Book Reviews

"Kennedy is one of the hottest new sensations in the romance genre." —Merrimon Reviews

978-1-4022-2990-9 • $7.99 U.S./$9.99 CAN